THE HERMIT OF BIG HORN COUNTY

ALSO BY JOHNNY WORTHEN

THE HERMIT OF BIG HORN COUNTY

A TONY FLANER MYSTERY
BOOK 5

JOHNNY WORTHEN

ROUGH
EDGES
PRESS

The Hermit of Big Horn County
Paperback Edition
Copyright © 2023 (As Revised) Johnny Worthen

Rough Edges Press
An Imprint of Wolfpack Publishing
9850 S. Maryland Parkway, Suite A-5 #323
Las Vegas, Nevada 89183

roughedgespress.com

Paperback ISBN 978-1-68549-327-1
eBook ISBN 978-1-68549-326-4

For Mick

THE HERMIT OF BIG HORN COUNTY

1

"SOMETIMES OLD IS BETTER."

"Not as often as you'd think," I said.

"Simple clears the mind," said Perry.

"Simple hurts the muscles."

"You're okay," said Standard, a bit too perky. I resented that. "You got the front seat."

"Don't dis the car, Flaner. You want to walk?" said Dara.

"Perry wouldn't kick me out just because he didn't bring a goddamn GPS. He'll need me for meat later."

"You need to relax," said Dara.

"He's working on a bit," said Garrett. "Good so far, Tony."

"No. He's wigging out. He's in withdrawal."

"I am not."

"You are," said Critter. "You've reached for your phone six times in the last ten minutes."

I reached for my phone. Still not there.

"You can't see me from there," I said.

"Can too."

"Can not."

"Can too."

"Can not."

"Tony," whispered Perry, "you're arguing with a hand puppet."

"Yeah? Well...well...you're lost."

"Am not."

"Are too."

"Am not."

"Are too."

"Am not."

"Take a breath, Tony," said Standard. "It'll get better. One day at a time."

I took a breath and focused out the front windshield for a moment. The car went quiet.

"Are too," I said.

We were somewhere in Wyoming in a 1992 white four-door Cadillac Seville. We were on our way back in time to an age before smartphones and computers, when power came from beasts instead of wall outlets, and food had to be cooked in situ because there were no phones to order pizza.

Perry had arranged it. Or maybe it was Dara after learning Perry got the cabin. Standard had something to do with it too. Something smug, but I don't remember. If I had had my phone, I might have checked my texts to find out. But I didn't have my phone. I didn't have my computer either. The car didn't have a GPS or technology that hadn't been obsolete for over a quarter century.

I seem to remember the pivotal moment happened in the Comedy Cellar, the bar we haunted like spilled draft.

"I bought a cabin up in Wyoming," Perry had said.

That had been yesterday. The whole gang was there: me; Dara Sutter, frail foul-mouthed elfin waif; Standard Flox, the most boring of the group; Garrett Corta and Critter, comic and puppet, not all there, though Critter seems all right; and Perry Whitehouse, the most successful comic among us who was near to getting his own Netflix special but mentally disturbed in a paranoid-phrenic-whirlwind-tinfoil-hat kind of way when not properly medicated.

I'd done a set that night, a bit of open mic where I worked on a bit about TED Talks, showing the proper way to steeple fingers on one's chin and nod consolingly while feeling sorry for the audience who hadn't figured out themselves that eating your own grass clippings was the future. It could have gone better. The audience wasn't paying enough attention for the full ride.

The bar was turning over, in between shows, with the night owls replacing the evening crowd.

"A cabin?" said Standard. He liked to be called Stan, so I always called him Standard.

"Up in Wyoming."

"What's in Wyoming?" asked Garrett.

"Isolation. It's off the grid," said Perry.

"I think the word you're looking for is 'secluded,'" I said. "You'll never make it as a realtor like that."

"The ad said isolated. That's what interested me."

"As in 'he wrote his manifesto holed up in an isolated cabin'?" I said.

"Remember the source," said Critter, nodding his felt head sagely. "This is Perry here."

"You on your meds, ol' boy?" I hadn't needed to ask him this in a while, which meant that he had been.

"Yes," he said.

"But you're depressed?" said Garrett.

"No."

"Why isolation then?"

"Well, you know. The future."

"Ballsy career move for someone trying to get famous," said Dara.

"Famous?"

"Cable special? Weren't we just talking about that? Netflix?"

"I'm thinking long term," he said.

"As in long-term isolation?" said I.

"It's in Wyoming."

"You're saying that like it's a good thing."

"It was a deal. The ad said he was selling for a divorce."

"Where did you see this ad?" I was piecing together clues. I am a detective.

"It was one of the websites I visit," said Perry. "One of the other contributors needed to sell his…erm, cabin. Fast. I kinda know him. We did an online Q&A about Element 115 a few months back."

"The flying saucer element?" said Dara. I was surprised she knew of it but then remembered that you really couldn't spend any time at all with Perry without some of the conspiracy rubbing off.

"Yes. It was a good Q&A."

"Is the cabin more like a house or a bunker?" I asked.

Perry had turned his beer glass one hundred and eighty degrees while not making eye contact with me. "He said it was really nice."

"Bunker," said Dara.

"Bunker," said Standard.

"No, it has windows and everything. A hunting lodge. With a bomb shelter."

"Your money," said Critter.

"You won't get a cable special deal by hiding in the middle of Wyoming," said Dara.

"Northern Wyoming," corrected Perry. "On the Montana border. Big Horn County."

"Audiences can't be any worse up there," I said, scanning my phone for new emails.

"So you're saying it could be a good career move?" said Perry.

"Hell no," we all said together.

Oh neat. A Groupon.

"Oh, yeah? Well," said Perry, chin set defensively, "what kind of a career would I have if I was a melted lump of smoldering flesh?"

"There it is," said Dara. "Prepping."

"Nuclear or alien caused?" I asked, wondering if I needed more a massage or a window cleaning.

Perry considered my question. Critter answered for him before he could decide. "A holocaust would be a bad career move too. Good thing you got a cabin in Bumfuck, Wyoming."

"Big Horn County."

"My mistake."

I checked the news. Nothing significant had changed since the last time I'd looked ten minutes before. No new texts, missed calls, tweets, mentions, links, likes, Google alerts, AMBER alerts, weather alerts, software updates, battery warnings, or alarms. I needed something, so I set an alarm for five minutes to remind me to turn it off.

"You got rattled after the dandelion joke flopped," said Standard.

"What?" I said. "Me?"

"Yeah. You pitched a dud and had a hard recovery."

"It was a callback to the lawn bit. Remember the good ol' days when only the performer had a spotlight?"

"What do you mean?" said Garrett.

"You've seen it," I said, filling in a row of Sudoku. "You're up on stage, doing your act, you look out in the audience and everyone is tuned into the light of their phones."

"Like you now?"

"You're saying I do that?" Got all the 7s.

"Yes, you're doing it now, dumbass." Dara.

"You're addicted," Garrett said in his best intervening tone.

I looked up then, scanned the faces of my friends, and saw sad, confirming frowns.

"Addicted to what?"

"Technology."

"I need technology. It's my job."

"I thought you were a detective."

"I do research on computers. They figure very prominently in not a few of my cases."

"You're on a case?"

I took a sip of my beer to buy time realizing only after I'd tipped it all the way up that I'd emptied the glass ten minutes ago. I refilled it and chugged it in one go for old time's sake. After a discreet belch that subsonically rattled the light fixtures over the stage, I said, "What was the question?"

"Case?"

"What?"

"We're all addicted to technology," said Perry. "That's part of the reason for the cabin. It's isolated and unplugged. A good place to be unnoticed. A place to get back to nature."

"Career suicide," I said.

"I'm not going to live there full time."

"Unless...?"

"Unless," he said.

"It's a good idea." I'm not sure who said it was a good idea, but it could have been me getting drunk and being shamed, staring into my phone, my attention split, wanting to steer the conversation away from my foibles. It all went on in a blur of beer and later tequila shots, good company, and comedy until now, the next day, where I found myself in a crummy car on a crummy road, having sworn off technology for the trip.

"This is going to be a dumb week," I whined.

"At least you got the front seat," said Standard. "Even after I called it."

"Butts beat bleats," I said.

"What is that supposed to mean?"

"I think he's saying that him sitting on the seat first, 'butts,' beat Stan calling shotgun, 'bleats.'"

"Exactly, Critter." That puppet understood.

"You made that up."

"The proof is in the privy," said I.

"Look." Perry pointed out the window.

"Antelope? We've seen a shit-ton of those." Which was true. I'd seen a lot of them, having stolen the front seat from Standard. I had a pretty good view.

"No, the sign."

"'Road closed 1/2 mile when flashing?' What's that, the tenth, eleventh one of those we've seen? Reminds me of Dante. Abandon all hope ye—"

"No," said Perry. "That sign. There. We're passing it."

"'Welcome to Big Horn County Wyoming.'"

Antelope watched us pass, showing as much interest as I felt, indifferently pooping on the plain.

2

"LOOK FOR FLOYD," said Perry. "Our turn-off is after that."

"Who's Floyd?"

"I'm hoping it's a town."

"Or a barber."

"Could be both."

Perry took the speed down to fifty-five to watch for turn-offs or signs or mile markers, buffalo tracks, snake scales—hell if I knew. He rolled down his windows. Maybe he was sniffing for signs. The car filled with the smell of sage carried on eye-scratching dust.

And a goddamn loud horn.

I jumped. Dara screamed in my ear. Standard kicked the back of my seat, Critter went flying into the air, and Perry over-corrected onto the shoulder, nearly putting us in a ditch.

It was an RV passing us, blaring its amplified horn like a freight train barreling in on a track-stalled school bus full of orphans. It looked like a spaceship of black glass and chrome as it came alongside, straddling the centerline. The machine was massive and made me think of a love child between a Peterbilt and a grain silo. This child was in a goth phase and huffed silver Krylon spray paint under an overpass. Poor parenting to be sure.

We were buffeted by its wind stream, but Perry managed to get our two tons of white American steel back on the road after it had passed.

Another camper, small by comparison but still longer than a boxcar, followed behind the first and passed us as well. No horn that time. The man behind the wheel gave us a pained, even apologetic look as he raced to catch up to the other.

"The hell?" said Dara.

"The hell?" we all agreed.

"Think that was Floyd?"

"I hope not," said Perry.

I suppose I should say something about how beautiful Wyoming is, but I won't. I live in Utah. I know what sagebrush looks like. We have better rocks and they have more rivers. Call it a tie. They have cowboys; we have Mormons. One for them. We have civilization and they have rampant fracking. Win Utah.

Of course I knew Wyoming from my trips to Evanston on the border to buy booze for cheap or when I passed through it on my way to Denver. I haven't gone far beyond the I-80 corridor. Up till then, I didn't think I'd missed much. More of the same. Farms stuck out among lots of nothing. Hay and cows. Antelope. Lots of those guys. So many in fact that I got to wondering if they were raised for meat. Free-range pronghorn steaks, coming soon to a Safeway near you.

Then it got green and nice. And pretty.

"Have we crossed into Montana?" I asked.

"I don't think so," said Perry. "This is just what the other side of Wyoming looks like."

I reached for my phone to find us on a map and came up empty. Critter who was now back on Garrett's arm shook his head in disapproval.

In a husky voice, I saw trees of green, red roses too. Farms and swooping valleys, crops, horses, little pink houses and American flags everywhere.

"Oh yeah," I said. "Isn't some holiday coming up?"

"The Fourth of July," said Standard.

"When is that?"

"The fourth."

"This month?"

"Yeah."

"What day is today?"

"The second," said Garrett. "Don't you know?"

"I don't have a phone or a watch or a computer, remember?"

"But still, you'd think—"

"Don't tell me what to think."

A sign proclaimed Floyd in one mile around a wooded hill. Even at thirty miles per hour, we were through it before anyone registered it had happened.

On the other side of town was a turnoff for the Bighorn National Forest. A mountain with trees. Beyond that was the Crazy Woman Campground with a sign saying they had vacancies, and reservations were not required. Bonus. Attached to a barbed wire fence separating the road from a big field next to the campground was a banner proclaiming 'Fourth of July Fair. Right Here! July 4th — Free Admission. Strangers welcome.' There were flags and fireworks drawn on it. Glitter. It looked like a middle school crafts class had made it.

Beyond the field, Perry pulled over.

"I knew it. We're lost," I said. "One paved road in the whole state and you—"

"Calm down, Tony, you're pissing me off. Get with it," said Dara. "This will be good for you, or I'll kick you in the nuts."

"I think I'm doing better."

"Not enough."

I thought I was chilling more. Maybe a third more. Before, I was hungover, missed my tech and was a little sick of the car. Now most of the hangover had oozed out of my pores, I only kinda missed my tech, but I was still really sick of the car. The drive had already been eight hours, and after every piss stop, I had to rush back to keep someone else from taking my front seat. A full-time job. If only there were some way to reserve it.

I told Allie—that's Allison Braise, my girlfriend—about the trip, and she thought it was great. I told her hoping she'd talk me out of it or maybe come with me. Having her around would give me something to do. She couldn't come. She had to work. She had to be at her ranch to rent horses and do animal stuff and be successful and all that. Nevertheless, she insisted I go.

"You've said yourself you thought you relied too much on technology," she said. "Remember when you left your phone at home and panicked for three hours?"

"They wouldn't turn the train around."

"And you don't even know my phone number," she said.

"Sure I do."

"What is it?"

"Top of my favorites page."

"From home?"

"Speed dial one. You're my special gal."

"From jail?"

"Um."

"You called your ex-wife last time."

"She had your number."

"Go with your friends," she said. "It'll be fun. Getting back to nature can be good. See how the old-timers did it."

"We're not going back in time."

"You might feel like it."

A long time ago, my hobby obsession took me camping, and I got back to nature many times over my famed seven months, but I was hardly roughing it. I had solar chargers, jet engine stoves, dried food, tents that could mount Everest on their own. My Therm-A-Rest could have gone with it and planted a flag. I knew this trip wouldn't be that challenging. Everest is hard, but still the guys had given us some pretty dumb rules for the extended vacation: one bag per person. No electronic technology.

The monsters.

Perry compared a hand-drawn map to the Wyoming atlas he'd bought second-hand. Perry said he was still on his meds, but he was acting paranoid. He didn't want The Man to track the book sale because it would give him away. He bought this car with cash and paid a friend named Ratchet to verify that it didn't have any trackers in it.

"What's the point of having a hideout if you show everyone where it is?" he'd said.

"But you're taking us," said Critter.

This conversation happened somewhere halfway across Wyoming and Perry didn't speak to anyone for an hour afterward. Then he said, "We can all use it, I guess."

"An hour? It took you an hour to say that?"

"Yes. Just don't tell anyone."

"I can't," I said. "I don't have my phone."

He raised an eyebrow over squinted eyes, obviously thinking he may have made a mistake bringing us to his secret bat cave.

"We won't tell anyone," promised Garrett.

"Okay."

Now we were lost. I guess that's a plus for a secret hideout, but my butt hurt.

As Perry twisted the map around in circles, first clockwise, then counter-clockwise, then turning it over and holding it to the windshield like a light-box, I measured the summer rainfall by the remaining glitter on the barbed-wired banner. Not much.

The buzz of a small vehicle came up behind us, signaling the eventual arrival of a four-wheeler. It was the first of a long file.

"Howdy," said the rider. "Lost?"

"We're looking for—"

"Shhhhhhh," said Perry.

She was a middle-aged woman—I put her about forty—with round hips and a red face that was more rosacea than sunburn, but some of that too. Taking off her sunglasses, I saw she had blue eyes and short medium-brown hair. She had jeans and a windbreaker. Her green baseball cap read "Crazy Woman Campground." She struck me as some kind of guide.

"Are you some kind of guide?" I asked.

"I'm Gail Larsen. I own the Crazy Woman Campground. I'm taking some guests out for an ATV tour. So I guess I am some kind of guide."

"They don't look safe," said Critter, eyeing the vehicle.

She did a double-take into the back seat, realized she was speaking to a puppet, then laughed and played along, thinking it was a joke. "Like all things," she said, "it's how you treat them. ATVs are as safe as their drivers."

"You ever heard of...shit. I actually don't know where we're going," I said. "Perry?"

"I didn't tell you for a reason."

"Sounds like you kids have some things to talk about," the woman said. "If you're around here on the Fourth, come on out for a show, shops, and fireworks." She pointed to the glitter-clad sign.

Perry squinted and rotated the map again.

A bevy of ATVs pulled up behind her and waited.

"Perry, we're losing our Samaritan."

He sighed and whispered, "I'm looking for the old Kayshaw place."

"Don't know the names, but I know all the back roads and then some. May I see?"

Someone gave an anemic honk behind her as she took the hand-drawn map and studied it.

"Go up a ways and look for a fallen willow that half conceals a road—a pair of tire tracks really—but that should be that road there." She pointed to a place on the map.

"Thanks," I said.

Perry snatched the map back and tucked it into his shirt. He was in a hurry to hide it, but I thought he could have folded it first.

Gail and her ATV headed forward, trailing the long line of others. Each of them slowed down to gawk into our car. Critter gave them the stink eye, Dara the finger. Perry hid his face, and I wished I could check my email. One of the riders, a darkly tanned guy with dark glasses and no hat actually stopped and, leaning against the car, looked at each of us in turn as if trying to memorize our faces.

When they were gone, Dara said, "The Kayshaw place, eh?"

Perry looked abashed. "Yes."

"Not the family who killed all those people?"

"What?"

"She's dicking with you," I said. "That was the Mansons."

"Oh, right."

He started the car, drove a ways up and found the road just as Gail Larsen had described it. We turned off and quickly lost sight of the paved highway behind us.

The trail we followed would have challenged a Humvee. A tank would have balked. The Cadillac bounced and bucked like one of those cow things those one guys ride in those shows they do out in Wyoming.

"I thought I was sick of the car ride before, but now I think I'm actually going to puke," I said.

"We're almost there," said Perry. "And the cabin has everything we need. Food for years, beds, fire, water—everything."

"Neck braces and aspirin?" asked Garrett.

"Military-grade first aid kits and a full MASH-level triage center."

"What does that mean?"

"I don't know."

Another bend, another bounce, another burn where the seat belt cut into my shoulder.

Then we saw the moon.

And the man it was on.

He was standing in the middle of the trail. Just beyond him, we could see a structure of some kind, but all eyes were on the man. The naked bent-over man.

He straightened and turned around as Perry slowed the car.

Above his wild confused eyes was a bush of wild long brown hair. His beard was the same but had gray streaks, equally a mess. His mustache had been trimmed, I assumed by his teeth. More brown hair surrounded his pelvic region, where a seriously long penis hung between his legs. He was dirty and scratched and scabbed, and, like I said, not a stitch of clothes was on him.

He shifted his weight from leg to leg, his impressive manhood swaying as he did.

"You out here for no good?" he demanded to know. "Everyone's living lies here. You come to do that or just visiting?"

"Is that Mr. Kayshaw?" I asked.

"Look at you in that thing," said the naked man, pointing to the car. "What good is that to get back to the source in? I ask you? Well?"

"Why are you naked?" I said. "Are you a crazy person?"

"I'm not crazy. You're crazy. I'm not naked. You're naked."

"How you figure?" I got out of the car. I would walk to the cabin from here. Or home. I was done with the Caddie for a while.

"Naked means wrong. Clothes are wrong. I'm as God made me. You're the abominations. You're not being true. Liars. Bureaucrats. Deceivers. Con men. FDA hacks."

"We can see you have nothing to hide," said Dara, getting out as well. "You got a license for that?"

Garrett climbed out after her, holding his hand over the puppet's eyes.

"I don't need no license or no permission. You just remember what I said. Memory is everything."

"Is that the old Kayshaw place?" I asked, taking a step forward, and as I did, he leaped back and screamed. He crouched a moment, then jumped into the air, his pecker slapping his belly as he did. A half turn and he landed on the pads of his feet. At a dead sprint, he disappeared into the trees like a well-endowed white rabbit who was late for an appointment.

3

YOU'D THINK a visit from a crazy all-naked porn star refugee would have gladdened my spirits, but I was tired and cranky and wanted a roof over my head that didn't threaten to break my neck bouncing over boulders. As irony works, the final fifty yards of road to the cabin were smooth and grated. I walked anyway and as such arrived only after the gang was already inside.

"There's no furniture," I said.

"Thank you, Hawkeye," said Dara. "We were wondering what was wrong."

"Perry, didn't you say that it was fully furnished with food and water and, well, furniture?"

"That's what was agreed upon."

"Is there a phone?"

Dara stomped her foot. "Dammit, Tony! Get with the program."

"I'm thinking of Perry maybe calling Mr. Kayshaw and asking what's what."

"Oh."

"No phone," said Perry.

"They took that too?" asked Standard.

"Dammit, Standard!" I said. "Get with the program."

"What?"

"This is about cutting wires, not stringing them. For hell's sake."

"Feel better?" Dara asked me.

"Yeah, a little bit."

There were switches, but they didn't work. Nevertheless, with light streaming through uncurtained windows, we could see it was a big house. The main room had a Pergo floor and log walls—the back sides of the same rustic logs we'd seen on the outside. A river-stone fireplace reached thirty feet up to a vaulted ceiling, which effectively halved the upstairs space suggested by a stairway. I glanced at a door up there and a few on this floor suggesting other rooms or a confusing interior design motif. Like true Scooby-Doo detectives and doomed 80s teenagers, we decided to split up and explore.

I found my way into the kitchen, which wasn't far from the main room. The house was big. My ex-wife, Nancy, would have been able to tell me the square footage within a dollar, but I only knew it was bigger than my house. It had more the vibe of a vacation cabin than a survivalist bunker. If it got some furniture and internet, it could host a writing retreat or a drunken orgy. Sometimes the same thing.

There was something strange about the kitchen though. It was shadowy on the north side, and I pushed open some shutters above the sink to let the light in. There was a fridge and a microwave, but they weren't working. There was a pantry, a big walk-in one, with empty shelves and six mouse traps. There was a gas oven and a double stainless steel sink over a granite countertop. I noticed then what was wrong: there were no plumbing fixtures. Nope, not there. Not stolen—never installed, and nothing to suggest they ever would be.

The sinks were depressions with holes at the bottom emptying into darkness below. Opening the cabinet, I found it empty—no pipe to take runoff but maybe enough room for a bucket to catch stuff, but of course there was no bucket. Since there were no faucets, it all worked out.

I left the kitchen in search of a bathroom and found several big empty rooms with mousetraps, some of which were already used.

"You guys find a bathroom?" I yelled.

"I found something, but there's no toilet," came Critter's voice.

"How about you, Garrett?"

"Same."

"Mirror and vanity and washbasin," called Dara from upstairs. "No toilet."

"Perry?"

"I found it," he called from some undisclosed location.

"Is it outside?"

"Yes."

I followed his voice out a back door and saw a shed with a half-moon on it. I went over to it with Perry and opened the door.

"A four-holer," I said, holding my noise. "Top of the line."

Perry seemed concerned but not brick-biting pissed, which would have been the normal reaction.

"Did you know about this?"

"I suspected. It's off the grid."

"Off the grid doesn't mean no toilets."

"No sewer."

"Septic tanks aren't gridded."

"Those require running water," he said.

We walked around the side of the house until we came to a path. It was a path, or had been, but now was overgrown. Holding still, we could hear the murmur of running water a little ways away.

Perry pointed to the side of the house. "In the picture, there were barrels there."

"Dara's not going to like this," I said.

"Flaner," came Dara's voice from an upstairs window, "I'm on board with you now. This is shit. And it smells like it."

We pointed to the outhouse.

"Ewww."

"Claim your rooms," said Perry cheerfully. "First come, first serve!"

Dara and I stared at him. Another window opened and Standard stuck his head out. "I call dibs on the one on the main floor."

Garret reported that he and Critter would take the northeast, upper room.

"You do know we can't stay here, right?" I said.

"Why not?" said Standard. "It's off the grid. It's just as advertised. Simple."

"It is not anything as advertised. Where's the furniture? Food? Water? MASH kits?"

"There's water down at the creek," said Perry.

"And nothing to bring it up to the house in. I'm not expecting pipes. No, nothing so bourgeois, but a bucket would be nice, or a towel maybe. A thimble?"

"What's your point?"

"Seriously? Dara, back me up here."

"Seriously," she echoed.

"We'll run to town and pick up a few things," Perry said.

"Floyd?"

"Why not?"

"You got ripped off, dude," I said.

"Yeah, looks like it, but the house isn't in my name."

"Not in your name?"

"A dummy corporation linked to a shell trust linked to a deposit box and a numbered—"

"I get it."

"There's a bomb shelter."

"Where?"

"Somewhere. I was told there's a secret tunnel."

"You ever thought of investing in bridges?" I asked.

"No. Tell me more."

We went back into the house. "Was the door locked when you got here?" I asked.

"No."

"Check if your key fits."

He did. It did.

"Left open, though?"

He nodded.

It didn't take long to find the tunnel. It was in the master bedroom closet, ready for a layer of shoes and dirty laundry to complete its camouflage. Very ingenious.

Perry lifted the wooden hatch revealing a stairway descending steeply and ominously into thick, gloomy, treacherous darkness.

"We need light."

I reached for my smartphone, which has a really excellent LED light, but came up with nothing. I gave Perry a cruel squint.

"We'll check it out later," he said.

Harder squint.

He lowered the door, and we went back to the great room.

"Looks like they even took the chandelier that was there," Garrett said, pointing to a chain dangling from the tall ceiling.

"It was probably tacky."

I went outside to relieve myself but first visited the car for some napkins. I reluctantly dragged myself to an official twenty-first-century four-hole outhouse to answer nature's call.

Like most people these days, I treasured my nature moments as a guilt-less pleasure where I could take my time, playing Tetris or surfing the web, following idle thoughts and questions. Who *is* buried in Grant's tomb anyway? Not having my phone now didn't seem like a big deal. I couldn't bear down hard enough to get out of that mini horror show as fast as I wanted.

I staggered out, gasping for air. Because I knew I had an audience, I fell to my knees, twisted and fell over, then turned my face upward, gasping to beseech the heavens to deliver me. Then I collapsed lifeless to the ground.

Unimpressed, Perry went back inside.

I followed the path down to the creek to wash my hands, expecting to find a picturesque little stream with faeries and sylphs dancing in silks. It was picturesque, but there was only a big black cow sitting in a wallow, a big muddy pit on the opposite bank.

I washed my hands with sand, moss, and giardia. For those of you without quick access to the internet, which is a terrible sucky state to be in, let me tell you, giardia is a parasite that causes giardiasis, a nasty infection of the intestines, causing diarrhea and total misery, often spread by cow shit in water supplies.

When I got back to the house, I was sweating from the walk. "We'll have to boil the water before we drink any of it," I said.

"Perry found a place for a generator," said Garrett.

"Over there." Critter pointed to the end of the house I hadn't seen yet.

"A place?" I said. "Not a generator? No. Of course not."

On the side of the house, we found Perry puzzling over some cables.

"It's so pretty out here," said Standard, jogging over. Jogging. What the fuck?

Dara slogged after him. I was with her. This was looking much harder than just not having Google.

"It is beautiful," agreed Perry. "A person can really get lost out here."

"And the wildlife," I added.

"Yes."

"With long schlongs."

"Oh, right. That happened," Perry said.

"Hullo!"

The voice was deep and resounding and actually came to us before the buzz of the ATV it was riding. Behind the voice, which I assumed came from the big-bearded man in an over-tight muscle-stretched T-shirt, was a smallish woman. They appeared from a stand of trees where a hint of a trail might be discerned if one was discerning. They both waved at us like we were old friends.

The ATV pulled up, and the two got off it like they were dismounting from a Clydesdale.

"At least they're clothed," Garrett observed.

"Hi," said the man, poking his hand into our midst but not at anyone in particular.

"Clothed?" said the woman. "Who wasn't clothed?"

The man shot her a glance.

"So you're the ones who bought this place," the man said to Standard.

We all pointed to Perry, who watched warily from the back.

"We're the Rawly family, James and Kim."

"Kimmy for short," she said.

"That's longer," said I.

She looked me over as if sizing me for a fit. Then she looked at Perry, Dara, Standard and fell upon Garrett, whom she drank in like a cool drink from a non-giardia-infested stream. Critter shuddered.

"Folks call me Rawly," said the big man. "Sally said the place had been sold."

"Sal and Sally," said Kimmy. "Divorced."

"I bought it from Sal," said Perry, leaving out the dummy corporations and tax hideouts.

"I heard," said Rawly. "Sally was just here last week with movers cleaning the place for the new owners."

"How thoughtful," I said.

"Didn't think they were in trouble," said Rawly, scratching his short cut hair.

"I knew they were doomed," said Kimmy, still watching Garrett. "Never thought it would last."

Garrett smiled but glanced around for help.

"You all got any furniture? We could help you move in," said Rawly.

"You're neighbors?" asked Perry.

"We sure are. Just a ways up that trail." He smiled and laughed hard like he'd discovered nitrous for the first time.

"How'd you find us?"

"We were just in town buying, um...supplies and we saw Gail, the gal at the campground. She said you were here." Another gassy grin.

"What are your names?" asked Kimmy.

We are nothing if not ill-mannered. Of course we hadn't introduced ourselves.

"I'm Stan," said Standard, always the boot-lick. "That's Perry. He bought the place."

"Hi," said Perry.

"Dara, Tony, and Garrett and his pretend friend Critter. We're comedians. We do comedy."

"Thanks for the clarification, Doctor Dictionary," said Dara.

There are times, a lot of them actually, when I have to wonder about my choice of career. Not comedy, that's a hobby that one day might bring me fame, glory, a late-night talk show, condoms with my name on them. No, I mean detective. Sleuth, surveyor of surveillance. Okay, that didn't work. But noticing things is a generally accepted requirement for the position. It was only after Kimmy extended her hand out to Critter as if presenting a ring for kissing, a pope thing, I think, but it was only then that I noticed the gun on Rawly's belt. I wondered why he had it.

"Why are you wearing a gun?" I said.

"Can't never be none too careful."

I stopped to calculate the quadruple negatives, looking for a meaning.

"You'd call us preppers," said Rawly.

"You mean the dance club at high school with the short skirts?" said Garrett. That made Kimmy smile so hard.

"No," said Rawly, not noticing or possibly trying not to notice his wife's smile. "You're thinking of Pep Club. We're survivalists. We came out here to get off the grid."

"Same as the Kayshaws," said Perry. "I get it."

"More, though. Harder. Real prep, not this half-ass luxury mansion stuff."

"There's no running water," said Dara. "How is that a luxury?"

I waited for a tale about walking to school in the snow uphill both ways, but Rawly shook his head as if rattling answer BBs into little holes. "Don't get me wrong. It's a nice place. We're just more buttressed."

"We have barbed wire around our place," explained Kimmy. "But there are places—"

"Kimmy," said her husband. "We don't want to scare these people. They just got here. They might not see the end of the world coming the way we do."

So much for not trying to scare us.

"We'll need to get some supplies," said Perry.

"Like what?"

"Like everything," he said. "Do you know if I can buy a generator that fits this in town?" He held up a cable.

"In Floyd?" said Rawly. "No. Maybe Lovell or Sheridan, but I'll tell you what. I have extras. I'll let you have one for what it cost me."

"You have two generators?" I asked. "I thought you didn't have luxuries."

"Eight. We use one. The others are backups. Everything important needs a backup."

"That would be great," said Perry.

I didn't like the gun on his belt. I thought of Chekhov, which made me think of phasers and then the Horta. What a lovely animal. Kimmy winked at Garrett, and I was on to green dancing women.

"I'll go fetch it," he said. "It's a good one. It's just like the one I use. I've been here for four years, and it runs as good now as it did the first time we lit the camp."

"The camp with the barbed wire?"

"We have chickens," he explained. "I don't like them to run amok."

4

GARRETT, Critter, Dara, and Standard would wait on Rawly and the generator while Perry and I went to town to buy what else was needed, which was everything.

Perry, still cheerful, I think just to piss me off, commented how the road wasn't as bad going back as it was coming up. "Maybe it's the less weight." He'd made us put our bags in the house before we left to claim our rooms. I got what could have been a study in another world on the main floor. Perry kicked Standard out of the master bedroom, and he went upstairs with Dara and Garrett.

"Maybe the car is being nice because it thinks we're going home."

The car was like the house. A new purchase through a series of dummy companies hiding its true owner, Perry. He liked it because it was half invisible and had absolutely no modern electronics that could be hacked or tracked. "Driving incognito," he explained.

"You've got issues, Perry," I said.

"So do you."

"Yeah?"

"Yeah."

"Touché."

We found the paved road after too goddamn long and turned back toward what passed for a town in this wilderness. The four-wheeler caravan from before was nowhere to be seen. It was afternoon, but I didn't know what time exactly because the car didn't have a clock, and I didn't have my goddamn phone. Or a watch.

We were careful to drive slowly so we wouldn't accidentally pass the town again. A thickening of traffic and a few buildings suggested we were there. The sign "Welcome to Floyd" was suggestive too. I could have verified our location precisely if I'd had…yeah, you get it.

We cruised the town once, then turned around and did it again. Both trips together took about a minute. We saw one building that was a small strip mall with a real estate office next to a store called Prospector Paradise, a beauty salon called The Sophisticated Cowgirl, and a sheriff's office. Across the street was a gas station with a convenience store, a Grab & Git, and a bar called Floyd's Old Times Saloon. A couple roads led away from the highway and disappeared behind some rare trees to who-knows-what wasteland.

"Pull into the real estate office," I said.

"Why?"

"Because you need to talk to someone about your lack of plumbing."

We parked in front of the strip mall.

The car was complaining. I think something was knocked loose underneath, or maybe hanging off it, like a tumbleweed in the axle trying to pry open the oil pan with a riveter.

He parked next to a ubiquitous white pickup truck, and before he'd turned off the engine, a man was loping out of the real estate office, excited to greet us.

"You must be the people who bought the Kayshaw place," he said.

"Nothing like isolation where everyone knows who you are and all your business," I said with a glance to my friend.

Perry scowled.

"I'm Jack Mandel. I helped the Kayshaws list the place."

We got out of the car. Perry looked underneath for Rosey.

"You insured?" I asked Jack Mandel.

"What? Why?"

"There is the little problem of the house being wholly and utterly unlivable. How it ever got permits to be built is a question the county will face as you're dealing with fraud and false advertising charges."

"What?" His smile fell away. "Everything was fine. The property was sold as property with a note of some outbuildings. Not a home."

"Perry," I said to my friend as he pulled out a hunk of road-burned shrub from under the car, "I think I know why you got it so cheap."

"It was pretty cheap," agreed Mandel. "So, you're the owner? Perry, is it?" He reached his hand out to shake and was given a branch. "I expected you to be more tan coming from the Caribbean."

"Cayman Islands?" I inquired.

Perry averted his gaze. "We need to locate a few things," he said.

"Like what?"

"A bulldozer?" I suggested.

Perry scowled again.

There was something about Mandel that didn't look right. I crooked my head to give my eyes more angle, a bit of vertical, a trick cats had taught me.

Then I saw it. He wasn't dressed like a cowboy. Or a country boy. Or a normal person. His suit gleamed. His shoes were spotless. His tie was amazing. Not a grease spot on it.

"Going somewhere?" I asked.

"Just work," he said.

"You look great."

"Thanks, I feel great."

Perry asked, "Any place to get furniture around here? Beds? Maybe a table?"

"Food?" I added.

Mandel's smile had returned, kinda. "There's the outpost down Stubbins Street."

"Stubbins Street?"

"Named after the town founder. Floyd Stubbins."

"Why not call the town Stubbins?"

"I have no idea."

Perry asked, "How did you know who we were?"

"Rawly radioed up with the info. Described your car and everything. News travels fast in a town like this."

"Described the car and everything…" I said to Perry.

He gave me another scowl, or it might have been the same one as before or the one before that.

"I can understand if you want to fix up the place, make it a home," said Mandel. "I can help with that."

"How is it listed on the deed?" I asked. "If you know, Mr. Mandel."

"Tony, are you trying to make this worse?" said Perry. "Wait—don't answer that."

"The structures are outbuildings," Mandel said.

"Out of what? What does that mean?"

"The secret bomb shelter is storage while the cabin can technically be called an outbuilding for taxes. You're allowed to camp in an outbuilding, like to hunt and such. Old law."

"You know about the secret bomb shelter?"

"Of course."

"Not so secret then, is it?" I said.

Mandel looked confused. "I guess not."

Perry, squeezing the bridge of his nose, said, "Kayshaw didn't tell me it was listed locally."

"It was," he said. "I gave them a break on my commission since they found the buyer themselves."

"Did you know about the stuff left inside?"

"They came and got it last week," he said. "I helped Sally arrange for the truck."

"Sal said he owned it all." Perry was now rubbing his temples. "He said it came with all furniture."

"I guess he changed his mind."

"They divorced two months ago?"

"Sal and Sally?" said Mandel, surprised. "Well, I never. No. Wait. There were those rumors. Yeah, come to think of it, I should have seen it coming."

"Sally took all the furniture," Perry said. "All the chairs, provisions, guns."

"Guns?" I said.

Perry squirmed. He knew I didn't like guns.

"Sal and Rawly are two of a kind that way, both of them preparing for some catastrophe or another."

"She took the stuff out of the cabin," Perry said, trying to make his point.

"You'll need to take that up with Sal and Sally," he said. "Let me know if I can help or if you want to list it again."

"First street for the outpost?" I asked.

"Stubbins Street. Just a ways." He pointed up the road a ways. A ways is how you measure distance in Wyoming.

A white SUV with a sheriff's badge on the door pulled up to the mall.

"Hey, Craig," said Mandel. "Guess who this is."

"I know who it is."

He parked beside the Caddy and got out. He stood maybe six-foot-three in his heels. Cowboy boots. He had sun-squinted eyes that were probably blue, but I was too far away to be sure. His skin was tan and lined in an I-never-use-lotion-or-sunscreen kind of way, and his hair was tawny brown, straight where it wasn't shaped by his white straw cowboy hat that he plucked off the passenger seat and slipped on. His hands looked rough as sandstone, a thin wedding band on one finger. I put him in his mid-sixties or seventies for all the creases on his face. He rolled his neck to get the kinks out. I'd seen this show before. Perry must have too, because he decreased in mass by about forty percent, trying to melt into the gravel. Cops and I have issues, but we communicate. Perry has a full-on phobia of The Man. It's the kind of thing that will lead one to buy a plumbingless house in the middle of Nowhere Bumfuck, Big Horn County.

"You're the new owner of the Kayshaws' place, ain't you?" The cop's drawl seemed a little put on, but then again, he might really be an ignorant slack-jawed third-grade-educated hick and not just a manipulative power-abusing brownshirt tool of the oppressor class. Time would tell.

"Yep, Sharrrff," I said, and for punctuation, I scratched my ass and spat on the ground but missed, finding his snakeskin boots instead.

He looked at me as if planning where to plant his baton.

"Actually, Craig, Perry Whitehouse there is the new owner of the Kayshaw place. I'm not sure who this is."

"You got any ID?"

"You got any cause to see it?"

"Let me guess. You know your rights? You wonder if you're being detained?"

"You've seen the act before?"

"I have."

"Award-winning," I said. "As in monetary awards from municipalities that fuck with it."

"Tony," said Perry, worried.

"What?"

"Be nice."

"I don't feel nice," I said.

"Show me your ID," said the cowboy cop.

"How about I tell you who I am?"

"Who are you?"

"Judge Antony Burgess the Third, Fifteenth District Court of Appeals on vacation. Who are you?"

"I'm Craig Carter, deputy sheriff, and there isn't a Fifteenth District Court of Appeals."

"Don't you mean there ain't none?"

He smiled a reptilian grin.

"Hick," I said.

"What was that?"

"Sorry. Something I ate. I have the hiccups. Hick, hick, hick. See?"

"You're one smart-ass." He stepped toward me. I think he was reaching for his handcuffs. What had I done?

"He's Tony Flaner," said Perry. "A private investigator from Utah. Maybe you've heard of him."

"I don't think I have," he said.

"What's going on here? We're all friends," said Mandel. "Neighbors."

I remembered then that the sheriff's office was in this very building.

"He's right, Deputy Sheriff," I said. "I overreached. I thought you were here to lean on us. You know, hassle the strangers. I—"

"I am," he said.

"What?" said Mandel.

"The Kayshaws were shady. Survivalist types. Like the Rawlys. Dangerous gun nuts. Unabomber types. Paranoid. Are you paranoid?"

"I'm not," I said.

"Am I being detained?" asked Perry.

"Do you welcome everyone to your town like this?" I asked. "It's kinda passé and cliché and dické. We haven't done anything. Yet."

He took a deep breath to speak, but I cut him off.

"Let me guess, you run a quiet little town here in the boonies and you like it like that? Don't want no trouble, right? 'Cuz you don't cotton to that?"

"Tony, is it?" said Mandel. "Maybe you should be on your way."

"The wrong people settling in attract more of the wrong people," explained Deputy Sheriff Carter.

As if he'd planned it, as if some great director like Kubrick had staged it, just at that moment we heard the roar of motorcycles. We all looked a ways up the street and saw two big bikes and a Jeep cruising toward the bar. The Jeep had a full-sized Confederate flag attached to its roll bar, and the driver had facial tattoos that went to his fingers. Three others in the car, all bald, I noticed, hung their heavy Doc Martens out the sides and waved to the sheriff as they passed. The bikers, similarly inked, saluted.

"Friends of yours?" I said.

He snorted, then turned back to us. "You're paranoid survivalists, right?"

"Private eye."

Carter looked at me again as if finally registering what I was. His look told me he had the usual cop disdain for PIs.

In a weak voice, Perry said, "I want to leave now. Am I being detained?"

"Watch your step," said Carter. "No one comes here for long unless they got serious business or are running away from something."

"Have you considered getting a Shake Shack?" I said. "It's a great franchise opportunity. Really put the town on the map."

"I'm just the humble sheriff," he said.

"Deputy sheriff," I corrected him.

"He works for the town," interjected Mandel. "It's a small town."

"It's a bar and a real estate office," I said. "You're about as far from a town as Deputy Sheriff Carter here is from getting a medal for gallantry."

"You want to spend time in jail?"

"Oh, you flirt." I fluttered my eyelashes. "Thanks, but no. I have a girlfriend. And standards."

"He's only visiting," said Perry.

"And you?"

"I'll be no trouble."

"You'll be the nice quiet neighbor we all hear about after the mass killing?"

I could see Perry was tharn—that state of staring into your doom, rabbits into the headlights of an oncoming truck. See *Watership Down*. "Let me handle this," I said.

"Okay," he whispered.

I took a deep breath, choosing my words carefully. "Listen, you dead-ended glorified mall security associate, you better start displaying a little bit of civility because we aren't from around here. We know people. Nice people, and they don't act like you. It's the goddamn Fourth of July, and America says we're innocent until proven guilty. We intend to stay in this little shit-stain town a while, free of the glorious internet, to see how the other side lives without running water, flushing toilets, and in your case, mouthwash. While we do, we don't want to see your big-bad-cop, tiny-penis-compensation act. Save it for the sheep and the padded tweezers you keep on the bedstead by the tissues."

I'm not sure what I was thinking. Maybe I was hangry—you know, hungry so you're angry. Or maybe I was just cranky from an eight-hour car ride, a shit in a box, and a cow in my washbasin. And how could I forget the naked nature lover with earwigs in his beard shouting about memory? I also recalled I had no real place to sleep—never an uplifting prospect. There was also that gun-toting neighbor with his cotton-eyed wife, and this shyster realtor, none of whom had helped my mood. Skinheads are never a good look outside a maximum security prison, and now this cop was being a dick, an actual dick. I wasn't making it up. He was being a dick. So I'd let him have it.

He was, however, a cop.

Out came the handcuffs.

"Tony..." said Perry.

"How'd you like to spend the night in jail for being a public nuisance, smart-ass?" said Carter.

"What's the jail like here?" I asked Mandel.

Alarmed and confused, he said, "A concrete room, lumpy cot, and a blanket. No seat on the toilet."

"But it flushes?"

"Yes."

Sheriff Carter twirled the cuffs on his finger, waiting for me to say something.

"Eat shit."

5

WE DIDN'T HAVE FAR to go. I was cuffed and perp-walked past Mandel's real estate office, next to the Prospector Paradise, turning just before The Sophisticated Cowgirl, where I could get my nails done. The glass door said simply "Sheriff." I think it was a sticker. Past the door waited a woman behind a reception counter in a tan uniform and shiny badge. I stopped, knowing the routine, waiting to be processed, but Deputy Sheriff Carter pushed me forward and down a hall, then made a left through a door into another hall with three cells. He put me in one of those.

"What about my—" but Deputy Sheriff Carter was gone, and I was alone.

I'd had a chance to study Deputy Sheriff Craig Carter in more detail as we'd come in. By his gray roots, I figured his hair color was from a bottle. Maybe The Sophisticated Cowgirl could help. He was fit for his age, which I still pegged on the wrong side of sixty. Physically he was in better shape than me, which probably isn't a good metric. I'm not a physical guy. He was a cop and looked like it—Roman nose, sharp chin, squinty pale eyes, and windblown cheeks. He reminded me of an older Longmire, but that was probably because we were in Wyoming, and he was a big-hat-wearing lawman. I wondered how close Absaroka County was to Big Horn.

The cot was better than most. I kicked my shoes off and sat down. I noticed I still had my laces. That and my quick walk past the receptionist deputy told me I wasn't really arrested. I was being harassed. I didn't mind. I was where I wanted to be. Well, maybe not that. More like I was not where I didn't want to be. A cold cell for the night with a warm blanket and flushing toilet sounded a lot better than picking out furniture and most likely building it before I could sleep in Perry's outbuilding. I like to arrive to parties late and leave early; that way I don't have to set up or clean. Perry's new place had a lot of setup in store. I'd let them do it without me, get blisters from hex wrenches, sound out Swedish names, hoping they're not really chanting Cthulhuian spells to summon the Old Ones. I'd get a bologna sandwich, maybe a PB&J; they'd get beans and burns from steno cans while picking splinters out of their asses from that stinking four-holer. I didn't have my phone or computer, but my butt had porcelain, and theirs didn't. Win for Tony.

Now don't misunderstand. My friends are all flakes too. If they'd been thinking and seen the opportunity as I had, you can bet your bottom dollar they'd have jumped at it. Physical labor is not on the menu for these people. Even if Perry found built furniture and hired husky men to move it in, they'd be bitching at having to cut the plastic away. And food? We can't agree on onion rings or jalapeño poppers without knives being drawn. Whatever Perry had in mind to keep the gang sustained had surely been overturned by the lack of having anything in that cabin at all. I suspect he'll find a pizza and a lot of beer and lock his door tonight.

I lay back on the cot and reached for my phone to while away the time.

Shit.

Without blessed blue light distraction, I was forced to fall asleep all on my own, which I shockingly did right away.

I was woken up by the woman I'd seen before. "Here you go." She slid a TV dinner through a door in the door.

"Oooo, Salisbury steak with corn niblets. My favorite."

"Really?"

"If it weren't for this, I'm sure I'd be eating bugs."

"You don't look homeless."

"There are different kinds."

"Carter said you'll probably be out tomorrow. You're not actually being booked."

"What's for breakfast?"

"Cereal and a banana."

"Orange juice?"

"And coffee."

"See you then."

She left me with my shoelaces, plastic utensils, and mystery meat. I savored every bite, thinking of which one of my friends would try to cook something in that kitchen, wondering if they knew what the early symptoms of carbon monoxide poisoning looked like. I wasn't sure myself. I tried to look it up on my phone.

After the peach cobbler it was good and dark, and I was good and tired. I cuddled up on the cot and slept for real this time, thinking this was how real pioneer public disturbance desperadoes spent their nights.

In the morning, I had regrets. I didn't have a toothbrush. The toilet was nice—don't get me wrong—and the little steel sink stuck to the wall was a level of magnitude better than Disease Creek, but I wished I had a toothbrush. I wondered if I'd even packed one. I didn't remember doing so.

"Hullo," I said, rubbing my gums with my finger. Without more calluses, I wondered what good it would do.

"What?" It was Carter

"When's breakfast?"

"You're leaving," he said. "All sobered up?"

"I was never drunk."

"Sure you were."

He came in and opened the door with a key. How quaint.

"It's nine o'clock. You can get your own breakfast."

"That early? What are we doing up so early?"

He thought I was joking, but really, nine o'clock is pretty early.

Carter gestured for me to leave. I put on my shoes and flushed the toilet again just because I could and wandered out the way I came.

The sun was up, so maybe Carter was telling the truth about the time. I had no way to check.

"What am I supposed to do now?" I asked him, standing on the sidewalk.

"Have a nice visit in Big Horn County. Then leave."

"I was thinking more immediately."

He shrugged. "You want to call your friend to pick you up?"

"Yeah—wait. I can't. No phones."

"That's too bad." And with that, he went back inside the strip mall deputy sheriff's office.

It was a nice morning, I guess. Not too hot, not too cold. Fourth of July was coming up tomorrow, and the street was bleeding red, white, and blue. Someone was making a killing on American flags. Insert partisan political joke here.

I walked up the side road, Stubbins Street by name, leaving the desolate main drag, looking for a McDonald's. I still had my wallet—they hadn't taken a thing from me. Hadn't even searched me. I had McMoney if I got McLucky, but I didn't hold my McBreath.

A block beyond the highway, on the other side of concealing poplars, was a town. A real town. There was a hardware store, a library, and a big modern-looking school. There were churches. Plural. I saw an "outpost" and boxy little houses all older than sliced bread. I thought I remembered that sliced bread was invented in 1928. I reached for my phone to confirm it, but...

I'm not saying Floyd was big, but it was more than the little row of commerce the highway suggested. Not a lot more, but more. Houses. People. Trucks. ATVs. Lots of trucks. Lots of ATVs. The air was full of the doppling sound of coming and going quad cycles and rumbling trucks.

Walking down the quaint road of this picturesque town out of time, my mind wandered and then went through a subconscious rebooting checklist and registered nothing in my pocket with a healthy jolt of lost-phone-adrenaline panic. This happened like three times. It wasn't enough that I had to suffer not having my bionic buddy when I needed it, but its missing presence was harshing my calm. And I was listing to the left for the loss of the 6.84 ounces usually ballasted in my side pocket. There was a physical as well as psychological thing happening here.

I liked using my computer much more than my phone. When I had work to do, research or games to play—computer all the way. The phone was a substitute for when I didn't have my computer. When I was waiting for something, like dinner to come, a bus to arrive, or a light to change to green —in those moments, I'd pull out my phone toggle through email and messages, check out a headline, stock prices, weather, figure a number on Sudoku and then flip off the guy behind me who was honking to get me to notice the light had already changed. It was habit.

There was this issue of new versus old. In the old days, people remembered things. Now we have computers to do that for us. I used to know all my friends' phone numbers. I'm not even sure I know my own now. I haven't needed to. The omniscient cloud knows it for me. I don't need to recall how to cook my famous cinnamon chicken because the recipe is in my recipe folder. I've made it a million times but still check it to make sure my garlic isn't to toxic levels. It's a crutch. They even say that people today know less than our ancestors. I believe it. We don't have to carry it all around. We don't need to be Mentats. We are cyborgs instead.

It's cool, in a *Terminator* kind of way, but still kinda creepy. No one likes to be dependent on a thing, be it coffee, drugs or electronics—three of my favorites. And the trade-off of instant communication is that you can be communicated with instantly. That can mess you up. It's habitual and plays off the same instant gratification as the microtransaction games. *Oh, I got a text. I win!*

And then there are the early adopters. The bleeding edgers. The people with RFID implants under their ears, Google Glasses and *Ready Player One* haptic suit lust-fellows. God bless them, they get the bugs out before Apple sells them to me in working order. Sometimes.

I have to remind myself, or maybe it's forgive myself, that it's not just the new tech. If I didn't have an electronic address book, I'd have one on paper. If I didn't have paper, I wouldn't need one because we didn't have addresses that far back. It's a moving stream and those that go ahead and those that lag behind are the definition of fringes. We're all there sometimes. The good ol' days for me were the unfathomable future for my parents. New and old. It's all perspective. It's all moving, and it's going so fast we can't keep up for long.

Perry hates this. He sees danger. He thinks Siri is spying on him. He's right, but how else am I to get a good recipe for pancakes? Perry was warning people about the technological military-industrial complex since before I knew him. In the twisted logic of a crazy comedian, he needed to be famous but wanted to be anonymous at the same time. He had people putting his name all over the internet, on TV, radio, even using the ancient alchemy of newspapers, but Perry won't have cable at his house. He had a pirated T1 cable for a while through which he watched the machinations of the monster before getting rid of it and moving three times. I could see how his "cabin" was a step along the same road. He wanted a place to truly hide, to be wholly off the grid, unknown, and as he figured it, safe. I don't know if he really thinks the end of the world is coming, at least not more than the average person who, in all honesty, should be scared shitless twenty-four-seven over current events, but a retreat from the world sometimes is a good thing. If your retreat has a bomb bunker, bonus. No water? I think that's a bit much. But what do I know? I just tried to search bomb bunker effectiveness but came out of my empty pocket with a handful of lint and a ticket stub.

I'd seen how it irked Perry that the entire town already knew who he was, where he was, and what he had. Damn these friendly neighbors all to hell! And I'd made it worse. Not only had I gotten tossed in the pokey as his only known acquaintance for an award-worthy tirade against the town's law officer, but I'd goaded him every time a petal fell off his imagined flower of anonymity. Now there's a labored metaphor, but you get what I mean.

What can I say? I was cranky.

These were the thoughts that guided me as I wandered the quiet, well-flagged streets of small-town America. I found a café called Ginger's Café and went inside. It was packed with people, all local, if flannel is any indicator.

Like a black-clad desperado fresh back from cattle rustling entering a saloon, all conversation stopped and everyone's eyes turned to me, the stranger.

In pure Sergio Leone, I squinted as I panned around the room, my fingers twitching at my side. "Howdy," I said.

"Sit anywhere," said Ethel, a shrunken old lady with a Sharpie'd name tag.

The floor was linoleum; the table plastic-topped on spindly steel legs, the kind of thing that made the '70s a forgettable decade. I sat at one in a rickety vinyl chair with similarly spindly legs and, after wiping syrup off the menu with a paper napkin, found they offered breakfast.

I ordered coffee and three eggs and bacon, side of toast, flapjacks, sausage—both kinds patty and link—an English muffin with rye and white toast and extra butter. I wanted to sample the array of single-serving jams they had.

Conversation picked up, and while I waited, I read a brief history of the area on the back of the menu below the gravy stain that had seeped under the torn lamination. It said Big Horn County was home to Cheyenne before they were driven off. It figured in the infamous Johnson County War. I guess I was supposed to know what that was because that's all it said about that. Floyd got its name from Floyd Stubbins, someone who also figured in the infamous Johnson County War but was similarly not expounded upon.

Then my food came.

I fell into a familiar habit of overeating and loving it. Only three or four times did I notice I didn't have my phone with me and had to reread the back of the menu.

"You with that Perry fellow that bought the Kayshaw place?" asked Ethel, refilling my coffee and changing its perfectly tan color to something else.

"News travels fast."

"You the one that mouthed off to Sheriff Carter?"

"Deputy sheriff."

She spilled coffee then, first on the saucer, then the table, then, still pouring, she aimed toward my crotch.

"Ahhh!" I jumped up just in time. It was the infamous slow roll. I couldn't believe it was happening. It was beyond deliberate. In slow motion, I just watched, unable to believe that Ethel would do such a thing. Luckily, thanks to my tortoise-like reflexes, I barely saved my boys from a boiling.

"Oops. I'm sorry," she said flatly.

"You don't like strangers, do you?"

"Not really," she said. "This town is as it should be. We don't like people trying to ruffle things up."

"I'm not ruffling."

"You didn't mouth off?"

"I'm just visiting."

"We don't mind visitors. Spend yer money and git."

"But don't mouth off?"

"You're upsetting the standard quo," she said. I didn't correct her. "We take offense to people trying to put their ways on us. We like things the way they are."

"I bet the Cheyenne felt the same way," I said under my breath when she left. No need to give her a second chance with the coffee.

6

WITHOUT MY PHONE and with the ire of an entire cafeteria, I ate quickly and left. I had no idea what time it was or how I was going to get back to Perry and the gang, or if I really wanted to. Did they have buses back to Salt Lake from Floyd? A stagecoach?

There wasn't much traffic: a couple of ATVs filling the air with noise pollution, white trucks, a big smelly van marked Magnus Meats that reminded me of feed lots and outhouses.

Listing to the left, I walked past a fireworks tent and into the hardware store as if drawn by magnets. Again everyone shut up like I'd burst in on a planning meeting for D-Day with a steaming tray of sauerbraten.

I went first to the lumber section and admired fence posts. Then I found a very convenient pile of scraps in the garbage next to the saw. Leftovers.

I perused them, but even after I cut a few with the help of a pimply-faced boy named Kyle, I found nothing that would do.

"Whatcha trying to make?" he asked after our fourth unsuccessful try.

"A pacifier."

"Oh. Okay."

Then I found the masonry section and a piece of gray tile with the right thickness. I had Kyle shave it a few times until it was the right shape. I bought it along with some high-grit sandpaper and left.

While sauntering a ways, because that is what you do in a western town, I softened the edges of my tile to a simulated beveled finish. I retraced my steps until I was standing again outside Mandel's real estate office. No one was in.

I slid my tile into my pocket and jiggled my hips to see how it felt. It was a pretty close approximation to the size and weight of my missing phone. At least my balance was back.

Pacifier complete, I walked to Floyd's Old Times Saloon like the outlaw the town thought I was. No one cared. There were six patrons and a barkeep. No one looked up from their drink when I entered. The barkeep, however, noticed me and then glanced at the others in the room as if expecting them to do something. He was young and slim and tan. He had a Middle Eastern vibe about him. The patrons, however, were all sunburned white guys with different stages of alcoholism, hair loss, and diabetes. Four were sitting together, one alone, and there was something else at a table by a window. It didn't quite register and before it could, the barkeep spoke.

"Howdy, stranger," he said.

"Howdy."

The patrons noticed me then. The four *Bonanza* rejects got up and skedaddled, leaving the anomaly and the single cowboy nursing three shot glasses of rye.

Just inside the door was a staple-plagued bulletin board advertising cars for sale, missing cattle, river fishing, a 'Keep Wyoming Coal Country' flier, and an open invitation for the Fourth of July festivities a ways up the highway—'Whole county welcome! Even strangers.' How thoughtful.

I squinted, taking in the decor which can be summed up succinctly as "cowboy." Horns and horseshoes, ropes, spurs, oil paintings of bison, that famous Otto Becker's lithograph of "Custer's Last Fight" that Anheuser-Busch published by the millions. They also had a framed comparison of seven different kinds of barbed wire—for the connoisseur. It was cool and dark and intimate, the way any good saloon should be. I wondered if the furniture was break-away balsa wood for the inevitable bar fight.

I sat down on a stool, and the barkeep, Amir, if you believe these Wyoming name tags, put a napkin in front of me. "What'll you have?" he said.

"Fresca."

"Fresca?"

"Fresca."

"You want anything with it?"

"Yes."

"What?"

"Ice."

He chuckled and brought me out a can of nostalgia and poured it over the rocks. I usually have gin with Fresca, but I was hot, having actually walked that morning. Exercise sucks.

The woman I'd met the day before on the ATV, Gail Larsen, came in and slapped dust off her pants. It was a good look. If she'd squinted too, I'd have given her perfect marks.

She sat down at a table like it was reserved for her, one with a good vantage point of the bar with her back to a wall. Outlaw style. Amir had a drink in front of her before she'd settled in. It was a Manhattan if I had to guess.

From the bar, I saw the anomaly was a white bald guy with a black face. A skinhead like the ones I'd seen drive by the day before. His head was shaved and reflective, but his face was a menagerie of tattoos. Teutonic symbols, swastikas, crosses, lightning bolts, and other charming decorations. He was drinking alone, but he was here, and nobody was punching him in the face. So I got a measure of Floyd's Old Times Saloon.

"You're the guy who got arrested for mouthing off to Carter," said Amir.

"This town needs to apply to host the NSA," I said. "No secrets here."

"Oh, there're plenty of secrets," he said. "They're just secret."

I admired the picture over the bar, the valiant death of a genocidal general. Such were the memories of the West.

"It's just a ways up the road," said Amir.

"What is?"

"The Little Bighorn Battlefield."

You'd think I'd have put it together before then. Big Horn County, The Little Bighorn, but I hadn't. Now, if I'd had access to a computer...

"It's just over the border in Montana," he explained.

"I'll have to check it out. Get myself a souvenir. Maybe a smallpox blanket."

Amir glanced around as if looking for a reaction from the room.

"So what are the secrets?" I asked.

"I'll tell you one. Some guy who claimed to be a detective in bad clothes got shut down by the law for disrespect and public nuisance."

"No way," I said.

"Uhm hum."

"Sounds like a hero of the people."

"Some say a fool."

"Some people call me Maurice. Others, the gangster of love."

He raised an eyebrow. I was dating myself and totally misreading the bar. I should have used a Tammy Wynette or Toby Keith reference instead. Like I had any of those.

"I'm Tony Flaner."

"Amir Rahal. But people call me Eddie."

"Why?"

"It's my name."

"That's not what your name tag says."

"People like to call me Eddie," he said. "And I like to see people's reactions to my real name."

"Looking for trouble?" It was an honest question.

"Why would I do that?"

"What else is there to do around here?"

He shrugged.

"Hey, I've got a secret for you," I said.

"Oh? Do tell."

"There's a crazy man without pants running around in the woods."

"Dasher the Flasher," he said.

"So it's not a secret?"

"Not to folks around here."

"The town character?"

"The town nuisance," said the drunk cowboy. He looked like a rancher, but he might have been a redneck cosplayer, hamming it up with shots and spit.

"What's his story?" I asked the rancher.

"He's a pest," he slurred. "He might have been funny once, but he ain't no more. He poisons the culture. Brings idiots to the area. And we're not very fond of strangers 'round here. Don't like nothing uppity. This ain't a tourist town."

"Really? I've felt nothing but welcome since I got here."

"Then you ain't paying attention."

"Roddy," said Eddie Amir. "I think he was making a joke."

"What?"

"Roddy, Roddy Dean there, owns the Double Dean Ranch down a ways," explained Eddie.

"A ways," I said.

"A ways."

"That wild man is cutting my fences." Roddy punctuated this proclamation with a shot. "He's letting cattle loose from all the ranches around here. Beaumont lay in wait for him last month in a blind, but he's a wily one."

"Wily?"

"Cows go missing," said Eddie.

"I bet he's butchering them," said Roddy. "It's gotta be how he survives the winters."

"How many cows can a man eat a year?"

"Plenty. He eats what he wants and leaves the rest to coyotes. Dozens and dozens we lose every year because of him. Fence-cutting bastard. Pervert. Carter said to let it go, but that man's a menace."

"He steals," said the skinhead.

"That's Varg," said Eddie. "Varg Jayger. Another local character."

"Shut up, Amir," said the Varg.

I heard the threat, but Eddie didn't seem to.

"Varg Jayger? Wow," I said. "Now there's a name." I tried to associate that aggressive nomenclature with the meek little man I was looking at. Though he was sitting, I guessed his height at maybe five-four, five-five in jackboots. He had skinny arms and I imagined a sunken chest beneath his wife-beater T-shirt. Only his glistening scalp and hate art connected the man to that name.

"People live here to be left alone," he said. "If Dasher did the same, we'd all be happier."

"What's he stolen from you?" I asked.

"He broke in."

"And?"

His eyes widened, and he searched the corner of the ceiling for a lie. "Stuff," he said. "He noses around everywhere. You'd be hard put to find anybody who likes that creep."

"I don't mind him," said Gail. "Some of my people come just for him."

"Your people?" I said.

"Gail owns the Crazy Woman Campground. Tourist trade."

"Ah, that's right. So who is Dasher the Flasher?" I asked.

"A hermit," said Eddie. "He was here before me. I've only been here a year."

"Why are you here?"

"Working at a bar."

"That checks out," I said. But really, I wondered what the hell he was doing here.

"He was here before me too," said Gail. "I've been here two years. Another drink, Eddie."

"Coming up."

"He showed up 'bout seven or eight years back," said Roddy Dean, the rancher. "But then that dumb reporter did that thing. What? Three years ago? And now we get lookie-loos and bad company in town."

Roddy was looking at me and not the skinhead.

"Ouch," I said.

"Lookie-loos keep Gail and me fed," said Eddie. "If Gail didn't get business, how could I sell her drinks?" He placed a fresh one in front of her.

I know tourist towns. I own a house in one. This was no tourist town. This was an antiquated hickville with delusions of interest. People came here to be off the grid, and I couldn't imagine a better place to do it.

"I've never seen him myself," said Eddie, getting back behind the bar. "But I love the stories."

"Rain dance," said Roddy.

"What's that?" I said.

He upturned his last shot and Eddie refilled them all.

"I heard that he dances in the rain."

"How romantic."

"Medicine wheel when there's thunder."

"What?" said Gail.

"I never heard that one," said Eddie.

"I can just see it, him jiggling about in the rain calling the lighting down like the freak he is. Maybe that's how he washes."

"He breaks into people's cabins," said Varg, "and steals things."

"I heard that was you and your friends," said Roddy.

The skinhead cracked his knuckles, impressing me with the acoustics of the room. They should get a band.

Eddie poured me another Fresca without me asking.

"Why'd you go off on the sheriff?" he asked

"He was leaning on me."

"We don't like strangers," said Roddy. "We don't want what you're selling."

I glanced up at the lithograph again. "Better put some gin in this, Eddie."

"I hear you," he said.

He poured a double. Coming from Utah, where bartenders use eye droppers to measure booze in cocktails, I was surprised to taste a drink as strong as the ones I made at home.

"Sheriff seems pretty uptight," I said to no one in particular.

"He's doing his job, and the town's behind him," said Roddy.

"You're pretty chatty today," said Eddie. "What's gotcha riled?"

"Riled?" I asked.

"Riled," he said.

"Mind your own business," said Roddy, and another shot was gone.

"What does the deputy sheriff have against preppers?" I asked. "Don't they mind their own business?"

"Weirdos," said Roddy.

"Have you met Rawly?" asked Eddie.

I nodded.

"Kimmy?"

I nodded again.

He nodded.

I shrugged.

He wiggled his eyebrows.

I squinted.

"Anything that disturbs the peace in Floyd is on his radar," said Eddie.

"Rawly buries caches," said Gail.

"Cash?"

"Caches, like supplies and such. A while back, we had a wildfire in the park, and one of them blew up. Box of ammo, some dynamite."

"Shit."

"The firemen were...concerned," said Gail. "They couldn't prove it was Rawly, but Carter had a talk with him."

"And?"

"Don't know. Ask Carter."

"I'm sure he'll tell me. We're BFFs."

Gail giggled.

"What brings a sarcastic urbanite like you to a place like this?" asked Amir. "Eddie" Rahal.

"To drink in a bar."

"That checks out."

"Actually, I'm here for the cure," I said.

He looked at the empty gin and Fresca glass.

"Screens. Computer time. I'm off the grid for a while after a stupid pledge to my stupid friends to come to this stupid—I mean lovely and unchangeable paradise—of North Bumfuck, Wyoming."

"Big Horn County."

"Oops."

"You got a bad attitude," said the skinhead.

"And you have shit for brains," said I.

The booze had reopened my cranky box. As a rule, I don't like skinheads, racists, fascists, knuckle-crackers, and dick-heads. If there was ever one I might be able to beat up in a brawl, it would be Varg Jayger. That couldn't be a real name.

Eddie was on alert. Maybe he was worried about the furniture. Varg squinted at me for a moment and then smiled. He was drinking beer out of a brown bottle with a torn label.

The sound of a motorcycle came from the road and then stopped very near the entrance of the bar.

"That was fast," I said. "You got your backup on speed dial?"

Varg stood up and strutted toward me, then he made a hard right and went outside.

"And to think the sheriff didn't like you," said Eddie.

"I know, right?"

The motorcycle started up again after a minute and was joined by another motor, something smaller than a truck, more than a lawnmower. I figured an ubiquitous ATV. We listened to the pair of them drive off.

"Mrs. Larsen?" I said.

"Miss."

"Gail?"

"Yeah?"

"Any chance you can give me a ride up the road?"

"How far?"

"A ways."

7

GAIL SAID I could ride double on her ATV, and she'd take me a ways. I said that was mighty neighborly.

We finished our drinks—I paid and still forked out less than I would have for one drink at the Comedy Cellar. Another difference was that I felt these. Even atop my pancakes and breakfast meats, I felt a glow.

Coming out of the dark bar, the sunlight was unwelcome. I averted my eyes and cowered, screeching, "Burnses! It burnses!" Until I thought I might lose my ride.

"Are you a crazy person?" she said.

"That's what I said to Dasher. Dasher the Flasher," I said. "You know he has a huge penis, right?"

"Is this how you talk to strangers?"

"We're neighbors."

"Get on before the sheriff hears you."

Her ATV was an inline mini bike-like thing with four wheels and too-wide seats so riders could work on their bowlegs without needing a bag of oats. A trailer was attached to it, loaded with boxes of fireworks, groceries and bug spray. She only had one helmet. She pulled it over her head and told me to hold on.

"Why does everybody have an ATV out here?" I asked.

"Trucks are big, horses are too much work, and golf carts look sissy." With that, she revved it up and took off, sending a spit of gravel into her trailer, chipping off black paint, and putting me in a dust cloud.

I held onto the handles on either side of the seat. I guess I could have put my arms around her, but I have a girlfriend. Remembering Allie, I reached for my phone to text her that I missed her and stared at a brick tile.

We went right on the road. You'd think an unseatbelted, roll bar-less ATV would be content putzing along the shoulder, safe from semis and semaphores, but she brought the beast up to sixty miles per hour and we were flying on asphalt.

Sneaking peeks around her head, I saw hay fields and trees, then a ditch with water in it. A cow. Another cow. RVs screaming past us going the other way, cars and eighteen-wheelers. Squinting as I might, my eyes were blown to tears from the clear country face-slapping air.

After a while, I relaxed and tried to enjoy the ride. Visions of childhood summers riding double on a bike with friends tried to manifest, but that shit never happened. My short-lived child bike life was a one-seater, not *The Brady Bunch* banana seat with a flag. I tried mountain biking in college, but it turned out to be too much like exercise so I gave it up.

We were cruising at sixty miles per hour, breezy and nice. A brisk breeze from the mountains cut the heat of the sunburn I was nursing. I liked that. Fresh clean country air. It probably meant rain was coming or a road-closing blizzard as so many signs had prophesied, but it felt good then, and I leaned my head around Gail and caught it fresh on my face.

Do you know what a June bug is?

It's a nickname for a kind of flying beetle with a long Latin name—a scarab-like thing about the size of a fifty-caliber bullet. I bring it up because there are lots of them in Big Horn County. Now there was one less.

The fucker hit me right above my left eye just at the brow on my forehead.

I thought I'd been shot. I reached up and pulled down wet fingers expecting blood and brains and saw clear guts and carapace shards. I felt goo running horizontally across my face to my temple, aiming for my ear, steered by the wind. Stupid wind.

I wiped the back of my hand across it and already felt a serious goose egg coming on.

I was very sick of the ride suddenly and looked around Gail to how far we still had to go.

There are these pretty white butterflies all over Wyoming. They frolic in fields of wildflowers and sometimes crossroads. They taste like bitter licorice.

I decided to stay in the draft of Gail's armored helmet and wait it out.

"I gotta drop this stuff off," she said, turning her head. I could see bug splats all over her visor. "I'll take you up to your place after that."

"Sounds good." I leaned in so she could hear me.

Wyoming farmers often use commercial beehives to pollinate their crops. Thousands of bees in each hive. Not all make it home.

I learned later that Gail Larsen's Crazy Woman Campground was named after an actual crazy woman. It is local lore around the county, but only 70s film buffs know it outside of the area. Remember *Jeremiah Johnson?* Robert

Redford in the mountains killing Indians? There's a crazy woman in that film, and that's her claim to fame outside of Wyoming.

The movie got part of it right, or maybe all of it. I only read the folktale, and who can say how accurate those ever are? For all I know, Sydney Pollack nailed it, and what I'm about to tell you is so much antelope poop.

All right, just so I don't have to tell you more about my bug barrage, once upon a time the Morgan family—John, Mary, and two daughters of unknown age, but probably younger than John and Mary—left Missouri because who wants to live in Missouri? This was before the Civil War with Quantrill and Bloody Bill Anderson bleeding Kansas and all that, so the Morgans were ahead of the curve, early adopters of the wilderness lifestyle.

They set up a trading post along a creek in Wyoming called at the time something like "Not Crazy Woman Creek Yet." Later the name would be changed.

John and his family traded with the Indians because they were the only regular customers. The area was Crow territory but Sioux were nearby. One day the Crow got it into their heads that John was selling guns to the Sioux. They didn't like that. I'm sure John Morgan tried to explain modern economics to them, supply and demand, other retail outlets, competitive outposts, and Adam Smith's invisible hand of free market capitalism, but they were unmoved.

To show their displeasure, they massacred the family. John and the girls were killed. Mary was clubbed unconscious at the door, and then everything was set on fire.

According to legend, this is when a handsome blond mountain man with dreamy blue eyes and a future in film festivals found Mary and pulled her out of the rubble. There was no little boy to later meet a terrible fate and trigger a vengeance arc. Hollywood would correct that.

Still, Mary was not well.

The trauma was more than she could handle, and even after her wounds healed, her mind would not mend.

Jeremiah Johnson, the mountain man who found her, built her a hut to live in and then left.

Yeah, he left her. Alone. Angry Indians in the area. He just left her.

Chivalry has its limits.

The Crow miraculously left her alone. They knew she'd survived, but they also saw that she was crazy as a batshat banana and it was "bad medicine" to harm a crazy person.

Anyway, Johnson left this broken woman in the bluffs. To his credit, or excuse, he'd leave her supplies every once in a while. He wouldn't actually take them up to her, but she'd leave one of her daughter's charred ribbons tied on a tree as a signal and he'd leave her a cracker or something. I'm not impressed with Johnson, if you can't tell.

One day, the ribbons stopped appearing and the shit Samaritan mountain man decided to check on her welfare. Finally. She was dead, of course. Frozen to a tree, partially eaten by animals. Let's say by a grizzly bear to stay on theme.

He buried her, and she became a folktale. The Crow said they saw her as a spirit along the creek and in the woods, moaning and crying for her dead family, or maybe just begging for somebody to help her, maybe take her back to civilization to family and doctors. Some pancakes maybe. We'll never know. Somewhere along the line, from either the Crow or a confession of Johnson's sickening neglect, the river was named Crazy Woman Creek.

The story of the West is full of great tales like that. It's colorful and tragic, just like the Western expansion.

Gail's campground wasn't particularly close to Crazy Woman Creek. I'm not sure it was even on the same side of the park, but the name was catchy and people came to stay with her and take ATV rides.

I felt the ATV slow and dared to peek one eye around her to see if we were there.

Gnats are a thing in Wyoming; big thick greasy swarms of gnats.

Gail maneuvered down a gravel road and stopped in front of an actual building. 'Office' was whittled in a plank above the door.

"What happened to you?" she said, taking off her helmet.

I pointed to the splats on her visor.

"You want to clean up?"

"Please."

She pointed me down to a cinder block building. "There're showers in there. Sinks, some soap."

"Med kit?"

"I'll see what I have." She went inside.

I passed a board showing a big colorful cartoon map of the campground. There were pull-ins for campers, good spots for tents, hook-ups for RVs and even some cabins. The cinder block bathroom I was heading toward was one of two. There was a big area in the middle called 'the field' with a fire pit and over-happy cartoon campers standing around it, like a Druid ceremony with marshmallows. The dumpster was up front. There was a pool.

My forehead hurt and my mouth had a strange chalky licorice taste I wanted to wash away. My eyelids were glued half shut with gnats. I headed for the showers.

There weren't many people camping then. I'd say about a third of the places were taken. But there, about twenty yards beyond the shower, in campsite #15 was an old friend. There was the RV that had nearly run us off the road. The sleek silver and black silo was unmistakable. The sides had been pushed out, probably doubling the already huge indoor area, and an awning offered shade over a carpeted patio with a gas grill and a La-Z-Boy. I did a double-take when I saw a car parked underneath it. You know where Greyhound buses store luggage on those long piss-fragranted journeys across state lines? Instead of duffels and trunks, there was a sports car—a red thing with a low profile. I watched it float down to ground level on an elevator and then move laterally over the grass.

A blonde woman in shorts, thin with narrow hips but sporting overinflated boobs, called inside, "It's down, Penn. I'm going for a ride."

Something landed on the back of my neck. I slapped it and had new bug residue squished between my fingers. I went inside to wash.

Just as I expected, I had a huge goose-egg above my eye, red and rising. Angry as hell. The bruise was already reaching into my eye, spawning a bruise about the size of a silver dollar, one of those old ones—not the new gold-colored ones or Susan Bs, but a big ol' Eisenhower dollar bruise—hefty, full of warning about the rising military-industrial complex. In the middle of that came the egg, a raised red lump three-quarters of an inch off my head. It looked like a big button: push to cause screaming.

I washed it tenderly and tried out the screaming function. I washed my mouth out with water, then soap because of all the swearing I'd done trying out the button. I fished a bee out of my bonnet, or rather my stinky day-old slept-in T-shirt and scrubbed an unidentified winged mass from between my ring and pinky fingers.

I looked longingly at the shower, thought of the stream up at Perry's with the cow, the toilet into a hole. I looked at my face again, saw the despair waiting for the despair awaiting me when I left this building. I'm a modern man. I understand immediate gratification as well as delayed misery. It was a no-brainer. I stripped off my clothes. Hot water awaited.

I opened the first stall and jumped when someone said from within it, "Not bad, but mine's bigger."

8

"THANKS," I said. "What are you doing in there?"

"Lurking," said Dasher the Flasher. "Why were you screaming?"

I pointed to my head. "I didn't know anyone else was here."

"Did you check?"

"No."

"Then you have no one to blame but yourself," he said.

Dasher was squatting in the corner of the shower stall. He hadn't washed. Hadn't put a stitch on. While I wondered how to answer the blame game, not wanting to admit a crazy hermit was right, he stood up and carefully peeked out a high back window on tip-toes.

"Woods are busy," he whispered. "Used to be quiet out there. Stuff going on now. I see it all. I have the secrets. All the secrets. I see, and I remember it all. I have a great memory. Enhanced. Secrets are painful, though. Gotta find a time and place to tell everyone everything. Are they still doing TED Talks?"

"Out here? I doubt it."

"Maybe a soapbox then."

"Speaking of which, hey, look at this."

He turned. "What is it?"

"Soap." I offered it to him. "Go nuts on your nuts."

He shook his head and turned back to the window. "Resistances," he muttered.

"Are futile?"

"We're weak. Our immune systems can't handle shit. We get addicted to antibiotics, soap, and computers."

"Et tu, Dasher?"

"I see everything," he said.

I remembered then that I was standing there buck-naked. I'm no exhibitionist, but for someone as out of shape as I am, I have, at times, an unrealistically positive body image. I'm not proud and I'm not ashamed. I was able to walk into the showers in high school while other boys cringed by their lockers. Of course I was thinner then. A dare to skinny-dip was no dare to me. I dipped, though not always skinny. Still, Dasher telling me he sees everything brought my hands down over my naughty bits. He hadn't even bought me dinner.

"I like your style, Dasher. Confidence is key. But you gotta know that every time someone sees you, it's a crime. Well, outside of shower stalls, I guess. Public nudity gets you on a sex offender list, and if you have a Twitter account, it's a meltdown. You can get arrested for nudity. I've met the sheriff and he seems like the kind of guy who without a pause would toss you in the pokey for showing your poker."

"No one can catch me. I know the hills. The ways. The secret herbs and spices."

"Ah, the KFC defense. New twist on the Twinkie."

He ducked as if someone had seen him. "Guns. Guns everywhere," he said.

"This is Wyoming. 'Nuff said."

"Good point."

I thought he was crazy as a bedbug, but in the realm of diagnosing and judging the dangers of psychological conditions, I knew I had to bow out. My friends were all crazy, and some people have accused me of missing some Legos. He seemed harmless. He was intense and maybe paranoid, but most people I've met who are intense get things done, and paranoid might just be a keener understanding of current events. If you can keep your wits about you while all others are losing theirs, you probably don't have all the facts.

"Dasher, my odd acquaintance, I'll use another stall," I said.

"You'll ruin your immunities," he warned me.

"I'll use a dirty towel."

I left him, wide and squatting, for another shower. I hoped he was potty trained but doubted it.

In the next stall, I was delighted to find hot water. Though hopeful, I'd expected a frigid glacier-fed tributary, but I got a nice suburban wash. The bar of used soap I'd taken from the sink did most of the work, and someone had been kind enough to leave a bottle of Head and Shoulders dandruff shampoo, so I wouldn't have to worry about flakes.

"Girl or boy?" came a deep voice from the doorway.

Dasher, if he were still there, didn't answer. It occurred to me then that this was a unisex shower. How progressive.

"Plumbing is a boy," I called back.

"Coming in."

Around the plastic shower curtain, I thought I saw the guy from earlier on the ATV, the guy who'd checked us out like he was looking for his mom. I'd thought him summer tan but saw that his tan was genetic. A Black guy, strong and muscular, judging by his calves.

As I was finishing my toenails, I heard another shower fire up.

I got out and wished I had a towel, dirty or not.

Dasher was gone. He had not left an organic calling card as I'd feared. See? He wasn't all bad.

I saw the man's fluffy blue towel on top of his clothes, and knowing the law of the West was to share, I patted my forehead with it. Just my forehead. I had an injury there and needed it more than him. Just my forehead. And face. A little down my neck. I have chest hair and if I didn't pat it down with the stranger's luxuriant soft cloth, it would take forever to dry. It was just water. And a little bug juice. Such is to be expected in a Wyoming campground unisex shower milieu.

That's when I saw the telltale black leather holster.

My towel buddy went around strapped with a big-ass gun. A revolver. A silver thing. I don't know guns. I don't like guns, though I do own a gun. I am a white male in America, so owning one was required before they'd issue me a library card. Also, I thought private eyes needed one. I even had a concealed carry permit, which you can get for twenty bucks in like twenty minutes at any of the bi-weekly gun shows in Utah. My gun was a revolver, but not that big. This one reminded me of the big-ass metal beast that Rick Grimes popped off at zombies in *The Walking Dead*. Remind me not to go to Georgia.

"Anyone out there?" came the voice from the shower.

I carefully folded the towel back up and placed it on the gun as I'd found it. Then I tiptoed away back to my stack of clothes.

As I found my undies and was sliding them up, I noticed Gail at the door. I don't know how long she'd been there.

"I've seen better," she said when she saw I saw her. She saw.

"That's not a nice thing to say."

"Come up to the office when you're done," she said. "I won't be able to run you up, but I have a plan for you."

With that, she left.

The shower turned off.

I hopped into my dirty clothes and sped out of the building.

The girl in the sports car was gone from the super camper. Under the awning, I saw a big older guy with salt and pepper hair around a bald spot. He had a respectable belly and stick legs. He was with a slim, middle-aged guy in slacks, so I had no idea how his legs were holding up. There were also two kids, probably ten and eight, boy and girl respectively.

The slim guy I recognized as the pained RV driver who followed the behemoth past us on the freeway. His RV was parked next to it. Between the two campers, they occupied three sites. There was also a big six-seater ATV painted in brown leaves and aspen camouflage. It didn't fool me, though.

I heard the distressing words "What the...?" from the showers and scooted across the road to the campers.

"Nice camper you got there," I said and angled myself out of view of the shower building.

"Should be," said the man. "Cost enough. But what's money when you're doing what you love?"

"If you love spending money, it's a win-win."

"Camping," he said. "Well, glamping, really. The best of the outdoors and the in. Old and new. All here."

"Glamping?"

"Glamorous camping. Symbolized by an electric massage chair set up by the fire."

I looked into massage chairs once. I tried one in a mall and thought it was great. They're not cheap, and they're not light, and this one was top-of-the-line and top-of-the-scale. I could follow its power cord under the big Persian rug connecting to a bank of plugs in the side of the silver beast.

The boy ran up to me with a Nerf gun, a rifle thing with multiple shots in a magazine. He proceeded to line me up in his sights and let one fly right at my face. He hit me square on my scream button.

I screamed.

"Why you screaming? Was that you before?" said the man.

"What the actual hell?" I said.

"Oh, that's just Terrence's way of saying hello," said the man. "Terrence the Terror, we say."

The next shot was in the neck. "You're still dead. You're a trophy now. Get the camera, Dad," he said.

The big guy laughed. The other man, the slim one in pants, gave me his patented pained look.

"I'm Penn Cromby," said the man, grabbing my hand from where I was wiping away tears and shaking it like gems would fall out. "You've met Terrence. This is Bunny."

"You're ugly," said the little girl.

I was planning a comeback that wouldn't involve a comment on her lineage when the guy from the shower walked by.

"Maxine just left," Penn went on. "That's all of us."

"I'm Tony Flaner," I said, wondering what the slacked man was, if not 'us.'

"Oh, him? That's our butler. Cheeves."

"Lynson," he said. "Ralph Lynson." He offered me his hand, and we shook like normal people.

"Sorry," said Penn. "Just a little joke there. We're still getting used to each other."

"Cocktail, Mr. Flaner?"

"What do you have?"

"Everything."

"I'll take one of those."

Lynson smiled and retired to his camper.

"Which campsite are you in?" Penn asked. "Have you seen any grizzly bears? Black-footed ferrets? Canadian Lynx, which is a dog-sized cat with long legs?"

"Saw a June bug. Kind of. And a cow."

"A cow? A bull? Wild?"

"It had a tag on its ear. Might have been on sale."

"No good."

Terrence shot me in the back of the head, execution style. Bunny stomped on ants.

Lynson returned with a tall glass and a bag of ice on a tray. "A Long Island iced tea," he said. "And an ice pack for your head."

"Thank you, Ralph."

"Call him Lynson," said Penn. "Or Cheeves!" A big laugh.

Lynson and I exchanged looks as Penn's face went red from the exertion.

"And go get Bunny a can of bug spray," he said.

Lynson nodded and went back into his camper.

"I'm actually not staying at the campground," I said. "I'm staying at an... uh, an outbuilding up the road."

"Dad, I saw a squirrel. Can I have the TrackingPoint Precision Guided AR-15?"

"That's way too much gun," he said.

"But it never misses."

"That's the shooter, not the gun," Penn explained. "Practice with your toy one. We'll break out the .22s later."

Lynson appeared with a black can of Raid chemical death spray and gave it to Bunny. She coated the hill in a thick white foam and stomped on it again for good measure.

"I gotta go," I said.

"You hardly touched your drink," said Penn, wiping his forehead with a white handkerchief.

"Oh." I downed it. Long Island iced teas are nothing if not smooth. Lynson took the glass, and I carefully held the ice bag on my forehead.

"Thanks for the hospitality."

"It's what the Crombys do."

"What do the Crombys do?"

"The best we can!" He laughed, and it was almost a nice laugh. Almost. "We're into the finer things."

"This is dirt here, you know? Real dirt. Dirty real dirt."

"But it's rare dirt. A dying lifestyle here. Rare. Unique. Going extinct. Get it while you can. Before someone else does."

I glanced at the RV, the sports car garage, the satellite dish, the massage chair, the butler, and cans of bug spray.

"You must be rich?"

"Not to speak of," he said. "But yes. I'm rich."

Seeing the shower guy was nowhere to be seen, I handed the glass back to Lynson. "I gotta go," I said. "Thanks again." I trotted off toward Gail's office.

"Take care, now." Penn Cromby waved back with the handkerchief. It looked like a surrender. "If you see any of those critters, let me know."

A Nerf dart fell short in the dust.

"Fuck!" said Terrance.

Gail was on the porch with an iPad.

I drooled.

She looked up. "When I said clean up, I didn't mean shower," said Gail. "You know they're reserved for paying guests."

"I bought your drinks."

"Okay. For today."

"What's your plan?" I said. "You said that you couldn't run me up."

"You could walk," she said. "It's only..." She trailed off when she took a harder look at me. "Here's what I can do."

"Do tell."

"I'll rent you an ATV. Seemed to me that you people up in that cabin should have one. That Caddy is no kind of car for that road, and I can't lend you my truck."

"Oh," I said. "That's very kind of you."

"The rental is fifty dollars per day. I know you have a credit card. I'll require insurance. I'll just get the forms."

Before I could say anything for or against, she was gone. She had a point about needing something other than the DeVille. The white beast might do for our daily trips to the bar—I already figured that would be the game plan —but I'd like a ride of my own if only for the shower. I'd need to ask Gail what she'd charge me for a shower or if it came with the rental. Was there room to negotiate? Did she have a menu? A punch card?

Gail came back and handed me forms on a clipboard. She was reading something on a phone, a lovely sparkly iPhone like the one I'd left at home. I felt in my pocket for my tile.

She handed me a pen. It used to be attached by a ball chain somewhere but was free now to steal.

I filled out the form using my home address in Sugar House and my MasterCard. I went ahead and took the full medical insurance along with collision, no-fault, and a whole-life rider. I passed it back.

Gail pointed to where I'd forgotten to sign.

I signed and she took it back into the cabin, her face still in her phone.

I saw the red sports car from before zip by on the highway, top down, wipers on full, spraying glass cleaner by the ineffective gallon on the bug-gut-splattered windshield. It was a slathery red blaze under a clear blue sky.

Phoneless, Gail returned with a set of keys twirling on her finger. "Follow me."

She led me around the building to a stable of ATVs. "This one," she said. "It's one like we were on today. Safe and easy. Don't go over twenty miles per hour."

"We were going sixty."

"Got it to seventy-five, but I know what I'm doing. Yours is throttled to twenty."

"What if I need to go faster?"

"You won't be able to."

"Right."

"Make sure you bring it back topped off with gas."

"Is it topped off now?"

"I don't know. I would take you up, but I have way too much to do here for the big event."

"What's that?"

"Independence Day."

"Oh, right."

"Next door there." She pointed to a big empty field where only now trucks were pulling in. "There'll be barbecue and drinks. A carnival. Fireworks and corn dogs. Your whole group is invited."

"Is there a gate fee?"

"Not this time."

I looked at the ATV, its fat wheels, single headlight, dusty seat. "Where's the helmet?" I asked.

"You want a helmet?" she said. "Let me get those forms."

"With a visor," I yelled after her. "A thick one."

9

THE HELMET WAS A DEAL. A dollar a day, but I had to buy insurance for its loss or breakage. A washing deposit was required too. She was a pro.

Gail sat me down on the machine and explained its operation. I could tell she'd done this before and often. She treated me like I didn't know what a brake was, which insulted me, and a throttle, which was news.

"You've got no cage," she told me. "If you roll, it's your neck."

"My neck?"

"Your neck. As in wheelchair at best, casket more likely."

"Why do people ride these?"

"I told you. Golf carts look lame."

"You did say that, and I can't argue there, but are these so much better?"

"Some have big throaty engines like a motorcycle. They're macho. They can go fast. They can crash."

"Macho? I don't know about that, but crashing is a selling point?"

"It is in Wyoming."

"Okay."

"These things put more people into the emergency room than all the combined animal attacks, weather effects, and domestic violence of the county, which is saying something out here."

"Where are you from?"

"You don't think I'm from here?"

"Should I?"

"Wish you would."

"I hear California."

"San Fernando. But keep it to yourself. I'm a country gal now."

"Got it."

"Bring your friends tomorrow," she told me. "It'll be a good time."

"I'll have to check our social calendar."

"I understand. This is Wyoming."

"Big Horn County."

I slid the helmet gingerly over my skull, careful not to push my button. I lowered the visor, admiring the scratches and pock marks all over it, then drove my ATV straight into a ditch. Long Island iced teas may be smooth, but they pack a punch.

Gail helped me pull the machine back on the road.

"You going to be all right?" she asked.

"Nothing like a near-death experience to sober you up."

"You had something since the bar?"

"The Crombys. Penn, Kimmy and their kids, Mayhem and Malice."

"I see."

"How many ditches can there be between here and there?"

"You filled out the insurance form, right?"

"I did."

"Happy trails."

This time I didn't go into the ditch. I peeled across a piece of lawn in front of the office. Gail's attention was directed to the distance where storm clouds were plotting something.

I'm sure there are rules, some might call them laws, about how and where to ride glorified go-carts on Wyoming roads and state highways, but no one had told me any. I tested the twenty-mile-per-hour limit and found I could go nearly twenty-four. Our little secret.

I kept to the shoulder where the beast seemed most comfortable.

The machine had a lot of pickup, but the ditch had warned me that I didn't know what I was doing, so I didn't press it. This also meant that most of the bugs had time to get out of the way before they painted my insured helmet. Most of them.

I passed the turn-off to Perry's place and didn't notice it until I was quite a ways too far, clued in by the change of scenery. When I saw desert plains, treeless and rolling, I realized my mistake.

The ground was like that. There were these little oases of trees and woods, mostly around natural water features, while the rest of the land, not under cultivation, was pretty sparse of shade. Low bushes and grass. Not the sea of the Great Plains but not far from it. I saw some antelope strutting around like people didn't eat them. They regarded me as I made a U-turn like I was a tourist. I reached for my phone to take a picture of them, but it didn't work out.

I heard somewhere, probably during my diet days, that it takes five weeks to form a habit and only three days to break it. I had a serious phone habit, and I was only two days into my cold-turkey off-the-grid tough love. I just had to DT it out.

But it wasn't just the phone. Driving back to the turnoff to Perry's cabin, I knew that once I was indoors, I would go through withdrawals from my computer. The phone was a mobile fix, but my real screen addiction is my Mac. I daily spend hours skipping between news sites and shopping pages, book reviews, how-to videos, hobby pages—been thinking about getting into fused glass—and Facebook to check on how the rest of the world is doing better than me. Then I'd find a video game, one to play or one to watch. One to buy and never play. I'd stream a movie and write up an invoice for a case I'd finished last month. I'd check my bank balances and wonder why it was so low before remembering to actually send the invoice. I checked out what acts were coming to town. Update myself on the never-ending street repair in the valley. There's a tornado warning in Tulsa, a fire in California, glaciers melting, fascism rising, and dandelions can be used to make a delicious and medicinal tea. I thrive on information blasting me like a firehose every day. It's a dopamine gold mine, and the best thing is I don't have to remember any of it. It'll all be there when and if I ever need it. The quick 'I'm smarter now' feeling is enough, like filling out a row in *Candy Crush*. I want more, and the last thing is so last thing.

In this way I know I'm like most other plugged-in Americans. I've been looking at getting one of those smart watches. I put one in my shopping cart a couple weeks ago and then found out it's really about physical fitness and not surfing. So there it has stayed.

The grid has made boredom a choice, not a condition. Immediate gratification on demand. Screen time.

It's odd that I haven't seen more rants from older generations about this phenomenon. Few of the expected tirades about how 'in the good old days we played outside and knew our phone numbers.' Maybe it's because everything changed so fast, or maybe those generations too have been sucked into all this and haven't found time to consider it the way I was then on the back of an ATV without computer screens or even music. Or maybe they realized that if they said anything, they'd be big fat dummy hypocrites. Our screens are faster, brighter and flatter, but they had theirs too. Like most Americans, my babysitter was a TV set. My parents got sucked into sports shows and soap operas, news, and made-for-TV melodramas that took two hours to pay off instead of the twenty seconds we afford YouTube videos now. The two hours thing might give them a little clout in complaining, but it's all just a continuation of the same movement. God knows attention spans have—

A squirrel crossed the road into the campground, and I realized I'd missed the turn-off again.

It couldn't have been an accident that the road was so easy to miss. I had to figure it was part of the prepper plan to hide from the roving masses of massing rovers massing and roving the countryside in the end times, all looking for the well-stocked hidey-hole of a survivalist who could be overrun by the roving masses. If it weren't so green, I could imagine Cormac McCarthy's *The Road* where—

Shit.

I passed it again.

At least I was narrowing the window. Five or six more passes and I'd have it.

Luck and a moment of concentration showed it to me at last. Never let anyone tell you that paying attention isn't a good quality to have.

I turned off the road and followed the car tracks up and around and over and past stuff until I could smell smoke and see the cabin.

I pulled next to the white Cadillac and admired the scratches along its side. Most of the smoke seemed to coming from the chimney, which I took to be a good sign.

I peeled off the helmet and shook out my hair like a shampoo commercial.

Dara stepped out the front door. "Flaner. How in the hell do you look so fresh?"

She hadn't showered. Dara has a special power of having her hair go all crazy in the mornings. It had to be past noon, and her hair was a sideways Mohawk on the right and a flat squash on the left.

Standard came out after her and his hair had been combed, but the lack of soap and product meant he looked like it'd been sprayed on his head. "You showered."

"How was jail?" Garrett sauntered around the side of the house with Critter. He was smiling and had wet hair. I remembered the stream was that way. I wondered if he'd met the cow.

"Where's Perry?" I said.

"Inside, trying to burn the place down," said Dara.

"Good thinking."

"He's actually making his world-famous cabin chili," said Standard.

"In the fireplace," added Dara. "And he's never made it before."

"Breakfast, lunch, and dinner," said Garrett, inspecting my rented ATV.

"One meal for everything. Just like the pioneers had," said Dara. "You know, the ones that died of dysentery."

"I remember that game. I didn't know you played it."

"What game?"

"What happened to your head?" said Garrett. "Cops?"

"Bugs."

"We're not sure that the water is safe to drink," said Critter.

"I said it wasn't. I told you to boil it first."

"That's a good idea."

"I said it."

"To whom?"

"You guys."

Critter shrugged.

I said, "Tell me you haven't been drinking from the stream."

"We purified it with whiskey," explained Perry, appearing in the doorway. His face was lined with soot, and his hands looked like he'd been juggling coal.

"What the actual hell?" I said. That could become a catchphrase.

"I had to climb up the chimney to open the flue. It was jammed with dead animals."

"Is that what I smell?"

"Partly."

"Do I want to know?"

Dara shook her head, her hair bobbing like a decoy in a river.

"Did you break out of jail?" said Standard. "Did you steal the bike after a daring battle with the evil sheriff?"

"No. I rented it after a nice breakfast, drinks at a bar, and a shower."

Crusty, envious stares.

"Come inside, Tony," said Perry. "See how we've fixed it up."

"You look like you've crawled through a chimney."

"Oh, right. Garrett, did you bring up some water?"

"I forgot," he said.

Critter looked away.

"You've been gone a long time," said Perry.

"I forgot," he said as Critter inspected the scratches on the Caddy. "I took a dip and forgot, that's all."

"Can you get it now?" Perry asked. "I could use it for the cooking."

"Boil it."

"Oh, yes."

"I'll go," said Garrett. Then he and Critter trotted off down the trail. Yes, trotted.

We watched them go and then went inside.

I'd wondered how Perry would decorate his outbuilding. One step inside and I could see that he had chosen to go the bold direction of modern green plastic patio furniture.

"Très gauche," I said.

"It works. I didn't have a lot of choice or a lot of help picking it out."

"Yeah, sorry about that."

"Perry said you really gave it to the law," said Standard.

"He was looking for a mattress," said Dara. "I'm right, aren't I?"

"No comment."

"Took two trips," said Perry.

"Then Dara borrowed the car and went for food," said Standard.

Perry said, "She came home with cereal and liquor. No milk."

"Kept us alive, didn't it?"

"Did either of you think to stop by the jail? See how I was doing? Make sure I wasn't being tortured?"

"Nope."

"Nah."

"Were you?"

"No. I had a flushing toilet, though."

"Lucky."

"Speaking of which, where are we on that front?"

Standard said, "I went to town this morning and got some paper plates."

"Did you think to—never mind."

"The lights are working."

I turned a switch. Nothing happened.

"When the generator is on."

"Why isn't it on?"

"Needs gas."

"Ah."

"Rawly said he had lots and would give us some, but I guess he forgot about it."

"Beds?" I asked.

Smiles on my friends' faces. Chill down my spine.

"Oh, that was easy," said Perry.

"Cots?"

"Better." He led me into the room I'd claimed.

There I saw my suitcase, opened and riffled through, my stuff tossed around like I'd been robbed.

"Why is my suitcase open?"

"We thought you might have brought some food."

"Did I?"

"No, but your shirt made a good pillow for Dara. I also noticed you brought chargers. Why?"

"I did? Habit, I guess."

"What the fuck is that!" Dara pointed to the bulge in my pants.

"I'm getting a lot of comments on that today."

"No, you liar. That." She poked my pacifier.

"No way," said Standard. "You cheater."

"You disappoint us, Tony," said Perry. "We all agreed."

"Hold your pitchforks. It's not what you think it is."

"What is it?"

As if under the red laser dots of snipers, I carefully reached into my pocket and pulled out my tile.

"A brick?"

"A tile."

"Why?"

"You try it." I handed it to Standard. "Put it in your phone pocket."

He did.

"Oh. Oh. I see. Oh, that's nice. Yes. Yes. Brilliant, Tony."

"It's a brick," said Dara. "Don't cream your shorts over a brick."

"Does that count as cheating?" said Perry. "Let's have a vote."

"Fuck that. He can have it," said Dara. "Now it's my turn. Hand it over, Stan."

Reluctantly he did, and Dara slipped it into her pocket, wiggled her hips and smiled. "Umm, yeah. I like it too."

"What's going on?" said Garrett. He and Critter stood in the doorway with a jerry can of gasoline.

"We're using gas cans for water?" I asked.

"No," said Perry. "Plastic buckets."

"This is the gas from the Rawlys," said Garrett. "I forgot the water again. I'll be right back." He dropped the can in the hallway and was gone again.

"Is it me, or was he skipping?"

"His hair looked messed up from last time," said Dara.

"Critter wouldn't make eye contact," said I.

"His fly was open," said Perry.

We all looked at the Rawlys' gas can.

"Dara and I will get dinner going," said Perry.

"That's sexist," she said. "Just because I'm a woman you think I can cook?"

"We know you can't," said Perry. "But you said you wouldn't get caught dead playing with the generator."

"It exploded a little," explained Standard.

"A little?"

"Spilled gas, electricity. Woomph. No biggie."

"He lost all the hair on his arm," said Dara.

Standard showed me his two arms. One was hairy and manly, the other smooth as a baby's bottom.

"No biggie," he said.

Perry puffed up like a ranger. "Standard, you get the generator working."

"What's Flaner going to do?"

"Tony needs to get started on his bedroom."

"What is there to get ready?" I said. That's when I noticed a sleeping bag and an air mattress, both still in their original packaging. Maybe for collectors.

When they all grinned at me again, I knew something was up.

10

THE LAST THING I remember that first time was the taste of rubber in my mouth and the room spinning like I was drunk. The bed became floor, became walls, ceiling, and then, a while later, Standard stood over me.

"Keep going, Tony," he said. "It gets better."

"How?"

"I don't know."

Then he left me in a cloud of alcohol fumes to the company of my air mattress.

Perry explained it like this: "I figured I'd splurge on big air mattresses because I knew you guys were disappointed by not having beds."

Sleeping bags and an air mattress. That was our reward. A warm –10° sleeping bag and a Wyoming king-size air mattress. Not just king size, not California King, which is bigger than a king-size, but a Wyoming king-size mattress. It's a hybrid between a huge bed and a cruise ship life raft. It'll hold three adults and pets according to the picture on the side of the box. Could be cats. Could be cows. And for "extra softness and comfort," as the box promised, this Wyoming king was a double-stuff mattress, thicker than usual. All told, there were 141,120 cubic inches of comfort.

And we had no inflator.

Everyone had to blow up their own mattresses. Standard said it was a rite of passage. Dara had chosen pine boughs rather than fill hers. I was told the others had theirs to some degree of firm. Standard bragged that you could bounce a dime off his. Garrett had his to a "soft" half-filled bladder that he said gave him nightmares of *The Blob*, the original, not the remake. Perry was somewhere in between, but he admits it took him hours to fill it and he passed out several times.

I felt my lips chafing as I puckered and latched onto the nipple again and blew. And blew. And blew. Nothing seemed to be happening with the rubber bed. It was getting dark. I blew, and I blew.

Then Perry shook me awake.

"It's kind of like getting high, isn't it?" he said.

I'd passed out again. This time, I'd fallen awkwardly on my right arm and it was all pins and needles.

It wasn't getting dark for real. I'd just thought that.

"I hate you so much," I told him.

"Dinner will be ready in about an hour," he said. "Keep going until then. You should be good by bedtime."

"So much."

He left and I went back to blowing.

I was either hyperventilating or suffocating. I'm not sure which. I kept getting dizzy. Too much oxygen or not enough, I wasn't sure. My body was a bellows. I learned after the first two blackouts that once the room started to spin, I should take a rest. Lie down and curse the universe.

I had a headache.

I blew and got dizzy and only after I had visible inflation did it occur to me to go get an inflator. I bet Gail had one I could borrow. Or rent. Probably rent. Floyd would have them by the shelf-full probably right next to the one with the sucker bait Wyoming king-size air mattresses. I might have seen one in the hardware store. I imagined seeing it before me, spinning like a flashback.

I screamed.

"What the hell?" Dara in the doorway.

"I fell on my scream button," I said. "When I passed out. Again."

This time it was getting dark.

"How are the pine boughs?" I asked.

"Like sleeping in a nest," she said. "If the nest is full of ticks and earwigs."

I glanced at the mattress, half full. Maybe. "Are they nice ticks and earwigs?"

"I put an hour into my mattress yesterday, another this morning. After dinner, I'll give it some more and sleep in the car."

"Good idea," I said.

"Dibs. And I'm locking the doors. Pervert."

Back to the nipple.

In and out. The room spinning. Gravity subjective. Migraine named Gary. Gary the Migraine.

"Dinner!"

I woke up staring up at the light fixture with a dim bulb behind a frosted dome.

My leg was twisted under me; drool had pooled in my ear.

I plugged the nipple, admiring how little I'd done, and I then crawled out into the main room.

There were my friends, sitting in lawn chairs around a card table, spooning chili into paper bowls one plastic teaspoon at a time.

I found a reclining chair and reclined.

"See what fun you missed?" said Standard.

"I wish I were in jail."

"We are, Tony. We all are."

"What's with him?"

"Wisdom in simplicity, my friend. Work and experience."

"He's gone all Thoreau, hasn't he?"

Everyone nodded, Critter's googly eyes rattling over the sound of snapping wood in the fireplace.

Perry brought me a bowl of chili and a beer.

The chili was hot and good. The beer was cold and excellent. Finishing a bowl of one and a bottle of the other, I helped myself to seconds and chased Gary the Migraine away.

I told them about my day, about the jail, the restaurant, and the hardware store. I let everyone take another turn holding my brick. Perry wasn't interested.

"There's a big Fourth of July party tomorrow. The whole county should be there if Gail is to be believed."

"Gail?" asked Garrett.

"The woman who runs the campground."

"First name basis?"

"Riding two to a bike?"

"What would Allie say?"

"What is wrong with you guys?" I said. "You know I'm devoted to Allie."

"We've also seen you melt when any woman with eyelashes flutters them at you," said Dara.

"Or man," said Perry. "You've told me."

"I have a mate."

"What happens in the woods is transcendent and secret," said Standard.

"Listen, we're here to cold-turkey progress, not to have sex."

"It's what vacations are for," said Garrett. "To relax."

Critter nodded enthusiastically.

"We're just giving you shit," said Dara.

"I'm not sure I want to break the serenity of this place with a loud holiday," said Standard with a far-off look in his eyes.

"Did you guys bring pot and not tell me?"

"You didn't ask," said Dara.

"The serenity is everything," said Standard. "Serenity is serene."

"We knew you needed all your lung power, or we'd have offered you some," said Critter.

"Still do," said Perry. "You're not halfway through that mattress yet."

"We should definitely go to the Fourth of July party tomorrow," I said.

"Hicks and shit-kickers? No way," said Dara.

"Patriotism is the last refuge of a scoundrel," quoted Perry.

"I might have plans," said Garrett.

"Serenity should not be tossed aside for—"

"There're showers nearby," I said.

"Fuck yeah! Let's go," said Dara.

"I'm there," said Perry.

"The stream wasn't great," said Garrett.

"Flushing toilets?" asked Standard.

"Probably."

"Okay."

"Plus it's a party. With burgers, beer, cotton candy, fireworks, and maybe a petting zoo."

"You had us at shower."

I sipped my beer.

"Good job getting the lights on, Standard," I said.

"I just had to become one with the greater generator."

I squinted at him under the light. "Where are your eyebrows?"

"Certain sacrifices had to be made."

"We tried the bomb shelter," said Perry. "But there's a lock on it. I was hoping you could pick it."

"Me?"

"Can you?"

"Probably."

"Then do it."

"I might."

"Yeah?"

"Yeah."

I'd taught myself to pick locks even before I was detective. It's come in handy with the job not a few times because ethics are for dopes and obeying the law is for losers. I was okay at it. I knew some tricks, knew the theory, but usually found rocks, crowbars, and a ten-dollar lock-pick gun to be the most effective.

"I'll tell you what, I'll pick the lock and you finish blowing up my mattress."

"It'll wait."

Perry pulled out a bottle of vodka from a white Styrofoam cooler chest and passed it around.

"Here's to friends."

"New and old," said Garrett.

"And serenity."

"And hyperventilation highs."

"And why isn't the vodka to me yet?" added Dara.

We gulped and ate and laughed and tried not to think about the combination of strong spicy chili and a splintery cold outhouse holes.

At some point that night, while blowing up my mattress, Gary the Migraine returned. My breath was coming shorter in alcohol-laced bursts, and he had an easy route in. When I blacked out again, I just went with it and crawled into the sleeping bag and pretended my under-inflated mattress was a waterbed.

It gets cold in northern Wyoming, by the way. Even in July.

The sleeping bag did fine, but where my hip touched the floor through the sagging mattress, I got a chill. I tried to sleep on my back, hovering in the depression, but my own snoring kept waking me up. Several times that night, I wished I were still in jail.

I had a dream I was talking to Dasher. He was telling me about the power of organic enhancers to make people better, stronger, faster. I asked about a bionic eye, and he got mad. "To go forward, we must go back. The old ways for the new. Eat the natural berries and be reborn."

I woke up holding my tile like the alarm had gone off. I touched it and tried to open it, tapped in my code until everything finally got quiet.

Perry stood with a pan in each hand. He looked at me, nodded once and banged them together. "Get up if you want bacon," he said.

The smell of sweet fatty life-sustaining pork wafted in and I got up.

"Why'd you open your window?" Perry asked. "You're lucky some animal didn't get in here. Oh, I spoke too soon."

There on the floor in the corner was a little pile of brown nuggets.

"Antelope?" I asked.

"Through the window?" said Perry. "Groundhog probably."

"Marmot?"

"Same thing."

He used a flap of cardboard from the air mattress box to scoop up the pile and tossed it out the window before locking the latch. None of the windows had screens. I mean, why would they?

I wanted a shower, but I needed to brush my teeth. I hadn't brought a toothbrush, and the vodka and beer and chili had done nothing for my breath but coat my teeth in latex.

Perry was again working over the fireplace. The kitchen was a glorified pantry. The fridge was working as long as the generator ran but without water, or propane for the stove, that was the end of it.

"Kimmy says Sally took the big propane tank when she took all the other stuff," Garrett explained over a breakfast of thick bacon and greasy eggs, i.e., heaven. "I think they're expensive."

"You're talking about that big Tylenol pill thing that everyone has?"

"Yes."

"Are you going to get one of those, Perry?"

"I don't know."

"Yeah, what are your plans for this place?" I asked.

"I'm undecided. It was better in theory."

"It is a noble experience, true to itself. One needs only embrace the s—"

"Stan, if you say 'serenity' one more time, I'm going to kick you square in your round balls." Dara meant it. Her tone said 'serious,' even though her plank hair spike disaster said ridiculous. She could well kick Standard in the yarbles. She does things like that. She'll take advantage of us that way, thinking that we won't fight back being as she's a girl and smaller than us. Truth is, we all know she could tear our ears off with her teeth and not even want mouthwash afterward.

Standard shut up and slurped his eggs off the side of his plate, having broken his plastic fork earlier.

"It'd make a great vacation cabin, but it's got no plumbing," said Perry thoughtfully. "And it would make a great survivalist cabin if it was more secret and had fewer windows."

"It's pretty," I said. "Rustic."

"Needs furniture," said Critter.

"And something to do."

"TV."

"Wouldn't hurt," said Dara. "But some books or games wouldn't be amiss, or are those too close to modernity for the 'experience'?"

"It's a good idea to unplug," said Garrett. "Everyone needs to get out of their comfort zones and have new and unexpected experiences."

"After breakfast, let's go to the party," I said. "Spend the day out of our comfort zones, having new and unexpected experiences."

"And showers."

"And flushing toilets."

"I need a toothbrush," I said. "Might look into getting a battery-powered inflating thing."

"Don't you dare!" said Standard. "It's a rite of passage."

"How many times do I need to pass out and freeze before I'm part of the club?"

"Just don't you dare."

"Perry, I need a ruling on this. It's not a computer screen. We have to allow some technology. I mean, there are stairs here."

I don't remember the exact promise we'd all made about this weekend, I don't think anyone did. There was something about no screens, no phones, no internet, no communication that wasn't face to face. Beyond that, I was blurry. There was probably more, something about toilet paper maybe, technology and "old ways," but I couldn't remember. I think my mind kind of shut down after the idea of unplugging for a week took hold. And we'd been drinking.

Perry put on a stern and patient face, echo of an Old Testament sage. "But you're so close," he said.

"I hate you so much."

11

ALL HOLIDAYS HAVE BECOME POLITICAL, but the Fourth of July, also called Independence Day by the literate class, is unabashedly that. It began well enough, a remembrance of when a bunch of deadbeats got out of paying their taxes, but it's morphed since then. I suspect it was once a day of unity. I see park pavilions with brass bands, parasols and barefoot boys with frogs chasing shrieking pig-tailed girls while another kid, a younger one, in Buster Browns, coaxes a rolling hoop down a dirt road with a stick. No coloreds allowed. Then came the First World War where the male populations of whole towns were wiped out in a single gas attack, falling dead in a ready-made grave called a trench for reasons not quite clear. Who was the Kaiser and why did we care? Political holidays lost some of their flavor after that. Then the Second World War happened with clearer reasons and objectives, and a good humanitarian validation at the end. It was a good war, if there can be such a thing.

Then came all the other wars, rising social consciousness, and civil unrest. And here, the holiday really got hairy. It became anything but a unifying event. It became an appointment to 'out-patriotic' the other side and was finally usurped to become the 'America: love it or leave it, we can do no wrong, please pay no attention to the man behind the curtain' day.

But we can all enjoy the fireworks.

Francis Scott Key probably made that happen with his "rockets' red glare" lyric. It's like blocking hidden in Shakespeare: "Is this a dagger which I see before me?" Hey, look, we have to have a dagger on a wire dangling in front of Macbeth's face. It's in the script. The audience will love it. Make it spooky and try not to poke the actor's eyes. It is a dangerous play.

I love fireworks. Always have. Thus, and therefore, e pluribus unum, lorem ipsum, the Fourth of July is one of my favorite events. Fireworks, beyond being way cool, are appropriate to the holiday. An unignorable distraction of light and smoke, explosions, shock and awe—what can be more American?

The lot next to the campground had gone from field to fest since I'd seen it the day before. What had been an enchanted glen was now a loud yard party of red, white, and blue.

Perry drove right by it into the campground and parked by the office. I'd taken my ATV because I was paying for it. I parked it beside the Caddy.

"Where're the showers?" said Perry.

I led them down the road past the dumpster, around the big sign, to the bathhouse. The air was full of music wafting in from the party next door.

At the shower building, I held everyone up. "Let me just go in and see if everything's okay," I said.

They were having none of it. Before I could take a step, they rushed past and took all the shower stalls before I had a chance.

"I'll just wait my turn, then, shall I?" I said. "Jerks."

Knowing I had some time, I dusted myself off like I'd seen Gail do in Floyd's Old Times Saloon and strolled across an empty campsite toward the party.

There was a midway at the festivities, places to buy food and souvenirs, games with prizes, sponsored booths. Maybe one of them a Walgreen's. I can dream, can't I? I really needed a toothbrush.

It wasn't the whole county. There were bigger towns that would be having bigger celebrations with bigger crowds, but for this corner of nowhere, it was a good little gathering. I guessed most of Floyd had come, so a hundred people. Still, with outliers and strangers, it was a bustling place and had the feel of a county fair with buskers and cotton candy, screaming kids and the smell of sheep. There were big circus tents, an arena in the back kicking up dust, and a bandstand off to one side.

The crowd was lively, and the scene had a specific and strict decorative theme: red, white, and blue. Not Belgian red, white, and blue, not English, Norwegian, or North Korean, but American red, white, and blue. Flags, eagles, guns, apple pie, rifles, more flags, banners, balloons, more guns, a truck, a horse, a guy with a revolver on his hip, a guy with an army rifle standing under a Confederate battle flag—also red, white, and blue—talking to three bald tattooed skinheads who also had guns. And beers. And long knives. Flag pins on their vests.

America.

The traditional patriot theme was in ascendancy, but coming in a close second was camouflage—khaki green on bland green, tan on tanner tan, gray on other gray, traffic-cone orange on brighter traffic-cone orange. I assumed those last ones were for urban blinds, hunting snipes in the suburbs hiding behind a 'Road Work Ahead' sign. There were variations:

pine versus elm, combat-worthy and the snowy, swampy, deserty, foresty ones, but it was all of a trope. There were camo jackets and pants. Camo shirts, shorts, and blouses. There were camo tube tops. Several, actually. One was interesting. One was being worn by a woman who had no business wearing tube tops. And then to make it all perfect, I saw a red, white, and blue camouflage print dress with eagles and flags. I saw a lot of people in camouflage but I had to wonder how many I couldn't see. There might have been many more people there than I originally thought.

Beyond the old patriotic designs and new camo chic, I saw the expected cowboy hats but found them to be outnumbered by baseball caps without baseball logos. Fertilizer companies, truck lines, and gun manufacturers, many in camouflage, were in high fashion.

The dress code wasn't enforced, so I walked right in even though I had no hat of any kind. Not even a tricorn, which I've always wanted and wouldn't have been out of place there on that day, especially if I stuck a little flag in it. I was dressed in a Royal Danish Cruise Line windbreaker over a Rick and Morty T-shirt and dirty jeans. I had sneakers instead of boots, an unintentional three-day growth of beard, and a chunk of tile in my pocket. I was ready to party and moseyed down the midway taking in the sights.

I was surprised at how many people I recognized, thus proving something about small towns. That they're small, maybe. It would suck to live here where everyone knows everyone and sees everyone all the time. How could someone live down shame in such a place? And there is always shame. Or at least there used to be. Big cities offer that anonymity the modern world needs to survive, at least they used to before the internet shot that to shit. Things to ponder.

I saw the butler Lynson with the woman from the red sports car, Mrs. Cromby, I figured. With her was the little ant-crusher Bunny but not Terrance the Terror or Mr. Penn Cromby. Lynson held two melting snow cones and stood behind Bunny as she shot BBs at paper cups. Mrs. Cromby peeled money off a roll of cash the size of a Reuben sandwich and slapped dollars down each time the child ran out of ammo. Lynson gave me a pained look of recognition. I waved and moved on.

Mandel the realtor had a booth that wasn't selling real estate. It was a free booth for the kids next to the face painters, where he taught youngsters as old as seventy-three how gold prospecting works.

"Sideline?" I said.

"Hobby that brings in some money," he said, and then recognizing me, "You're going to be nice today, right?"

"As long as the sheriff is nice. If he isn't, then I'll—" The look on Mandel's face said it all. "He's standing right behind me, isn't he?"

He nodded.

I turned around. "Deputy Sheriff Craig Carter, as I live and breathe."

"Your breath stinks," he said.

"Still running for chairman of the tourist board, I see."

He adjusted his hat and strolled away.

Back to Mandel, I admired his panning pans, sluice boxes—new and old —divining rods and metal detectors. "Are you selling this stuff?"

"Nah, just showing it off today."

"You ever find anything?"

He nodded. "Amateur prospecting is legal in Wyoming."

"Good to know," I said. "I panned for gold once up in Alaska."

He looked at my cruise ship jacket and said, "I bet you did."

So much for impressing the locals. I moved on.

I saw Roddy the rancher in an argument with a young man that could have been a carbon copy of the grouchy old guy if you took fifty years off the top and poured him into jeans a size too small.

The Cromby boys materialized for a second, decked out in woodland camo, but then I lost them in the crowd of other woodland camo.

The Black guy from the shower was poking around, looking inconspicuous as the skinhead from the bar eyed him across the midway. The bartender, Eddie Amir, was skulking in the background, watching them both until he saw me watching him, then he checked out the dunking booth.

I found a stall called Pioneer Products. It was just the place to buy spurs and bonnets. On a lark, I asked for a toothbrush.

"We've got something," said the clerk. I felt sorry for her. She was in a full-length prairie dress with a bonnet and period shoes that went up to her knees. I saw them as she hiked her skirt and moved around the counter. She was sweating. "Though you must know that the modern toothbrush wasn't patented until 1857."

"What did they do before that?"

"Chewsticks."

"Chewsticks?"

"Chewsticks."

"Show me."

She gave me a stick.

"What now?"

"Chew it," she said. "But chew it and you own it."

"How much?"

"Ten dollars."

"For a stick?"

"Yes."

"It is a nice stick." It was, as far as sticks go.

"Lasts about a week."

"Not very economical."

"It's meant to be a souvenir, not a replacement."

I felt my teeth with my tongue and looked longingly down the road toward Floyd.

"Always wondered," I said, "what did the pioneers use for toilet paper? Pine cones?"

She gave me a Sears and Roebuck catalog.

"Original?"

"Oh no, it's a reprint, but it works just the same."

"How much?"

"Forty. Also takes the place of smartphones while you're doing your business."

"Do you take credit cards?"

"Chip, swipe, PayPal, Venmo, Square, and ApplePay."

I paid her fifty dollars with a piece of plastic. She put my purchases in a blue plastic bag that wouldn't decompose in my great-grandchildren's lifetimes.

I chomped on the stick.

"Trying it out, huh?"

Chomp. Chew.

"Use one end as a toothpick," she explained, "and the chewed side should brush you clean in no time."

Nibble. Gnaw. Masticate and mosey on.

There is a lot to be said about technological advances. Take for example the humble toothbrush. We take it for granted. We take brushing our teeth at all for granted and miraculous toothpaste that brightens and whitens and kills germs before they can build plaque redoubts at our gum lines. I found out later that the chewstick was a common solution for many cultures facing the heartbreak of halitosis. The Chinese invented a toothbrush, but without pharmaceutical reps they couldn't distribute them for any impact. It was a luxury item, the way my teeth are luxury bones for my "comprehensive" health insurance company that would require a separate policy with ungodly deductibles for cavities and crowns.

But I digress.

The American toothbrush patent went to some American in the late 1800s, and animal hair took the place of stick bark as the dental cleaner of choice shortly thereafter. It was an advancement. I could see, or rather, taste and feel, why sticks were used, but it was a far cry from minty freshness and nylon bristles. And though I was speaking without direct concrete experience, relying on my imagination, I believed double fluff Charmin bathroom tissue would be unequivocally better than page 240 of the Sears and Roebuck catalog, even if I was in the market for a new banjo. As for reading material, the catalog had its charms, but Reddit still commanded my love for those lingering moments of bathroom oblivion.

But I digress.

Rawly found me chewing a stick contemplating getting a cotton candy for its abrasive properties. "You seen Kimmy?" He was wearing camouflage and a gun in a matching holster. Oaktree pattern.

"I have not."

"Is that weirdo friend of yours here?"

"Perry. Yeah."

"No. The other one."

"Girl or boy?"

"Boy."

"Puppet or not?"

"Puppet."

"That's Garrett," I said. "I left him and the others in the Crazy Woman Campground shower."

He peered between tents in that direction. "If you see Kimmy…"

"Yes?"

"Never mind." Weaving into the midway, he left me.

A cloud passed overhead, which isn't saying much, because, I mean, where else would it pass? On the right? A Hail Mary to the end zone?

The momentary shade made for a surprising chill, and I felt a breeze threatening to become a wind. I saw Gail at the end of the midway scoping the skies with a concerned expression.

"I see you have a concerned expression," I said. "What's up?"

"Hey, Tony," she said. "Have you tried the elephant ears?"

"God, is that what I'm smelling? Heavenly scones. Where are they?"

She pointed. "Get it soon. Looks like we're getting that storm."

"What storm?"

"The one they talked about on TV."

I stared at her blankly.

"It was on the internet."

Nothing.

"Phone alert for possible flash flooding?"

I showed her my tile.

"It's going to storm," she explained.

"Does that mean no fireworks? Tell me it ain't so."

She shrugged. "It could blow over. We often have these afternoon squalls. Cloud burst, thunder, lightning."

"Very, very frightening?"

"Sure," she said, brushing off my hip charm offensive. I felt deflated when she did.

Dust kicked up in the wind from the rodeo arena, blinding me for a second and filling my pores with grit. When I could open my eyes again, Gail was gone, and the corral had riders galloping horses around fifty-gallon drums like they were being chased by very fast snakes.

I paused for a moment and assessed why I'd put on a charm offensive for Gail. It's my usual thing, but the bigger question was why had her rejection deflated me? My choices were: 1, I was hitting on her and my masculine identity was threatened, B, I'm an insecure person who goes to extraordinary lengths to endear myself to others and was thus psychically wounded. Or, third, it just wasn't funny, and I have no censor.

"What's that about a censor?" The Black man whose towel I'd used before stood beside me watching the horse and snake show.

"Just talking out loud."

"Best way to do it."

He had mirrored sunglasses under his brows and a lean physique under his shirt. He gave off a vibe of danger. It might have been he was dangerous or he was in danger. He was the only Black person at the fair.

"I'd agree that I am," he said. "Wyoming isn't known for its diversity."

"Shit, did I say that out loud?"

"Shit?"

"No, the Black at the fair thing."

"Yes," he said. "That's how I heard it."

"Shit. I got issues."

"You know the old joke about shit and Shinola?"

"Yeah."

"What are you standing in?"

I looked down. I was standing in shit. Horse by the shape, fresh by the texture. Alfalfa-fed by the fragrance.

"Shit."

"Excellent." He lifted his glasses up to look at me. "You're not an idiot. Neither am I. I prefer to towel off with dry towels, as a rule."

"What a coincidence. Me too."

"The name's Boone," he said.

"Really?"

"Yeah."

"Are you a hunter on the wild frontier?" I said without thinking.

"Something like that." Then I remembered that I'd seen his gun with the towel and he knew I'd seen his gun with his towel and my clever joke about American pioneer heroes had deeper and darker implications.

"Like what?" he said.

"Shit," said I.

"The man with no filter."

"The name's Flaner, Tony Flaner."

"Take it easy, Tony Flaner," he said. "Stay out of trouble."

He walked away with a style I could only admire, a nice easy stride that made him look hip and cool, confident and smart.

"Thank you," he said.

"Shit!"

12

A WORD ABOUT SHIT.

There's a lot of talk about simpler times. The times without polluting cars, mind-sucking internet, phones and sparkly games, when people read newspapers and books and rode noble steeds to work. But let me say that we have to balance all that idyllic fantasizing with shit. In the good ol' days, shit was a real problem. Some people's jobs were to wander the streets of major cities, pooper-scooping up tons of horse droppings. Tons and tons and tons of it. Everything smelled like a stable, and not one of those sawdust Hyatt Regency stalls you see backstage at the Preakness, but overflowing garbage cans of organic waste, hot in the sun, fly-bothered and bubbly. And dog shit. It's only been the last while that people were asked to pick up after their pooches. In school, I remember scratching dog mess out of my sneakers every day with a stick—a stick, not unlike the one in my mouth, I realized. I thought even then that dogs were pretty shitty. Or maybe it was their owners. Anyway, dog shit is nasty. If you have a dog, have pity on sneaker-wearing kids and barefoot babies. Take a cue, maybe from modern horses in modern cities that have to wear diapers because the shit-can man is now installing cable. And horses died all the time, along with cats, dogs, rodents, hobos, and dreams of a just society. The smell was bad. People wore boots out of necessity, not for style. As I stood there with one foot up to my ankle in fresh green patty, I contemplated the advances modern society had made.

It was a simpler time, the imaginary history I dreamed up to try to put my soiled shoe into some kind of flattering light. But I was in sneakers and the slurp my foot made when I lifted it reminded me that I was a child of my time, and just didn't think random piles of shit in public spaces were a good decorating decision.

The wind blew more dust into me, coating my foot in a tan patina, cemented on with a different kind of equine-based glue.

I saw Boone going up the bleachers. I noticed too that he wore a jacket that could have concealed his big-ass gun, but I don't think it did. It was open and loose so I figured he didn't have his big-ass gun. Lots of people watched him out of the corner of their eyes and I wondered if he wished he did have it.

I stand corrected. He was not the only person of color there. Lots of rednecks to liven up the place—red is a color—and one Arab-American bartender named Amir "Eddie" Rahal who followed Boone to the bleachers but at a discreet distance.

Huh.

With new dust in my hair and moisture seeping through my shoe, I was glad I hadn't showered yet. It gave me something to look forward to. The tempting smell of greasy scones was harshed by less appealing organic ones, and I wandered up the bleachers where all the cool people were.

The horse and snake races were paused when I got there, and a man in a black hat, shiny boots, and red, white, and blue vest took a microphone and walked to the center of the ring. The air was fragrant with the smell of leather and dust, hot dogs and beer. And horse shit.

"Big Horn County is coal country!" the man yelled like it would open a cave of treasure. When he didn't get the reaction he wanted, he yelled it again but added a big "Yee-haaaw!" to the end of it. The secret word triggered some western Pavlovian response, and the bleachers popped with yips and howdies.

"We got tradition around here," said the man, pouring the accent on thick. "Our fathers found coal, and sold coal, and coal made America great!"

"'Murica!" came a call from somewhere.

"America is Wyoming and Wyoming is coal country because this is America!"

Hard to argue with that logic, I thought, unless I was conscious.

"I need your help in November," the man went on. "We need to keep coal country, the greatest country in the world. Vote for America. Vote for the Friends of Coal."

"But coal is killing the planet," said someone.

Everyone turned to look. Gasps.

"Coal's a cancer. Renewables are the future. They've already eclipsed fossil fuels for cost and efficiency, even in Wyoming."

All silence but the whispering wind, dark stares of threat and hate. A crackle in the microphone.

"Coal is an American tradition!" said the man in shiny boots.

"Tradition is just peer pressure from dead people."

"Commie," yelled someone. "Socialist," spat another, and then the ultimate epithet— "Liberal!"

"Tradition is no reason to keep going on with a bad plan. Consider the shit problem."

Shit.

It was me. I was the one talking. I was the one getting all the stares.

"Shit," I said.

"What about it?"

"It's a mess and there are better solutions."

"Like cars for horses?"

"Mass transit is better. Electric vehicles powered by renewable energy, if we must."

"Boooo!"

"Bleeding heart!"

I got hit in the back of the head with a freedom fry.

"Renewables?" said the guy in the middle of the arena. It was a modest audience, intimate arena, small town, so he'd been privy to all my uncensored arguments. "That technology ain't none been proved. Early adopters always get burned. One day maybe you'll be onto something, but are we going to sit in the dark by candlelight waiting on it?"

"Candlelight is a tradition," I said, not knowing when to shut up. "Don't cherry-pick history to ignore facts."

"Shut up, tourist!" Roddy, the rancher.

"Fuck off." Varg Jayger, skinhead.

"Get out of there, Tony!" Dara?

"Big Horn County is coal country!" Unknown.

"Friends of coal! Friends of coal!" Man in the arena.

"Liberal!" Multiple concerned citizens.

"He's got a point." Eddie?

"Sumbitch!" Several.

"Filter your damn self!" Boone for sure.

"Windmills cause cancer!" God only knows.

"Read the room, Flaner. Get out of there!" That one was Perry. I saw him with the gang at the bottom of the stairs, stage left.

Amid a shower of ketchup packets, corn-dog sticks, beer cans, and other assorted sundry, including paper clips, taffies, and lit sparklers, I hastily exited the bleachers and met up with my friends behind the fortune-teller's tent.

"Making loads of friends, I see," said Garrett.

"I have a knack."

"Seen Kimmy?"

"No, but Rawly's looking for her too."

"There she is," said Perry, pointing down the midway. "With the sheriff."

"Probably turning you in for public nuisance," said Standard.

"I think I'll take my shower now," I said. "Can I borrow someone's towel?"

"No."

"No."

"No."

"No."

"Thanks."

"What's that smell?"

Wiping ketchup from my hair and dragging my foot in the dirt, I took the shortcut across the field back to the campground. Behind me, I heard rodeo doings, cheers as able-bodied men got their spines compacted on the backs of pissed-off animals. Ah, tradition.

It was later than I thought, or at least it felt later. The sky was now fully gray. No rain yet, but the wind made promises it was coming—real promises, not like those snotty Girl Scouts I chased across the parking lot who promised to bring me six boxes of Thin Mints and some Samoas. Little liars.

The Cromby camper was lit up. Lynson was in their "yard" wrestling the electric massage chair into cover. The sports car was not to be seen, but the undercarriage garage was closed, so it could have been there in the shuttle bay.

"Where's my ghillie suit?" screamed the terrible boy.

"Look by your light-up shoes," came a man's response, Penn Cromby I was sure. "Oh, wait. No. It's here with mine."

Progressive American Western holiday apparel now transcended from just camo to full-on ghillie suits. Progress. It made sense. Next-level camouflage and complete one-upmanship in the boonies. If anyone saw them parading around looking like shambling shrubs, they'd be the envy of the day, but of course, no one would.

Lynson saw me and gave me his patented pained look. If I'd had a cookie, I'd have given it to him.

I snuck into the showers, sadly disappointed that Gail hadn't caught my friends in there. It would have served their towel-hogging mugs right to money up a cocktail or whatever it cost for hot water in Big Horn County, friend of coal, 'Murica! But the joke was on them. I didn't need a towel. I had the most absorbent product known to nineteenth-century pioneers—a Sears and Roebuck catalog.

I stripped and put my dusty clothes on my shitty shoes. Still chewing my stick, I climbed into the shower and felt a pang of fear and freezing flow as I wondered if my ignorant friends had bogarted all the hot water. Before I could get to cursing them to their third generations, it warmed up, and I relished the meditative splendor of heated water.

If civilization has a symbol, it is hot water out of a spigot. Oh, and air conditioning. And ice. Hell yes, ice. Ice for sure. But hot water too. How many times had I taken a hot shower, cranked up the air conditioner or drank something with ice in it? Dozens, I'm sure. Sometimes doing it all at once.

I found a sliver of soap and used it on myself. I was shocked at the color of the water going down the drain. Either I'd opened a mud hose, or I had been much dirtier than I'd thought. I tasted the water coming out of the spout. No mud. It was me. Modern Tony isn't used to being so dirty. A hundred years ago, I'd have probably been good for a wedding like I'd been, but my contemporary sensibilities were alarmed.

The lights blinked and a moment later came a roll of deep thunder. I finished up and tried to dry myself with my new book and then took another shower to wash off all the ink smears. Again the water ran black down the drain.

I dripped-dried while rinsing my shoe in a sink. Don't judge. Outside, I caught a breathtaking sky. Distant clouds popped and sparkled with internal lightning over diagonal streaks of ozone-scented rain connecting cloud to ground. Low rumbles, throaty and awesome, rolled down a few moments later. The storm was making an entrance to remember.

As soon as I could, I slid clothes over my damp skin, got dressed in my dusty duds, and headed back to the fair. Fireworks were coming.

I didn't run into anyone else I knew as I retraced my path back to the bleachers. There'd been some rain and lightning, and it had apparently scared most people away. Maybe they knew something I didn't. But I would have my fireworks.

The rain had cemented the dust down into little dime-sized tiles of dirt clods, and the wind couldn't pick it all up as before. The smell of animals was replaced with that fresh scent of rain and wet sage. A much better smell, in my opinion.

The first rocket went up as I reached the bleachers in the dark.

I looked around for anybody I knew and saw no one, and luckily no one saw me. I'm sure there were coal friends around still. I found a seat near an exit.

A note on fireworks.

I had a friend once tell me that fireworks are boring because they're always the same. Nope. I disagree. Every year I'm surprised by the new designs those clever bomb-makers come up with. They can now do smiley faces, for crying out loud. Louis XIV never saw such a thing in Versailles. And the ones that pop and then sizzle in amber cascades—man, I love those. I could sit through a whole hour show of just that. I also love those big ones that go like chrysanthemums, big as the horizon. Those are classic and only getting better. A fountain for background, a whistler, white zoomies—all improved from when I was a kid. Fireworks might be old, but they definitely have evolved for the better.

Almost.

There's one new firework that sucks. Once I was surprised by it, then I was hurt by it, then I was annoyed and hurt by it, now I'm just pissed off when I see it. And I see them a lot. They must be cheap because every show I've seen in the past ten years has a ton of them. I'm sure they're marketed as fireworks, but they're really grenades. Flash-bang grenades. You've seen them, I'm sure. They go up and then burst in a very bright light, the kind of light that singes your retinas when your eyes are dilated, like in the dark watching fireworks. And the boom isn't a pop, it's a goddamn shockwave of eardrum-puncturing malice. They hurt on many levels. They injure you with the eye burn, then insult you with the decibels. They're weapons-grade munitions. You could use them to storm a bunker, which I'm sure they were originally designed for. This night, they were only about five hundred of them. I got to where I could guess when they were coming about one out of three times by the spark trail. So forewarned, I was only partially blinded and deafened by the pyrotechnic onslaught, but I think I missed some of the good ones while hiding from those.

The show went for twenty minutes, which is pretty good for such a small town. About halfway through, the lightning clouds put up an awesome background for the fire streams. The kaboom of fireworks was joined by the low approaching rumbles of thunder, which then joined the show with strike and roar. From horizon to horizon, the sky was alight. The mesas, mountains and trees were struck in momentary sizzling silhouettes, a sky of kaleido-scopic crackling colors. It was surreal, menacing, and awful, in the awesome sense of the word. You couldn't have planned a better or more spectacular show unless you cut back on those goddamn grenades.

After the fireworks, the remaining crowd dispersed in droves. Lots of droves. And trucks and ATVs, but mostly droves. I looked for my friends and tried not to be looked at. I wasn't recognized, and I didn't see my friends. I joined a drove in the back and followed it through the collapsing midway. I rushed to the elephant ear booth just in the nick of time and got the last honey butter-slathered deep-fried flap of heavenly dough. I ate it while I took a second shower on my way to the campground where I found my soaked, rented ATV next to an empty parking place. My friends had left me, which was their prerogative since we had different vehicles, but I wouldn't have turned down a ride in a vehicle with a roof since it was rain-ing. Hard. And cold. At night.

The ride back to Perry's cabin in the cold dark rain sucked as badly as you think it could. My headlight wasn't great, my driving sub-par, but the mud was thick and splatterful. I wondered why they even put fenders on the thing. Oh wait, they hadn't. The back wheels shot muck up my back, the front ones crap into my face and neck. They needed to make a helmet with wipers. I flipped up the visor so I could see to make it home. The wallow creek was sounding pretty good when I finally pulled into view of the cabin.

It appeared in a flash of lighting. There were no lights on. No Cadillac.

I dismounted and slogged—literally slogged into the house. The lights came on when I flicked the switch and stayed on long enough for me to peel myself naked in the living room. Then they flashed twice and went off with a loud clunk from the generator outside.

"Screw it," I said and felt my way into my room.

By lightning flash I crawled into my sleeping bag on the half-filled air mattress. By thunderclap I fell asleep in Big Horn County mud.

13

I WOKE up with more scratches than an orphan's Pinewood Derby car. Tossing and turning in my grit-filled bag was like sleeping in a rock tumbler. I was polished in places I'd rather not speak of.

The sun was up, the day looked bright and cheerful, and the only thing missing to make the morning the complete shit-fest I thought it was, was a hangover, but alas.

I brushed the sand and gravel from my knees, shook it out of my butt crack and put on some clean clothes before going in search of booze for the missing hangover.

"Hey, Perry, when's breakfast?"

No answer.

In the kitchen I found a bottle of vodka in the freezer. It was warm.

"Standard, are you going to fix the generator?"

No answer.

"Dara? Garrett?"

No answer.

"Marco—"

No Polo.

I went out on the porch to look for the Caddy. It wasn't there.

Huh.

I found my chewstick and matched it with the eighty-proof Russian mouthwash for a cleaning only Stalin could envy.

Over the crunch, gulp, and splinter of my new back-to-earth alcoholic morning routine, I heard the crackle of tires coming up the road and sat on the stoop. Vodka was a good substitute for coffee, I thought, as I put together a suitable tirade to unleash upon my friends.

It wasn't the Cadillac. It was a police cruiser.

I went cold. Cops in general are bad news. Cops in the morning when your friends are missing is a potential nightmare.

I took a deep swig as Deputy Sheriff Craig Carter pulled up, got out, and adjusted his hat.

"Mr. Flaner," he said.

I was mister now.

"Ah shit," said I.

"What?"

"Just out with it."

"There's been a death."

"Only one?"

"Yes."

My mind went to Garrett. "How?"

"Shooting."

"Was it Rawly?" I asked.

"I don't know."

"What do you know?" I took another swig.

"Hey, take it easy on that."

"Fuck off. You have a county of heeled hicks and one of them killed my friend—my best friend."

"He was your best friend?"

"Damn right he was," I said, though in fact I'd never considered him my best friend. I don't have many best friends. My current one was undoubtedly Allie, but right then, it was Garrett.

"I didn't know you knew him."

"Damn right I knew him."

"Did you know him before this weekend?"

"Of fucking course I did, you—wait. Who are we talking about?"

"Dasher."

"The hermit? Goddammit, you stupid-ass cop. You could have opened with that. I'm here pissing myself seeing a cop pull up, and then you tell me someone's dead—murdered no less—and you don't identify them? What kind of shit-for-brains sensitivity training do they give you out here? Pepper spray and a baton?"

"Hey, hold up."

"And why are you telling me about this? Am I a suspect? Or are you some kind of Paul Revere with bad news? One if a murder, two if by flood? Don't you have phones out here? Smoke signals. Pony Express?"

"Calm down. You've got a bad attitude."

"You just figuring that out?"

"Listen, if this is about me throwing you in jail—"

"Nah...how could that have affected our relationship? Do you think me that shallow, you tin-plated dictatorial shit-kicking dickless artifact of oppression?"

"What?"

"Why are you here?"

He took his hat off and scratched his head. He then held it in his hands, almost modestly.

"I've got certain pressures on me," he began.

"Just rub one out. You'll feel better. You can use our outhouse. I've got a catalog you can use. Nineteenth-century lingerie do it for you?"

"Listen, Mr. Flaner. I had to make a show of leaning on you. This town expects it of me. Requires it. We ain't no tourist town, and I was told to keep it that way."

"So coming up here and scaring me was another sick joke you are contractually obligated to perform? What a town. And here I thought Wyoming didn't have a sense of humor."

"I need your help."

I stared at him. Usually when I chew branches and drink vodka before ten in the morning, I'm jovial. Actually, that's not true. When I drink vodka while chewing kindling in the morning, my experience has been that I'm pissed off. Of course I only had this one incident to base it on, but even so, statistically, I was acting perfectly normal.

"What. Do. You. Want," I said.

"I looked you up on the Google."

"And how is the Google these days?"

"It said you really are a detective."

"Gosh."

"I want to hire you on the QT."

"You're kidding."

"As a favor."

"Ha ha ha." I chuckled. "Really?"

"Really."

"Ha hahahahahahaha," I roared, and then for emphasis, I threw myself onto the porch and writhed on my back, kicking the air. I spilled some vodka, but it was all for a good cause.

"Mr. Flaner…"

"Almost done."

I gave it about three minutes. Maybe four, with a couple of false stops only to laugh harder the next time.

"Mr. Flaner."

"Okay, okay. What in your pea-brain mind thinks I want to help you?"

"The stories I read about you made you sound like an okay guy."

"I am an okay guy. Hell, I'm a great guy. You, however, are an ignorant slack-jawed hick. My original question still stands."

"He was murdered," he said.

"Dasher the Flasher?"

"Yes. Now shut up, or I'll—"

"What, 'Mister Do-me-a-favor?'"

He took a deep breath and counted to ten, actually counted. After another deep breath, he said, "Dasher was not liked around here. Most folks will be happy he's gone, so happy in fact that many will think his killing was a community service. It will not look good for me to investigate this too much."

"And you wonder why people think small towns are corrupt."

"You're not making this easy."

"Oops."

"I understand. We got off on the wrong foot. But I can't let this stand and I can't do much about it. I need your help."

"He was the town crank. A nobody. Why do you care?"

"I liked him," he said. "And since when do nobodies not deserve justice?"

Going for my moral bone. "You don't know me," I said.

"No, but Allison Braise does."

"What are you talking about now?"

"I called her. I saw her mentioned in the story about the Moab thing. She said you have a good heart."

"When did you do that?"

"This morning, after we found the body and I looked you up."

"That's kinda creepy," I said, "calling a guy's girlfriend."

"She is? I didn't know that. I just wanted to know if I could trust you."

"How do you know you could trust her?"

That stumped him for a minute. "It backed up what I already thought."

"Pu-lease."

"Mr. Flaner. Are you doing anything right now?"

"My friends are missing."

"No, they're not. They stayed at the Shady Tree Motel in Floyd. They were having breakfast when I saw them last."

"Did you talk to them too?"

"Only to ask them how long you were all staying and what plans you had."

"Did they tell you all the fun we were having and how we were leaving right away?"

"They said at least a week, maybe two, and they had absolutely nothing on the agenda and were scared to 'fucking death' that they'd die of 'fucking boredom.' That was the girl who said that."

"Don't let her hear you call her that. She's more of a woman than you and me together."

I suddenly wasn't so interested in seeing my friends right away. I looked

down at my scraped knees, felt my empty stomach and my abandonment—
all of it heating up with cheap vodka.

"I usually get paid," I said.

"I can handle that. Ms. Braise told me your rates."

"What did she say?"

"Two thousand dollars a day plus expenses."

Allie had my back. That was twice the best rate I'd ever gotten before.

"You have that?"

"Yes."

"How?"

"I'm rich."

"Now there's an enlightening answer."

"Will you take the case or not?"

"Watch your tone, young man."

"We're wasting time."

My tummy grumbled, my scuffed knees stung. I had a mouth full of
lighter fluid and tree bark. I could look forward to a week of staring at a tile
shard and getting sick of my friends, or I could do this. A true Hobson's
choice.

"Who's Hobson?"

"Errrgh."

"What?"

"Okay, I want the week in advance and a contract," I said, "notarized and
mailed out of the county in case you get uppity."

"Uppity?"

"Uppity."

"Sure, that's fine. You'll take the case?"

"What if I need some help of the official kind?"

"I'll do what I can, but keep me out of it. I have to live here."

I sighed, then dropped my half-chewed stick into the vodka bottle to
sterilize it and left it on the porch. Dibs. "Drive Hobson and me to the crime
scene," I said.

"Who?"

"Crime scene. Let's go."

Carter held the back door open for me, the one without inside handles
and fenced off from the front seat. I gave him a look, and he opened the
passenger door.

"Sorry. Just a habit."

The cruiser wasn't what I was used to. The days of the old Crown Victo-
rias were past and might never have gotten this far into the boonies anyway.
Four-wheel drives were the name of the game here. It was a Ford Explorer,
recently washed, low light bar, ram plate and side-mounted flame throwers,
or something like that. He handled it like he was born in it, disregarding the

whole wear-a-seat-belt thing, and driving with his wrist on the wheel as he splashed down Perry's road to asphalt.

"I'll admit I'm not sure what to make of you," he said as he turned away from town.

I cracked open the glove box and found some gloves. Behind them were some forms, a box of bullets, a big bottle of antibiotics, another of vitamins, some heartburn medicine, and throat lozenges. Eucalyptus.

"Tell me about it," I said. "Here I thought you were just a hick cop, but now I think you have the clap and a vitamin deficiency brought on by strep."

He pushed the compartment closed. "Focus," he said.

"Me?"

"I guess you work with partners?"

"Like cops?"

"You mentioned Hobson."

"He's involved in a lot of my cases."

What I've been referring to, if you haven't already looked it up, is the famous "Hobson's Choice." It's an expression from jolly old England circa seventeenth century. Hobson had horses, which undoubtedly made lots of poo all the time. He had a stable of them and rented them out. When a customer came for one, he said they could take the horse in the stall closest to the door or fuck off. I guess he rotated them so the best ones wouldn't get overused or he just liked ye olde bait and switch. So the deal was take what was offered or nothing. An appearance of variety, but really a binary take it or leave it. The illusion of choice. In my case, I could do what the deputy sheriff wanted me to do or I could do nothing. It fit my usual motivation of push and pull into things. Pull, something to do that even paid; push, flee boredom in a plumbing-less house in the middle of nowhere watching dirt erode with my flaky friends for a fortnight, all the while going cold turkey off an entrenched technology addiction. Push/pull, Hobson and the gang. So I drove into the woods with a cop who, a day earlier, I'd have sworn would have punched me, hoping this wasn't all a ruse to lure me to a quick-lime-filled hole in a dark gully. Strange that thought hadn't come to me before I'd gotten in the police car with the small-town tin-plated dictatorial cop who'd been such a dick before.

"Where are we going?"

"The body was found up by the little medicine wheel."

He turned off the highway and began to ascend the mesa that loomed on the horizon. I looked around at all the sagebrush and grass.

"How can anybody be a hermit out here? There's nowhere to hide," I said.

"Mostly he kept to the forests in the park. There's plenty of canyons and caves and whatnot up there."

"And when he comes down to do mischief?"

"What mischief do you mean?" He sounded defensive.

"Let cattle go, steal shit, flash tourists his respectably large schlong."

"Hell if I know. He had his ways."

"Huh," I said.

"When we get there, I'll tell anyone who's there that you're a suspect."

"What?"

"As a cover."

"Let's not."

"Flaner, I can't be part of this."

"Tell whoever asks that I'm working for the USGA. You're transporting me as a favor."

"The United States Golf Association?"

"USDA?"

"Department of Agriculture?"

"Shit. Okay, who oversees the forests and stuff?"

"Forest Service?"

"There we go."

We pulled to the side of the road where a gravel parking lot was filled with emergency vehicles and another sheriff's car.

"We'll have to walk from here."

"Shit."

"It's just a quarter mile or so."

"Double shit."

And so, against my lifestyle choices and desires, that day I got some exercise. Oh, the humanity.

"The body was discovered by tourists this morning around six."

"Six?" I panted. "Who's up that early?"

"They biked up from Floyd for the sunrise."

I looked back down the steep mountain road and wondered what madness was in the air to make someone want to do that.

"I got here around seven," said Carter, breathing normally. "Secured the scene, got statements, and went back down to make some calls."

"The air is so thin up here," I said. "How can...breathe..."

"Almost there," he said.

The sign said half way.

I found a bench and fell into it. "Let me take in the scene," I said.

Pretending I wasn't gasping and sweating like an out-of-shape suburbanite on a mountain hike before noon, I steepled my fingers on my chin and scanned the area.

"What do you see?"

I took a deep breath. Then another. And a third for good measure until I could speak calmly.

"Um," I said. "Is this the only way up here?"

"I doubt it."

I pointed. "Tracks."

"Those are probably from the bikers."

"How many were there?"

"Five."

There were a lot of tracks.

"Is that allowed?"

"Nothing motorized past the parking lot. Bikes are okay."

"There are footprints."

"Sure to be."

"What did you find in the parking lot?"

"The rain washed out most of what could be there, but we think there'd been some kind of vehicle parked in it last night. Probably pulled in before the rain, left after it."

"So the killer?"

He shrugged like the true professional investigator he pretended to be.

I got up and found my pace again, which was slow and plodding. Eventually we got to the top of a flattened hill and I beheld the little medicine wheel.

What I saw were pale rocks placed in a circle about twenty feet across with spokes running to the center, where they all met at a low mound of the same pale rocks. The smell of pine and sage and what I can only call fresh air, stranger than I was to it, perfumed the scene with an eerie peaceful calm.

"This isn't the famous wheel," said Carter. "That one's farther along a ways. This one is smaller, less frequented."

"Unadvertised? For locals only?"

He nodded. "Exactly."

"Dasher?" I said.

Carter pointed to a higher mound a few yards farther up. "Dash is on the hill," he said. I noted the familiarity in his statement but left it alone.

Another deputy sheriff met us as we approached the body.

"Hey, Jake," said Carter. "Mr. Flaner here has been hired by those pinheads at the USGA to look into this thing. He's a detective."

"Hi, Jake." I offered the man my hand. He didn't take it. Instead he scowled and menaced.

I pushed past him. "Mind if I play through?"

14

NO ONE HAD COVERED the body. Jake had been stationed to keep the critters away. In true Western form, birds flew above the peak in slow lazy circles, waiting for the buffet to open.

Because I play detective, I've seen more dead bodies than most people in modern America. I mean real dead bodies, not the wall-to-wall corpse parade on cable television. Did you know in Europe you get an R rating for killing people, not loving them? There, boobs are fine. Ripping someone's still beating heart out of their chest and showing it to them is considered in bad taste. Go figure.

For all the video game and R-rated movie preparedness, real dead bodies are a thing unto themselves. The dead in situ are the worst. No funeral home furnishings or mortician's makeup to hide the brutal reality of the end. This is death as it happened—just happened. Being there before cleanup and sanitation is rough. The experience is unlike anything else. There's a mortal creepiness to it, a sorrow and a warning, almost as if seeing someone dead suggests you might be dead one day too. Maybe soon. Probably soon. And then there's the idea that someone out there did this. Murderer doing murder. It is unnatural, hurried, and this case shitty.

"Is that shit on his chest?" I asked.

Carter caught up to me. "I'll help you only so far, Mr. Flaner," he said very loudly. "We don't need no one like you poking around..."

He went on, but I tuned him out.

There was Dasher lying dead on his back. I counted three bullet holes in his upper chest, a loose grouping, mid mass. And a pile of shit on his sternum.

His face looked oddly serene. His lids were half open, in a groggy peaceful kind of way, like he was falling into a nice dream. The rain had washed much of the dirt away, and he was still naked. His unfairly large penis was slack and tucked between his legs. His feet were rough and calloused, a deep crack in his left heel that must have hurt like hell. His beard and hair were tangled with sticks and leaves, but again washed a bit from the summer storm.

"Hey, Carter!" I called.

"Shit," I heard him say. "Looks like I gotta go babysit." He trudged up the hill like he was going to a time-out.

I gave him my "I'm unimpressed" look.

He glanced back down at Jake and, seeing him watching, barked out, "What?"

I moved to the far side of the hill, where Jake couldn't watch.

"Are you back to yourself now?"

"I told you, I've—"

"I want the money in cash and the contract in blood by tonight. Wire it to my account."

He rolled his eyes.

"What kind of scat is that?" I asked. I used the outdoorsmany name for shit to impress him.

"Human."

"How can you tell?"

"I'm a country boy," he said as explanation. "Might be a dog, but a dog wouldn't crap on a dead body."

"Bear?"

"No."

"Wolf?"

"That's a kind of dog."

"Can we get it tested?"

"No."

"Why not?"

"For what?"

"DNA."

"Not from scat. Might be able to tell you what the person ate, but that's it."

"Happened after he was dead," I said to myself.

"That's some real meanness there," said Carter.

"Any shell casings?"

"Haven't found anything recent."

"Recent?"

"You can find old cartridges most everywhere. Folks been shooting here for over a hundred years."

Spent gun cartridges were like cigarette butts, I reasoned—they didn't count as litter somehow.

"How did the bikers find the place if it's locals only?" I asked.

"One of them is a local. High school kid training for some race in France."

"Some race?"

"Yeah."

"Probably the Iditarod."

"Yeah, I think that's it."

Unable to look at Dasher's body anymore, I scanned the surroundings. It wasn't the highest peak, but there was a pretty good view from up here. It was just a little bald hill above another with rocks in a circle.

"What's the significance of the medicine wheel?"

"It's an Indian thing."

"And?"

"And the Indians do it."

"How do the whites view it?"

"We leave it alone."

"Cultural sensitivity?"

"Yes."

"Does—did Dasher respect them?"

"Oh yeah. In fact, one time the Crook boy was up here and moved some of the rocks around to say some profanity. Dasher followed him down to his farm and broke every window in the place and let their chickens loose."

"Did that stop him?"

"That and a good talking-to by the town fathers."

"Why would they care? I mean, in a normal tourist town, I'd get it, but Big Horn County seems positively isolationist."

"You're saying we're backward?"

"Sure."

"You're right. There's still a good fear of Indians out here. Indian spirits and hoodoo and such."

"Hoodoo is—ah, never mind," I said. "Could the Indians have done this to Dasher?"

"Hell no."

"How are you so sure?"

"He was touched. They revere crazy folks like Dasher. You ever hear the story of Crazy Woman Creek? Same thing. They'd no sooner harm him than desecrate their own medicine wheel. If there's one group of suspects we can positively remove, it's the Indians."

"So who do you like for this?"

"There's a list," he said. "All of them got some standing in the county. Even asking them about this is a political hot potato. That's why you're here."

"Who? I need names."

"Everyone and no one. Most folk have some grudge against Dasher, even if it's made up. He's the boogeyman. Easy to make a scapegoat and ridicule, but I never thought any of my neighbors were so mean as to do this."

I looked back at the body. There's a way that a dead body flattens against the ground that live ones never do. The muscles are so relaxed it appears like they're already soaking into the ground. I shuddered.

"Whoever did this was right pissed off," said Carter.

"Or just pissed," I said. "As in drunk."

"That opens the door even wider."

"Can you at least order an autopsy?" I said. "Also ballistics on the bullets. Fingerprint him too. Let's find out who he was."

Carter was about to say something, maybe something about wasting county resources, but he nodded instead.

"This would have been a great place to see the fireworks from," I said.

"And the storm," added Carter.

I walked around the other side. "There's another trail here," I said.

"I know it. It's rougher. Leads out behind the Rawly place."

"An ATV could use it. A bike. A horse."

"In the dark? In the rain? I wouldn't do it."

"Mule?"

"Don't know any."

"It would get someone here unnoticed," I said. "The other way is a major well-used highway—major and well-used being a very relative term out here."

I walked down the hill a ways to the mouth of the trail looking for tracks. I couldn't find much since the rain had washed it. Something had been there recently. I could make out some impressions, bent grass, a squished rodent.

"Someone was here recently." I pointed to flattened fur.

Carter nodded, impressed with my tracking skills.

"There are at least four different tracks, we think. One is barefoot. The rain obscured more than that. At least one came up the trail from the parking lot, but the rain and the bikes ruined anything more than a maybe."

"You can place the tracks at the time of the murder?"

"No. Could have been anytime yesterday."

"Useless."

Shrug.

"You say this trail goes down to Rawly's place?"

"And your friend's. It meets up with a service road that connects to about everywhere."

"That's what a road does. Any tracks there?"

"We haven't looked, but I doubt it."

"It's a good thing we didn't look then."

He ignored me.

"They might have been here waiting," said Carter. "Maybe hiding there behind that rock."

We walked over to a boulder by a bush. It was about fifty yards from the body. It gave a good overlook of the medicine wheel and a good view of the hill where Dasher lay.

I moved aside the bush, and it came up in my hand.

"Well, this isn't at all suspicious," I said.

"Dammit," said Carter. "It's a hunting blind."

"What do people hunt out here?"

"Legally? Nothing. Not now. Not here."

"You'd have to be a pretty good shot," I said, measuring the distance.

"You don't know much about guns, do you?"

"Just testing you. What's your take?"

"A scoped rifle with someone who's used it before couldn't miss at this range."

"Exactly. Well done. You get a cookie."

A medical team with a stretcher arrived. They looked as tuckered out as I had, but they had the excuse of carrying up a metal stretcher and boxes. I'd brought only my stretch marks and boxers. Not quite the same.

"Can we take him?" one called.

Carter looked at me. I nodded.

"Go ahead."

They fitted him into a body bag, shit and all. We waited for them to finish, then I examined where the body had been. Where it had been was dry.

"That's a clue," I said.

"What?"

I pointed to the ground where the rain had made an outline of the body better than chalk ever could, particularly on grass and dirt.

"He was killed before the rainstorm, not after," I said. "Actually, maybe just as it began. Aren't those raindrop craters?"

"Craters?" said Carter.

"In small scale. Baby moonscape. Use your imagination."

"All right. I'll give you that."

"It's a time of death."

"I get it."

"The rainstorm happened down below just before the fireworks. When did it happen here?"

"My guess is during or after it began, but I'll check with my weather guy."

"You have a weather guy?"

"Yes. The weather's important out here."

"You get a lot of it, huh?"

"Can you not be a smartass?"

"No."

He sighed and adjusted his hat. "People die out here from heat, from cold, from flood, die from—"

"I get it. I get it. Weather is a thing. So you have a weather guy? Good. Get us a time of death."

"Localized burst, shouldn't be too hard."

"Do you think a gunshot up here would be heard down below?" I looked at the distant road, the farmhouses, the field where the fair had been, Floyd in the distance.

"Yeah," said Carter. "We get calls about it during hunting season. Ignorant tourists think there's a gunfight behind their motel, but it's miles up these canyons."

"But we had thunder last night. And fireworks. Double cover."

"If I'd have wanted to kill a man up here, I couldn't think of a better time for it."

"Did you have a reason to kill him?" I asked.

"What? I said *if*."

"Since you're not giving me much to go on, I have to start somewhere."

"But I—"

"You're a prime suspect, Deputy Sheriff. Getting rid of a nuisance like Dasher would be just the kind of thing the town would expect you to do. Have they, or have they not, asked you to deal with him?"

The medical workers slowed their work and were listening. Jake too was coming up.

"Yes, but not to kill him."

"They told you specifically to run him out of town? Lean on him like you did me? Or were they less specific? Leaving it up to your judgment?"

"Less specific."

"Do you own a gun?" I asked.

He blinked at me as his hand slid to the revolver on his belt.

"Do you know how to shoot a gun?" I said.

"Yes."

"Where were you last night during the fireworks show? When the storm was there but not here and Dasher was killed?"

Carter glanced at the others and glared at me. "Doing my job."

"Exactly."

He flushed. "If you've got an accusation to make, make it, but you better have some goddamn proof." There was real indignation in his voice. I was taken aback. I just wanted to needle him a little, but I hit upon a real motive and means, and he knew it. Now he was evasive about the opportunity.

"Don't leave town," I said.

"I live here."

"Should be easy for you, then. How about you, Officer Jake?" I said. "Where were you?"

"Craig, do I have to—"

"Humor him."

"I was in Lovell. It's where I'm stationed," he said. "I live there."

"Can you prove that?"

"Yes."

"Is it far from here?"

"Yes."

"Do you have a gun?" I was just dicking with him then, but he wouldn't be dicked with. He drew his revolver and aimed it at me.

"Yes, I do," he said.

"Is there anyone in Big Horn County who doesn't have or know how to use a gun?" I asked, staring down the loaded weapon.

"You," said Carter. "Put that away, Jake. It gives a bad impression."

He slid his gun back into his holster, then pulled it back fast in a quick draw.

"Of course," I said.

He put it back as Carter gave him another look. Then the ambulance men lifted the body onto the stretcher and headed down the hill. I could tell they were surprised by how light it was.

"Do you know these trails well?" I asked Carter.

"What are you implying?"

"Are there maps?"

"Not really," he said.

I pulled out my phone to take some pictures of the area and then put back a brick.

"Did anyone take pictures of the area?"

"Jake?" said Carter.

"Yeah, I got some. Why?"

"Have there been any formal complaints about the deceased guy?" I said to Carter.

"Oh, yes."

"I'll need to see them. All of them."

He rolled his eyes and gave out an exasperated sigh. "They're at the office."

"And the pictures. I'll want prints of them all."

"Why not the files?"

Why not indeed.

"I like hard copy," I said.

"Sure I can't just send them to your tile?" said Jake.

"Listen, shit-weasel." I walked right up to his quick-drawing macho chest. "You keep fucking with me, and I'll have your badge for breakfast and your fat fanny in a federal prison so quick you won't have time to say 'I'm an inbred dumbass hick shit-weasel who doesn't know who I'm dealing with.'"

"That quick, huh?"

"That quick, shit-weasel." It was a good burn, worth a repeat. Feel free to use it.

He looked to Carter, who did something to back my play. I don't know what; my eyes were firmly on Jake. I have a thing about cops. Maybe it's because one shot me once. Not a good introduction. I couldn't blame Jake too much for his attitude. He was taking after Carter's "act" of keeping undesirables out of town.

Jake averted his eyes and stepped back.

"Come on, Carter, take me into Floyd," I said. "I've seen all the shit there is to see here."

I turned and stepped in a pile of brown pellets of poop just to ruin my point.

"Guess you had a little more left," Jake said under his breath.

15

IT WAS ANTELOPE POOP, and I was told it was everywhere. "Antelope are everywhere," Carter explained. "That reasons that their scat would be everywhere too. It's very common. We call it 'Pronghorn Brand prairie fertilizer.'"

"It looks like candy."

Carter coughed and stumbled. I didn't think it was that good a joke. Cowboys have different standards, I guess.

Back in the Explorer, Carter said, "Are you serious about seeing the complaints?"

"I am."

"I'm not sure I have that many written down," he said.

"Why?"

"Things get lost."

"Do they, now? Well, how's your memory?"

He coughed again. "Pretty good."

"We'll make a list together. It'll be fun. Do you have crayons at the office?"

"I'm sure we can find something."

"Do you have maps at the office, or is that all memory too?"

"I have some. Also have a computer."

I hesitated. "I'll start with the maps," I said, "but first breakfast."

"How about I park you at the office and then go get you something? My treat."

"Okay. Better be good, though."

"You want something healthy?"

"I said good."

The police office was empty except for the same woman behind the desk. Even police put pretty girls up front as receptionists. Kinda creepy really.

"Back again so soon?"

"You make the best Salisbury steak in town," I said.

"Veronica," said Deputy Sheriff Carter. "Mr. Flaner has been hired by some government agency to have a quick look into the Dasher thing. Show him every consideration." His words were delivered with such venomous contempt I wondered if he wasn't really asking Veronica to beat me to death with a rubber hose when my back was turned.

"Sure thing, Craig."

He gave me a loathsome stare and then left the building.

"He really pours it on," I said.

"Um-hum." She was wearing a gun, part of the standard American police oppression outfit. I assumed the hoses were in the desk.

"Don't kill me," I said.

"Okay."

I stared at her. She stared back. She cleared her throat. I cleared mine.

The niceties being handled, I ventured to hope.

"Uh, Carter mentioned you had some maps here?"

She reached into her drawer, and I pulled back, angling toward the door because I know that in modern times most rubber hose torturers don't remove the threaded brass ends, liking the modern addition to the traditional weapon.

She came up with papers.

"He died up at the medicine wheel?" she said.

"Was murdered," I said.

"Yes, that's what I meant."

"But not the big one. The little one. The local one."

"Oh, that's right." She folded the map back, fished in her drawer again, took out a length of rubber hose, found another map, and replaced the hose.

I wet myself a little.

On a table behind the counter, I laid the maps out and tried to get a sense of things. The first map she gave me was actually the more useful. It had roads, landmarks, points of interest, but no little medicine wheel. That was the only advantage to the second map, except for maybe a few trails drawn in with pencil.

When Veronica sat down and brought up a game on her computer, I remembered Google Maps was a thing. A public, easy-to-access satellite view of the whole freaking planet, often with pictures from the streets themselves with blurred faces of onlookers, animals, and Greek statues.

The deal I'd made to avoid screens sure seemed like an impediment to my investigation as I tried to visualize elevations by looking at lines like some backward savage. I considered seriously just calling up the ol' internet and using it the way I was used to, but if I did that before I'd had a chance to shame my friends for them falling off the cabin wagon first, I'd lose months, if not years of teasing them. I stayed with the papers and lines.

Looking at the maps told me that most of the county—I mean like 99 percent of it—is absolutely barren and uninhabited except by things that shit outside, like antelope, snakes, and hermits. I'd felt like I'd hardly had a moment alone since I got here, but I saw that that was only because I'd never left the 1 percent with people in it, which weren't many. Politicians from the Middle of Nowhere could come to Floyd, feel its unwelcoming culture, check out its empty landscapes, verify the nothingness on these maps, and then go home to run on a platform of "at least we're not Big Horn County."

If there was ever a place to hide, it would be here. The corollary was probably more useful; if there was ever a place to hide a body, it would be here. And yet Dasher was left where people would find him. Maybe not so soon as the morning after, but within a day or two. The area was not advertised, but neither was it unfrequented. I didn't know what to do with that.

Most of the human structures were clustered around Floyd. I found Perry's cabin on a map by tracing the road past the Crazy Woman Campground. A deceptively passable dashed line led up to the square of the "outbuilding." There was even a little square in the back where I'd left my catalog. A couple of dotted lines led away in several directions. One to a square that I assumed was Rawly's cabin. There were two other buildings linking to the highway with dashes, and to the wilderness with dots. All the dots leading toward the park grouped up eventually into a dashed line behind the cabins that in turn broke into a spray of smaller dots once inside the park boundaries. One of these lines of dots led to the little medicine wheel, near an actual line that I assumed meant road. My eyes blurred as I tried to imagine what kind of machine could print that small, that layered, fine and subtle. USGS maps are goddamn works of art. I wished I had a microscope to see if the tiny dots were scale footprints. I bet they were. With a smug air, I realized that no satellite map was half as useful as this framable masterpiece of surveyor sweat.

"It's so beautiful," I said, my eyes watering with tears of joy and strain.

"I think that one's really good," she said. "The other is for tourists. That's the real deal."

"Where can I get a copy?"

"The tourist one is at the store."

"No, the beautiful one." I choked up.

"Actually, those aren't sold in Floyd."

"What?"

"You can get one in Lovell or Basin probably."

All I could do was wipe my red eyes and say, "Why?"

"Some places just want to be left alone," she said.

"Et tu, Veronica?"

"We like it the way it is."

Carter burst in then with food.

"Are you almost done?" He practically spat the words at me.

"Uh...no?"

He sighed audibly and dropped the food on the table before disappearing into a back office.

"See what I mean?" Veronica said. "Trouble ain't welcome here."

"Who is?" I said.

Breakfast was a cheeseburger and fries, a chocolate shake and a slice of apple pie. Veronica's eyes went big when she saw how much food I had.

I dug into the chow and studied the map, trying to put as much of it to memory as I could because I didn't think I'd be allowed to take it out of the building. It's not like it was something common, like an original copy of the Declaration of Independence. But maybe it was a drug, a controlled substance. It was hypnotic, and I mused about pioneers with Indian scouts and modern-day heroes who'd mapped all this with stick and scope before Sputnik and Skynet.

When the pie was done and the foam box licked clean, I got up and folded the maps. I walked around the counter. "They go in here?" I said to Veronica, pointing to a filing cabinet.

"Botton drawer."

I opened it, stuffed both maps down my pants, then closed the drawer.

I crinkled as I walked to Carter's door, where I knocked.

"Come in," he said.

I opened the door.

"Oh, it's you," he said contentiously, loud and menacing. He was beginning to piss me off.

Leaving the door open for Veronica, I spoke loudly. "Thanks for the lunch," I said. "But now, deputy one-bullet Barney Fife, you're going to cooperate with me in every detail with a goddamn smile on your shit-eating kisser, or I swear to God I'll bring a stew of federal alphabet soup down on you and this town so hard you'll be pulling vowels out of your ass for a month of Februaries. Do I have your attention, shithead?"

His face went blank.

Veronica dropped a coffee mug of paperclips, which made a most satisfying sound. Crash, crack, and sprinkle.

I closed the door.

"You really want to keep playing this game?" I flopped into the chair in front of his desk. I put my feet up and noticed the absolute unit of a desk he sat behind. It was a 50s metal box with green enamel sides, the kind of thing that would actually have had a chance of protecting someone if a nuke went off.

"I told you—"

"Pull it back," I said. "It's hurting my feelings."

"It's not doing me any good, either," he said. "You're vicious."

"I've been a little cranky, I admit. But you're lucky. You should talk to my friend Dara. I'm a pale shadow to her unholy wrath."

He lowered his voice. "Find anything?"

"A masterpiece of geographical representation." I wiped a tear away.

"What?"

"Who do you suspect?" I asked.

"You need to—"

"Uh-uh. You have a suspect in mind. Save me a step."

"I can tell you who made complaints against Dasher."

"Written complaints that were lost?"

He nodded.

He eyed the bottom of my shoes. I dropped them to the floor but used the momentum to lean forward and pick up a half-sized legal pad from the edge of the desk and a pen from the decorative holder in the middle that proclaimed 'Twenty Years' Loyal Service to the Community.'

I tore off the used pages, tossed them on the desk and checked the pen. Carter just watched.

"You got a pen that works?" Naturally that one didn't. They never do.

He opened a drawer, and I saw gardening in my future before he gave me a Bic.

"Like I said," Carter began, "Dasher didn't have many friends."

"He had one."

He looked somewhere else and said, "First, Varg Jayger."

"I've met him."

"You have?"

"Yes. Another local character I'm sure the town wouldn't mind losing."

"Actually..."

"Ah...really?"

"It's Wyoming. White Nationalists are up here. There was a push not too long ago to found an independent country."

"Ick."

"Jayger complained that Dasher broke into his cabin and robbed him."

"Where's his cabin?"

"Just a ways from the cabin you're staying at," he said.

"It's an outbuilding."

"Right."

"Is his the one just beyond Rawly's, or the second one past?" I had just seen the super secret map and felt it crunch in my undies as I shifted my weight.

"Second."

"Who owns the first past Rawly?"

"It's for sale. Empty, I think."

"What was stolen?"

"Jayger didn't say." I could tell that Carter thought he was the most likely suspect.

"Do you think he's the most likely suspect?"

"Wouldn't you?"

"I take it you're not that sort."

"Sort?"

"A Nazi."

Carter shook his head.

"Really? You should go into acting."

A look of shame crossed his face and I realized I'd hurt him. Cowboy cops have feelings? Who knew?

"Who else?" I wrote down notes on the pad, a swastika by Varg's name. Varg. What a name.

"There've been a lot missing cattle in the county. The rumor is that Dasher's stealing them or just letting them go free."

"A PETA activist?"

"Dasher had leanings."

I was going to ask him how he knew this bit of personal and political information, but he cut me off.

"The most vocal accuser has been Roddy Dean."

"I've met him too."

"How about his son, Beaumont?"

"I think I saw him."

"You get around."

"What's with Beaumont?"

"His son."

"Hitman doing daddy's dirt?"

"No."

"Okay..." I hung the word out for him to latch on to. He didn't.

"Then there's Jack Mandel, the realtor. He made a big stink not long ago, saying Dasher's 'unbridled hijinks' were holding down property values."

"Unbridled hijinks? Heavens to Betsy," I said. "And he dresses so nice." At least he did the first time I saw him. The last time at the fair he was in country casual. Jeans and flannel. Probably boots and a buckle big enough to serve Thanksgiving turkey on—I couldn't remember—but I do remember that suit he was in that first day. Fashion envy.

The observation caught Carter by surprise. His forehead wrinkled and one eye squinted as he stared into space. "Yes. He does dress nice, doesn't he?"

I ground my teeth, put out a mental Help Wanted sign for a new censor, 'overtime pay guaranteed,' and said, "I'll put him on the list."

"He's a friend—hell, they all are, except Jayger. Jack was pretty upset when he came to me. Really upset. I think Dasher might have broken into that empty house."

"And…"

Again the opening was ignored.

"James Rawly had a beef with him too," Carter said.

"Burgling again?" I said.

"No. It was personal."

"How?"

"Rawly didn't like him."

"Why?"

"He had reasons."

"He told you these reasons?"

"No."

"But you know about them?"

"Yes."

"Who told you?"

"Rather not say."

"Kimmy?"

"You've met her?"

"Of course."

He sighed. "Okay. There are others who might have thought it would in the public good to get rid of the man, but those four stick out to me."

"Isn't doing the public good your job?"

"Listen, I've told you. I'm trying."

"I just have to put you on the list too," I said. "It won't look good if you're not on it."

"I'm a lawman."

"And lawmens don't shoot folk?"

"This isn't the Wild West."

"And modern cops don't shoot folk? Have you heard of cable television? YouTube? Reading?"

He grunted and furrowed his brow. "I'm the one hiring you."

"Excellent cover," I said. "You wouldn't be the first villain to hire me as an alibi."

"Really?"

"No. I totally pulled that out of my ass, but there's always a first time."

"I didn't kill him!" He slammed his hands on the desk to make the point and then looked sheepish. He fiddled with his wedding ring as if it was reminding him to be a better person. He said, "Sorry."

"Still, for appearance's sake, you're on the naughty list. Unless you'd prefer to be on the friends of the flasher list."

He thought for a moment and shrugged.

"By the way, who else could be on the friendly list?"

"Nobody," he said. "No, wait, maybe Gail at the campground. She said that documentary brought in business, and then there's that Arab guy at the bar. He's always asking questions."

"Being curious makes you a friend of the hermit?"

"Different from what usually happens. Complaints."

"Do you have a copy of this documentary?"

"There's one at the library. Do you have a VHS player?"

"I have a tile in my pocket."

"What does that mean?"

"Forget it."

"Gladly."

"I'm going to head to the library."

"Sounds good."

"Have you considered that the killer isn't from around here? Maybe it was a random thing?"

"Clear those four, and I'll say you're right and close the case."

"I didn't say anything," I said. "And I thought you wanted answers. It looks to me that you're more concerned with the suspects than the victim. Which, frankly, is weird because the four you gave me aren't exactly area luminaries."

"Compared to Dasher, they're dukes."

"You didn't answer my question."

"There was a question?"

"Am I clearing suspects or finding the killer?"

"Well…"

"Listen, Matt Dillon, stop dodging."

"*Gunsmoke* reference? Dodge City?"

"Good. Give yourself a cookie. Suspects or killer?"

He leaned back in his chair and took a deep breath, all the while holding me in wrinkled cowboys eyes. I gave him my Eastwood squint and pretended to move a cigar stub from one side of my mouth to the other.

"Mr. Flaner," he said, "get the bastard."

16

I KNEW the way from jail to the hidden town. It was just behind the trees a ways, just a ways, but safe from the prying eyes of civilization. Only serious pilgrims could get breakfast or buy bricks in Floyd. It was so conveniently hidden that it gave off a cult vibe if you thought about it too long, so I didn't. Instead I figured Google Maps would be the great equalizer for the future downfall of Floyd. Thus reminded, I retrieved the purloined maps from my perspiring loins and waved them like semaphores to air them out as I walked.

I looked around for Perry's Cadillac but didn't see it. I hoped the library was open and friendly. Not all libraries are friendly. It depends on the librarians. In my experience there are two kinds: the helpful energetic enthusiastic lover of letters, all too willing to chat about books, recommend resources, and order stuff in from across the globe with a smile, and the burned-out bureaucrat who thinks everyone who comes into a library is either an idiot who wouldn't know their chin for Chaucer or a hobo looking for shelter. Such functionaries condescend with alacrity, fervor, and dispatch by all the thesauri.

She was young and pretty, blonde hair pulled away from her face. I put her in her twenties, wearing round glasses that made her eyes look big, warm, and welcoming. My heart leaped hopefully, a friendly face in a wild place.

"What are you, some kind of bum?" she asked.

"Ee-gawds," I said.

"You can't sleep here. Do you want me to call the sheriff?"

I looked at myself. I had jeans, tennis shoes, and a comfy tie-dyed T-shirt.

It was not Floyd fashion, but it wasn't bum, nouveau-slacker maybe, but not bum. Not really.

"I'm just visiting."

"This isn't a public space."

"Yes it is. It's a public library."

"Are you going to make trouble?"

"Could be fun, but I probably don't have time."

She picked up the phone. I watched her. She narrowed her eyes and stuck out her chin.

"Veronica? This is Susan at the library. We have a bum here who won't leave."

She listened. I thumbed through a copy of *Welcome to Wyoming!*, an annual publication put out by the Wyoming Tourist Commission. This one was eight years old.

"Yes," Susan said. "Yes, that's him. I'm sure he's the one Craig put in jail the other day. He's—"

And here I smiled at Susan, waiting for the shoe to drop.

It dropped on her face. Her big, warm, squinty eyes looked lost and upended. She glanced at me, at the door, the cup of pens, the *Welcome to Wyoming!* pamphlet and then turned to look at a wall behind her.

"But—" She repeated the sentiment a couple times. "But..." and "But I—" and "But Veronica..."

She hung up without turning to face me.

"I don't have it," she said to the wall.

"No, you don't, but I'm sure there're finishing schools back east who are looking for a challenge."

"I mean the video tape you're looking for. I don't have it."

"What's going on here, Susan?" The voice belonged to an old woman, hunched over and limping. She had a mud gray shawl around her shoulders, a skirt that would have been fashionable at a Dust Bowl mortgage sale. Her hair matched her shawl and was tucked into a bun so severe it pulled her ears into near Vulcan points. She looked at me with beady eyes through cat-eye glasses connected around her neck with a beaded chain. Her lips pursed into a frowning pucker, the lines around her mouth deep and many, reminding me of a satellite photo of mount doom.

"Ms. Severe," said Susan. "This...man...wants to see the documentary tape about the hermit. The sheriff said we should help him." She said it like she was explaining that I'd just shit the bed and the manager had sent them in with a wet wipe to deal with it.

"Is this true?" said Ms. Severe.

"What part?" said I.

"Any of it?"

"Except for the shit tone of little miss stuck-up, yeah, it's pretty close."

"What was that about a wet wipe?"

"Errrr," I growled, while I waited for the old witch to spread her arms and summon winged monkeys. I glanced around for a water source and only found the drinking fountain. It'd have to do.

"Where is it?" said Ms. Severe.

"It's checked out," said Susan.

"Put a hold on it for when it's returned."

Susan rolled her eyes and went to a computer and tapped the keys.

"I'm sorry," Ms. Severe said. "We only have one copy of that newscast. We used to have more, but they kept disappearing."

"Why'd you let this one leave, then?"

"We're a library."

"Oh. Right."

"Can I help you find something else? We have an extensive section of westerns."

"Go figure."

"Lots of romance." She giggled. That's right. Ms. Severe giggled. "Some nastier than others. The ones with the six-pack torsos usually do the trick for me, but we have clean ones too."

"How about local history?"

"Oh, yes," she said, nearly jumping out of her orthopedic shoes for joy. "Let me show you."

Like I said. There are two kinds of librarians.

Ms. Severe led me to a history section and pulled down a dozen books she said I just had to read. "Cowboys and Indians, cattlemen and settlers. Wyoming is so young, it's like yesterday," she said.

I held off making a joke about her age. "Can you find out when that video is due back?" I said instead.

"Of course. Do you need paper or pencil?"

"No, I'm good." I showed her my purloined legal pad and extorted Bic. She nodded eagerly, pursed her frowning lips into something up-tempo and skipped back to the front desk.

I sat down and learned a little about Big Horn County, Wyoming.

Founded when the Earth's crust cooled, what is now called Big Horn County, Wyoming, originally didn't have a name, or if it did, it didn't survive the Pleistocene period. Rains fell, dinosaurs gnawed, plants grew, bugs did their bug things and years later James Clavell would pad his books with it. I'll skip ahead to the coming of people, leaving out the mountains rising, beavers swimming, and logs logging and all that.

The first people to arrive in the area were not white people—really—and they were there for a long time before the white people showed up, but you might not get that impression from the few books the library had on that subject. The Clovis people were there twelve thousand years ago. The Folsom, ten thousand, and a group I never heard of called the Eden Valley

People were there eight thousand years ago. What adventures they must have had.

After these ancient guys, there were a bunch of peoples who didn't get their own designation in the encyclopedia I had. They were big game hunters and traders. These Yellowstone obsidian dealers had customers as far away as later New England.

Nomadic peoples, they came and went. One group would dominate for a while, then another. Some for decades, others maybe for an afternoon just after lunch. Some were surely forced out by others, some just left remembering they were late for a glacier. It was like a millennium-long game of musical chairs but with plains instead of ass-numbing folding metal seats. When the music stopped at the boom of a Monroe Doctrine crescendo, the area was home to the alphabetized plain Indians: Arapaho, Arikara, Bannock, Blackfeet, Cheyenne, Crow, Gros Ventre, Kiowa, Nez Perce, Sheep Eater, Sioux, Shoshone and Ute tribes.

Trappers and mountain men were the first European invaders to meet the locals. Lewis and Clark visited what would become Big Horn County in their travels, but not the Wyoming one. There's a Big Horn County just over the border in Montana. That gets a bit confusing. I was confused for a while. A long while. Locations, like history, like the arbitrary borders Wyoming politicians would eventually put on the dry lands of northern Wyoming, were fluid and hard to pin down to any one place. The area had a history; the county was just a label for some of it. This history was icky. Most history is, since history is usually just a list of calamities. This was no exception.

Western expansion is the celebrated American myth that played really well until recent times. Later audiences, separated by the distances of time and cultural evolution, look on it less romantically. Count me among those.

Indian-wise, the history of the area had two notable moments from the white point of view: the aforementioned tragedy of the Crazy Woman and Custer's comeuppance. These were the exceptional moments during the grinding day-to-day killings of the tribes by starvation, disease, and finally by bullets when there was a hurry.

Exit the Indians. Enter class warfare.

Progress, I guess.

I fell into reading about the infamous Johnson County War, a little slice of hellish American exceptionalism that lasted officially from 1889 to 1893. It was followed by the comparatively quaint Tensleep Raid of 1909. And here I thought Utah had a corner on the real shit-shows of the Old West. Nope. Wyoming was right there too.

Then I noticed that Mormon colonists entered the area in 1885 and so were actually instrumental in—

"Ahem." It was Ms. Severe. "We're closing soon."

I saw the orange rays of a coming sunset out a window and blinked to regain myself.

I'd been nose deep in books, turning pages in a trance, engrossed in history, style, and character. Forgetful of time, I'd become part of the stories I was reading, as only reading can do. Like the stolen map from Carter's office, I was immersed and impressed by the skill and simplicity of the paper media. I can't remember a time I'd ever been so drawn in to anything I'd read on a computer screen, but connecting it all then, I remembered hundreds of times books had done that for me. Books are cool. There's a reason they're still around.

"What time is it?"

"Nearly five o'clock."

"You close early." I rubbed my eyes.

"Sometimes," she said. "Did you find what you were looking for?" She beamed with pride as if I were her A+ student handing in extra credit.

"I don't know," I said. "I kinda got drawn in."

She pursed a pruny smile and nodded.

"That Johnson County War was something else," I said.

"Oh, wasn't it, though?"

"What did you find out about the tape?"

She consulted a blue rectangular card like the ones I'd seen in the back of all the books she'd shown me. "It's checked out. Due back next week. We'll hold it for you."

"Who has it?"

"We don't share that information," she said.

"Even if the sheriff asks for it?"

"Especially if the sheriff asks for it. He needs a warrant, and then we'll probably lose it before he sees it."

I think I was falling in love with Ms. Severe.

"I'd like to check out a couple books," I said.

"Sorry. You have to have residency in the area or piggy-back on a local's card."

"That happens?"

"It does."

"The cards are quaint," I said. "Very retro."

"Dewey decimal is doing fine. We use computer when we *have* to.""

It occurred to me that this library was somewhere between yesterday and tomorrow, just not today.

"Hey, you know what I just thought?"

"What?"

I leaned on the table too hard and my reading spilled onto the floor in a literary crash.

"Oh dear," said Ms. Severe.

As I'd hoped, she put down the cards and rushed to pick up the books, three-second rule and all.

I sidled over and peeked at the card.

Action News Wyoming Report: The Hermit of Big Horn County. Video checked out to Gail Larsen for Penn Cromby, July 2nd.

As Ms. Devere, on her aged knees, stacked the books back on the table, I looked at other checkout cards: *Fifty Shades Darker, Outdoor Family Activities that Don't Suck, History of S'Mores, Endangered Animals of Wyoming, Gun and Dagger Annual* and *Resumes that Get the Job.*

All were out on Gail's card 'for the benefit of Penn Cromby,' but I had a feeling they weren't all for him personally.

"Would you help me here?" asked the librarian.

"What do you need?"

"How about some help picking these up?"

"Sure thing. Susan!" I yelled.

"I was beginning to like you," she said.

"Sorry. Too good to miss."

I got down beside her and collected books.

When we had them back on the table, I helped her up. She looked appraisingly at the tidy stacks we'd made, then glanced over to the cards she'd left on the other table and glared at me.

"Did you get everything you needed?" she asked, her attitude less warm.

"What do you know about the medicine wheel?"

"One of the oldest in the country. Dates back to 1790."

"Have you heard about the little one?"

"Have you?"

"I'm Tony Flaner," I said. "I know things and—"

"The detective?"

"You've heard of me?"

She nodded. "Are you on a case? Is that why Carter said to help you?"

"Maybe."

"How exciting," she said. "The little medicine wheel's only been around for about forty years, maybe a little less. It mysteriously appeared one day and it's been there ever since. I find it quite—" She cut herself off.

"What?" I said.

"Are you looking into the death of that pervert?"

"Um, pervert?"

"You are."

"I'm not really—"

"I saw him up in Miracle Canyon last year. He grabbed himself indecently and...ohhhhh, I've never been so disgusted in all my life. That foul exhibitionist, shit-eating, Dashiell—"

"So the little wheel only goes back thirty, forty years? That's interesting."

"We're closing," she said, collecting the cards I'd looked at. "You have to leave. Now. Have a nice day."

17

I WANDERED out of the library without a destination, my mind swimming with bipolar librarians, visions of new ancient Indian traditional spaces, rustic perverts, tales of cattle barons and homesteaders, shepherds and crooked governments. I tried to piece it all together as if they were all part of the same puzzle but then fell to marveling at how little I'd needed my faux phone that day. I'd had books, maps, conversations—ancient technologies—well, less modern technologies. Still, they'd worked just fine.

Although screen time abstinence was the rallying cry for this trip to Wyoming, I realized with my head full of book learning that thematically, this trip to Perry's outbuilding was really about new versus old. Old tech versus new tech. Which is best? Have we gone too far? Are the old ways better or are we happy to be rid of them?

That reminded me. I needed a real goddamn toothbrush.

I am a creature of my time, and my time has been unparalleled as far as change. The internet has done that. Information comes at light speed, paradigms are old before I realize they were the new ones. Keeping a face to my computer screen kept me in the loop at least. Taking the time to read a book or two, a chapter, an article, a real map in my fingers, had been like a trip down memory lane, a nostalgic vacation to simpler times when I could keep up. I was over thirty, closer to forty. The writing was on the Facebook wall: I was not keeping up. I could never keep up. Maybe no one could.

In a flash of understanding, I saw Floyd as an attempt to halt this daunting and relentless advance of information and change. A familiar line in the sand. It was a false line, sure to be washed away by the flood of modern life, but I could appreciate the attempt. It reminded me of an old *Twilight Zone* episode where idyllic simplicity lured an unhappy man to his ultimate death.

That got dark. But I think you know what I mean. It's a universal dream of 'the good ol' days' where one believed they understood the world they lived in.

But it doesn't last. It's still musical chairs. Change happens, and the people who made the change demand that change stop after them because they'll be the victims the next time. Case in point, the infamous Johnson County War. It all began—

"Well, if it isn't the troublemaker."

I looked up and saw the man from the rodeo, the guy who made the speech in shiny boots. He blocked my way on the sidewalk.

"Well, if it isn't the cancerous cancer killing the planet," retorted I.

"What is that supposed to mean?"

"It means I have comedy training. K's are funny. Cucamonga. It also means you're a moron."

"What?"

"A moron."

He stared at me. I stared back.

"M-O-R-O-N," I offered.

"You're on thin ice," he said. "Who sent you? That liberal solar company? The windmill conglomerate? Democrats? Or are you some self-styled do-gooder, a tree-hugging bleeding-heart troublemaker?"

"Mo-ron." I said it really slow so he could keep up.

That's when he slugged me.

He didn't slug me hard, but he did find my diaphragm, which meant my lungs emptied, and I was in a familiar doubled-over pose. I was on a case, all right.

I straightened up and sucked in a breath. I'd been punched plenty of times, and I was getting sick of it.

"You know what?" I gasped. "This happens to me all the time."

"I'm not surprised, smartass. Looks like I'm not the first in the county to get you." He pointed to my scream button and pushed his thumb into it.

I screamed and backed a step. I sucked air through my teeth. "I am learning new ways to deal with this, though," I said.

"Like what?"

I kicked him in the balls.

He hovered for a moment, his balance shifting left to right. A little squeak escaped his pinched lips and he listed to starboard, found the ground, and assumed the traditional fetal position.

It wasn't a gunfight at high noon, no six guns, but it still felt like a duel. I was sick of all the animosity in this town. Was it my shirt? Does tie-dye trigger rednecks?

I watched the man writhe, astonished that I'd actually done that to him. I too was surprised. This wasn't like me. I stick up for myself but not physically. Not usually. That's probably why I get beat up so often. My weapons of choice are words, though I have been known to force lattes up people's noses. That was in defense of the species, not me specifically. Still, this was a departure. Was I regressing to some animal state, a victim of some rural devolution, turning feral from the mountain air and lack of twenty-four-hour news? Should I buy a pair of boots?

I pondered this as I left the man to fish his testes out of his abdomen.

The assault had diverted me from a toothbrush. The devil and the deep dark dust drew me toward Floyd's Old Times Saloon.

I rounded the corner and ran into Mandel coming out of his office.

"So you're looking into the killing?" he said.

I tried to gauge his interest and excitement, but once I took in the tailored suit and wingtips, I couldn't get past the emerald pinky ring.

"How is it selling real estate up here?" I asked.

"Meh."

"But you're doing well?"

"Meh."

"Meh?"

"Meh. Real estate is slow, but the prospecting is good."

It registered then. "You run the Prospector Paradise?"

"Yeah, it's a sideline. I sell panning stuff like you saw at the fair."

"That's tourist trade, isn't it?"

"Some buyers there, but there are enough locals to keep the lights on. I sell the gear and buy the gold. The markups keep me going."

The sun caught in the emerald ring and blinded me like a laser into a Cesna's cockpit.

"One day I'll be out of here," he said.

"Where would you go?"

"Seattle. My fianceé lives there."

"Long-distance romance?"

"Long-term," he said. "What about the killing?"

"Just started snooping."

I could see that the word jarred him. "Okay." He moved toward a ubiquitous white pickup.

"Where were you last night?" I said. He straightened up like a roving proctologist had just hit pay dirt.

"Am I a suspect?" He was suddenly sweating.

This was going to be the shortest case of my life. "Answer the question," I said.

"Uh, you saw me at the fair."

"After that?"

"I watched the fireworks."

"From where?"

"The bleachers."

I shook my head. I hadn't seen him there. And I looked.

"Maybe the parking lot," he said.

"We gotta do better than that."

"It wasn't me."

"Then who was it who watched the fireworks?"

"Huh? The killer?"

"The killer watched the fireworks? You can swear to this?"

"No." He brought his shaking hand up and made a fist on his chest. Hadn't seen that one before. "I'm not the killer."

"But you know who it was and that they were watching the fireworks?"

"You're so aggravating."

"So, who's the killer?"

"My money's on James Rawly."

"Gotta do better than that too."

He looked around to see if anyone else was watching. "He's violent and untethered," he said. Then he got into the truck. "Gotta go."

In the bed of the truck there was a tarp. Once I lifted it up and looked underneath, I couldn't help but notice a pair of muddy boots beneath it.

"Excuse me," Mandel said. I put the tarp down and stepped aside.

He backed up in a three-point turn and then dramatically spit gravel as he sped out. If he was aiming for me, which would have been the move, he missed. The gravel spray kicked up over the wooden sidewalk and broke the front window of his real estate office.

Mandel didn't stop.

I crossed the street and went into the saloon. I blinked to adjust my vision to the cool murk for the warm sunset.

"Tony. There you are."

My friends were all at a table, drinking.

"Yes. And there you are you, you rotten bunch of oathbreakers, black-guards, and scoundrels. J'accuse!"

Amir "Eddie" Rahal at the bar leaned in to watch, his ear turned toward us, a glint of sweat on his forehead.

"That's pretty harsh," said Garrett.

"We promised we'd rough it."

"I'm drinking straight rum," said Standard, holding up a glass.

"No umbrella in my gin and tonic," said Dara.

"I asked for a dirty glass," said Perry.

"But we don't do that here," said Eddie.

I glared.

"You know about the hotel?" asked Garrett.

"Uh-huh."

"We had a good reason," explained Perry.

"Can't wait to hear it."

"The usual?" asked Amir from across the bar.

"Sure," I said.

"And what is that?" he said.

"Fuzzy navel with three maraschino cherries. Blended."

"What?"

My friends were at a corner table, not the one Gail had had, but its sister, a little farther back, nearer the kitchen. On the other side of the bar at the same table as before sat Varg Jayger, his inked face, bald head and bad attitude shining in the dim light slipping in between the curtains of the window. He sat alone as if waiting for someone.

I joined the gang in the gulag.

"So you're looking into the killing of that naked dude," said Dara as a way of hello.

"You know about that? How do you know about that?"

"It's all over town," said Eddie, appearing with a Fresca. He had remembered.

"Yeah, it's all anyone is talking about," said Perry.

"The restaurant, the hotel, the bar," said Garrett.

"So it's true?" said Eddie.

"Can I have a pickled egg to go with my Fresca?"

"We don't have pickled eggs."

"Then you can go."

Eddie scowled but went back to the bar.

"Is it true?" asked Garrett.

"Yes. Amazing how fast news travels. He was killed last night, early this morning. The sheriff found me at the cabin, all alone, lonely, with no one else there, and..."

"And what?"

I realized I'd nearly said too much. I'd almost mentioned how I'd got the case, spilling the sheriff's secret to my friends. My friends were flakes and big mouths, so even though they were temporary and tourists, they were not to be trusted. Such are my friends.

I sipped my cool refreshing grapefruit-like beverage and said, "Where's Critter, and what the hell happened to you last night?"

"Are we suspects?" asked Perry. "How could you think such a thing?"

"Critter was with me all night," said Garrett.

"I didn't kill anyone," said Dara. "Last night."

"Thanks for the clarification," I said.

Standard looked concerned. "You're jealous, aren't you? This is about me finding peace in the woods and you not. It's about my soul being opened to the majesty of fresh air and running water while yours is bitter and envious."

"More likely it's about us not getting him out of jail," said Dara. "And making him blow up the mattress. Ditching him in the storm."

"I knew it. He's framing us for murder," said Standard. "Such a lost soul."

"Tony wouldn't do that," said Perry. "Would you?"

"You're tempting me."

They all looked at me in horror.

"Have you all lost your ever-garbled minds?" I asked.

"You're not really going to frame us for murder," said Standard.

"What's going on?"

"Standard said you'd be royally pissed and get even with us for stuff," said Garrett.

"What have you done?"

"We stayed in the Shady Tree Motel."

"I know."

"You do? How?"

"It's all anyone is talking about."

Standard's lip quivered, a tear formed in his eye. "Forgive us—we watched TV. *Gilligan's Island.*"

"For hell's sake."

"Told you," he said to the others. "We *are* oathbreakers."

"And you think I'd come at you for vengeance over that?"

"You trusted us. We let you down. This whole trip was to help you get over your addiction to technology."

"I thought it was for us all to see Perry's new place and find spiritual wellness in the simplicity of older times."

"Well, that too."

"And everyone said they wanted to go screen-free for a while."

"We were doing it for you," said Dara. "We don't have a problem."

"The hell you don't."

"Well, we didn't think we did," said Garrett. "We kind of all thought we were here to help you. An intervention. But then we got here and it rattled us."

"Rattled you enough to think I'd come and frame you for killing someone?"

"It sounded better last night with the reefer."

"We were watching *The Fugitive,*" said Dara. "It got us thinking."

"I dreamed of one-armed men all night," said Garrett.

"You mean it got your drug-addled minds going paranoid?"

They all looked sheepish. Garrett pulled Critter out of his pocket, and the puppet looked at me with big sad eyes.

"It's like this," he said. "Everyone's a fish out of water here. None of us has been our best selves. Perry's embarrassed at his cabin and paranoid as usual. Standard is over-compensating. Dara is unfathomable to mortal beings, and Garrett is borrowing trouble. The technology blackout is preying on all our minds. Plus Dara's pot was pretty potent."

"So what happened last night to trigger your complete and humiliating breakdown of moral obligations to friend and quest?"

"You're being harsh again," said Standard.

"Danger," said Critter. "We were warned off."

I saw Varg's eyes go large as Garrett's hand spoke.

"Garrett's fault," said Dara. "He can't keep his dick in his pants."

"It was that woman who owns the campground," said Perry.

"She recognized Garrett and warned him," said Perry. "I don't know how."

"Was Critter there?"

The puppet nodded. "Maybe she's psychic."

"What did she say?" I asked.

Perry said, "She told us that Rawly—Mr. Rawly, the husband—was in a terror and we better not go back to the cabin."

"In a terror?" I asked. "Because of Garrett and Kimmy?"

"And Critter," said Dara.

Critter looked away. A puppet can't blush, but he tried.

"A ménage à trois," said Dara. "Hurts the cerebral cortex just to imagine it."

"They were having sex?" said Standard.

We all turned to stare at our clueless friend.

"What? I was communing with nature."

"What did Gail say exactly?" I asked.

"She said that Rawly was in a terror."

"How'd she know about Garrett and Kimmy when I didn't?" asked Standard.

"Maybe she has eyes."

"Gail and Kimmy are friends," said Garrett. "And um, the last time we—"

"The last time?" said Standard. "How many times have there been?"

"A couple."

"A couple?"

"A few."

"Different times or multiple events at the same appointment?" asked Critter.

"My brain is hurting," said Dara.

"What happened the last time?" I asked.

"Kimmy said that her husband suspected she'd been running around. She said he was capable of doing rash things."

"Did you see Kimmy yesterday?"

"Not in the evening." Critter cleared his throat.

"Gail said that Rawly was in a terror," said Garrett.

"That's why we stayed in the hotel?" asked Standard.

"Why'd you think?"

"To piss off Tony."

"Thoreau has nothing on you," I said.

Over Standard's shoulder I saw Varg suddenly come to alert. He stood up at the sound of a throaty car outside. Smirking, he went to the window and peeked out. His smirk melted and he pulled the drapes shut before going back to his table. While upending an IPA, he saw me looking at him and scowled. He checked his watch, got up, and after collecting a khaki green rucksack from the floor, left through the backdoor in a hurry.

I wasn't sure if that was strange or not and looked at Eddie to judge his reaction. Eddie was not looking at the back door, not cleaning, not stocking. He was staring straight at me.

18

"WHAT'S WITH THE BARTENDER?" said Perry. "He's looking at you like you were a science experiment."

"He does that to everyone," I said and realized it was true.

"Does Tony's little moonlighting mean we don't get to go home?" said Dara.

"Leaving? You're already talking about leaving? It's been three days."

"We're fucking bored. There's a reason alcoholism is rampant in places like this."

"What do you mean places like this?" Eddie was back. He'd magically created a plate of nachos and put them on the table.

"We didn't order these," said Standard.

"On the house."

Eddie stood by and waited for someone to try them.

Standard was the first, Dara quickly after him.

"I heard a couple more steers were lost last night," said Eddie, just making conversation.

"Roddy must be in a fury," I said, stuffing warm cheese, salsa, and crisp tortilla chips into my face. "Theesh are pwetty goobd," I said. "Thwank ooo."

"You're welcome," said Eddie, "But it wasn't Roddy Dean's herd this time. It was another rancher. Mr. Pilana. He owns the Bar Shield ranch."

"Do you do onion rings?" asked Garrett.

"Happened sometime yesterday night," said Eddie.

"Maybe one of those onion bloom things? Critter and I really like those."

"Pilana's lost a bunch of cattle this year. But he came in this morning happy as a clam saying that he'll lose no more now."

"Shit, Tony, are you going to at least act interested in any of this?" said Dara. "He's trying to tell you something."

"I know he is."

"You don't look very interested," said Perry. "You look bored. And ravenous."

"You don't know the first thing about interrogation," I said. "More guac, if you have it."

"He's right," said Eddie. "The best way to get someone to talk is to offer them silences."

"So no onion rings?"

"Where's the Bar Shield, Eddie?" I said.

"Out a ways toward Montana, but he said the cattle were taken off a range that abuts the park against a dirt road not too far from your place—just on the way to where the body was found with shit on it at the little medicine wheel if you're coming from the north. Someone cut the fence and took two prize steers the night of the Fourth. Ollie and Hardy."

"They had names?"

"Prize winners. Each a thousand pounds on the hoof."

"How do you know so much?"

"Why did you have to include that detail about the shit?" said Garrett.

Eddie shrugged.

The door to the bar opened and a couple walked in. They were in their late sixties, I'd guess. The man had streaks of gray in his dark hair at the temples; she had her hair in a scarf and wore sunglasses as if they'd been cruising Tampa in a convertible, not Wyoming at sunset. He was thin, walked like a retired golfer, moseying down the fairway in a baby-blue polo shirt and tan khaki shorts. Black socks in his sneakers. She was in plaid slacks with no pockets that did nothing to diminish her very wide hips. Her blouse was untucked. She smelled like citrus perfume and pine air freshener.

"Excuse me," said the man. "Is there a hotel in town?"

"There has to be," said the woman before anyone could answer. "This can't be all there is."

Eddie walked slowly back to the bar.

"Excuse me," said the man again.

"The Shady Tree Motel," I said. "Take the road across the way called Stubbins Street, and it'll snake you into something closer akin to civilization."

"Thank you." The man gave Eddie a glare. Eddie glared back. "Very kind of you." I heard a Midwest accent.

"Michigan?" I asked.

"You betcha," said the woman, perking up. "We're the Isaaks. Ada and Sherman. Glad to meetcha."

"Are you staying here long?" asked Eddie.

The couple turned to look at him. Eddie squinted and polished a bottle of

Pabst Blue Ribbon with a dirty bar towel. I drink beer, and used to tend bar, so I know that PBR can not be made worse by a dirty bar towel.

"Don't mind Eddie," I said. "He's up to something, but I don't know what it is yet."

"He is?" asked Perry.

"Duh."

"Couldn't he just be weird?" asked Standard. "People are weird sometimes."

"Do you think it's about the murder?" asked Dara.

"What murder?" asked Mrs. Isaaks.

"A man was murdered last night," said Garrett.

"Who was it?" said Mr. Isaaks, visibly concerned.

"No one knew his name."

"So he was new here? A tourist?"

"No," said Eddie, finding his tongue. "He's been here a while, but no one knew who he was."

"Oh lord," said Mrs. Isaaks. "Sherman…"

"I think I saw a sheriff's office across the street," said Mr. Isaaks. "Come on, Ada."

The couple turned and ran outside.

The gang turned to stare at Eddie.

Eddie turned his back to us.

"He could just be weird," said Critter. "He's acting weird."

"He's up to something."

"You know I can hear you, right?" said Eddie to the back shelves.

"What are you up to?"

"I'm not from around here," he said.

"Finally," said Critter. "A plain answer."

Eddie moved his bar rag to the draft handles.

"That puppet is disturbing," he said.

"What puppet?" asked Critter.

"So you forgive us?" Standard asked me.

"For breaking our sacred blood oath and leaving me to go back to the cabin where there was forewarned danger?"

"Yes."

"We figured the Cadillac was the giveaway," said Perry. "If the Caddy wasn't there, Rawly would pass the cabin by."

"No car was like blood over the door?"

"Exactly."

"We were talking about leaving," said Dara. "Are you ready?"

Perry's face fell.

"You don't want to leave?"

"We haven't even seen the bunker under the house yet."

"He has a point," said Critter.

"Shhh," said Garrett.

"I'm on a case now."

"There are buses," said Dara.

I squinted at her malevolently.

"No, there aren't," said Eddie.

"Do you mind?" I said. "We're trying to have a conversation here."

"Can't help it."

"Because you're nosy?"

"Great acoustics."

"Bullshit," I whispered.

"Really. It's the best thing about the bar."

"You're acting very suspicious," I said and went to the bar.

"So are you."

"No, I'm not."

"Yes, you are."

"No, he isn't," said my friends.

"Well, I'm not either."

"Yes, you are," we all said together.

And just like that, the argument was won.

"I'm just a fly on a wall."

"Why?" I said.

"I need a reason?"

"No, but you have one." He looked positively astonished. "How do you know that?"

"You're not from around here," I said.

"And that—"

"Answer his fucking question, barkeep, or I'll smack you into Colorado." Dara had my back.

"There was a question?"

Dara bolted up from her seat, ran across the room and leaped on the bar, crashing glasses and spilling everything as she crawled purposefully and bloodthirstily at Eddie.

"Whoa whoa whoa." Eddie backed into the counter, adding to the broken glass.

He looked around for help, but there was only our group in the bar, and we knew better than to get between Dara and her prey.

On hands and knees, eyes steely and locked, Dara moved ever closer.

"Shit. Shit shit. Call her off."

If Dara had had a bloody knife in her teeth she couldn't have looked any scarier. Like my friends, I could only watch.

"Keep her away!" The pitch in Eddie's voice was finding new heights.

"You better talk," I said. "I think she has rabies."

His hands came up.

Dara paused, drooled.

"Promise you won't tell anyone," he said. "I could be in danger."

"As opposed to where you are now?"

He made to reach for something under the bar. Dara growled at him. He jumped back, this time knocking over a bottle of gin. Sapphire. Good stuff.

"I'm doing a research project," he said, cowering to the floor as little Dara Sutter stood on the bar top and leered down at him.

"What kind of research project?"

"'Conservative attitudes toward minorities, outsiders, and people of color in a modern rural America small town: a field experiment.'"

"You're studying rednecks?" I said.

"My adviser advised me not to use those words, but yes, that's basically it," said Eddie. "It's my doctorate thesis in sociology."

"What's your methodology?" I asked.

"Attitudes and reactions to hostile and non-hostile strangers of color and minority status. I'm the guinea pig, a minority outsider, with Arab heritage, taking a job from a local."

"You took less pay than a local would?"

"Actually, I'm paying the owner to work here."

"Worse than a fucking intern," Dara said. "Have you no class consciousnesses?"

"It's for science."

"That's the stupidest thing I've ever heard," said Standard.

"I don't know," said Perry. "A good scientific paper exploring racism and xenophobia is always useful, and rednecks as a class are a widely unstudied group."

Garrett said, "I don't think 'rednecks' is the politically correct term."

"It could be argued that since the subject is not politically correct, the usual niceties in civility of terminology could be adjusted in the study to reflect the truth on the ground."

"Also, it's not a protected class," said Eddie.

"Because it's an acquired mindset," explained Perry.

"Exactly."

"Jesus," said Standard. "I may be ready to go home now."

"You can't go," said Eddie slowly standing. Dara glared at him as he did, her little hands flexing in and out of fists. "Tony—can I call you Tony?"

Dara growled.

"Mr. Flaner," he went on, "has to look for the killer."

"What is it to you?" asked Critter.

I understood and explained, "I'm the new minority outsider. A fresh new guinea pig."

Eddie nodded. "Plus when we find out who killed Dasher the Flasher, I'll have a whole chapter on the town's reaction about the killing and the arrest."

Dara climbed down off the counter.

"I agree with Stan," she said. "This is the stupidest thing I've ever heard."

"No, it isn't," I said.

She thought for a second.

"Okay, not the stupidest, not with you guys as friends, but it's stupid enough to be true."

We all nodded. I could hear Critter's jiggling eyes loud and clear from across the room. The place really did have good acoustics.

"You know, Floyd isn't normal," I said to Eddie. "I've never been to a more isolationist place in my life that didn't speak Dutch."

"I know. It's a complete exaggeration. It's why I chose it and why I will be careful not to use the term 'typical' or 'normal' in my paper. The data will back up my hypothesis of an intolerant backwater berg of bigots."

"So you'll alliteratively overstate the data to match your preconceptions?" I said.

Eddie nodded.

"I mourn for the state of scholarship."

"Everyone does it."

"Mourn, I say. Mourn! Gnash teeth and keep the dead from spinning tunnels in their graves to the Galapagos."

"Why does Tony have to be your guinea pig?" said Standard.

"Because the town has accepted *him*," I said, tilting my head to the barkeep.

"To me, everyone's been pretty nice. Even behind my back," said Eddie. "However, I do hear them run down others all the time, Dasher being a constant subject."

"Go on."

"You have to promise not to tell anyone. My safety's involved here." He looked genuinely worried about that, more even than the prospect of Dara ripping his skull off his spine.

"We don't care," said Critter. "Do we?"

"It'll ruin a year's work if it gets out."

"Mum's the word," I said, and he visibly relaxed. "Now, tell me what else do you know?"

"Oh, there are all kinds of secrets in a town like this."

"Such as?"

"What do you want to know?"

"Who killed Dasher?"

"I don't know that."

"But you think it might be Pilana?"

"Him or a dozen others."

"What's wrong with Pilana?" asked Perry. "You got a grudge against him?"

"No," Eddie said, getting excited. "I have this corollary theory that newcomers, in order to fit in, will overcompensate the area's tendencies. Thus, a newcomer like Pilana would be the most likely to act against another newcomer or outcast in order to show affiliation and service to the main group."

"Like you with the Isaaks?" I said.

"What?"

He was oblivious. "Do you have anything to back that up? Asking for the Nobel Committee."

"No, I just thought of it this morning. It's pretty good, though. Maybe I'll get a psychology minor."

"Are there more nachos?" said Garrett. "And we never got an answer on the onion rings."

"What can you tell me, Eddie? What do I need to know?"

"I don't know what you need to know. Ask me something."

"Could it have been Roddy?"

"Yes."

"The sheriff?"

"Yes."

"You?"

"Yes."

"Yes for you?"

"I don't have an alibi for the night." He gave me a little smirk that I didn't know what to do with.

"I saw you at the fair," I said.

"I was there, but when the murder happened, I have no alibi."

"How do you know when it happened?" I asked.

"Ah, good one, Tony," said Perry. "You got him."

"I heard people talking about it. Some deputy from Lovell said it was probably around when the fireworks went off."

"So where were you?"

"I'd rather not say."

"Did you know Dasher?"

"I'd seen him around."

"When?"

He thought for a moment, his lip between his teeth. I stored the hesitation with the grin for later analysis.

"Once he was behind the bar at closing time," said Eddie. "I didn't see him. I sat down with my recorder and reported what I'd heard in the bar so I wouldn't forget. Dasher jumped out from behind a dumpster, naked as he was, and um…he berated me for needing a recorder to remember things. That's it. He called my mind 'modern mush.'"

I leaned over the bar and looked where Eddie had made a grab. Yeah, there was a gun there. Right next to a cassette tape deck slowly turning. As for the gun, it was a snub-nosed revolver. I withdrew it and noted a .32

etched in the barrel. Since when are serial numbers in decimals? I opened the cylinder like I knew what I was doing. Bullets fell on the floor with a clatter.

"Oops."

I picked them up, noting that several had been fired.

"What's up with the spent bullet things?" I said.

"You always do that," Eddie said. "One empty beneath the hammer and the next one too so you don't accidentally shoot anyone."

"Really?"

"True that," said Perry. "Remember *Young Guns?*"

"No."

"Well, it was there."

I smelled the barrel. "You need to clean this," I said.

Eddie watched me with great interest, doubtlessly sensing my skill with the weapon and fearing I'd accidentally murder the whole room. I held it up to the light looking for a watermark, turned it around and upside down, smelled gunpowder again in the muzzle, and tasted the sights.

"What's this block thing under the pointy part?"

"That's a laser sight."

"Ah, très chic," I said. "Tradition would say you should have had a sawed-off scatter-gun under there." I spit on the floor for effect.

"Hey," he said.

"Missed the spittoon."

"We don't have one."

"See what I mean?"

"Onion rings?"

"Where were you, Eddie?" I said. "Let me cross you off my list. You have means with this science fiction pea-shooter, opportunity since you were near the crime scene, and motive."

"What motive?"

"Dasher knew what you were up to, overheard you reporting your observations. If word got out about what you're doing, you'd be tarred and feathered and ridden out of town on a rail, or then again, maybe something bad would happen to you."

"I didn't kill him."

"So where were you?"

The door opened again, flooding the room with the last light of the day. Bars don't like light, even the pretty kind.

"Hey, Eddie, did you hear about Dasher?"

It was the guy I'd seen with Roddy Dean. I assumed this was the rancher's son Beaumont.

"Are you Beaumont Dean?"

"What? Yeah? Who—"

"Yeah, I heard about it," Eddie said. "The usual?"

"Sure. Set me up." Beaumont walked to the bar and leaned against it. "Who're your friends?"

"This is the guy looking for Dasher's killer."

"A detective?" He moved next to me. Eddie set him up with a shot of Jim Beam.

"In Wyoming?" said Beaumont.

"No, I'm from Utah."

"So you're not actually licensed in our great state?" he said. "Just a guy nosing around?"

"Well...um..."

"Then what makes you think you have any authority to do anything in Big Horn County?" He gulped down his shot for emphasis like a badass or someone really thirsty.

I didn't have an answer.

"They were just leaving anyway," said Eddie. "Since we don't have onion rings."

19

"WHAT GOT INTO YOU?" Standard said as we got in the car.

"Yeah, Dara. That was pretty intense," I said. "Intense, but effective. So I thank you."

Perry had parked behind the bar to hide the Cadillac. From me.

We climbed in and I got the passenger seat without issue. The gang was feeling sheepish about their behavior, and I let them.

"It was something to do," said Dara.

Perry pulled around onto the highway.

"It was more than that," said Standard.

"No. It was something to do. This place is the geographical center of boredom. I've only been here a couple of days and already I'm pulling my hair out. Even the TV sucks. The motel could use some roaches for some excitement."

"I've been entertained," I said.

"You're on a case and that's why," said Dara. "That spices things up. We'll help you."

"Wait, um. Could it be dangerous?" asked Garrett.

"Will it threaten my calm?" said Standard.

"I'd rather not draw attention to myself," said Perry.

"What else are we going to do?" said Critter.

"I honestly don't know how people live out here," Dara went on. "I get it that this is about the good ol' days, but if the good ol' days were that great, why didn't we just stay that way? I can tell you: because they sucked. It's boring."

"I suspect they had lots to do," said Perry. "But it was stuff we'd call work. Like chopping wood and not starving."

"Good pursuits," I said. "Noble."

"I say we stay," said Standard. "We all agreed to help Tony through his terrible, debilitating addiction of—"

"Excuse me, Professor. Or are you channeling Gilligan?"

He scowled.

"I'm for going home," said Garrett. "And you were too, Stan."

"I just—"

"Let's stay," said Dara.

"What?"

"Yeah. Tony'll make it interesting. Garrett's doing his best to do the same."

"I'd like to stick it out a little longer," said Perry. "I have a lot to do, and we can't take Tony away from his case."

"It's not like I'm married to it," I said.

"You'd quit?" said Standard. "See, another one of Tony's terrible addictions."

"Whoa."

"Who hired you?" asked Perry.

Not wanting to lie and unwilling to be truthful, I changed the subject. "Turn into the park," I said. "It's something to do."

Perry steered the big white car onto the road that snaked up the plateau into Bighorn National Park. It really wasn't a park. In my whole time there I didn't see a single swing set or slide, but everyone called it a park, so to be like the locals, I'd adopted it.

"He's doing it for something to do," said Dara. "Tony's also bored. And he's a professional defective."

"I think you meant 'detective.'"

"Sure I did."

"Maybe," said Perry. "But it's just like Tony. He's always in it for the little guy. The underdog. I understand the hermit was not well liked, but he didn't deserve to die like that. Of course Tony's going to step in. It's a matter of honor."

I hadn't thought of that. Would I have stepped in if the sheriff hadn't been so insistent? Perry knew me better than the others, and his vote of confidence moved me. It also made me a liar for not coming clean about the sheriff.

"I have a client," I said.

"Who?"

"Can't say."

"You know that whole confidential client thing is bullshit, right?" said Dara. "You told us so yourself."

"It was somebody who liked him," I said. "There aren't many of those."

"I got the feeling Eddie liked him," said Garrett.

"How?"

"He seemed excited to hear that someone not affiliated with the town or sheriff was looking into it."

"Who'd he say this to?"

"Us. Before the skinhead came in. About an hour before you showed up."

"Where are we going?" asked Perry.

"For a drive," I said. "Let's look around. It is pretty here."

It was pretty. The sun was down, but the air still harbored enough clouds to color the sky in warm summer light.

The gang fell into reverie at the magic hour light, and I joined them.

I began to understand why people would want to live here. The cliffs were sharp and sure, the trees, emperors of their spaces. Pines and scrub brush fought for a toe hold around one bend and were thick as bristles the next. The sky was wide open, shading blue and kaleidoscopic. It pulled your gaze to the heavens and the smell of it all, pine needles, soil and rain, plus a hint of ozone from lingering lightning, was an intoxicant.

Standard was not wrong in thinking one could find peace here. Just a drive up a mountain and I felt somehow more harmonious. I laughed, thinking how unplugging my life had made me feel more connected. A person could lose himself up here, and I had to think that was a lot of the draw.

I didn't know Dasher, but I didn't see any reason to kill him. The motives I'd been presented with were all pretty low on the usual list of motives, but who knew what exaggerations and twisted realities could come from too much time in isolation. The Unibomber came to mind. His cabin would have fit right in here.

I broke from my peaceful contemplation for a quick berating from our sponsor. "What is wrong with me?"

"Where do you want us to begin?" Dara said in a quiet, dreamy way. It was a good joke, but her tone told me she too was falling for the place.

"Sorry. Talking out loud," I said. An old joke most people told without knowing it.

Carter had told me that he thought Eddie Amir would be an ally in my hunt and that Varg Jayger was high on the list of suspects. I'd managed to slide Eddie onto the suspects list and, except for a few crusty stares, I'd failed to interact with Varg at all when I had the chance. Sometimes only half of my detective centers are operating, if they're operating at all.

I should have stayed and pumped the barkeep for information. He'd be the storehouse of gossip in Floyd, an unofficial historian in an acoustically enhanced interrogation room. Instead, I'd scared him. Well, Dara had scared him. I'd probably only alienated him. He looked pretty alienated when I left him. Big eyes, gray skin, Area 51 hall pass on a lanyard. Okay, I made the last one up, but my mind was going places.

The key to most murders that aren't completely random—and I was hoping this one wasn't one of those nightmares—lay in the victim. I didn't know shit about Dasher the Flasher except he could have had a career in blue movies. He didn't strike me as dangerous. A definite curiosity, yes, but harmless if you averted your eyes. I think I'd be safe to say he was on the spectrum somewhere. Probably closer to all-out insanity than collecting paper clips. He struck me as educated. A radical perhaps, hopped out on the reefer twenty-four-seven. Or magic mushrooms. Or ayahuasca. That would be cool. Maybe he had a secret underground growing operation in an abandoned mine somewhere. What were the chances of that actually happening? Oh. Right.

Somebody had told me that Dasher arrived in the area relatively recently, a few years ago—eight, I think. That's more than a few. If I were a good detective I'd remember who told me that and pump out more information with a cattle prod, but I'm Tony Flaner and I couldn't even remember how I knew that. Regardless, I had to find out more about Dasher, like where had that name come from? Was it self applied? That could be a clue. I'd assumed that The Flasher was a nickname for obvious reasons, but what about the first part?

"It gets really cold here," said Perry as we passed a little patch of sooted snow on the shoulder. "Twelve feet of snow is not uncommon."

"Glad we're here in the summer."

"How could you survive in the winter?" I asked.

"Exactly," said Dara. "If this is the good time, imagine finding something to do when you're snowed in. How much masturbation can one person endure?"

The car went silent.

"I don't want to know," she said.

"I was actually thinking about Dasher. How could a nudist survive out here in the winter? I froze last night myself. How'd he handle twelve feet of snow?"

"What could he eat?"

"He'd hunt," said Critter. "Squirrels and deer. Antelope and wildebeest. Whatever they have out here."

"Cows," I said.

"Yeah, cows," said Garrett. "Hamburger bushes."

"Do they still hang rustlers out here?"

"They hanged cattle thieves?"

"When I'm in a better mood and want to ruin yours, ask me about the history of this area," I said. "The Johnson County War."

"Check."

We crested the summit and found a view area pullout. It hadn't been a long drive, but we all shuffled out and stretched and marveled at the coral sky. For five and a half comedians to be together and not bantering like a dozens marathon is a thing of wonder, yet we had been quiet in the car and now were silent as the landscape drew us in and made us small.

We sunk in the benches and let it play out in the crisping pine-scented air until the horizon was just a blue green line, a false aurora of dying light.

"Wow," I said.

"Wow," they all agreed.

———————

Our usual selves returned slowly on the drive back to Perry's cabin. No one wanted to leave anymore, at least not immediately.

"What about Rawly?" I asked to sour the mood. "Maybe he was after Long Schlong Silver. And got him."

"Is Rawly a suspect?" asked Perry. "Do you have a list of suspects yet?"

"From what I've heard, it could be anyone in the county."

"Do you think it was Eddie?" asked Dara.

"I didn't before I talked to him."

"What about Rawly?" Garrett asked.

"He's on the list. It doesn't look good that Gail heard him make threats and then someone turned up dead."

"That's a reach," said Standard. "Are you saying Rawly was jealous of Dasher?"

"Wouldn't you be?"

"Dasher and Kimmy were a thing?"

"Well?" I said. "Garrett, Critter, any information here?"

Garrett looked out the window at the passing reflectors. Critter spoke. "We got the feeling that she got around."

"With the hermit?"

"Maybe."

"You should probably get some shots," I said. "You too, Garrett."

"Yeah," they agreed.

Still aglow in the wonders of the old simple pleasures of fresh air and mountain views, the cabin was a rude reminder.

"What did you do to the generator?" Standard was pissed. "I had it working."

"I existed."

"Well, don't do that. Now we have no power."

Perry handed out candles and lit a fire in the fireplace with damp wood from outside. It took a while, and by the time the room was warm and inviting, everyone but me and Perry had already gone to bed.

"Buyer's remorse?" I asked him.

"A little. It's more than I'd hoped for and less than I'd thought."

"Indoor plumbing is overrated," I said.

"No, it's not."

"No. It's not."

"I made promises about this place, about this trip, and I feel like I've let everyone down."

I know Perry was manic, but depressed was new and scary. I wanted to ask him about his meds but held back.

"We all signed up knowing that you hadn't been here and couldn't honestly know everything. There are a few bugs to iron out, but that happens. It's like we're early adopters of a new thing."

"You adopted only because I said it would be fun and rustic and easy. It's not been that."

I honestly couldn't remember what promises Perry had made about the place. "It was a spontaneous decision. You don't owe us anything."

"That's not what Dara thinks."

"Don't ever, ever ever ever listen to Dara. You know that."

He poked at embers with a stick. We didn't have actual fireplace tools.

"Standard seems to be finding it restful," I said.

"Yeah, there's that."

"And Garrett found love."

"And Critter."

"Let's not think about that part."

"Okay."

"And I have a case that will keep me busy and make my intervention more manageable."

"What about Dara?"

"And you?"

"What? No, I'd never—"

"I meant, are you finding anything here? Besides guilt at not keeping the grand promises you think we all believed but knew were bullshit from the start, if we remember them at all?"

"I feel like I got ripped off."

"The missing furniture is the kicker."

"Yeah," he said. "You said early adopter? That's me. I am the first to believe any story."

"Are you talking about Area 51 again?"

"No. Yes—but that one is real," Perry said. "I'm talking about stuff like new products."

"And crazy theories?"

"They're only crazy until they're proved right."

"Don't get defensive."

"Well, it's like the ad for this place. There weren't any actual lies, but the lily was gilded. I could have come out and checked it first, but if I didn't, he'd have certainly sold it to someone else. He said he had a list of people waiting to buy it but wanted to give me the first crack at it."

"You fell for that?"

"I fall for that all the time," said Perry. "Late-night infomercials will be my financial ruin. I have a closet of kitchen conveniences that have since been recalled due to safety concerns. I have memory enhancing pills and vitamins that the FDA said were literally shit, and don't get me started on doomsday accessories."

"Doomsday accessories?"

"I said, don't get me started."

"Start anyway."

"I have enough MREs to feed a city for a week."

"Those military lunch packets? Where do you keep them?"

"In an undisclosed location."

"Naturally," I said.

"The biggest is gold," he said. "It's shilled on every website."

"I've seen the gold shills. I don't get it."

"It's dumb. For some reason people think that if civilization collapses, shiny metal will be the way to go."

"You'll have more treasure with the MREs."

"I know, right? Still, I feel like an idiot. I bought Krugerrands."

"Those South African coins?"

"Solid gold."

"It's easy to get caught up in hype. Those kinds of things prey on fear."

"It's how I paid for this place."

"Krugerrands?"

He nodded.

"Well, there you see. Your hobby is paying for itself."

"A dead end investment traded for—"

"Real estate," I said. "Always a good investment. For the future."

"If there is a future."

"What else could there be? More past?"

He shrugged noncommittally, and I realized there were many people wanting just that.

Perry threw his stick in the fire and watched it light. "When something sounds too good to be true," he said, "it will probably be recalled by a governing body."

"Nice new twist on an old adage," I said.

"I can't live here for more than two weeks per year."

"What?"

"Outbuilding rules," he said. "That sheriff told me he'd fine me if I went an hour over and then every hour after that."

"Really?"

"Yeah," said Perry. "He's kind of a jerk."

20

I SLEPT TERRIBLY AGAIN. I'd shaken most of the grit out of my bag but still hadn't turned the Wyoming king into a real sleeping platform, and my hips hurt when I got up.

I'd also forgotten to get a toothbrush. Vodka stick, day two.

The worst part was the want of a shower. I just need one every day in the morning. It's the daily baptism, me becoming a new person by washing my hair and privates. It's me time. Without it, I felt like a grease trap under a fish and chips shop in Soho.

Feeling at odds and ends, sticky, salty, and re-abraded from the lingering sleeping bag sand, I fell into the familiar pattern of push and pull. My life in microcosm. Push, I wanted a damn shower; pull, Gail was on my short list of people I was told might help me find Dasher's killer. My chariot awaited.

On the ride over I found that I could handle the modern horse ATV well enough that my mind could wander and I thought about what Perry had said about early adopters. I wondered what the first person who brought one of these dune-buggy wannabes to Big Horn County went through. Sure, they'd eventually be everywhere, but I bet he got a ration of shit to go with his road rash. They were originally three-wheelers, if I remembered right, and then they were notorious—more notorious—for injuries. Early adopters are guinea pigs, like Eddie in his research, just more so since he knew what he was getting into. Human guinea pigs usually don't and are lured in by promises.

Snake oil came to mind on that associative Wyoming morning road. What is more originally Western Americana than the snake oil salesman? Roll into a struggling town on a wagon filled with promises. Toothache? I gotcha covered. Bullet wound? Here's my tonic. Bad love life? Boner enhancement made from porcupine quills. From snake oil came patent medicine and from that came the FDA after a couple of really terrible moments of unregulated pharmaceutical malpractice. Someone finally decided that claims needed to be substantiated, and testing for side effects wasn't a bad idea either. Of course the vitamin industry, nutritional supplements, herbs and such don't count. I don't know why. Most are harmless wastes of money, but some have dreadful side effects, whole populations breaking out in multi-level marketing schemes and other insanity. It's frightening.

I'd forgotten to bring a towel again, not that I had one. I realized this as I pulled into the campground. Also, as luck would have it, through the bug splatter of my visor I saw Gail Larsen sitting on her porch. She saw me and waved me over. I wondered how much a shower cost. Had she told me and I forgot? Could I get a towel?

"I'm glad I ran into you," I said.

"You were going to sneak a shower, weren't you?"

"Maybe."

"Go ahead. When you're done, come in for some coffee."

"Really?"

"Yeah."

"Can I borrow a towel?"

She laughed. "Yes, you can. Do you need shampoo? Soap? Toothbrush and paste?"

"Yes, yes, oh hell yes, and yes, please."

"You were never a Boy Scout, were you?"

"I had an interview to join once, but I arrived unprepared."

"You some kind of comedian?"

"Some kind."

She laughed and went inside. That wasn't even a good joke. Wyoming has low standards. Or Gail did.

Gail returned in a moment with a care package—all the toiletries one could want. Even a razor. My legs were pretty shaggy. I said thanks.

The shower was its usual transformative ritual. The shampoo and soap went far to make me feel human again. The towel made the end game pay off, but my dirty clothes put the stink back on me.

I gotta get my shit together.

"I don't suppose you have a laundry?" I said as greeting when I returned to Gail's office.

"There's one in Floyd," she said. "Stubbins Street."

"Of course."

"Come in."

The building was a cinder block affair with a wide porch where a row of lazy rocking chairs would not go amiss. There was a little bistro table and two chairs, a matching wicker bench and an industrial-sized garbage can. A large glass pane window looked out over the porch with an *open* and a *vacancy* sign both illuminated in red. The door was commercial and glass and opened into a reception area with a desk, computer, chairs, and a wall display with more pamphlets than a Jehovah's Witness's scrapbook. She led me past all that and through another door and into a living room.

"Thanks again for the towel and stuff."

"You can keep the stuff. The towel is mine."

I gave to her. She laid it over the back of a chair.

"I looked you up on the internet. You're quite the man."

"I was only on those forums for research," I said.

She giggled.

The room was simple and clean. A fabric couch with a pastel abstract design sat in front of a coffee table holding a stack of magazines. There was a matching side chair, a corner table, and a TV that didn't take up an entire wall. The air smelled of oregano marinara and Nag Champa incense.

"So you smoke pot, huh?" I blurted out.

"What?"

"Sorry. Joke. That incense always reminds me of smoking pot in college. A long time ago. When I was young and not mature like I am now. That very limited youthful time of experimentation that I in no way condone today."

"How do you take your coffee?"

"Black. With lots of cream and Splenda. Lots. Lots and lots."

The magazines were all of a kind: *Modern Entrepreneur, Business Weekly, Working Woman Today, The Executive Female*. There were newsletters—actual paper ones—that predicted future trends from solar energy to fashion crazes. Pleather will take the world by storm next year.

Books on her modest bookshelf were similarly corporate. *The Power of Yes, You Can Do it! Really You Can!, What Color is Your Parachute?* All good reads for the long boring nights of a Wyoming winter when dreams of cities and central heating haunt the snowbanks like bad choices.

"Here you go." Gail had two mugs of coffee. One was an over-large orange Garfield mug, the other some corporate swag thing with an owl logo and wouldn't hold enough coffee to be useful. She gave me the big one.

"You are a life saver." I took it and sat down on the couch.

She sat down next to me.

She'd changed clothes from when I rode in. I seemed to remember her in overalls and a work shirt. Now she was in slacks and a blouse. Comfy shoes and her hair was combed.

"I hear you're going to be around for a while," she said.

"What did you hear?"

"I heard about the hermit getting killed. Heard you're some kind of FBI agent looking into it."

"Finally," I said.

"What?"

"The Floyd rumor mill gets it wrong for once. God, I was thinking the whole town was connected by telepathy for how quickly and accurately news spreads. It was freaky weird. Had a whole *Village of the Damned* feel to it."

"White-haired British children?"

"Yes."

She laughed. "Not much new to talk about out here. When there is, it's like Christmas."

"Does seem like it gets boring."

"It is different. Some people really like the pace." She said it flatly, and I couldn't tell which side of the question she was on.

"Where are you from?" I asked.

"All over."

"Army brat?"

"No, just chased opportunities my whole life. Born in New Hampshire. Spent time in Dallas, Seattle, Denver. Finally settled here to get out of the rat race."

"How long have you been here?"

"Two long years," she said.

The couch wasn't in such good shape as I'd imagined. It seemed to sag in the middle and drew Gail closer to me. Our hips touched.

"What did the rumor get wrong?"

"Only the FBI part. I'm not FBI."

"I didn't think so. The internet says you're a private investigator. A pretty good one by the looks of it."

"Don't believe everything you read about me unless it's flattering," I said.

She laughed.

"I'm a private investigator in Utah," I said. "I have to remember that. My license isn't valid here. Not sure if that'll matter. It's not like it does me any good back home."

"What would you like it to do for you?"

"Get me some truth. But I can't handle the truth." I channeled my best Jack Nicholson. It was automatic.

She laughed again.

"You seem to be one of the few people who didn't absolutely hate Dasher's guts," I said, remembering my mission.

Gail took a long slow tonguey sip of her coffee with closed eyes. She had put on makeup, I noticed, and wore a lavender scent that mingled well with the Nag Champa.

"He brought in business," she said after the sip. "This town isn't doing anything to bring people in, so I'll take any visibility I can get."

"There was a documentary about him. Did you see that?"

"That's what I'm talking about. And it was actually just a news report. A couple minutes, but it put Floyd on the map. That's when I heard about it."

"Don't suppose you have a copy of it, do you?"

"No, but the library does. One of my guests checked it out."

"The Crombys," I said.

"How'd you know about that?"

"I'm a detective. I know things. I drink and I know things." Now I was channeling Tyrion Lannister, or maybe Sam Spade. Either way, I have issues. "You wouldn't happen to have a VCR, would you?"

"As a matter of fact I do," she said. "I have a lot of movies if you want to watch something. I have this great trilogy from Holland."

"I'm thinking more for when I get the tape from the Crombys."

"Okay. So as a detective, have you ever had to get rough with someone?"

"Physically? Never. I couldn't. But I hurt people in other ways. There was this one guy once. He wasn't telling me what I needed to know so I reminded him that his younger sister had done more with her life than he had his. She was married, had a better job, nicer house, vacations, and was the hands-down favorite of their parents. It wasn't pretty, but after the crying I got what I came for."

"Brutal."

"Sometimes you gotta pull out the stops."

"Tell me what you want," she said slowly.

"Talk about the hermit."

"Um. Okay. Can you be more specific?"

"Was he dangerous?"

"Crazy people are always dangerous," she said. "Danger is an aphrodisiac. Your job must be dangerous."

"So there's something to the rumor that he slept around?"

"Um. What? Uh, yes."

"Tell me about it."

"The rumor goes that he paid visits to willing recipients. Some of them are pretty saucy."

"Not to be too personal, but—"

"No. Hell no. Not my type. I learned that lesson. I like clean men. Did you like the soap?"

"Yeah, it was really nice. Better than I expected. I really like this coffee too. Thanks for the big mug."

"I like nice things. I have them sent in. I'm a health nut. Don't let my few pounds fool you, I'm healthy as a horse. I can go for hours."

"Clean air and clean living too, huh?"

"It's hard to do up here, but with internet and UPS, I survive. Lots of dust, though."

"You don't buy local?"

"Oh, I do for some things. Vegetables."

"Beef must be pretty reasonable. Lot of cattle ranches out here."

"Not really. Everyone has contracts to sell them to a central buyer. I remember a restaurant guy showed up once trying to get a deal and he was sent packing."

"Got ugly?"

"It became something of an ethical question about loyalty, contracts and promises."

"Cows?"

"They're a big deal out here. I'm glad they sent him packing."

"Is the cream fresh?"

"From a dairy near Basin. Big teats on those cows."

"Do you know the little medicine wheel?"

"Honey, I know every path and trail for a hundred miles. I can guide you anywhere."

"Oh, that's right, you do the ATV safaris."

"I know all the back roads, honey, and I'm not afraid to go there."

"Yeah? Any idea where the hermit holed up? Did he have a den?"

"I never found it."

"He had to have a cave or a hut or something. It would be lonely but shelter, at least."

"Loneliness is a big problem. People seek shelter where they might, with whom they might."

"Are you suggesting the hermit had outside help?"

She huffed as if frustrated. "I don't know," she said. "He might have. Probably did. If the rumors of his sexual exploits are to be believed."

"You mentioned saucy exploits before."

"Now you're asking the right questions."

"What did you hear he did?"

"Who?"

"Dasher the hermit."

"What about him?"

"Exploits?"

"Hermit stuff."

"I ran into him in your shower on the Fourth."

"You did? What was he doing? He wasn't showering?"

"Nope. He was complaining about guns," I said.

"Boys' stuff," she said. "I like boys."

Realization finally hit me. I let out a long sigh. "Oooh wow, am I dense or what?"

"Nothing that can't be forgiven," she said.

"Here I am looking for a killer, and the victim himself mentioned guns right before he was shot and killed."

"That's what you finally figured out?"

"Pretty obvious, don't you think?"

"Sometimes people can miss the most obvious clues," she explained.

"I guess I just wasn't paying attention."

"You?"

"It happens."

"I'll get us more coffee and a Danish."

She got up, and I couldn't believe how dense I'd been. It should have clicked the instant he said it, and if not then, how about after he was shot and I got the case? Man, not my best day.

"What it means, or rather, suggests," I said into the kitchen doorway, "is that Dasher might have known his killer or at least seen him in this campground."

Gail returned with a Mr. Coffee carafe and a box of pastries. They must have been kept high up on a shelf or something, a place hard to get at because her blouse had come undone a button or two. That happens to me sometimes when I reach way up for something, not that I wear buttons that often.

"Have any of your guests left since the killing?"

"Why?"

"I might want to talk to a couple of them. Maybe arrange to keep them around."

"But you don't have any authority."

"I should at least talk to them."

"Let me look." She went into the office.

"Oh, and Gail?"

"Yes?"

"One of your buttons came undone."

"Thanks for telling me," she said, though she didn't sound overly grateful to know.

21

BOONE HAD LEFT. The Crombys were still around and scheduled to stay for another week. Gail's shirt was buttoned.

"Anything else?" she asked from the doorway.

I ate a second Danish. Raspberry.

"Where were you the night of the killing?"

Her eyes went big. "Me?"

"Where were you?"

"I was at the fair, then I came back here to do some things. Saw the fireworks while fishing a dead badger out of the pool. Threw it away with the roadkill."

"Did anyone see you there?"

"I don't know. Wait. I don't like where this is going. Do you suspect me?"

"Did you see anyone?"

"I don't think so. Do I need an alibi?" Her mood was much less friendly. It's weird how people always get defensive when you try to tie them to a murder.

"I'm not accusing you," I said. "I'm looking for witnesses. Did you see Roddy Dean that night?"

"The rancher?"

"Yes."

"Not that night. Maybe during the day. I saw his son Beaumont, though, in the evening."

"How about Rawly?"

"Oh, you've talked with your friends."

"We do that."

Next one was blueberry.

"I talked to Kimmy earlier in the day, and she said James was on a tear and to batten down the hatches. She was staying away herself, she said. Had a rendezvous."

"Did she say with whom?"

She shook her head.

"Can I get more cream and sweetener?"

She went into the kitchen.

Lemon.

"How about Mandel, the realtor guy?"

"He had that stupid gold prospecting booth," she said. "He'd have been there until twilight at least."

"What do you know about him?" I doctored my coffee.

"He sells real estate and runs a scammy prospecting store."

"Why do you say it's scammy?"

"The only person I've seen make money on looking for gold out here is him."

"Don't dig the gold; sell the shovels."

"Yes. But he's done well with it. In the last couple years he's gone from tater tots to filet mignon."

She sat down in the chair away from the couch and picked up her mug.

"What about the skinhead, Varg Jayger?"

"I saw him in the parking lot talking to a guy on a motorcycle. Not sure when."

Bear claw.

"Those are your suspects, huh?" she said

"Some. I have a couple of outliers too."

"Who?"

"Boone and Cromby and the bartender."

"Eddie?" she said. "I don't see him for this. But then again, he plays everything close to the vest. I've known him for a year and know almost nothing about him. Seems nice. Good listener."

"Did Boone say he would be leaving today?"

"No. He was open-ended, had been here for a while, paid up through next week," she said. "But you know what? I did see him on the night of the killing. He was rushing around the campground like a crazy man."

"A crazy man at the Crazy Woman."

She was unimpressed with my witticism. Her mood had definitely darkened.

"It was before the fireworks when I was coming back. I saw him run from the toilet to the shower and back to his camper. Run. Not walk, run."

"And?"

"And nothing. I dealt with a dead animal. And when the news of the killing came, he listened, packed up and left."

"I have a new number one suspect," I said.

"Because he's black? Don't be racist."

"No. Because he was acting suspiciously. How'd you find out about the murder?"

"Carter came by and asked questions for half an hour. Asking if anyone had seen anything or anyone. He seemed pretty broken up about it. I didn't think he did a particularly good job interviewing, but maybe he just hasn't had a lot of practice. Or maybe he really wasn't looking for the killer. The hermit put a black eye on the town."

"Not for you."

"He did a little bit. Families didn't like it. Weirdos did. I get weirdos. Now I doubt I'll get anything. Probably time to pull up stakes and try something else. I'm done here."

"Back to corporate America?"

She smiled. "It's hard for a woman to rise in traditional workplaces. Easy to fall. It is unforgiving out there. I have to keep my eyes open for new opportunities. Get in the bottom floor where my skills can be used effectively. Maybe start something myself."

"You could sell Danishes."

"To starving people like you?"

"We came very unprepared."

"I would think it was Rawly if it was anyone," she said. "His cabin abuts the back road to the little medicine wheel."

"So does ours. If I'd have been there earlier, I might have seen someone."

"And miss the fireworks?"

"Good point. Do you have an address for Boone? A phone number?"

She went back to the office. Apple fritter time.

"His real name was Barney Burger," she said, reading off a card. "He says he's from Cheyenne."

"How long was he here for?"

"Two weeks."

"Alone? Isn't that weird?"

"Like I said, I get the weirdos."

"How about the Crombys? Did you see them on the Fourth?"

"I saw the woman and the butler. Maybe the little girl, but I don't remember Mr. Cromby or that boy brat."

"They're all brats."

"No argument here."

"What have they been doing? What is there to do?"

"I don't spy on my guests."

"Mind if I do?"

"Please don't ask me that."

"Just kidding. Mind if I take the last maple bar?"

"Go ahead."

I did. The caffeine and sugar rush were firing my little gray cells.

"There are a couple ways up to the little medicine wheel," said Gail. "The back trail is really tricky. The main road is safer. Particularly in the dark."

"And rain."

"Which way was used?"

"The rain erased that vital clue."

"Vital? Really?"

"Hell if I know. I'm feeling around in the dark."

"You had your chance."

"What?"

"Nothing," she said. "My safari trip visits the trail up there, so there's that."

"Gotcha," I said. "Thanks for everything, Gail. I gotta get to work. I'll try to find a way to repay you for all your generosity."

"The way to a man's heart," she said cryptically.

"Yeah, great pastries."

"Great," she echoed, but again enthusiasm wasn't there.

Outside, I moseyed a ways to the Crombys' site. I saw no one there.

"Hullo," I said. Then tried "Howdy." Seemed appropriate.

No answer.

The place was set up more or less as before. A big Persian carpet taking the middle of three spaces between the modest camper Lynson used and the monstrosity the Crombys stayed in. The vibrating easy chair was there as before, a table with glasses, a bar set against the back. The under-camper garage wasn't open. I didn't see the big six-seater camouflaged ATV from before, but it might have been there.

I was pretty full on pastries, but I do declare, I saw a rather inviting pitcher on the bar.

"Hullo and howdy," I called again.

Mint juleps.

It was already getting hot, and the iced pitcher sweated cool drops of temptation. I knew that if Penn and Maxine were there, they'd offer me one, so I poured myself a glass and garnished it with a mint leaf. I lifted it to my nose but pulled back before sipping.

Instead of the crisp smell of pickled mint, I smelled dead thing. You know the smell, that rotten meat road kill stench.

I bent down to look under the trailers thinking they must have hit something and it had stuck underneath in the chassis and was now decomposing. Nothing.

I followed my nose around the back of the smaller trailer. There I found a tarped-off area. Tarps on high wires between the camper and a power pole. It made a little open roofed room. I wondered if it was a privy and maybe they'd all had bad curry for a week, maybe raw lard.

I went in because that's the kind of thing I do.

Inside was a sturdy camp table with a board on it and next to it was a trash can. The air stank and buzzed with flies. It looked like there was blood on the table. Some of it not so old.

I stared at the garbage can. It was one of those old metal ones with a lid. It stank. Garbage cans have played an integral part in my life as a detective, and I suspected this one would as well. Holding the glass with my cupping hand, I lifted the lid.

Guts.

Bloody guts.

I'm no expert on guts, but they were guts, you can believe me. I know fish guts from a short-lived hobby of mine involving tying flies and embedding hooks in my thumb, so I didn't think these were aquatic. The foot also was a hint.

I reached in and scattered the cloud of flies that had descended and pinched the paw up.

It was a paw from a cat. A big one. A big tannish brown one. It had a big gash at the ankle. Cats have ankles, right? It flopped lifeless and large between my fingers. I dropped it back inside, scattering the flies again.

The stench was killing me so I went to put the lid back on the can but hesitated when I saw something stuck on the underside of it. There was blood on it, that's what made it stick the way it did. It was a color photo of a man blown up and printed on white paper with running colors, proving my theory that they hadn't used non-blood-soluble printer ink. Amateurs. Even if the tight grouping of bullet holes through the paper body hadn't been there, I doubt I'd have been able to tell who was on the picture. It was grainy and ink-smeared. I could however tell it was a human shape. Sasquatch?

"What are you doing in our garbage can?"

The voice naturally made me jump and shriek and throw my glass into the air while simultaneously dropping the lid with a crash onto the can.

"Yeaouw!"

The glass crashed onto the bloody table, shattering in mint leaf and Kentucky bourbon. The lid was a cymbal to accentuate my scream. Perfect.

"You shouldn't be here," she said.

It was the little Cromby girl I'd seen before. She was in a swimsuit with her hair in a towel. I tried to remember her name.

"You're Kitty, aren't you?"

"Bunny," she corrected me.

"My mistake. The kitty is in the can."

She scowled.

"You're trespassing. Daddy says that the campsite is our home and we can defend it with guns and kill anyone who makes us stand our ground."

"Good thing you don't have a gun."

"But I do have one," she said excitedly as if just remembering. "I'll go get it."

She rushed out of the tent thing. I followed her out but not into the motor home; out to the road as fast as I could.

I literally ran into Lynson, the butler guy. I sprayed his ankles with gravel as I skid to a stop.

"Were you just in our campsite?"

He was dressed in a yellow swimsuit and green flip-flops. His towel was around his neck, and he carried a float tube shaped like a llama.

"Been swimming?"

"What were you doing in our camp?" he said.

"Fleeing Little Miss Murder. Bunny wants to shoot me."

"Why does she want to shoot you?"

"Don't they want to shoot everything?"

That gave him pause.

"Where are they, by the way?"

"Penn and Terror are out reconnoitering. Maxine took the car to find a casino and see how quickly she can lose her allowance. I'm watching Bunny."

"Did you hear about the murder?"

"The hermit? Yeah. Wait, are you the FBI guy looking into it?"

"Who told you I was working for the FBI?"

"I don't remember."

"Where were you all on the Fourth?" I asked.

"I got my gun!" came a shout from between the campers. "Hey, Mister...Mister?"

"Let's talk behind the privy." I guided Lynson and the llama behind the cinder block toilet.

"Mister! Where are you?"

"What kind of gun does she have?"

"Her favorite is this little .22 derringer with mother-of-pearl, My Little Pony grips."

"How rich are these people?"

"Rich enough."

"Rich enough to get away with murder?"

"I doubt she'd actually shoot you. Probably."

"Comforting," I said. "So where was everyone the night of the killing?"

"When was it exactly?"

"We think during the fireworks, right after the rain here but before it was there."

"Where's there?"

"The little medicine wheel."

"Where's that?"

"You didn't go on the ATV safari?"

"No. As a servant, I stayed here."

"But the others went?"

"Sure. I got to clean...up."

"It's in the park, over there up the mountain. Not too far." I pointed. "A ways."

"Must be nice," he said.

"So where was everyone? And don't change the subject again."

"It was you changing the subject."

"Was not."

"Was too."

"Was not."

"Was too."

"Hey, Lynson, hold him! I'm coming."

Bunny was at a dead run, barreling toward us.

"Excuse me, I gotta pee." I ducked into the bathroom. "Boys only!" I yelled.

Through the door I heard Lynson talking to her.

"No, Bunny put that away. What did your dad say about gun safety?"

"But he was in the cleaning room."

"But he's not there now."

"He's just in the bathroom. We can wait for him to come out."

"I'll be in here a while," I called. "I'll let you know when I'm done, okay?"

"No. You'll run away."

"You've done a good job, Bunny. You scared the man away from the campsite. That's good."

"But I want to shoot him," she whined. "Terror always gets to shoot, and I don't."

"Go back to the camper," he said. "Go play GTA. You'll feel better."

I heard shuffling feet recede.

"It's all right to come out now," Lynson said.

"Your bosses encompass the best of both worlds," I said, drying my hands on my shirt. I'd not wasted the opportunity of a bathroom visit. Coffee, you know.

"What do you mean, both worlds?" said Lynson.

"Gun nuts and rich fucks."

"No comment."

"Why no comment?"

"Part of my job description."

"There you go again, changing the subject. I want answers. Where was everyone? Do I have to pull my FBI on you?"

"You're the one who—"

"Where?"

"Okay, fireworks," he said, readjusting the llama. "I had a break and watched the fireworks talking with another camper, the Black guy. Terrence and Penn were reconnoitering. Maxine and Bunny were back at the camp watching the fireworks from there. Maxine had four screwdrivers and Bunny two Shirley Temples."

"Reconnoitering?"

He nodded.

"You gotta do better than that," I said. "Once I show you an FBI badge, there'll be paperwork." Like I knew.

"That's what Penn calls it. He goes out in the woods and looks around."

"Hunting?"

He shrugged.

"Hunting game?"

Another shrug.

"Hunting the most dangerous game?"

He blanched and looked away. I didn't like that at all.

"Tell me," I said. "What are they looking for?"

"Stuff."

"A-hem…" I reached into my pocket and felt my phone tile.

"Animals. Game. He likes to reconnoiter game."

"With a gun?"

"No comment."

I knew the answer of course.

"What's in season right now?"

"I don't know," Lynson said, shifting his weight on his hips.

"Does Penn Cromby?"

He sighed then shook his head. "I doubt it."

There was the sound of a gunshot from the campsite.

"I better go see what that is," he said.

"You're pretty calm."

"Third time it's happened," he said. "She probably shot the TV. Again."

He moved to leave.

"I'm okay!" came Bunny's yell. "Teddy was trespassing."

"Not the TV," Lynson said.

"How did you get involved with these people?"

"I work for a service company. Butler by the week."

"You're kidding."

"I wish I was."

"Why?"

"Some people have a hard time keeping good help," he said. "I gotta go."

"I'll be seeing you," I said.

"Me?"

"Your group."

"Figured," he said, and left me.

22

GLAD I HADN'T BEEN SHOT by a nine-year-old serial killer in training, I decided it was time to leave. I crossed to the other side of the loop and headed back toward the office. I saw the empty campsite where Boone, a.k.a. Barney Burger, had been. At least, I thought that one was his. It was next to the pool, which looked inviting on that warm July morning. A family of six were playing Marco Polo. Two of them were out of the water, a dangerous strategy that didn't pay off. "Fish out of water!" called Marco, and the twins were both nabbed. They didn't admit to it, of course. But justice prevailed with the little brother narcing them out.

The last time I'd been in a pool, I'd forgotten to take my phone out of my pocket. That's how that went: a six-hundred-dollar dip that no amount of rice could fix. It ruined the swimming day, technology again taking a toll.

I boarded my little four-wheeler and started it up. Gail was on her porch. She'd changed back into her overalls. I waved. She waved. I left.

I mulled over my talks as the bugs splattered arrhythmically on my grimy visor. I thought of some poor family whose cat had been killed in a Cromby reconnoiter. I thought how Gail had been friendly and then not. I nearly drove off the trail into a ditch when it finally occurred to me.

Could she have been hitting on me?

She could have been. Maybe.

Were there any clues? Cues? Innuendos?

Ah shit.

She totally had been.

Duh.

Goddammit. How do I miss things like that? I'm a detective.

Not my best moment, but at least my cluelessness kept me from temptation and answered my earlier worry that I might have been hitting on her. Nope. No interest, not even subconsciously. I was in a committed relationship, and my stupidity proved it. Goes to show that you don't see what you're not looking for.

So I was feeling pretty noble and stupid at the same time. Distracted, I drove past the turnoff to Perry's cabin. As I was looking for it, I wondered as I found myself turning into a side ride road for an easier U-turn.

I remembered my stolen maps. I kept them in my pocket now, folded up. Maybe 'wadded' would be a better word. They were thick when folded small enough to pocket.

Anyway, I had the maps and I checked them out.

As near as I could figure this trail—calling it a road was a stretch—led to the empty house Mandel was selling. A trail behind it connected with Rawly's cabin and then to Perry's. In the other direction it went past Varg Jayger's and then eventually connected to the little medicine wheel. It also connected to Kennebunkport, Maine, Nome, Alaska, Acapulco and Peru, if you thought about it.

Because that way offered shade and I wanted to see the back trails anyway, I rode on. I followed parallel ruts that were more gutter than guide, and after about half a mile I pulled in behind a white truck.

I took off my bug catcher and killed the motor. "Mandel! Howdy and hullo. Friend here. I was just a-moseying by, pardner." I still didn't know how country folk announced themselves. "Got any chaw?"

There came no reply.

"I'm here about the listing," I said, though I hadn't seen any signs advertising it for sale—not here, not on the road where people might see it.

It wasn't as grand as Perry's. No big windows. More like an unattached garage. There was a door up three concrete steps. Beneath a big peephole hung a sign. Written in blood-red paint with a shit brush on what I think was a broken piece of weathered two-by-four read 'Trespassers will be summarily executed according to international law.' That's one I wasn't familiar with. A new reverse psychology sales technique possibly.

I walked around the side, wary of international executioners. I found windows, but they were barred with steel shutters. They had little slits in them just the right size to push a gun barrel through or grilled cheese sandwich. Up close I saw the walls were concrete as was the arched roof. In the back, beneath an open steel mesh door, was a stairway leading to a basement door that looked like it had been liberated from C-block at Rikers Island. A trail of mud ran down the concrete steps and disappeared behind said door.

I stopped and listened.

Nothing but nature in the morning. That means bugs. I heard bugs. Buzzing, chirping, high-pitched mosquito-rich bugs.

The mud was curious and so was I, so I went down and tried the door.

It pulled open on a squeaky hinges that made me pee myself a little.

There were international executioners about. The door was two inches of thick steel with a barring mechanism that secured it to the roof, floor, and thick concrete walls with a single turn of a submarine-worthy wheel. I pulled out my phone for the flashlight and showed the room my tile.

It smelled like oil and gasoline and I imagined a cache of Molotov cocktails waiting for a spark.

I went in a couple more steps and waited for my eyes to adjust as they would. Eyes can adjust to dark areas. Really. I saw it in a movie. Most people don't know that these days because there really isn't any reason to. Light is as common as internet in most places.

It took a while, but after said while, I could make out shapes in the room. There was a gas can on the floor and several empty oil bottles. There were also digging instruments, two shovels and a pick. One of the shovels had a broken handle. The other was new and still had the sticker on the blade. Otherwise the room was big and empty, like an unfinished basement but with concrete columns instead of wood framing. A door in the back promised to lead upstairs.

I jumped nearly out of my skin as I thought I saw a man standing by the door. When he didn't execute me, I realized it was just a suit of clothes hanging on a coat rack. It was too dark and too far to see more than that it was a man's suit.

I took a few steps farther in, but the door behind me creaked on its hinges, and I decided it was time to leave.

As I got to the door, I remembered the mud. I saw that it extended into the center of the room and chunks of it had fallen to the concrete floor. It was dry and cracked on the steps, but still had a bit of moisture on the floor.

I'm no Apache tracker, but I think I'm safe in thinking that a two-wheeled vehicle brought the mud in and then drove over it again, probably today. Bicycle? Broken ATV? General Lee from the *Dukes of Hazzard* on its side with one of them Duke boys hanging out a window calling for Roscoe? No. Probably a motorcycle.

I pushed the door closed and hiked up the stairs. At the top I stopped again and listened, this time trying to discern the whine of a dirt bike from the din of crickets and critters crawling up my pants leg.

Nada.

There was a trail behind the house with, go figure, motorcycle tracks in it. It led, I remembered, to the other trails, which led to the Magic Kingdom and Bolivia.

A mosquito bravely landed on my forehead, right in front of my eyes, bold as you please. I squashed it and screamed. I comforted myself by thinking that I wouldn't forget the June bug goose egg scream button on my forehead again because now it hurt like a sumbitch.

Feeling properly Wyoming, I carefully pulled the helmet back on and took the ATV behind the "house" and onto the trail.

For being a back road, it looked to get more than its rightful share of traf-fic. In fact, there were parallel tire ruts made by covered wagons, Or maybe cars and jeeps. More probably those. This was no trail, it was a dirt road. I wondered if I shouldn't update my map, call someone at the USGS or tell Google. No, they'd know already.

I turned north, away from Perry's, remembering there was Varg Jayger's cabin next and then somewhere between there and Montana was suppos-edly a pasture with a cut fence from whence Oliver and Hardy had been snatched.

I kept to a reasonable speed, one that let the smarter insects avoid their deaths on my face but made the mosquitoes work if they wanted to land on me. Butterflies, though beautiful, are not smart insects. Their guts are translucent yellow, by the way.

After a while, I passed a side trail that I think might have been the way to Varg's cabin. A 'No Trespassing' sign with a swastika also gave me a clue. I turned onto it.

I should mention that though much of the area of Big Horn County and environs was pretty desolate, shrubs and grass with the rare occasional noble tree, around Floyd and the cabin district there were trees. The creek probably had much to do with that. As such, I was maybe fifty feet past the 'No Trespassing' sign when I got my first whiff of something other than clean air. Window cleaner. Strong window cleaner, ammonia and vinegar. It passed and I was hit with more fresh air and a cloud of gnats for good measure. Then it came again.

I could see smoke rising ahead and plodded forward, my little ATV maneuvering the trail leading to the house.

The smell again came and with it the smell of wood smoke. And a sound. A sharp sound like a gunshot, but muffled. And another. And there was Varg standing on the trail maybe twenty feet away with a huge rifle making those muffled sounds and moving his lips.

I stopped and took off my muffling helmet.

"Are you even listening to me?"

"That's a hell of a way to start a conversation," I said.

"Get. Off. My. Property." Varg held his gun one-handed at his shoulder, aiming up. It was an M-16 or something like it. His shaved head was a little bristly today, but it still caught the light in a sweaty glow. His face was flushed, lines around his mouth. I thought maybe he'd been huffing paint, except there was no color. Maybe nitrous oxide. I knew a guy—

A burst of shots filled the air. These weren't muffled by my helmet but loud as murder. And a burst. Not a single shot, but a bunch. He leveled his gun, his machine gun.

"Last warning," he said.

I started my machine.

"Can I just ask you one thing? Do you have a wet wipe? Wait. That's two, isn't it? Oh. Now it's three questions—"

From the hip, like Pacino in *Scarface*, he grinned and let go a fusillade of fire. I saw flash and flame burst out of the muzzle of the gun like a four-petaled flower, strobing in time to shell casings rainbowing out of the side.

I cranked the gas. The ATV lunged forward, nearly throwing me off. I stayed on, though, and made a mental note that ATVs are capable of wheelies. I turned around in a long clumsy circle, not half as fast as I wanted to, trampling shrubs and sending up waves of grasshoppers. Varg snarled, and the bottom of his gun appeared to fall out. He had a spare in his pocket, though, and plugged it in lickety-quick. He pulled back a lever and again with the hip action sprayed fire my way.

Pointed the right direction, the air full of muffled automatic fire and grasshoppers, clutching for my life, I popped another wheelie and raced back to the road.

23

THE ROAD WAS A WELCOME SIGHT, blurry with bug splatter, but welcome. The machine gun fire hadn't stopped, muffled malignant pops still too damn close for comfort. I turned hard, again nearly chucking myself into a ditch and sped on to the right.

After an hour or so—it could have been less—the shots stopped. For another hour, also could have been less, I went as fast as I could. The road led out of the wooded area to low rolling plains and pasture that were more the rule than the trees. I slowed down to a non-bug splatter speed and then, topping a hill, stopped to get my bearings and assess the damage.

I was unhurt, physically. Emotionally I was not so certain. I think I would have evacuated my bowels if I hadn't done the deed at the campground. I guess I had Bunny Cromby to thank for clean pants. Joy.

The maps were worse for wear. A couple of tears on the edges. The creases were about worn through, moistened from my machine gun-scared butt sweat. Not a good thing.

There should have been a turn off to the left into the park just after Varg's place. I'd missed it. Other things on my mind, I guess. The way I was heading led to Montana and Canada, the Bering Sea. Jamaica. I saw a truck, another ubiquitous white pickup a ways down the road.

Everything's a ways up here.

Not in a hurry to go back to Pork Chop Hill, I headed down the road and wondered what the hell I was thinking crossing a Nazi 'no trespassing' sign. I guess I thought that since I'd kinda met Varg Jayger, we were pals. Never mind that I'd insulted him and he'd scowled at me, that we were on opposite sides of the political divide and I was in the rural America famous for gun fetishes, and 'stand your ground' perverts, in an area populated by paranoid doomsday preppers and jumpy neighbors. Oh, and there was a murderer running around. Oh oh, and Varg was a fucking Nazi. When the gang heard about this, I'd never live it down. It was a miracle I was unshot. I'd deliberately wandered into the little Führerbunker and faced not one but two clips of automatic weapons fire and came out alive. Maybe there was a medal to be had.

Someone was walking toward the truck from the pasture on the right. The park was on the left. It was a rising plateau with trees and rocky cliffs. The road disappeared in dirt ruts up a ways around a low green hill.

In the bed of the truck, an ATV not too different from the one I was riding was lashed down.

The man paused at the fence line and waited for me. As I got closer I thought I recognized him, which wasn't easy through that besmirched visor. It was Roddy Dean's son, Beaumont. In true Western fashion he was leaning against a fence post with a stalk of grass in his teeth and his thumbs in his belt with crossed cowboy boots.

"Howdy," I said, taking off my helmet.

"Someone hit ya?"

I guess polite greetings were not the Big Horn way.

"No, he missed," I said.

"Doesn't look like it." He pointed to his forehead.

"Oh, that. Yes. Wyoming did that."

He wore a long-sleeved shirt, but the buttons were down pretty low. His jeans looked new and hugged his hips like they were painted there. His belt buckle was the size of a tea plate. His hat—of course he had a hat—was of the tan cowboy variety.

"You're Beaumont Dean," I said.

He shifted the stalk to the other side of his mouth.

"And you're still that guy from Utah looking into the killing. But now I hear you're FBI. That true? What are you doing here?"

"What are you doing here?" I rudely ignored the question. I can be rude when I want to be. Ask anyone.

He squinted and shifted the stalk back to the other side.

I saw that where he was standing by the truck, the barbed wire fence had been cut.

I walked over to take a closer look. Beaumont didn't move, but tracked me with his beady eyes. Well, squinty at least. The sun was pretty bright.

Yep, it was cut and rolled back, leaving an eight-foot gap any bovine could wander through.

There was an area that had been trampled down to dirt a couple yards in around what looked like a dented brown cinder block. I could see lots of hoof prints, or maybe post holes, deep and clear even after the rain. There were no vehicle tracks in the pasture.

"What are you doing here, I said?" he said.

"And I said, what are you doing here? See how that works?"

"No."

"I also said 'howdy' at the beginning. You failed to reply politely. That'll have to go in my report."

"Report?"

I'm not sure if he was naturally surly or defensive or just slow. Hard to tell. I put him in his twenties, low to mid. An uppity age.

I walked into the pasture, and Beaumont finally left his post perch and followed.

"Are you now some kind of law, then?"

"You know anything about these missing cattle?" I asked.

He paused.

"Well?"

"I'm here to see what happened," he said. "So it don't happen to our cattle."

I squinted at him. I had to. I had no sunglasses or hat, and the sun was shining bright the way it often does.

"Private eye, then I heard FBI. Are you now saying you're a cow cop?" He shifted his weight. Not sure if it was swagger or nervousness. I glanced up and all was retinal damage.

"I'm Tony Flaner," I said.

Nervous now for sure. He took his hat off and ran his fingers through his hair, his luxuriant dark hair.

I bent down and inspected the thing in the middle of the dirt. It wasn't a cinder block. It was thereabouts the same size, but it was a rock, a polished rock that looked like it had once been a block.

"What kind of rock is this?" I bent down to get a better look.

"That ain't a rock. That's a salt lick."

"Really?"

I licked it. It was salty.

"I can't believe you just did that," said Beaumont.

"What's it for?"

"Cows lick it for salt."

I spit.

Honestly, what is with me? Remember how I often don't have a vocal censor? Apparently, I don't have much of a physical one, either. I thought of giardia.

"Checks out," I said and kicked at the stone. I uncovered something shiny beneath it. I picked it up and wiped spit off it.

It was a gun.

It was a tiny little thing, silver with a white handle. An automatic. It was dirty.

"How'd this get under this salt lick?"

Beaumont shook his head. "Could have been out here a while."

"But under the block?"

"Cattle move those things around all the time," he said.

I looked out over the pasture. It was big. I could see a ribbon of highway between two hills.

"You know anything about these cows that were stolen?"

"Steers," he said. "Is it related to the killing?"

"Do you know about the steers that were stolen?"

"Big prize monsters. Best in the county. Shame Dasher went and killed them."

"He killed them? How do you know this? Have the bodies been found?"

"They're never found," he said. "He probably leads them into a cave or something and kills them there."

"That's what people think?"

"Yep."

"Why would he do that?"

"Mean-spirited, I guess," said Beaumont. "Maybe he eats them." He didn't sound convinced.

"He ever steal any of your cows?"

"Steers. Sometimes."

"Same way? Cut the fence and lead them away?"

I walked back to the road, looking for telltale hoof prints. I saw none.

"What are you going to do with that gun?"

I looked at it again. It was mud-encrusted, the barrel a dirt clod. "Sheriff might be interested in this."

"You have any suspects?"

"For the gun?"

"For the killing," he said. "You know everyone had a grudge against Dasher."

"You did."

"What? No. I liked Dash just fine." His eyes found the horizon. "He never hurt no one. He was all right, had his heart in the right place. Friendly enough."

"Except when he stole people's cows?"

"Steers," he corrected me. "Yeah, except then."

"Does he always only steal steers?" I said. "What's the difference, by the way?"

He laughed. "Steers are boys, cows are girls. Cows we keep to make more animals. Steers are fattened up and sold."

"Can't you sell cows too?"

"Can, but only when they're no longer making calves."

"What about Oliver and Hardy?"

"They were the prize bulls. They were the fathers of lots of stock."

"More valuable alive then?"

"Yeah," he said with a little regret. "Real shame for Pilana to lose them.

And the county."

I knocked the dirt out of the gun barrel and ejected the magazine. I cycled the chamber but nothing came out. That's gun talk for it was not ready to fire and probably had not been fired. There were bullet boys in the bullet box, but not in the barrel place. I put the pieces in my pocket.

Beaumont looked uneasy.

"What?" I said.

"Suspects?"

"Your father is high on the list."

The news didn't shock him.

"You don't look shocked to hear that."

"There are others who could have done it too, others with motives."

"Stealing cattle isn't motive enough?"

"Stealing? No. Not for Roddy. He wouldn't kill for that. But others might." And again he was morose. "Pilana was pretty pissed."

"Only after his prize bulls were taken. Which was the night of the killing."

"Yeah, that's true."

I tried to imagine a naked man gnawing through barbed wire in the dark, hustling out two enormous animals, chasing them up that plateau, and disposing of them before finding his way to the little medicine wheel, which had to be five miles from here, mostly uphill.

I leveled my squinting, watering eyes at the dude. "Do you know where your father was the night of the killing? Do you know where you were?"

"We were together."

"How convenient. Where?"

"We were at the fair. We watched the fireworks from the bleachers and then went home."

"You didn't ask me when Dasher was killed."

"I heard it was at night. That's what we were doing at night."

"Do you have any witnesses?"

"Lots of folks saw us at the fair."

"Lots of folks left when the first rain hit. Is that when you left?"

"We stayed through the fireworks. A little time after."

"Witnesses?"

"Everyone knows us."

"I saw you there."

"You did?" said Beaumont.

"In the afternoon. You and your father looked to be arguing. What about?"

"Just some family stuff."

"But you were all made up by the time the fireworks came on?"

"Yes."

"And went home hand in hand?"

"What do you mean by that?"

"Did you leave in the same car?"

"My truck."

"It's a nice one," I said, admiring the white truck. "You should wash it."

"Mud makes it look cool," he said. "A working man's truck."

"Très chic."

He swapped out grass stalks.

"Were there other cattle in this pasture, do you know?"

"No, just the bulls."

"Isn't it strange to keep bulls together?" I had no idea, but he didn't know that.

"Not if there are no cows around."

"Right. Where do the animals drink in this pasture?"

He pointed down a ways toward the road. "There's a trough down there, fed by a stream that comes from the creek."

"A ways out there?"

"Yep."

"There's a gate over there?"

"Yep."

"Why is the salt lick way over here by the far fence, you think?"

He paused and scratched his head again. Really, he had amazing hair even when shaped by a hat.

"Probably to encourage exercise. Make them move from the water to the salt lick."

"Is that normal?"

"No."

"Do you think Dasher might have deliberately moved the salt lick here to pull the cows away from the highway to this far side where he could get them?"

"Steers."

"I have a gun, you know."

"What?"

"I asked you a question and you understood it, so answer it, or it goes into my report."

"I don't know what Dasher thinks—thought. I guess you'd have to have asked him."

"Where does this road lead?" I said, pointing north.

"Montana."

"Gun."

"I don't know. Lots of places."

"Does it connect to the highway?"

"In a couple places. The closest is back the way you came."

"Which one did you use?"

"Which did I use?"

"Today," I clarified.

"What do you mean by that?"

"What?" All innocent face.

"I used one a ways up there." He pointed north.

"Where's your ranch?"

"Mine?"

"You're making this too easy, Beaumont."

"What?"

"Where?"

He pointed southeast. "A ways the other side of Floyd."

"Far?"

He shrugged. "Everything's far out here."

"So it's a ways."

"Yeah."

"So what did you find?"

"What do you mean?"

"You said you were out here looking for ways to stop this from happening to your cattle. Get any ideas?"

He shrugged.

"You really don't have anything to worry about now, do you, though?"

"I don't?"

"Dasher's dead. No more cattle rustling. It is called rustling, right? Stealing cattle is so urbane. It's rustling. Has a good hanging sound to it, don't you think?"

"Rustling. Yeah, rustling."

"And no more Dasher, so all's safe and will be cool."

"Yeah, I guess so."

I kicked a dirt clod and noticed that I was getting sunburned on my arms. At least the mosquitoes were gone. They liked the wooded glen, not the high prairie.

"How's raising cattle? Good money?"

"Yeah, it pays pretty well. It's why people do it."

"Is your family doing all right?"

"All right."

"Ever need any special spending money like for a trip or something? Maybe a new spittoon."

He squinted.

"Hypothetically speaking, Beaumont," I said, "what's to prevent one rancher from stealing cows—steers—bovine creatures of all makes and models—and selling them?"

"Brands," he said.

"Brands?"

"Yes, those burned things on a cow."

"I know what a brand is. Are they cursed? Is that it?"

"Yeah, kinda."

"Explain or I'll write this up in my report."

"What will you write up?"

"Uppity."

"That's not very professional."

"How about uncooperative? Suspicious?"

"Are you really FBI? Show me your badge."

"Tell me about brands."

He opened and closed the tailgate. I don't know why.

"You can't sell cattle without provenance. You know what that means?"

"I'm familiar with the term. It's usually used to talk about art, though, tracing the ownership of something to make sure it wasn't stolen."

"Same thing. If you show up with a cow that isn't your brand, you better have a bill of sale or no one will buy it and you'll be turned in. It's a big deal out here. Really big. Back east, I hear it's not so big, but here, it's behind-bars serious."

"Who buys the cows?"

"St—"

"Who?"

"We have auctions usually. Big deals at the end of the season."

"Can someone buy privately?"

"What do you mean?"

"I mean buy a co—steer, from an owner. Just hand over money and take one home. You know, for the kids."

"For the kids?"

"Beaumont, stop with the stupid act before I begin to believe it."

"Sometimes I've heard of people paying to have an animal raised and then buying them, but they're delivered butchered, ready for the freezer."

I knew of this too. Good way to save money on meat if you had a walk-in freezer or ten friends with an iron deficiency.

"So they could be sold that way?"

"I don't see it working like that," he said.

"How do you see it working then?"

"What do you mean?"

"Hypothetically speaking."

"I wouldn't know." He looked up at the sun as if using it to tell time. "I gotta go," he said.

"One more question, Beaumont. Why do you think your father would kill Dasher?"

I half expected him to round on me, fists a-coming for family honor, but he just paused, his hand on the door latch.

"He didn't like him," he said.

"But you did?"

"Yeah."

24

I WATCHED BEAUMONT DRIVE AWAY, heading north into the drylands, chased by a tan cloud of dust. I had a mouthful of that dust and after noting my sunburned arms made the obvious decision to turn around and seek shade.

I left the helmet off. It was hard to see through, it was hot, and it muffled sounds that could be useful to hear, like the telltale sound of gunfire. I'd be passing behind Varg's cabin on the way back to Perry's.

Riding an ATV is more physical than I'd like. It bounces and jars, and you have to use muscles to stay on and steer. Who needs that? Plus it was hot with the midday sun and all. I lost sight of all the majestic scenery and wished I'd brought a water bottle, or, as they used to be called, a canteen. Maybe waterskins, for the D&D players out there. I should have had less coffee and pastries and more water with Gail, but I didn't know I'd be taking a couple hours' detour to steer-snatching central along the Eastern Front.

I thought of Gail making a pass—passes, many many obvious passes at me—and how stupid I'd been not to see it. It must get lonely out here. The array of possible mates is not huge in this wilderness. Seeing how quickly rumors spread, I could also understand why she'd reach out to a tourist like me. I'd take her secrets with me when I left, if there had been any secrets. There hadn't been. Just so you know. You were there. You saw.

The coziness of a small town is a curse sometimes, and for some reason, maybe because I'd just talked to him, Beaumont came to mind. I thought of Kimmy. I thought of Eddie and the stories he knew but didn't tell me.

I found the turn-off into the park and stopped there. The trail led across a stream and then disappeared up a steep hillside around a clump of trees. Trees are in clumps, right? It was wide enough for ATVs but probably no good for anything bigger. In a bare and dusty spot, I saw the same kind of tracks that had led me into the scary basement of the deserted house. Remembering my western ways, I lay down and put my ear to the ground. I heard ants.

After shaking bugs out of my auditory canal, I looked longingly at a bubbling brook of tempting mountain water.

Came the sound of gravel rustling, if that's a thing. Someone or something was coming down the trail. Rolling. I took a couple steps up and then heard a faint engine sound just as a motorcycle barreled around the bend right at me being ridden by what I thought at first was a samurai.

I jumped head first to my right as you see in movies and activated my scream button on a patch of bare clay on the bank.

The bike veered, slipped and flipped, tossing its rider full-on into the stream beside me.

"Why are you screaming?" asked Mandel, pulling himself up from the muck. "I'm the one who got thrown."

"Hold on a second," I said, sitting up. I cleared my throat. "Aaaahhhhhh-hhh! Okay, now I'm done."

"You sure?"

I felt my button, gritted my teeth. Though I couldn't see it, I'd swear it had doubled in size since I first got it. "No," I said.

The backpack he'd been wearing had spilled into the water. He was quick to pick up the tossed things: a hand shovel, a bag, work gloves, batteries, flashlight, a screwdriver. What had made him look like a samurai were a long shovel and a metal detector he wore crossed over his back like two swords. Those were in the muck as well. I recognized the metal detector. It was a twelve-inch Deepsearch Spider Coil Pulse Induction Tech Treasure Hunter 8000. Top of the line. I had one just like it.

Mandel picked up the tools and slogged to the shore. I offered him a hand, but he didn't take it because he got out on the other side.

"Hey, why'd you park across the trail like that?" he asked.

"Oh, this is my fault?" I said.

He repacked his things.

"Hey," I said, "you didn't have a helmet on. Do you like the taste of bugs or something?"

"I can't hear with the helmet on."

"It does muffle. But I didn't have mine, and I still couldn't hear your bike until it was on me."

It's been my experience that motorcycles are loud. Some are loud, some really loud and some are so god-awful loud that they shake the fillings in your molars from eight blocks away. I see signs on roadways about no engine brakes, also called Jake Brakes because they're so loud. I'm not sure I've ever heard one of those, but Jake must have really pissed people off to get so many signs put up. I have to wonder what his recipe for auditory assault was that could rival the unsigned cruelty of blaring Hondas and Harley Davidsons. You know what I'm talking about: that full throttle apocalyptic roar of a screaming motorcycle shattering glass at fifty miles per hour in a doppleringly debilitating din. They must use amplifiers instead of mufflers on those things and communicate by sign language in their off hours. Mandel's bike was not one of those. It was so quiet, in fact, that I'd noticed it was quiet. It was quieter than my ATV, which sounded like an ATV. I don't have much to compare it to. Maybe a good lawnmower. When I sense a motorcycle, I naturally clench my teeth and cover my ears and say a prayer to the god of silence to strike the rider dead in their seats for rudeness. So Mandel's was so different that I noticed. I'd actually thought that maybe a small radio-controlled buggy was coming down the trail, not a dirt bike.

"Why is your motorcycle so quiet?"

"Is it?"

"Yes. I didn't even know motorcycles could be quiet."

"Oh, they can," he said, inspecting his machine for damage.

"Need help?"

"Hey. No, I got it."

"So how so quiet? Electric?"

"No. You can get quiet ones. It's extra, believe it or not, but they do make them. Just not trendy. I don't like the noise they make, so I got a quiet one."

I suspected there was more to it.

"I suspect there's more to it," I said.

He tested a lever. It squished. He pushed the bike forward. It rolled. "It's less disruptive to the wildlife."

"True. But that's not why you have a quiet bike."

"Why can't I have a quiet bike?"

"You can. You do. But it's not for the antelope. Maybe it's for you, but I think there's more to it."

"What are you talking about?" That line could have been delivered with more effectively, like if he'd put a harsher tone in his voice or made eye contact.

I sat on my ATV and stroked my chin in the classic, 'I'm thinking smart stuff' pose.

"You were out looking for gold," I said.

He didn't say anything.

"You ride a quiet bike so no one can easily follow you and jump your claim. You probably have a secret hideout where you store the bike and your tools. Probably on this road somewhere. Maybe in a deep basement of a house you're selling, one without a 'For Sale' sign anywhere to be seen."

His face blanched but his eyes widened. I love it when that happens.

"Or maybe you use it to track."

"Track?"

"It's a hunting term I heard on a National Geographic special when I was a kid. It's another way of saying 'sneaking up on.'"

He blinked.

"Am I close?" I asked.

"Yes," he said.

"And a bike will get you places that an ATV won't. Through narrows and in between trees and suchlike."

He nodded.

"Where were you the night Dasher was killed?"

He flinched as if I'd physically hit him. Words are so powerful. Gotta love words.

"What?"

"Don't think too hard about it."

"I told you."

His gaze went up and to his right as he formed a lie.

"Tell me again."

"I don't remember."

"Try harder."

"He was killed after the fair, right? I was at the fair."

"During the fireworks?"

"I was at the fair."

"But not at your booth?" Not sure why I asked that, but it got him looking at the horizon again.

"No, I took my booth down before then. I saw the rain coming and pulled out."

"Before the rain?"

"Yes."

"Did anyone see you pack up?"

"There was the woman who sold you an expensive stick."

"Great lady. Has integrity. Then what did you do?"

"I went to the bleachers and watched the show."

"Did you hear the guy talk about coal?"

"Sure I did."

"Did you throw a freedom fry at me?"

"What? No. Why would I do that?"

"Because of coal."

"I don't know anything about coal. In the park or out. Don't say I do, because I don't."

It's not very often I get to deal with someone as rattled as Mandel was then.

"What're the last four digits of your social security number?"

"Three seven eight one."

"Mother's maiden name?"

"Shlekovich."

"Spell that."

He did.

"What about the coal?"

"Hey, I told you I don't know anything."

I looked behind me to make sure there wasn't an interesting zeppelin on an attack vector. I didn't see any. Might have been camouflaged.

Another chin stroke.

"You've been prospecting around them thar hills for a good spell now," I said in Cowboy. "You found coal."

"It's a protected park. Even if I did know something, it's not like anyone can get to it."

"Until the upcoming vote."

"Didn't take you long to get into local politics, did it?"

"Now it makes sense."

"What makes sense?"

"Getting punched in the street and showered with condiments."

"I don't know anything about that."

I let a pause settle in, mostly to bask in my luck and good guessing, which I often pass off as investigation.

"Would Dasher have known local politics?" I asked.

"Dasher?"

"The dead guy."

"Hey, I know, um…" He looked down. "Hey, I really gotta go."

"Mandel—Jack, isn't it?"

"Yes, Jack. Jack Mandel."

"Sit your Jack ass down."

He did. On the ground. Just like that.

"Dasher?"

"I doubt Dasher got the newspaper," he said, now with some spirit. "Dumb question."

The sound of an oncoming vehicle turned our heads. Mandel collected his things, strapped the gear on his back as before, turned the bike around and shot up the trail in a cloud of quiet dust like he was fleeing a subpoena.

I waited, contemplating what had happened, anticipating what was to come. I was feeling pretty good until I realized that the sound could be a blitzkrieg from Varg's place.

I fired up my ATV and took aim to follow Mandel up the mountain when Rawly rounded the bend. He waved, and I stopped.

He drove up to me and turned off his machine.

He was in green camouflage fatigues pants that didn't really match the area but looked comfy. Around his waist he had a gun belt with the required gun in it, plus a bunch of pouches that would make Batman envious. Above this, he had a khaki green tank top, a sunburn, and a baseball cap with a Lexus Dealership logo.

"Howdy," I said.

"Howdy," said he.

I looked at his belt. "Got your shark repellent in there?"

"What's that?"

"Nothing. What brings you out?"

"I heard gunfire. Thought I'd check it out."

"Automatic gunfire?"

"Sounded like."

"That was like an hour ago. Maybe two."

"Whatcha getting at?"

I guess I couldn't blame him, but I did a little. I thought tough prepper guys like Rawly lived for the gunfight. I'd think the sound of it would draw them like flies to shit. I guess it did, just not quickly. Rawly wasn't an idiot.

"You're no idiot," I said.

"Who've you been talking to?" The accusatory and defensive tone unmistakable.

"It was Varg Jayger," I said. "The gunfire. I went onto his property and he politely shot me off it."

"With a machine gun?"

"Yes."

"Machine gun or automatic rifle?"

"I really don't know."

"Was it belt fed?"

"It had a strap on it."

"Was there a big can underneath it?"

"It was an army gun. Modern. It had a magazine that he emptied and replaced."

"How long for the changeover?"

"I'm not sure."

"Love to know how fast he is."

"He was pretty quick with the trigger," I said. "Not in the mood for talking."

"And fully automatic, huh?" He looked into the distance appreciably. "I wonder if he's got a permit for that."

"You'd have to ask him. But make an appointment."

"But look at you," Rawly said with a giggle.

"What about me?"

"You aren't dead."

"What? Really? Damn. Now what am I going to do with my afternoon?"

He wiped his sweaty forehead with a black handkerchief that had white skulls all over.

"How well do you know your neighbors?" I asked.

"Folks around here like to be left alone." He said it like it was some kind of sacred credo. I wondered if it wasn't the town motto.

"He had an M-16, if I had to guess."

"Oh. Well, at least it's American."

"Ra ra."

"Hey—you haven't seen my place yet. Do you want to? Come on. Follow me. We'll have a beer. We can talk. Get to be pals."

"Is there shade?"

"Yep."

"Let's go."

25

I'VE BEEN friends with Perry Whitehouse long enough to have experienced, at least second-hand, much of the fringes of society. Preppers are definitely that. Preppers prep, which I assume is short for prepare. Nothing wrong with that. Being prepared is good. There's a popular young men's paramilitary group based on the idea, the Boy Scouts, who have to sell popcorn to raise funds because no one would buy a cookie with "BS" stamped on it. If it's cloudy out, you might want to be prepared with an umbrella, not that any American outside of Seattle even owns one of those anymore. If there's a chance some asshat in a Chrysler will drive into you on the way to buy a lottery ticket, having your seat belt on is a smart piece of preparedness. Of course the odds are far better that you'll be bashed by the Chrysler than see an oversized PowerBall check with your name on it. Then again, Chrysler sales are down. More likely a Ford or a Toyota. Maybe a Hyundai. I've seen a lot of those around lately. Still, better safe than sorry. Good luck with the lottery ticket, by the way. Remember me if you do win. Preparedness saves lives and is an unquestionable good. But there comes a time when too much good does become questionable, if not, well, bat-shit-crazy-fringe–paranoid.

Preppers are not just smart squirrels stashing acorns under their bed like lighted toys, frugal rodents with a nut fetish. They are preparing for a certain event, and by certain I mean specific, not guaranteed. The long form of preppers in this context—not to be confused with 'prep cooks' who cut cucumbers for the salad bar—is 'Doomsday Preppers.' Thus enter the bat-shit-crazy-paranoid demographic.

There are those who will argue with me on this, and those people will probably be very well armed, so let me say that I truly love and respect the paranoid nut-jobs who spend their fortunes on missile silos and wheat germ kits. They are the best people in the world. Ever. What follows here in no way reflects the actual views and opinions of normal people or the author or characters in any way, so there's no need to get upset and shooty and put me on some kind of purge list.

We good? Okay.

Doomsday preppers are idiots. (If you are a prepper, please refer to previous paragraph.)

That's how I see it. Preparing for the end of the world should be about making amends, crossing things off your bucket list, eating s'mores until you puke. Enjoying life. Maybe finish that book you started last year. Positing things. Instead, these fanatics are all about hoarding food and ammunition, barricading themselves in a salt mine and learning to like the taste of their own piss. What's the point? Doomsday. The end of the world. It's over. Gone. End. You're part of the world too. Ergo, you'll be gone. If you really believe in doomsday, you're delusional to prepare for it. It's like buying green bananas on the Titanic. When pressed, however, preppers must admit that they don't think the world will really end, only some of it. Just enough to send angry hordes, roving bands, and stoned groupies hungry for MREs into the streets to break windows. Maybe there'll be some nuclear fallout. Maybe insects. Economic collapse. But most of them really want zombies. They're really hoping for zombies.

To prepare for the inevitable fall of civilization, they prep. They collect guns because nothing says 'a new tomorrow' like an armory with more firepower than a D-Day storage closet. They hoard food because grocery stores will be overrun by said hordes. They buy gold because they fell victim to some unscrupulous doomsday charlatan on a cheap commercial running between radicalized screaming radio programs spouting fear and telling them that when the end comes they'll need gold. Because gold keeps its value. It's so valuable. Gold. So useful. Never goes bad. Forget that there won't be any banks and that anyone still around will have as many guns as you have, and if they want your gold, they're probably going to get it. Gold is great. It's heavy and shiny and absolutely useless for everyday living. But it's gold, so...gold.

There is an old Chinese curse, I'm told, that goes, 'may you live in interesting times.' Interesting is bad, you see. Change is trouble. Uncertainty is icky. All this causes anxiety, which makes fear like gophers make holes. Fear is what drives preppers. They, like the rest of us, are living in interesting times but turn their confusion, anxiety, and pants-shitting fear into the practical preoccupation of buying things. What can be more American? Fear of the future turned into a shopping spree. Remember when George W. told us all to go shopping after 9/11? Same kind of thing. Still, it's better to be busy than not. It's hard to lose sleep over nerve gas attacks and the terrible commies trying to give you health care when you're too tired to stand after digging a twelve-foot moat around your foxhole and filling it with snakes.

Obsessions I understand. Hobbies I completely get. I'm not unsympathetic. Anything worth doing is worth overdoing. But it's just a negative vibe I can't get behind. When you put so much energy into fear and doom, you can begin to resent nice days. Every day that doesn't rain nukes, you look stupid. When the race war is postponed it gets on your nerves. This much disappointment has got to get into your head and make you bat-shit-crazy-fringe-paranoid if you weren't before, but luckily most of these people are bat-shit-crazy-fringe-paranoid already, so it's all good, I guess.

When Perry goes off on his newest conspiracy theory, I like to think that it's just his pastime, his way of letting off steam, like a model railroad set but with tinfoil hats and masked IP addresses. Usually his plot du jour is sidelined by a new day's offerings, and he doesn't blow too much sleep researching ley lines and gnomic necromancy. Most of his plots are interesting, make for good stand-up routines and anonymous blog posts, but some have the flavor of coming Armageddon and have been known to put my friend into a catatonic state and get him to buy gold off sketchy websites. In those cases it hurts him. I remember when the Mayan calendar thing happened, the prophecy that the world would end on December 21, 2012. Perry was convinced the world would end then. I bet him a hundred dollars it wouldn't. After he paid me, I asked him how he expected to have collected on the bet had he won. I think I made a point. It didn't last, though, as evidenced by him buying a survivalist cabin in Big Horn County, Wyoming.

Because I'd seen the syndrome before, the things Rawly showed me didn't break my brain. I could appreciate his twelve-foot-high razor-wire-topped fence with reinforced padlocked entry system and spiked booby traps. I thought the foxhole garden was practical and playful. They could double as ponds during the monsoon season. The compost heap was generous and overflowing, near the untended garden, not too far from one of six different sheds.

"I've only been living the lifestyle for a couple of years, but let me tell you it's so liberating," explained Rawly. "All this country air. Time to get to know myself. Me and Kimmy are just loving it."

He didn't show me into all the sheds, just a glance into a couple. One had farming stuff, unused. One a garage. One had boxes of canned food with the cardboard nibbled off at the corners.

"Got a lot of stuff," I said.

"Yep. I'll show you the cabin."

I trotted, no, skipped, to the door.

"I had the main building put up in six months, but left much of it raw so we could decorate and evolve as the situation led us."

The cabin wasn't a bunker like the empty one I'd been to that morning, but neither was it a glass-walled vacation home like Perry's. It was a single-story house, a rambler with stucco walls and a forest green metal roof. It didn't match the area at all. The roof would fit in in Oregon, and stucco is a thing of the desert. Out here, log cabins or siding was the way. The stucco did offer a single advantage—it could be painted, and painted it was. In camouflage.

"In the summer months, you can't see this place from the road," explained Rawly. "The pattern goes all around."

"What about the roof?"

"I'm getting a camouflage net for that."

"In the winter?"

"It's best to keep snow on the roof."

He took me around to a patio that had a grill and deck chairs, an umbrellaed table, two feeders swarming with hummingbirds.

"That's cool."

"I sit out here alone for hours," he said. "Just watching them come and go. They're territorial, you know. One will rise to the top and chase off all the others."

"Nice."

"Yes," he said without much conviction. "Want to see all my guns?"

"Sure."

"But first a beer."

"Of course. How can anyone be expected to handle firearms without a buzz on?"

"You know it," he said, but I didn't think he'd heard me. At least I hoped he hadn't.

Rawly took me inside, where the house was as comfortable and luxurious as any home I'd ever been in. Except for the thick walls, bullet-resistant windows with steel shutters, and cameras in every corner of every room, it was a Parade of Homes showroom. Marble tile, leather couches, huge television, modern art, and sconce lighting.

"Really nice."

"Yes."

"Shame it's only one floor," I said.

"Oh, it's got others," he said. "Underneath. They're accessible by that stairway." He pointed to a blank wall. "And another secret hatch in my bedroom and two out in the yard."

"I didn't notice them."

"They're hidden for security."

"Okay."

"One's in the vehicle shed, the other is out by the west side. That's the bug-out door."

"Can't be too careful."

I remembered Floyd's love of isolation, the 'mind your own business' credo, and felt sorry for Rawly. He was happy, no, actually *excited* to have someone to talk to. He wouldn't shut up.

"Beer goes bad so I get cases delivered every week. Try this one. It's Swedish."

"Thanks."

"It's a pilsner. My favorite kind."

"What kind does Kimmy like?"

A shadow weakened his smile which had turned genuine when showing me around. "She likes girly drinks with vodka."

"You were going to show me your guns."

"Yes. Yes," he said. The smile returned.

He pushed open a secret panel beside the blank wall he'd pointed to, revealing a keypad. He entered "1234" and I heard a latch click over. He pushed the wall and it swung open easily, revealing a staircase. Lights flickered on showing the way.

"Follow me," he said. "Only this level is built out. The bottom one is a bomb shelter and boring. We're still wondering what to do with that. Maybe turn part of it into a rec room. Been thinking an indoor pool would be good somewhere."

"You had all this built in six months?" I said, marveling at the high ceilings and open design of the dungeon level.

"Doesn't pay to drag these things out. Plus I was in a hurry to get out here."

"Why?"

"Um…I thought we needed a change of pace."

"Where were you before?"

"Indianapolis," he said.

"Are you rich?"

"Venture finance. Made a killing. Still have stocks in lots of startups. They pay the bills."

"What kind of startups?"

"Oh, anything. Computer, resorts, exploration, medicines. Whatever sounded catchy. The new thing always sells."

We walked down a long, brightly lit tiled floor. On either side were imposing metal doors made a little less imposing by having been painted in warm colors and decorated with bright flower power blossoms. He stopped at one, opened a little door and typed in the same inane 1234 code. The door unlatched.

"I was a local congressman," he said. "Sat on the arts council board. Chamber of Commerce."

He pushed in the door and the light snapped on. Inside was a large cluttered room. My first thought was that I was looking into a man-cave, one of those masculine nests where regular guys sit around in their underwear playing video games and watching porn with a 'no gurls allowd' sign taped to the door. This had that feeling, and there was even a video game console and computer with three monitors on one table.

Rawly saw me looking.

"I get satellite internet," he said. "Not bad, all things considered."

I felt a desire to sit in front of the monitors, bask in the glow of forbidden light, touch the sensual keys of the mechanical keyboard, shift the mouse on the rubber pad with delicate graceful motions. I felt for the tile in my pocket and squeezed. I felt the squirt of toothpaste and remembered I still had Gail's care package supplies in that pocket. The other pocket had a gun, so I guess I got off lucky.

"My armory is over here." Rawly stepped inside and walked to another door and pressed the same code to open a James Bond-worthy cabinet of weaponry. There were rifles and pistols. Lots of different kinds. It reminded me of a Walmart display, just without the underpaid clerk and useless safety glass. There were boxes of shells beneath each weapon, a crate marked 'grenades'; another promised C-4 and a third something in stenciled Cyrillic. Maybe tuna fish. Probably not. I'm sure Rawly would have told me the make and model of each thing on display, explained the Russian text, let me hold everything, maybe offer to let me play with them, but by then my eyes had fallen onto a side workbench.

"I have all kinds," Rawly said. "I prefer 9mm for all my small arms, but I play all the calibers for the big stuff. I have AKs and ARs and 5.7s for the main guns, as they say. And...oh, I see you've noticed my gold."

26

IT WAS STRAIGHT OUT of a cartoon, stacks of gold coins piled up like poker chips on a table ready for counting. Four stacks of gleaming gold disks, and one spilled on its side.

"Fe-fi-fo-fum," I said.

"What's that?"

"The treasure. It looks like something out of a fairy tale."

"They're Krugerrands," he said. "Take a look."

I'd never held a Krugerrand before. Perry hadn't let me touch his, so I was keen to hold one.

"They're from South Africa. Those guys really know how to have money down there. None of that fiat currency. Real gold."

"Fiat currency?" I shook my head.

"Modern money is backed by a promise."

"Okay…"

"Well, I mean, it's the government who makes the promise," he explained.

"I follow."

"Well…see? They can do whatever they want. When they need more money, they can just print more."

"Don't other countries do the same?"

"Most do, yeah, but it's worthless."

"I use money all the time," I said. "It seems to work."

"But it's not real. That's why gold is so good and why South Africa is so smart. America used to be so smart."

"We used to have gold coins?"

"Yes. I mean no. We had gold and silver certificates."

"Paper money?"

"Yes. I mean no. They were paper, yes, but you could always ask for the silver or the gold it was worth if you wanted."

"Did people do that a lot?"

"Yes. I mean no. Gold and silver are hard to carry around. Paper money is easier."

"Okay…"

"It's part of the banking cabal."

"Banking cabal?"

"Yes."

"You mean no?"

"Right. No. It's just how modern countries do things. Except South Africa, which actually has gold coins in circulation."

"They don't have paper money?"

"Yes."

"And no?"

"They have both."

I shuffled the coins like poker chips with one hand. I can do that. It intimidates people at card games.

"So the old paper money, which was good," I said, "could be changed into gold or silver."

"Yes."

"How did you get these Krugerrands?"

"I bought them."

"With fiat currency?"

"Yes, but see? That's how I tricked the system."

"Could you have taken some fiat dollars and, say, gone to a jeweler or some metals guy and bought gold and silver there?"

"Yes."

"So the fiat money still works like that old 'good' paper money used to?"

"Well, yeah. I guess so. But…but…oh. Here it is. They can't print more Krugerrands."

"But they can dig more up, right? Isn't that like making more money? I seem to remember that happening to Spain with all the New World treasure coming over. A bit of inflation."

"Really?"

"Yes. I mean. Yes. Surely yes."

"But gold is solid and real and has value," he said.

"Who gives it the value?"

"Those coins are worth about fourteen hundred dollars each. That's what I paid for them."

"Does the price stay the same?"

"No, it fluctuates."

"Like fiat currency?"

"No. I mean yes, kinda. But this gold has value. I can sell this for…"

"Goods and services?" I offered.

"Those, sure."

"Who accepts those for payment outside of South Africa?"

"Smart people."

"So not Macy's?"

"No. Nor Walmart."

"You're losing me."

"You have to remember these coins can appreciate in value."

"Do they ever go down?"

"Yes, that happens. But it's gold, see? It has value outside of governments." With that he smiled and folded his arms across his chest.

"Who gives it the value?"

"Governments buy it to…"

"Yes…"

"It's the eh…eh…the market economy. It's worth what someone will pay for it."

"So instead of a government meddling in money, you get speculators and collectors and late-night commercials?"

"What's that about late-night commercials?"

I took mercy on him. "So what's with all the ammo cans?" I pointed to a stack of metal boxes under the table.

"Those are .50 caliber boxes. They're what I put the gold in to cache them."

"Cash them?"

"No, not like getting change. I mean to cache them. Bury them. Hide them for a rainy day."

"Like a squirrel?"

"Yes. You see, the cans are government issue so they're dependable. I buy them surplus and put in a new gasket. I fill them with emergency supplies and cache them around for if I have to bug out."

"You'd leave?"

"The hordes will eventually figure out that I've got gold and supplies and they'll come here and try to take it."

"So you bury some of it?"

"Yes," he said, and then with more enthusiasm, "Yes. You see, it doesn't decay. Paper money can get wet and rot. And this isn't no bank cabal with electronic transfers of made-up money in computers. No siree, this is money. Real wealth. Solid. Heavy and stout."

"And it'll be useful when the banks and governments are gone?" I said.

"What else?"

"Love?"

"What?"

"Joking." I glanced back at the wall of guns. "I'm assuming that you foresee the fall of civilization and that's why you're doing all this."

"That's the idea," he said, but less enthused than before. "Mostly we just needed a change of pace from Indianapolis."

"What else do you put in the cans besides money?"

"Guns, ammo, maps, food, flares, fire-starting kits, snake-bite kits, compass, satellite radio, hunting knife, thermal blanket, fishing line, hooks, change of clothes, mirror, first-aid kit, amphetamines, a picture of Kim and me, sunglasses—"

"Amphetamines?"

"New addition. Had room when I stopped putting in explosives."

"Where do you get it?"

"The explosives, gold, or drugs?"

"The drugs. But also the gold. Maybe the explosives."

"Explosives are mostly war surplus. Lots of wars."

"Yep."

"I bought the meth from some skinhead bikers. They tell me it's meth, but I don't know. Haven't tried it."

"And the gold? From TV?"

"I used to do that, but I was told it would be suspicious. So now I go through Jack Mandel. He deals in gold and can trade without drawing the attention of the authorities. I probably keep him in business."

"You probably do." I did a quick count of the stacks on the table and came up with over eighty coins. I did the math in my head and came up with a lot of money in gold.

"Pretty, aren't they?" he said.

"They're neat."

"You can have that one." He put one in my hand.

"No. You can't give me this."

"Rather give it to you then have it stolen."

"You got robbed?" My thoughts went to Kimmy, but I didn't say anything.

"That hermit found one of my caches. He cleaned it out."

"Just one?"

"One I know about."

"Did you check others?"

"I checked out a couple others that I buried about the same time last year. They were fine." He didn't look convinced.

"What?" I said.

"I must have jostled them, because they looked jostled when I opened them. But everything was there."

"The money?"

"Everything."

"How do you know it was the hermit that took the one?"

"Who else is up in those mountains?"

"You came here to get away from people?"

"Thought it would just be Kimmy and me," he said forlornly. The man wore his emotions like a billboard.

"I really can't take this." I tried to give the heavy coin back to him, but he pushed my hand back and I dropped it into the fifty-caliber box with a bright plink.

He reached in and put it back into my hand. "Pshaw," he said.

"Pshaw?"

"That means my pleasure. Keep it," he said. "That coin might come in handy one day."

I wasn't sure he was right about that word, but I didn't have my phone to check the definition so I just thanked him.

"Thanks," I said. "I could always trade it for some fiat currency."

"Good one!" He laughed and slapped my shoulder like we were old drinking buddies when we were in fact only new drinking buddies.

"What about all the guns?" I said.

"You want one of those too?"

"No, why do you have so many?"

"Is this a lot?"

"It is to me."

"You should see some of the other guys."

"What other guys?"

"On the internet. I see how many other people have. I'm an amateur."

"It's a vibrant community on the net?"

"Not really. They're kinda paranoid, and some of them seem downright crazy."

"What about Varg?"

"He's a Nazi. Who likes Nazis?"

"Not me."

"Plus he's a loner."

"Isn't everyone out here?"

"I wish." He had that wistful look in his eye.

I followed him back out into the hall. The door closed behind us with a click and a red light on the key panel.

"Let me show you the storage rooms."

"Sounds like fun."

To another door with a numeric keypad. 1234. We were in.

"Who installed your security systems?" I asked.

"Pearson and Son Survivalist Security and Time Shares," he said, pointing to a sticker on the four-inch doorjamb. "They did Sal's place too."

"Survivalist Security and Time Shares." I had to read it out loud just for it to sink in.

"They're very good."

"Yes, they are," I agreed, but I'm not sure we were talking about the same thing.

No automatic light here. Like a savage, Rawly had to flick a switch on the wall to summon light. Fluorescents flickered and crackled, hummed and lit to show us a storage room.

What I beheld would make an organizer's pants grow tight. There were rows and rows and rows of shelves, each reaching from the floor to the ten-foot-high ceiling above. The back wall was barely visible at the end of a long vanishing point.

"This is...a lot," I said.

"This is all just toilet paper."

"Why?"

"Lesson learned from the pandemic."

"This is what you took from that?"

"What else?"

I was about to suggest hands washing, or mask wearing, or getting vaccinated, or even not to eat monkeys, when he opened a door and revealed an even bigger room.

"In this room alone we have enough to hold the two of us for ten years," said Rawly proudly. "Twenty if we eat the vegetables."

"Is the Ark of the Covenant back there?"

"No, but I hear tell of an alien body."

"With a glass head?"

"A crystal skull."

"God, I hated that movie."

"Didn't we all?" said Rawly. "Didn't we all?"

I was beginning to like Rawly even though he was an idiot prepper and possibly a murderer.

"I've got it all down here. The water is stored in a tank on the other side, but here I have powdered milk, protein bars, hard cheeses in cans, dehydrated beef, chicken, turkey, fish and pork. Tang, coffee, tea, butter, lard, and olive oil in those big industrial cans. Over there is wheat flour, Bisquick, shredded wheat, cereals by the bushel, corn, potato flour, rice flour, rice—lots of rice, oats, oatmeal, farina, crackers, cookies, pasta, raisins, dried mangoes and banana chips—I really like those so I have three hundred pounds of them made with coconut oil. Coconut oil, jams, jellies, canned fruit by the gross. I especially like the cocktail ones with the cherries. I have jars of vitamins—C, A, E, K—millet, eel juice, and I even got some of those discontinued memory-enhancing chocolates by Kiksuye. Those were hard to get, but I'm told they could be a lifesaver. Ebay has everything. Oh, see there, I have beans of all kinds, legumes—whatever they are—peanuts, cashews, pistachios, almonds, mixed nuts, salted nuts, nut flours, sunflower seeds, hazelnuts, trail mix by the quarter-ton, honey, sugar, molasses, salt by the bushel, pepper by the can, assorted spices in jars, chocolates—lots of chocolates—they store really well, I'm told. I have A-1, soy sauce, dehy-drated ketchup, mustard, mayonnaise, horseradish. Let me tell you about the vinegars I have, and…

I tuned out impressed I'd stayed with him that long. If you've stayed with me, you too are impressive.

Rawly walked the aisles reading the labels as he went. I nursed my beer and let him talk. He seemed so happy to have someone to tell all about it.

I perked up when he went through the liquors he had. He had a bunch. He found that buying in barrels was cheaper for the long hall, but he had a wine cellar behind one of the other doors.

"Kimmy likes the sweet stuff when she drinks," he explained. "I mean sweet." He cleared his throat. "You can get vodka in fifty-gallon drums. Bet you didn't know that."

"Doubles as emergency cooking fuel," I said.

"Exactly. It can burn in five of my eight generators—seven. Forgot the one I sent to your friend. I have five fifty-gallon barrels of vodka. Do you want to see them?"

"Do they do tricks?"

"No."

"I'm good then."

Understanding crossed his face and as if coming out of a dream. He blinked a few times under the bright fluorescent lights and then said, "Your beer's gone. Let's go get some more. And some steaks. Do you like steaks?"

"I do."

"Then you're in luck!"

27

TWO MORE GOOD BEERS LATER, I was sitting with Rawly on his deck, cutting into an inch-thick rib-eye. On his built-in fifteen-burner gas grill he'd also roasted corn in the husk and allowed me to cut up a watermelon so all the food groups would be present: meat, fruit, corn, and alcohol.

Rawly was on his fourth beer, and, like he needed any help, he was more talkative than ever.

"It's all about Kimmy," he said. "My life is about her."

This seemed to me to be the obvious opening for the obvious question. "Where is Kimmy now?"

"Well." He giggled, finished his beer, cracked open another and started to cry. "I don't know."

It was an awkward moment. I didn't know what to say, so I ate instead. The steaks were choice. He had a real talent at grilling and a knack for entertaining. I could see him pressing hands at Chamber of Commerce meetings, cutting ribbons, buying drinks for whole bars and then line dancing till dawn. Yet here he was, in the middle of nowhere, where people go to get away from other people.

To break the tension, I said, "You heard about the hermit's murder? I'm investigating that."

Usually announcing a murder investigation creates tension, but I could see Rawly was happy for the distraction.

"I hadn't heard that."

"Really? How have you not heard?"

"I don't have many—any—friends out here. Kimmy might know, but I don't know where she is."

"Maybe we should call the sheriff," I said.

"You think it's him?"

"The killer?"

"No. Do you think Kimmy is with him?"

"Uh, no. I was just thinking about putting in a missing person report."

From his pocket, Rawly produced a hip flask, unscrewed it and took a long swig. "Beer ain't doing it. Want some?"

"What is it?"

"Bourbon."

"Don't mind if I do."

It was potent. Burned my throat.

"I moved out here for Kimmy," said Rawly, miserably.

"She wanted to be a prepper?" If Rawly was a marooned social animal, what was flirty Kimmy?

"I couldn't keep her in the yard," he said.

I pretended this was news. "Oh? Really?"

"I was the laughingstock. All of Indianapolis…all…"

"Why not divorce her?"

"I love her."

"Of course."

"So I moved out here to be alone with her."

"How'd that work out?"

"Good for a while, then not so good."

I looked around the million-dollar bomb shelter and tried to imagine what brought Rawly here. I found a new reason for someone to be a prepper and to hope for the end of the world: a chance to be Adam and Eve. Rawly and Kimmy, the two of them together, no distractions or rivals. It was romantic in a desperate kind of way, a desire to return to the simplest, and I mean the simplest time imaginable.

I nibbled corn.

"It gets in your head, you know? Being cuckolded. It's enough to make a man crazy."

"Where were you the night the hermit was killed?"

"When was he killed?"

"The night of the Fourth of July."

I wasn't sure I believed that he didn't know this already. The rumor mill in this county was the best I'd ever seen. Twitter wasn't as quick as these mouths. Strange how a town of loners could do that.

"Wait, do you think I killed him?" He sat down.

"Did you have reason to?"

"What reason would I have?"

"Kimmy."

His face went hard, his eyes blanked. His jaw clenched.

"I'll take that as a yes."

Rawly's hand slipped to his hip. I remembered he had a gun on him.

"None of my business," I said.

He stared.

"Actually, Rawly, it is my business."

"How?"

"I'm a detective. I've been hired to look into the killing."

"You are? You have?"

"Yes. I said that."

"I'm drinking."

"And sharing. Thanks."

"Wait. So you're here under false pretenses?"

"You invited me," I said. "And your hospitality has been exemplary."

"It has been good to have someone to talk to," said Rawly. His hand came up for the corn and after rolling it in butter, he ate some.

"Kimmy and Dasher?"

"Dasher's the hermit?"

"Yes." Again I was dumbstruck that he didn't know this.

"Maybe."

"Maybe?"

"Probably. Yes. I caught them in the food shed." He pointed to one of the outbuildings he hadn't shown me. "He was naked. She was half so, putting on or taking off, I don't know. The guy's a beast."

I didn't know if he meant the smell or his penile abundance.

"Few people liked him," I said.

"I try not to think of him. Or any of them," he said.

I could smell the clouds of despair in his mind. Or maybe it was the grill. Despair.

"Denial is a powerful drug," I said. "It builds up. It can get to levels where it just blows and a man does something he shouldn't."

He looked at me hard and I realized I'd pretty much just accused him of murder. It's a special knack I have, a secret weapon to accuse suspects of murder, hoping they'll just confess. It worked more often than not for Agatha Christie. In the noirs though, a confession was usually followed by a gunfight, not a cup of tea. The real world was more noir.

"I looked for Kimmy that night," he said. "When I couldn't find her at the fair, I came back here and made a cache to take my mind off things. I'd just gotten those new coins you saw. I like to plant them before storms so the rain will wash away tracks and help hide it. I did that. Afterward I came home to my Kentucky friend and drank to blackout. I woke up the next morning soaked in foxhole 2A."

"Do you black out a lot when drinking?"

"When I over drink, yes."

"A lot then?"

"Yes."

"Kimmy ever show up that night?"

"She was in bed when I went inside."

His hand went to his side again. I changed directions.

"How much gold do you put in a cache?"

"Thirty Krugerrands. Why?"

I pulled out my tile to calculate how much that was worth, but it was covered in toothpaste.

"So about fifty thousand fiat dollars' worth?"

"A little less, but thirty coins is about the weight limit."

"How many of these have you buried?"

"Why do you want to know?"

"Curious."

"Fifteen. No, closer to twenty."

"So nearly a million dollars worth of coins buried in the hills? Man, you are rich."

"What else is money for?"

My mouth hung open. I gagged on a fly.

"I'm not as rich as I used to be," he said. "I think I have to pull back. The world isn't ending as fast as I thought it would."

"Never does."

"Yeah."

We ate in silence for a little while. Squirrels came near, and Rawly tossed them ears of corn. He'd made extra, and it looked like this was why. The squirrels nummied them down.

"Not to be too nosy, Rawly, but do you think, maybe, during your blackout you went and killed the hermit up at the little medicine wheel?"

He didn't blanch or react.

"Tony, my gun was empty when I woke up," he said. "I didn't see any shell casings in the hole. I must have fired them somewhere else."

"Huh."

"I don't remember doing anything," he said. "But I don't remember not doing anything either. The Kimmy situation has been on my mind lately. I..." He trailed off and took another stiff drink from his flask before offering it again to me.

I waved it off. "Do you know about the little medicine wheel?"

"Yeah. I go there sometimes to think. As a matter of fact, the cache I buried that night is on the trail that leads to it."

"Huh," I said. "Would Kimmy have a reason to kill Dasher?"

"She's not the jealous type."

"Any other reason?"

"I don't think so. You think she—"

"She's just someone else I don't have an alibi for."

"She wouldn't hurt a...harm...physically injure anyone unless that was what they were into. I don't think."

"She's low on the list," I said, and ate some fruit.

"And I'm high." It was a statement, not a question.

I had a near confession, or at least a declaration of no alibi with motive and means. Usually that goes pretty far to hooking people up to an electric chair. Most cops don't get that much. Still, Rawly didn't strike me as a killer. People are different when drinking, but not that different. He was getting drunk now, and though his hand had several times dropped to his gun, I still didn't pick him for it. He struck me as a lonely, desperate, unhappy man with a ridiculously unfaithful wife. That assessment didn't point to innocence, I realized, the opposite in fact. But still.

"How far is the little medicine wheel from here?"

"By vehicle, about twenty minutes."

"Walking?"

"An hour."

"Did you use a vehicle to get up there to bury your cache?"

"Yes."

"Did you see anyone up there?"

"I had been drinking, but I don't think so. I was on personal autopilot, I guess. If I think anyone's around, I don't cache. They've got to be secret. Only I know where they are."

"Okay."

"But I was drinking."

"You blacked out?"

"Maybe a little."

He returned to his beer, finished it, and started another. He then ate steak, which I took as a good sign. "I'm pretty careful when I go out and bury," he said. "I'm on the lookout."

"Paranoid?"

"Yes. I mean no. Careful. It's just that I'm on high alert, and sometimes I think I hear or see things because I'm so jacked."

"What do you think you saw or heard that night?"

"I thought I heard singing at one point."

"Like a radio?"

"It was probably just the storm. The wind was blowing. If it was singing, it could have come from anywhere on the wind. Most likely my mind. There're echoes up there, and I often think I hear other vehicles. Usually I imagine someone following me. Maybe I am paranoid. It's why I get off and walk a good ways off the trail first."

"Did you hear other vehicles that night?"

"I thought I did."

"Big? Little?"

"In the wind I thought I heard everything, but there for a while I thought I heard an ATV, but again where it was coming from, or if it was real, I don't know. After I stopped I didn't hear it again."

"Did you hear any gunshots?"

"Not to call them that. The rain hit just as I finished up and I was heading down the trail, hoping it wouldn't get too muddy. The lighting and thunder were pretty loud, and the fireworks from the fair carried over the wind sometimes."

"You saw the fireworks?"

"Some of them, coming down from the trail."

I took a big bite of steak. "You really have a talent for these," I said. "A real talent."

"Thanks, Tony."

"Anything else you can tell me?"

"Like what?"

"Distant lights? UFOs? Tracks?"

"Might have seen lights out past Jayger's place."

"What kind of lights?"

"Lit ones."

"Headlights? Flashlights? Fireworks?"

"Could have been a lightning flash in a puddle. I just glimpsed it as I turned onto the road."

"Is that road used much?"

"Not really. Jayger uses it sometimes, I'm sure. He comes and goes and doesn't pass my property."

"How do you know that?"

"I have surveillance cameras pointed onto the road."

"Shit. Why didn't you tell me before?"

"Why?"

"Can I see the tapes from that night?" I love technology. "Oh. No. Wait. I'm not sure I can. I made a promise."

"You can't. I don't keep tapes."

"Well, I'm off the hook, then."

"What hook?"

I told Rawly about the deal to go technology free at Perry's cabin. Then I told him about Perry and the gang, and stuff he really didn't need to know about, like how I was worried this one pimple was turning into a hemorrhoid, and how vodka and sticks actually isn't a terrible combination when the alternative is giardia and catalog paper.

"Everything is technology," Rawly said, leaning back. The food was all gone and the sky was dipping into ambers and pinks. The sky really is pretty in Wyoming. "Does that mean you can't use a fork?" he asked.

"No electric technology."

"No lights?"

"Nothing with personal electronics."

"Your ATV has a computer in it."

"Don't say that."

"It does."

"I guess computer screens are the thing I can't have. And running water or flushing toilets. Hell, I don't know. My friends have already given up. They're staying in the Shady Tree Inn."

"I hate that place," he growled.

I could guess why. "So far, though, it hasn't been so bad."

"You have a brick in your pocket. That isn't bad?"

"I'm keeping busy."

"Hi, honey!" It was Kimmy walking up to the house. She was coming from the main road, but I hadn't heard a vehicle. "Who's your friend?"

"It's Tony Flaner, remember, dear?" He stood up and blushed.

"Oh, you. You're the detective looking for Dash's killer."

"You've heard?"

"The whole town is talking about it."

"The whole town?" said Rawly.

"Nice place you have here," I said.

"I'm tired. I think I'll go to bed early," she said.

"Where've you been?" I asked. I didn't think Rawly was going to.

"I was hanging out with my new friends."

"New friends?" Rawly's ears were red.

"Calm down, honey. It's not what you think."

"It's not?" he said. "What could I have been thinking?"

"I love you, shnookums," she said.

Rawly smiled.

"I spent the day with Maxine."

"Who?"

"Maxine Cromby. They're staying at the campground."

"Rich people," I said to Rawly. He didn't seem to care.

"We drove around in that fabulous little sports car and went to an Indian casino. I won five hundred dollars at Roulette."

"Good for you," I said.

"But I lost eight at cards. Cards are hard."

"How'd Maxine do?"

"About the same."

"Did you have dinner?" asked Rawly.

"We ate at the casino."

"Okay."

"I might have a nightcap, though," she said, enjoying me with bedroom eyes.

"I gotta go," I said. "My friends will be worried."

"They aren't," she said. "I saw them at the casino."

"Sonova..."

"But the sheriff is looking for you."

"Why?"

"He didn't say."

"The sheriff?" asked Rawly. "He was at the casino?"

"No, he pulled us over for speeding through Floyd. The town's so small it's easy to forget it's there."

"Forget it's there," echoed Rawly as if in a trance.

"The sheriff really is a nice man," she went on. "He let us off."

"He wasn't so kind to me," I said.

"I know him better than you do."

"Where were you the night of the murder?" I asked.

"Tony!" said Rawly in full defensive mode.

"It's okay, James," said Kimmy, eating some watermelon. "I was at the fair and got a ride home afterward. I couldn't find you, sweetie."

"Uh, okay," he said.

"I'm going in. The mosquitoes are coming out."

She crossed to the sliding door.

"Who drove you back?" I asked as she got there.

"Checking up on my alibi, Sherlock?"

Rawly scowled at me.

"Yeah. Sure, why not?"

"I have an excellent alibi," she said. "Sheriff Carter drove me home that night."

28

I LEFT RAWLY to ponder his wife in his camouflaged rambler.

"Take the front road," he said. "It's easier than the back way. The code on the gate is 1234."

"Thanks."

I let myself out.

It was late evening, becoming night. I turned on the lights and, staying on the shoulder, navigated my way through insect abdomens and pollen-stuck beetle guts. I kept slow to limit the new additions and not to miss the turn-off.

Of course I missed it. Of course.

I turned around in the campground; that's how I realized I'd missed the turn. I thought of checking on the Crombys. I still had questions for them but thought better of it when I remembered Bunny's little gun and big bloodlust.

Under a light post in the corner I pulled up next to the dumpster and rearranged the contents of my pockets. I still had the little gun and my tile. I had a toothbrush and toothpaste but an empty tube. I scooped it out as best I could, and flicked my fingers like expelling boogers into the dumpster.

Dumpsters are a detective's best friend. That should tell you something about the job. A sign above the big smelly metal box stated that it was 'Okay to put fish guts and roadkill in here.' How very Wyoming.

Out of habit I poked around in there, noting half a dozen white kitchen garbage bags and as many industrial black ones. Some greasy bags of takeout were there, along with some spent sparklers from the Fourth. I pushed bags around and got a smell of old garbage, marinara and garlic. A melon rind. Fish guts. Icky, but not as bad as it could have been. I remembered the Crombys' can of gore and was glad they were holding onto that, at least for now. This can stank; theirs was malodorous. No, that makes it sound civilized. It was reeking. Yes, that's it. Reeking—reeking of greasy grimy gopher guts and goobers of gunk. Never had a grade school insult been so apt in one of my cases.

I dragged my fingers across the edge to scrape the last of the toothpaste off and instantly regretted it. In the amber light of the streetlamp, I saw bugs stuck to my fingers.

A quick jog to my favorite cinder block toilet and ten minutes with a powder hand soap, I was ready to relieve myself of some of Rawly's good beer.

As I was turning to leave, I heard someone driving down the road. I peeked out and saw Penn Cromby and his little monster Terrance pass by on their camouflaged four-seater. At least I think that's what they were in.

They pulled up to their campsite where they were met by Lynson, who helped Penn squeeze out of his seat while the terror hopped out himself and spilled red tubes from his pockets. He glanced at them, said something to Penn who said something to Lynson and then trotted out of sight around the camper followed by Penn, who carried a heavy burlap sack. Lynson watched them go and then picked up what Terrance had dropped.

It was far away, but I was pretty sure they were shotgun shells. About eight of them. Lynson picked them up and dropped them into the ATV before getting in himself and parking it.

I thought of going over there and saying hi, doing the detective thing, but I figured my friends would be worried about me. How their nerves must have been shattered when they didn't find me at the casino.

I trotted over to my ATV, got on and was about to start it up when Sheriff Carter pulled his big cop SUV into the campground. Though I was lit like the exorcist under the lamp, he didn't see me, and I watched him cruise up to the Crombys' site and stop. He got out, stretched, and walked behind the super camper, where I lost sight of him and interest.

Figuring I'd find out later what Carter was doing with the rich folk, I left. As I was getting onto the highway, I saw Gail watching me from her porch. I waved. She didn't.

I couldn't help feeling that she was mad at me. Oh, yeah. The attempted flirtation thing.

Back on the highway I drove the shoulder slowly until I found the secret turn-off to Perry's cabin and followed it through the dark forest, seeing Grimm wolves out of the corners of my eyes.

Turning the last bend, I saw the cabin lit up in real electric lights. I saw the white Cadillac parked in front and a low-profile red convertible next to it. Laughter and music leaked out of the windows. It made we wonder if the cabin would stand up against a nerve gas attack. Such had been my afternoon.

"Look who decided to come back," said Standard, raising up a red plastic cup in toast.

"I hope you didn't miss me," said I.

"Who?" said Dara.

"We figured you were out sleuthing," said Perry.

"A before-dawn stakeout," added Garrett. Critter wasn't with him. But Maxine Cromby was. She had a red Solo cup of her own and raised it to her lips. A smoldering cigarette was pinched between her fingers.

"Actually, it was well past dawn when I got up. Late morning, in fact," I said. "You guys are just lazy."

"It's the clean mountain air," said Standard. "It's so refreshing."

Maxine blew a cloud of blue smoke into the center of the room.

Perry brought me a cup from the kitchen. Blended margaritas in red plastic.

I found a seat on a lawn chair where I could see the fire and join the gang.

"We went to the casino for something to do," said Dara. "Since you didn't want our help."

"I heard."

"How?"

"I'm a detective."

She scowled.

"That's where we hooked up," said Maxine. "I'm Maxine Cromby."

"I know who you are and where you met my friends." It came out kind of ominously, and she pulled back a bit, sipped and smoked.

"Kimmy was there," said Garrett.

"I know that too."

"Stop it," said Dara. "Don't be a prick."

"Can't help it," said Perry. "It's one of his ways."

"He has a lot of ways," agreed Garrett.

"I was just down at the campground," I said to Maxine. "Penn and Terror are back."

"Terror?" said Perry.

"He means Terrance," said Maxine. She was on a new lounger that wasn't there that morning, the kind of thing you see orbiting Vegas pools. Someone had draped a towel over the back. "A spawn of one of Penn's earlier marriages," she said.

"Is Bunny yours?" I asked.

"Hell no." I could see her cheeks flush but couldn't tell if it was the alcohol or the accusation. "I'm done having kids."

"How many—"

"None," she said. "Not for me."

She was maybe thirty years old, at least two decades behind Penn. She was strikingly handsome; not beautiful, not soft, but sculpted and sure, the kind of attractiveness that lasts a long time even if weight comes, which hadn't introduced itself to her yet. She had dishwater blonde hair, keen blue eyes, and wore her blush well. Though I had rattled her, she recovered quickly with a self-confidence we stand-up comics spend our lives trying to fake.

"So how goes the sleuthing?" asked Perry. "Find out anything useful, or did you waste your day?" He threw a look at Dara, who snarled back at him.

"I actually made a surprisingly lot of headway," I said.

"What did you find out?" said Maxine.

"Stuff. Not sure where it all goes, but stuff. Okay, I know where some of it goes, but mostly just stuff."

"Is that an answer?"

"It's one of his ways," said Garrett.

"Where were you when the killing happened?" I asked Maxine.

"I was back in the RV having vodka."

"Can anyone vouch for you?"

"Yes, but why the hell would I want to kill a hobo?"

"A hermit."

"Oh, well now it makes sense," she said.

I began to like her.

"What do you know about it?"

"I got the generator working," said Standard. "It was a—"

"Shhhh," I said. "Grownups are talking."

He sulked.

"I know nothing about it," Maxine said.

"Even hearsay?"

She finished her cup and shook it. Standard rushed over to her and took it back to the kitchen for refills. I heard the sound of a blender breaking ice.

"I heard about it the morning after when the sheriff came by the campground. Gail, Miss Larsen, called all the campers together, and he asked us questions and told us about the killing."

"Did you ever see the hermit?"

"No. Where would I?"

"He was lurking around the campground before he was killed."

She shook her head.

"Would you know him to look at him?" asked Standard. He seemed to be a little smitten by the woman.

"How would I?"

"He was naked all the time and had the longest dick I've ever seen that wasn't CG," said Perry.

"There was that," said Dara.

"Let me try to remember. No, I saw no such thing."

"But you did know about him before the sheriff told you," I said.

"How would I?"

"The video tape from the library," I said.

I'd surprised her.

"You *are* a detective."

"It's another of his ways."

"Have you seen the video?" she asked. "It's only like three minutes long."

"I haven't," I told her. "But I'm interested."

"Penn had heard about him." She tasted the drink Standard had given her. "It's probably the main reason we're here."

"Go on."

"The video doesn't show much," she said. "Blurry picture of a naked guy far away. Reminded me of the Bigfoot footage from the '70s. Remember that?"

I glanced at Perry, who was about to launch into one of his Bigfoot conspiracy theories that experience had taught me would take the rest of the evening to complete. I waved him off it with both hands, holding my cup in my teeth.

"I remember it," said Standard.

"Still," said Maxine, stubbing out her cigarette, "he looked familiar."

"Yeah?" I said.

"But everyone does lately," she said. "I told Kimmy—you know her, right?"

"Not as well as some," I said. Garrett blushed.

"I think I met her and her husband once, but I can't be sure."

"Where?"

She shrugged. "Might have been a lot of places. James and Penn are in the same line."

"Bunkers?"

"Venture capitalists. We could have crossed paths a thousand ways."

"That's interesting," I said.

"And the hermit looked familiar. And Mrs. Larsen at the campground, and frankly you too. Have we met?"

"I'd have remembered."

"No you wouldn't," Dara said. "You've forgotten so much shit."

"It's one of his ways."

"Are we going to do s'mores or not?" asked Perry.

"S'mores?"

Perry ran to the kitchen and returned with an armful of stuff.

"You said Penn was back?" said Maxine.

I nodded. "They were camouflaged, but they made the mistake of moving."

She laughed.

"How was the casino?"

"A long ways away and not that fun," said Garrett.

"Seen one casino, you've seen them all," said Perry.

"He wouldn't shut up about the odds on everything," said Dara. "Kind of ruined the spirit."

"I really despise all the new computer games," Perry said. "Slots are computerized, but now also craps. What was wrong with an old-fashioned craps table with dice you can throw? Now it's all place bets on a screen around some plastic cylinder and push a button and the dice bounce."

"Seemed pretty efficient to me," said Standard.

"How can you be sure the game isn't rigged?"

"The dice are real," said Garrett. "Big and untouchable, but real."

"Isn't that suspicious?"

"Just trying to cut down on trained personnel," said Dara. "Same reason they only had a couple of live tables and acres of slots. More money, less overhead."

"I can't imagine it would be fun to play craps by pushing a button," I said. "Are you supposed to blow on the screen? All the charm is gone."

"It's the new thing," said Maxine. "Once people get used to it, they'll forget about the good ways, the party atmosphere, the people, the feel of the felt."

Her phone came to life in her pocket, a bubbly chirpy sound. "That's Penn." She quickly slammed the rest of her drink, shook off a freeze headache we could all sympathize with, and answered the call.

"Hi honey," she said with one eye closed. "How was...sight-seeing?"

"Eight? Nice," she said. "I'm hanging out with Kimmy's neighbors I met at the casino. They're nice...no, I'm good to drive...twenty minutes...no, go ahead and put them to bed. Kisses."

She ended the call and shook her cup for a refill. "No ice this time."

Standard fetched it and ran to the kitchen. Perry stuck marshmallows on an unspooled wire coat hanger and passed it to me.

"How'd he sound?" I said to Maxine as Standard came back.

"Who? Penn? Fine. Why?"

"Just wondering if he seemed nervous or upset."

She raised an eyebrow at me. "Why would he?"

"Eight," I said.

"No," said she with a worried look. "He sounded fine."

29

AFTER MAXINE LEFT, we ate the s'mores and all agreed that they were good but possibly the worst accompaniment to margaritas on the planet.

They told me about the casino trip, how it was lame until they met Maxine and Kimmy.

"They gambled real money, so we just watched," explained Standard.

"But it was exciting," said Garrett. "Smelled bad, though. No drinking but smoking, oh so much smoking."

"Like us, they were bored as all hell," said Dara. "Tell us you've got something for us to do tomorrow."

"Me? Since when am I the camp counselor?"

"More like a tour guide," explained Perry. "You and me are the only ones who actually have something to do."

"What do you have to do?"

"Get this place going."

"We stocked up the kitchen," said Standard. "It's pretty good now. We have provisions for a week. Longer if we can live on alcohol. Then probably a month or two."

Garrett nodded.

"Where's Critter?" I asked.

"I left him in the room."

"He was sassing Garrett about Kimmy," said Garrett. "Got a little ugly in the car."

"Do tell."

"Don't," said Garrett.

"Do," I insisted.

"Kimmy gave Garrett the cold shoulder at the casino. She had eyes on this big Amerindian fellow and hardly gave our lover friend a glance."

"We're just friends," he said.

"Critter told Garrett to get over it, that it was fun while it lasted, but it was over. C'est l'amour, c'est la vie."

"He said that?"

"Critter is very international," said Garrett.

"C'est la guerre," said Standard.

We gave him the required look.

"Kimmy is a modern gal," explained Garrett.

"What does that mean? A suffragette? She uses the pill?"

"Strange how modern gal sounds old and dated," said Dara. "Really. And don't call women gals. It's demeaning."

"I mean, she's a girl who—woman, she's a woman—who has a very progressive view of sex."

"You boys have to learn some manners," she said.

"Men," said Standard.

"Oh, really?"

"She explained it to me," said Garrett. "She made the rules clear. Our friendship was not romantic."

"Oh?" we all said.

"No. Not like that. We were friends...I can't say it."

"With benefits?"

"Yes."

"But not really friends?" said Perry.

"No, not really. It was all about the benefits. She's devoted to her husband."

"She has a shit way of showing it," I said, remembering Rawly's near apoplexy.

"I think she does, though. She just likes her...hobbies. Yeah, that's it. He has his hobbies and she has hers. I shouldn't have been surprised that she was like she was at the casino."

"Playing with fire," I said. "Rawly doesn't like her hobby."

"How do you know?"

"Didn't I say? I spent the afternoon with him. He has a great compound. Ready for zombies and the end of days. He also makes a mean steak. We talked. I think he's lonely."

"I wonder why," said Dara.

"He's an old-fashioned guy," said Perry. "Times, they are a'changing."

I shrugged. "I think they changed and then changed back. Infidelity—I mean *hobbying*—is not the fashion these days."

"Everything old is new again? How's that?" said Perry.

"I say, let grown-ups do what grown-ups do," said Garrett with not a lot of conviction. "It's a victimless crime."

"Tell that to Rawly," I said, and wondered if I couldn't include Dasher in that statement. Had Kimmy's hobby led to his death?

"Maybe the s'mores aren't so bad," said Perry.

"They suck," I said. "Give me another."

I told the gang about my adventures that day while crunching crackers and squirting melted chocolate onto my shirt. Perry was very interested in hearing about Rawly's and Varg's layouts.

"Rawly will give you the tour, I'm sure," I said. "I didn't get a good look at Varg's for obvious reasons."

"He sounds like a psycho."

"Sounds?"

"Maybe we don't want to help you tomorrow, after all," said Standard. "I thought I might go for a nature walk and write some poetry."

"God help us," said Dara.

"What are your plans tomorrow, Tony?" asked Perry.

"I'll decide tomorrow. It's never a good idea to be too prepared."

———

Once again, I was the first one up in the morning. Impressed at my gumption, I checked my tile to see what time it was to later brag and had to content myself with noting it was after sunup and before sundown. Probably closer to the former.

The gang had bought boxes of Pop-Tarts so I had breakfast. The toaster even worked. I found two kinds of orange juice and energy drinks in the full cold fridge. There were paper plates and red plastic cups and a supply of liquor Dean Martin would approve of. There were also four super coolers full of ice, three regular and one the dry CO_2 kind. There was a tower of bottled water pallets still in plastic shrouds.

Boonies these were, but the crisp morning country air had something to recommend it. I brewed a pot of coffee and had two cups but couldn't really get my day started without a shower. It was habit and I looked forward to the trip down to the campground. I grabbed a wad of paper towels and washed my visor with a bottle of Evian. It got the big things off and smeared the rest into a nice translucent oily sheen. I'd need something stronger. Maybe vodka. I'd ask Gail if she had something when I got to the Crazy Woman.

The sun was bright but clouds crossed its path enough to make warm and cold spots. I'm pretty sure it was sunshine and not pee, but I couldn't be sure. Animals had made the trail their toilet. A cow, if I could guess a pie without cutting it, and antelope pellets, if I could believe Carter. The best thing about them is that neither species is carnivorous. The air was only spiced, not polluted by the organic additions to the road.

It was a Sunday, as near as I could reckon without data, and I expected the highway to be vacated the way some Utah towns roll up their streets on that day. I was mistaken. The highway was very busy with a steady stream of campers driving south. The end of the long weekend, Fourth of July week. Good time to burn some PTO and get a vacation in.

I stayed on the shoulder keeping below my illicit twenty-four miles per hour and made the campground without being killed *Easy Rider* style or run off the road like in *Duel*.

Gail had fewer guests than the day before. Early risers leaving early. The Crombys' enclosure was still there and a bunch of those silver bullet Airstreams with Cold War nostalgia. I don't know if Airstream had just kept the same design from the age of Ricky and Lucy or if they were just the toughest damn campers ever built by man and had weathered the decades in glistening aluminum shells. In any event, they were there in some quantity still doing what they did. Maybe they'd all been gutted for a voice-actuated smart camper that could make martinis like the Jetsons' maid, or maybe they were all wool socks and pull-out bunks, but I had to admit there was something timeless about them.

I still didn't have a towel and I was in the same dirty clothes as yesterday, which were now dirtier from the shoulder ride and passing eighty-mile per hour wind gusts. The bugs, however, were noticeably lighter, maybe for the gusts, or maybe having been thinned out by the windshields of passing tourists.

I pulled past the office and dumpster and straight to the toilet. (Coffee.) After that, I went for my morning shower.

When I came out, applying my dirty clothes on my wet body—putting them on just isn't the right description—I found Deputy Sheriff Carter waiting for me. He was leaning against his cop SUV, legs and arms crossed, hat tilted like he was examining his belt buckle, which was silver and etched, or maybe his boots, which were lizard leather, heeled and of the cowboy variety.

"Posing for a Marlboro ad?" I asked.

"Listen, Flaner," he began.

"Don't go there," I said. "We're alone."

"I wasn't sure if anyone else was in there," he said, glancing at the shower. "How goes it?"

"Making progress. Got an alibi for one suspect."

"Who?"

"You," I said. "I talked to Kimmy."

"What did she say?"

"She said you gave her a ride home from the fair."

"Yes. I did that."

We let the moment hang in the air like a bad smell.

"I came to give you something." He offered me a plastic grocery sack. "I heard you were looking for these."

"What is it?"

He dug in the bag and handed me a tape. "The video report of the hermit," he said.

"What are all these other books?"

"The Crombys' other library stuff. I told them I'd take them back for them."

"Mind if I keep them for a while?"

"Why?"

"There's no TV at Perry's place."

"I'll need them back. Mrs. Severe will be furious if we lose them."

"You were talking to her, huh?"

"Small town."

"Thanks for running it out."

"I have some news," he said. "But first, I have to ask you something."

"What?"

"Did you kick the mayor in the balls?"

"The mayor?"

He nodded. "On the sidewalk up Stubbins Street?"

"That was the mayor?"

"Oh god." He put his hand to his forehead.

"He started it."

"How?"

"He hit me and literally pushed my button."

"Why would he do that?"

"He's an asshole?"

"That still doesn't explain it."

"It kind of does," I said. "Also he was angry that I ruined his rodeo show."

"That was you?"

"You heard about that?"

"I heard about that."

"The mayor's a little pissant for running and telling you. Tell him I said that."

"Should I also mention to him that snitches get stitches?"

"Would that work on him?"

Carter shook his head. "Flaner, tell me you'll have this thing wrapped up by tomorrow."

"I doubt it. Why? What's tomorrow?"

"A work day."

"Why would the mayor get so upset about a little environmental heckling?"

"I don't know. You should ask him."

"I'm asking you, Craig. You want this done fast, cover my ass and tell me what I need to know. And don't lie because—"

"You'll know it?"

"No. Because it'll hurt my feelings if I find out later."

A sharp pop came from the Crombys' campground.

Carter and I shared a glance that direction. "Gunshot?"

He nodded and turned to go, but just then Lynson ran out into the road. "All good," he said to anyone within earshot. Seeing the sheriff, he added, "Accident. Nobody hurt."

"A menace," he said.

"The mayor?"

"He's a politician."

"So?"

"So, this is Wyoming. We have resources and that means jobs."

"It means other stuff, too, but let's not think beyond the county."

"There's a ballot to open the park up for exploration."

"Does no one here read Naomi Klein?"

"Who?"

"Modern-day Cassandra."

"Who?"

"Never mind. Why take it so personally?" I said. "Talking about the mayor, not Naomi. I get why she's pissed."

"It's his job."

"Not like that," I said. "He has an interest in this. A corrupt, polluting personal interest. What party is he? Wait. I already know."

"I'll hold him off if I can," said Carter. "But you better not go around saying he's corrupt like that. It won't help your case or your health."

"Et tu, Carter?"

"I have to live here."

"Fine," I said. "Want to see this with me? Gail—Miss Larsen—has a VCR player. How gauche."

"Sure."

We walked up the gravel road to the office. I wanted to drive, but legs worked too.

"I got some reports back," Carter said.

"Yeah?" Our feet joined in a crunching gravel cadence. Another shot rang out from the Crombys' place. We turned and looked. A second or two later, Lynson was out again as before. "Another misfire!" he said. "All good." He didn't sound convinced.

"What did the autopsy report say?"

He reached into his shirt pocket, took out a folded piece of paper and opened it. He stopped and squinted. "Death by gunshots."

"Modern science—is there anything it can't do?"

"Yeah, pretty obvious."

"Anything else of interest?" We were close enough to the office that I could smell coffee.

"Nothing."

"Let me see it."

"I can't."

"Why not?"

He put it back in his pocket.

"You're not allowed to see it."

"Pretty pretty pretty please?"

"I can't."

"I won't kick the mayor in the marbles again if you let me read it."

"You wouldn't understand it."

"Do you?"

"Not all of it."

"I'll take my chances."

"Fine." He pulled a folded paper out and offered it to me. When he saw Gail on the porch he added, "Here it is, you meddlesome outsider. And you better be out of here by tomorrow."

"Because it's a work day?"

"That, and there's something else."

"Hey, Gail," I said. "Coffee smells great. Mind if I get some and watch a movie in your front room?"

Her face went from unreadable, to shocked, to smirking, to laughing. "You are something else, Mr. Flaner."

"Call me Tony."

"Oh, now it's Tony?"

"It always was."

"You got the tape, I see," she said, seeing the tape in my hand. "Sure, come in."

I turned to Carter, who wore an overdone scowl.

"Gail's good people. Cut the act."

He glanced at Gail. She smiled.

"So?"

"So what?"

"And they say millennials have short attention spans. What else is happening tomorrow?"

We went inside. I put the tape on the coffee table and marched straight into the kitchen. Carter paused and wiped his feet.

"The body's being taken," said Carter

I called from the kitchen, "Where are the mugs?"

"By the sink."

I filled three, looped them among my fingers, and put them on the aptly named coffee table.

Gail was fiddling with the VCR.

"Taken where?" I said.

"For burial. Someone's coming to get it."

"No kidding. Who claimed it?"

He shook his head.

"Come on," I said.

"I don't know."

"Could it be a medical college or something?" asked Gail. "Looking for cadavers?"

"No," he said, taking off his hat. "I'm told it's kinsfolk."

"Kinsfolk?" I said, tasting the word. "Well, fer tarnation!"

30

COWBOY, as a dialect, must have its roots in the Appalachian Mountains. Or maybe the other way around. I can't hear a word like "kinfolk" and not think of a long-bearded, overall-wearing, corncob sucking, bent-backed hick tending a still with a rifle close at hand ready to shoot varmints and Hatfields, which he'd swear were the same thing. I blame stereotyping cartoons or maybe the play *Li'l Abner* for my messed-up view of the Eastern Mountains. *Li'l Abner* started as a comic, which is like a cartoon, so there's that. One day I'll have to visit and see if I'm wrong.

"Ready to go," said Gail as the tape slid into the archaic machine.

"You've seen this, right?" I said.

"Three years ago when it came out. It was picked up by the wire searches and shown in countless places, not just Wyoming."

"It's what put us on the map," said Carter.

Gail offered me the remote.

"I can't," I said.

"You don't want to see it?"

"No. I can't push the button. I'm on the wagon."

"Seriously?"

"You push it."

Gail and Carter shared a glance at my expense. I'd already won whatever bragging was available with my friends, but I was also enjoying the challenge of the no-tech investigation.

"Really?" said Carter with some passion. "You're doing this with one— no, *two* hands tied behind your back? That's not why I hired you. Half-ass work may be the norm where you're from, but up here, we expect a little more from employees."

"Half-ass is my style."

He didn't look placated by my astute personal observation.

Gail bailed me out and pushed the button.

"In an isolated county of Wyoming, there is a new neighbor," said a disembodied voice over a view of the park mesa. It paused for a slow pan of the view, browns and greens, blue sky. A cloud all in bright neon colors.

Cut to an older woman with a scarf on her head and a microphone to her worried face, labeled 'Concerned Citizen.' *"It's scary now,"* she said. *"No one knows what's going on or what it's all about."*

A man in a cowboy hat and bolo tie, with eyebrows you could store nuts in, named 'Local Resident' said, *"It's crazy. Insanity, that's what it is."*

Another man, older, no hat, but a fine graying beard, 'Local Rancher' said only, *"Indecent."*

Cut to a reporter in a windbreaker with a forest behind him, 'On the Spot Dan Locum.' *"The strange new neighbor isn't a critter, it's a man."*

"The law's been too slow to stop this foolishness," said Concerned Citizen. *"He don't always wear clothes."*

I glanced at Carter. "He used to wear clothes more than he did at the end," he explained.

"The man lives in the hills somewhere behind me," said the reporter, gesturing to a clump of trees that could be anywhere. *"He's called the Hermit of Big Horn County, and he's raising quite the ruckus."*

"He coined that name," said Carter. "No one said that before that reporter. We'd always just called him Dasher because he'd run away so quickly. The flasher came later."

"I seen him up on a hillside eating bugs," said 'Boy Who Saw Hermit.' *"He told me to keep my brain sharp. That's what he told me."*

"I think we started seeing him around a couple years ago," said Local Resident. *"He might have been around for years before that, but that's when people started talking about him."*

"He's a harmless eccentric," said 'Melanie Oprit, Visiting Tourist.' *"Seeing an actual old-fashioned hermit in this modern age was the highlight of our trip to Wyoming."*

"Word is getting out about the stranger in the woods, and people are coming just to try to get a peek at him," said a young Jack Mandel, 'Local Businessman.' *"It's good for business."*

"A visiting tourist captured this video of the elusive stranger."

The video showed a hillside below a guard-railed road. It zoomed in, and the shape of a man came into focus.

It was Dasher, but he wasn't the flasher. He wore ripped beige khaki shorts and green flip-flops. No shirt. Squatting, he was eating something off the ground, grubs or bugs maybe.

He looked up and saw he was being filmed. His expression was clear, confused, and wild. He stood up and I recognized the pose from the bullet-holed still image I'd seen in the Crombys' trash can. They'd used a screen-shot from this report as a target.

Dasher spoke, but it was garbled. He pointed to his head, gestured to the area, pointed up and then to his head again. He laughed, a big Santa Claus laugh with his hands on his tummy, rolling with waves of giggles. Suddenly he sped away as if spooked by something. Then he was gone.

"*Actual sightings of the hermit are sporadic but unnerving,*" On the Spot Dan Locum told us. "*The Hermit of Big Horn has combed the hillside and wandered the west for a while now. Some think he's dangerous, others just another part of the Old West in the tradition of mountain men and loners from the past.*"

"*I think he's dangerous,*" said Concerned Citizen adjusting her scarf.

"*He's kind of part of the Old West coming back,*" said Local Resident, his eye-bushes fluttering in a breeze. "*Like in the tradition of the mountain men and loners from the past.*"

"Now there's some reporting," I said. "Sourced his material right away."

"*Some say he's a menace,*" On the Spot Dan Locum.

Local Rancher: "*He's a menace.*"

"*Others say he's good for business.*"

Mandel, Local Businessman, saying, again, "*good for business.*"

"This went on the wire?"

"Slow news day," said Gail.

"*Whatever he's doing, whoever he is, he couldn't have chosen a more beautiful place to be a hermit in. This is On the Spot Dan Locum, reporting from Big Horn County, Wyoming.*"

The segment ended with the same slow pan of the mesa in the bright noon light.

"Rewind to the hermit," I said.

Gail pushed buttons.

"It was Melanie Oprit, Visiting Tourist's footage they showed," I said.

"How do you know it was her video?"

"She was the only person to be properly identified."

"Good catch," said Gail.

"Tech savvy," I said. "There. Pause it."

The tape showed the hermit in blurry waving lines, but I recognized him.

"So seven years," I said. "That's a long time to be hiding."

"I don't think he was hiding, just staying out of the way," said Carter.

"I think he was hiding," said Gail.

His eating off the ground bothered me, but the flip-flops and shorts confirmed a theory.

"Okay. I saw it," I said.

"What do you see?"

"I saw the hermit story and have to wonder at the state of reporting in this country."

"There was another guy who came around trying to get an interview," said Carter. "From a big network. I helped him try to locate Dasher."

"Where did you look?"

"Down around the southern point," he said. "There'd been some sightings there."

"Uh-huh."

"He gave up after a couple of days."

"Again, the poor state of journalism on display."

"Do you want to see it again?" asked Gail.

"No."

"And?" said Carter.

I shrugged.

"Well that was anticlimactic," said Carter. "I thought you'd bust it open from that."

"Are there other pictures of Dasher on the internet?"

Gail nodded.

"Wait," said Carter. "Is this about you not touching computers?"

"No. I mean, yes. I don't need to look for the answer if you can tell it to me. It's the heart of gathering clues. Enlist help, like witnesses and laboratories and such."

"Which reminds me," said Carter. "We got the ballistics back."

"And?"

"Three shots at close range. Any one of them would have killed him. The slugs were from a .357. That's a handgun caliber. Most likely a Magnum."

"Like this one?" I said, pulling the gun I'd found the day before out of my pocket.

"Not even close," said Carter. "That's a peashooter. What gunned down Dasher was a hand-cannon."

"Oh, um, okay."

"And that's a pistol. .357 Magnums are revolvers. Do you know the difference?"

"You have to fan a revolver?"

"God help us," said Craig.

Gail smirked.

"Let me see that," said Carter.

I handed him the gun.

"How'd it get dirt all in it? Is this toothpaste?"

I'd switched it to the other pocket before a proper laundering. "So that's not the gun that killed Dasher?" I said to change the subject.

"No. This looks like Beaumont Dean's little pocket gun. He's always losing that. Where'd you get it?"

"I found it near Beaumont Dean," I said. "I think I'll take it back to him."

"That'll be neighborly," said Gail.

"Ain't it, though?"

"There's more on the gun," said Carter. He took a sip of his coffee.

"Yes..."

"It was involved in another homicide."

"Really?" said Gail. "How would you know that?"

"Ballistics."

"I agree with Gail," I said. "How the hell could anyone know that by the bullets?"

"Ballistics."

"Of course. What was I thinking?"

"A man was killed with it in Casper."

"Where's that? Wyoming?"

"Yes, Wyoming," said Carter. "You're the detective."

"It's not far from here," said Gail. "Not far at all."

"A ways," said Carter. "But close, by Wyoming standards."

"Who was killed?"

"A witness who was supposed to testify against his brother for murder."

"What happened to the brother?"

"Ran after the killing but was apprehended last year. He's in jail now. Trial hasn't happened yet. Scheduled for October."

"In Casper?" I said.

"Wait, I remember this," said Gail. "It was a big deal. The killer was a truck driver and they think he might be a serial killer. Kyle Poole."

"Yeah, that's him. The brother would have testified to that," said Carter. "But the brother is dead."

"Killed with the same gun that killed Dasher?"

"Yep."

"Do they like Kyle Poole for the brother killing?"

"Of course."

"Could it have been hired out?"

"Doubt it," said Carter. "I talked to Casper. They've added the brother's murder to the list against Kyle. They have witnesses of him going into his brother's house, hearing an argument, a gunshot and then they saw him race away in a white pickup truck."

"At least it wasn't camouflaged," I said. "No, wait. White pickup in Wyoming? It was."

Gail laughed.

I said, "How many shots to kill the brother?"

"One."

"You sure?"

"Single shot. That's what they said. Why?"

"Dasher got a hat trick."

"And?"

"I dunno," I said. "On a hunch, um, would this big gun look anything like the big thing that Rick Grimes uses in *The Walking Dead*?"

"Yes."

"Could it be that easy?" I said out loud. "No. Still don't know why."

"What are you talking about?"

"There was a camper here; a guy called Boone. He had a gun like that. He rushed out of here the day after the shooting."

"No kidding?" said Carter.

"I'll get his information for you." Gail left for the office.

I said, "I'm going to keep poking around," and got up to leave. Gail came out with the reservation card and gave it to Carter.

Our eyes locked for an instant.

"And thank you, Gail," I said. "I really appreciate your hospitality. I...I mean...um." Carter was standing at the door waiting to go out with me. Outside, not like on a date. Or maybe he was, and I had missed the signals again. Shit.

"I'll see you later. Thanks for letting us use your antiquated but useful VCR."

"You're welcome."

I followed Carter to his police mobile while Gail met a new camper in front of the office.

Carter looked around suspiciously, maybe afraid of being seen with me.

"Are you afraid of being seen with me?"

"Hell yes."

"Hold up a second," I said. "I gotta ask you a question."

"Make it quick."

I unfolded the autopsy report and scanned it. Blood work was included. I smiled.

Carter climbed into his vehicle.

"I take it Dasher's lair was on the north side of the park," I said.

"Why do you say that?"

"Because you showed the reporter the south."

"What are you implying?"

"Someone was helping Dasher," I said. "Maybe more than one. But I know I got one right here."

"Flaner, you're not—"

"Flip-flops and shorts?" I said. "Where'd he get those?"

"He could have stolen them."

"Or someone could have given them to him."

"Wasn't me," he said.

"I think it was," I said. "And I think you were the one giving him antibiotics and vitamins."

"What?"

"The autopsy report showed an insane amount of antibiotics in his system and a dissolving multivitamin in his stomach."

"So?"

"So, I saw the meds in your glove box." To prove the point I reached in and cracked open the glove box. There were the gloves, lozenges, and pill bottles as before.

"They're for me, I have the…"

"Clap. I know."

"What? No."

"Carter—Craig. Clap, man. You have to tell me things I need to know. I have enough shitty witnesses to wade through here, I don't need another. I might actually solve this by tomorrow if you tell me everything."

He stared through me as if troubleshooting my *Matrix* code.

"I don't know where his lair is," he said. "But on the north side. At mile marker twenty-five, there's a turn-out. Beyond that there's a deer trail. If you follow it about a hundred yards, you'll see flat rock. I left things for him there sometimes."

"How often?"

"Every new moon."

"Did you talk to him?"

"No."

"I don't believe you."

"Well, not to talk." He started the engine. "He jabbered, and I couldn't get close to him."

"Do you know who he is—was?" I said.

"Why do you have to—"

"Come on!"

"It doesn't play into it," he said, finding a gear after several tries. "But I'll tell you one thing. Getting this thing closed by tomorrow would be a good idea."

"Because of the mayor. I know."

"You know some of it."

"I'm going to smack you," I said.

He looked around again. "The proposition about the coal that the mayor is all hot about includes his exclusive rights to the north part of the park where no one's looked before. It's kind of hidden in the section descriptions, but it's there."

"Dummy company?"

"Yep."

"And you're a shareholder too?"

He blinked and lost some color in his tan cheeks. He recovered himself. "Dasher in the north could have been a problem with that."

"Shit," I said. "You're giving me more suspects."

"No. It was Boone."

"The Black guy? You're going to pin it on the Black guy?"

"His gun."

"I gotta get to work."

"How about some more?"

"What?"

"I wasn't going to mention it, not until you got this work done."

"What?"

"But now that we have it solved, I guess I can tell you."

"What?"

"Another case."

"What?"

"I'll tell you."

"Can you talk like you don't have all day to tell me?"

"There're some tourists in town," he said. "An older couple."

"The Isaaks," I said.

He looked surprised. "Yes, that's them. They're staying in the Shady Tree Motel."

"A shady motel. Got it."

"They're looking for their son who they say went missing up here. I mentioned you, and they'd like to hire you to help."

I smiled.

"What?"

"You are the worst client I've ever had," I said.

He reached under his seat and fished out a green three-ring binder. "Here," he said, handing it to me.

"What's this?"

"It's the Isaaks' case."

"You're kidding."

"They're very organized."

"Could they be Dasher's kinsfolk?"

He shook his head.

"Are you certain?"

"They insisted on seeing his body. They saw it. It's not their son."

"Who'd they insist to?"

"Me."

"Worst. Client. Ever."

He was about to object but chose to go the scowl route instead. He sniffed at me and peeled out like the indignant cop he was, flinging dust and gravel into my freshly washed hair.

31

THE COVER of the binder was a wanted poster offering $5,000 for information on the whereabouts of Uri Isaaks, Ada and Sherman Isaaks' son.

The binder itself was a photo album scrapbook showing pictures of a little boy growing up. There were shots of little Uri as a baby, in pre-school, middle school, high school, junior college, college. Two Michigan driver's licenses when he was sixteen and twenty. Double checking my math, I figured him to be twenty-four now. Time for a new license. There were also prom portraits, vacation pictures and holiday photos of the Jewish persuasion with Uri wearing a yarmulke and locks as a young kid and just the yarmulke when he was older. In many pictures he stood with an older girl who looked to be his sister. In those pictures, she always looked happier than him while he looked scared. One showed her holding some kind of award, her parents glowing with pride while Uri wore a grin more forced than a Palestinian resettlement.

There were job evaluations and report cards. "Uri is a great sweeper." That from Mr. Thomsen at the French Baguette Bakery. "Uri's a man with great drive but is too eager and prone to taking shortcuts." Professor Haddim, New York University Stern School of Business. Uri's grades were good up until college, then they were hit and miss. Lots of C's showing up amid A's. He seemed to have an aversion to B's, not getting a single one. His final semesters showed a lot of STEM classes: Biology C, Chemistry A, Physics C, Calculus C. Remembering that C's get degrees, I assumed I was working through the usual pre-med array of weeder classes picked by an overachiever, but I saw he'd double-booked his hours with business. C's in Business Ethics and Business Law; A's in Entrepreneurial Speculation, Market Analysis and Venture Capitalism.

Another venture capitalist. Rawly, Cromby and now this guy. Big Horn County was thick with them. I've heard venture capitalism called "the new Wild West," so I guess it was appropriate.

I took a long look at the most recent pictures of Uri and put the folder into my bag of books with the VHS tape of the news story. Carter had really loaded me up with media.

Next, I pulled out my stolen maps and tried to figure out where the Double Dean Ranch was. Beaumont had pointed that-a-way, south of Floyd. There were a few suspicious roads feeding off the highway in that direction. I didn't think it would be hard to find.

I then studied the area where Carter had told me he'd left Easter eggs for Dasher the Flasher. I couldn't help feeling a little indignant. He'd come down on me for trying to uphold my sacred pledge to my noble—uh, no…useful? Trustworthy? Erstwhile? Photogenic? Hygienic? Nearby? That. My *nearby* friends and he was holding out on me. He'd mentioned four possible suspects while simultaneously ignoring the elephant in the cream, the goddamn mayor. Shady land schemes are as common a reason for murder in the American West as wills used to be in English country houses between the wars.

Tracing the mile markers, I found the place near a place called Miracle Canyon, which I seem to remember hearing before. The closest road was the highway, and no trails were indicated nearby. The tight contour lines suggested steepness if not an outright cliff before it turned into just a sloped canyon begging for toboggans and flash floods at the other end.

I put the bag of reading material under a bungee strap on the back of the ATV and squeezed into my helmet.

I headed south on the highway, eating dirt and bugs when it was too hot for the visor. I got to Floyd and figured I might as well check on the Isaaks. If I took the case, I wondered if I'd have to give Carter a percentage of my pay. Was it a manager rate of 20 percent, agent rate of 15 percent, or head-hunter of 10 percent? How about nothing? Nothing sounded right. The guy was on my nerves.

The Shady Tree Motel was not a new or attractive establishment. L-shaped with doors facing the parking lot, cars matching the rooms like accessories. Not many there. Only two. It had the charm of an abandoned strip mall, but it was the only show in town.

It was easy for me to find the Isaaks. Their Michigan-plated car was in front of room five. It was a nice car. A big Lexus. The thick layer of bug-kill on the grill and windshield couldn't hide that the car looked like money.

Peeling off my helmet, I forgot about my scream button but was reminded by a clumsy shift of it.

"What was that screaming?" Kimmy burst out of room four.

"Just me."

"Do you need a doctor?"

"Just a bump," I said.

"It looks worse than yesterday."

"You look about the same," I said. "I'm looking for the Isaaks. They're in room five, I think."

"They left a few minutes ago," said Kimmy. "Looking for a place to print posters."

I wondered which one of the pictures they'd choose. Remembering all the skinhead Nazi screws around, I had to hope it wasn't one with a yarmulke.

"Shouldn't you be in church?" I said.

She gave me a long look before saying, "Mind your own business."

"I like Rawly. He seems like a good guy. A fish out of water, a duck out of his depth, a moose on the highway, but he has a good heart. He gave up a lot to—"

"Don't lecture me."

"I guess I'm just old-fashioned."

"Puritanical? That old-fashioned?"

"You trying to tell me that fidelity is archaic and you're modern?"

She looked me over appraisingly. "Are you an educated man?"

"Don't even try to seduce me. I'm oblivious to it."

"Is that the right word?"

"For me? Yes."

"Don't flatter yourself."

"Don't flatter me because then I might get seduced."

"I asked you if you're educated."

"A decade of college," I said.

"This modernness you accuse me of is actually just a return to the natural state. There have been studies that suggest that the natural condition of human sexuality is orgies."

"Studies of skin mags?"

"Monogamy is a recent hangup, not the natural state of human sensuality. My modern outlook is actually older than your Puritan one."

"Sounds like you've used this speech before."

"Rawly understands."

"Does he?"

"We love each other."

"Weird way to show it."

"You're judging again. People come to Big Horn County to be left alone," she said. "Mind your own business. Leave us alone."

I held my hands up in surrender.

"So the Isaaks are gone?"

"Left half an hour ago."

A white pickup pulled into the parking lot. A tall, swarthy but not unhandsome Amerindian stepped out. Eagerness turned to hesitation as he saw me.

"I'll talk to them later," I said. "Have...whatever this is."

"Grow up," she said.

I left Kimmy and her casino catch to their Sunday morning exercise and headed south in search of the Double Dean Ranch.

I hadn't seen the south side of Floyd since we'd passed it coming in. It was a lot like the northern side: lots of low hills and plains and the occasional coven of trees here and there plotting something.

The tourist exodus to places more civilized continued as car after RV after boat after trailer barreled past me as I navigated the garbage collected on the shoulder. Food sacks, broken coolers, shards of blown-out tires and the hellish pee-bottles truckers throw out their windows when full. What the actual hell is that about? The dust wasn't bad, but the midday heat meant that only the laziest and stoutest bugs greased my helmet.

I know there's a thing about bugs disappearing in the world, a sign of the next big extinction where mankind plays a prominent and probably doomed role. I used to see bugs everywhere growing up. October particularly was a horror film when boxelder bugs swarmed the house. They can bite, by the way. Not so many bugs lately. A fly here and there, nary a grasshopper in town. A moth if you're lucky. June bugs left the suburbs. But northern Wyoming hadn't gotten the memo. I noticed about six mosquito bites when I showered that morning, doubtlessly acquired during the nice outdoor dinner with Rawly confirming my thinking that at best, the outdoors is a mixed bag.

I found the Double Dean about twenty minutes out of Floyd, so a ways. A gravel road wove off the left side of the highway where a shorter ways down a wooden arch over stretched it. Two parallel logs, as big around as Goodyear radials held what looked like the residue of a flash flood. Intertwined sticks and smaller logs, bones, a rustic plank declaring "Double Dean" in burned lettering hanging from two chains in the middle. Antlers ran up both posts as if warning away errant deer, elk, and antelope. Cows too. Maybe weasels. Trick-or-treaters. There was a cardboard 'Keep Out' sign tacked to one of the posts, which totally went against the aesthetics so I ignored it.

I drove under the arch of death a ways, maybe two, until I saw a cluster of buildings on the left and a fairly modest house to the right. I expected to see a meadow full of cattle, but I didn't. The house had some cottonwoods, some grass. The outbuildings had dirt and looked like deserted aircraft hangars.

I saw a white pickup by the outbuildings, with its Wyoming-required occupied rifle rack in the back window, a kind of rural bumper sticker. The house didn't look occupied.

Their horse must have already run off because the barn doors were closed. They were big enough to pull a semi-trailer through with room to spare on all sides. Luckily there was a human-sized door down a ways from that, next to a window and a laboring air conditioner.

I went in.

"What the hell do you think you're doing?"

I'd walked in on Roddy Dean. It was an office. He was behind a desk going over paperwork and he'd jumped like I'd caught him watching hentai in church.

"I wanted to talk to you about the hermit's murder," I said in a way that sounded police-like, authoritative, in command.

"Get out of here."

"You're a crotchety old coot," said I.

In my usual circle of acquaintants this would be seen as a stylistic observation, but in cow country, thems were fightin' words.

He stood up so fast he jostled the desk, dumping a dish of paperclips, a Rolodex and a glass paperweight with a scorpion in it to the floor.

I took a step back. "I've been hired to look into it," I said.

"Not by me."

I bent down to pick up the fallen things to be a nice guy. He glared.

"Get down to Cheyenne a lot?" I said.

"What is that supposed to mean?"

"Magnus Meats in Cheyenne. Do a lot of business with them?" I held up a business card that I'd fished out of the Rolodex under M.

"Sometimes." Roddy grabbed the card from me.

"What for?"

"To sell meat. I'm in the meat business, you ignoramus."

"We hardly know each other."

"I know your type well enough," he said. "You're from the city with all your city ways."

"Do you know what you sound like?"

"Putting ideas into folks' heads, undermining the fabric of society. That's you."

"I do what I can." I offered him a paperclip. He didn't want it.

"What's up with this scorpion?"

"I don't want you here," he said. "You're trespassing. There was a sign."

"That was serious? Oh, man. Do I feel dumb. I thought it had just blown onto an alter point like some tumbleweed."

Still standing, he opened a desk drawer.

"The sheriff…" I said to stop whatever he was doing.

He paused.

"Said you'd lost cattle to the hermit."

"Along with a lot of other folk."

"That means you had a reason to kill him. Rustling is punishable by hanging."

"That's actually not done anymore. It's serious, but not serious enough for lynching."

"So the law of the West has been replaced by the law of the land?"

He hesitated. Fidgeted. Dare I say, worried? It was a question all backward gazing cowboys struggled with. To lynch or not to lynch? Hereabouts, it was a tossup.

"Where were you when the hermit was killed?"

"None of your business."

"Do you own a gun?"

"I own lots of guns."

"Compensating. Figured."

His face went red.

"Not to belabor the point, but do you own a .357 Magnum?"

"I do."

"Oh. Really." I don't know why I was surprised.

"I own two of 'em. Here's one." From the drawer came a big-ass gun. It looked like the one Boone had, but this one wasn't shiny silver. It was gun-metal blue.

The door opened, and in came Beaumont just as Roddy pointed the barrel toward my chest.

"Dad, what are you doing?"

"Man asked to see my gun. I was obliging."

"He was expressing his 'small penis syndrome.'" That didn't seem to help.

"You best get out of here," said Roddy.

"I think the word you're looking for is 'git.' Old West tradition, like being neighborly and hanging rustlers." That too failed to get a positive response.

"I think you better go," said Beaumont.

"I'll leave but not because you told me," I said. "I'm leaving because you threatened me and there is that trespassing thing. But before I go I want to say two things."

"What?" Roddy kept the gun on me.

"First," I said, scooting closer to Beaumont so if I was shot, I'd get his clothes dirty. "I'm heading off to Miracle Canyon to find the hermit's lair. When I do, I'm going to be on the lookout for cow bones. If I don't find any, that might make people wonder where all the cattle went."

Roddy and Beaumont both stared at me. Again, I'd failed to bring levity to the moment.

"And the other thing?" asked Roddy, casually clicking back the hammer on the hand cannon.

I reached into my pocket and slowly removed the pistol I'd found the day before.

"Here, Beaumont," I said. "You left this when we were together before."

Roddy's face went from mean and threatening to slack-jawed-surprised horrified. Really, his mouth fell open. The gun wavered, his eyebrows knitted and he looked at his son with a mix of accusation, sympathy, and contempt.

"Git out!" he barked. "Both of you. Git out!"

"That's more like it," I said, beating Beaumont to the door by a step.

32

BEAUMONT GLARED AT ME. His face was hard to read, like his father's—a mess of emotions. If I had to guess, I'd say it was gas.

"Here." I handed him the little gun.

He took it from me. His hand was shaking.

"Did that bastard in there kill Dash?" he asked.

"I didn't think so until a moment ago."

His mouth twitched as if silently practicing some new vocabulary, but he said nothing. He closed his fist around the gun, turned, and walked off toward the house.

I mounted my trusty steed and headed out, looking forward to seeing Miracle Canyon, glad to get off the Double Dean Ranch. Those folks got issues.

Like the saddle tramps of old, I ventured north into the wilderness, my mind wandering. I mulled over the events of the day. I thought about guns and Pop-Tarts, cows and steers, Roddy and Beaumont. Rustlers and lynching and the Johnson County War.

I mentioned before that this little incident ranks up there with all the truly terrible shit-shows of the Old West that aren't talked about today. There's a reason for that. This particular shit-show was a real shit-show, and the powers that were are the powers that still are, at least in spirit. There have been a few retellings, most memorably being the infamous 1980 Michael Cimino movie, *Heaven's Gate*, starring Kris Kristofferson, Christopher Walken, and John Hurt. An epic movie in all senses of the idea; grand concept, huge cast, enormous cost overruns. It was a shit-show to itself but I kinda like the movie. I didn't put it together with the case until the library visit, then I knew more local history than the inhabitants did. I also

got a sense of how little the country had changed since those Good Ol'
Days®.

The dates generally assigned to this little example of Americana capitalism and cruelty is 1889–1893, though the problem started before that and
trickled on for a while after. The West was tamed. The Indians had been
shuffled away by cavalry and disease, exiled to lands alkali found trying.
Big cattle was the name of the game. The plains were perfect for bovine habitation now that those pesky buffalo had been hunted to near extinction. The
first to get there got rich using free grazing land and imported moo beasts.
They organized themselves into a group called the Wyoming Stock Growers
Association, abbreviated to 'WSGA' or sometimes 'cattle barons,' or, more
accurately, 'fuckers.' I'll use these terms interchangeably. These fuckers were
an open range monopoly. They let their cattle prowl the lands—the public
lands—and once a year rounded them all up, checked for brands, branded
new ones, divvied them up, sold them and shipped them away.

Then four things happened. First, they sold so many animals that the
price fell. Second, to try to make up for the lost bazillions of dollars, they put
more critters on the range that was already at its support limit. Third, God
intervened with a terrible blizzard that killed gazillions of animals and was
followed the next year, fourth, by a terrible drought that did its own culling.
This coincided with Western migration driven by the Homestead Act.

Homesteaders and smaller ranchers moved in, set stakes, and went to
work. These homesteaders had the nerve to make legal claim on open lands
that the cattle barons had used for years—years! The irony of the displaced
natives was of course lost on them. The barons were there first. Such as they
had, it was the way things were, and they way they liked it, and screw
anyone who'd try to change it. Irony must not have been invented yet.

Water rights became an issue and fencing really pissed them off—what
good were a thousand head of cattle if they can't eat your neighbor's
vegetable garden?

Seeing this as a threat to their greed, disregarding God's subtle hints,
they went to war with the homesteaders, though the victims didn't find out
for a while. First, the newcomers were naturally excluded from the annual
roundup, which meant any of their free-ranging cattle were divided up
among the fuckers. Some might call that stealing, maybe even rustling, but
the barons owned the media and the new state government, so they got laws
passed to support this shit. Remember legality and morality are not often
related.

Rustling was a big deal to the barons, however, and they used laws
against it to persecute the homesteaders. There was surely some going on,
but they made it out to be some kind of economic apocalypse. The barons
hired 'detectives' to look into it for big rewards to catch miscreants. They
were a bit too enthusiastic and caught innocent people who were tragically
acquitted by fair juries, which incensed the WSGA no little bit. Munching on

big smoldering cigars in The Cheyenne Club, they fumed and plotted while the newcomers tried to make new lives.

Detectives were sent out again, this time vigilante style. Today we'd call this terrorism, but back then they called it...probably terrorism. They were sent to make a point, and boy did they.

In 1893, detectives caught two people and hanged them for rustling. Normal day in Wyoming, maybe, but this time they broke one of those aforementioned laws of the West. They hanged a woman. Her name was Ella Watson. She wasn't a rustler. She was a homemaker trying to survive on the Wyoming plains. Naturally the barons-owned newspapers libeled her to high hell, making stuff up out of whole cloth, like she was a prostitute and Jim Averell, who shared her tree, was her pimp. Really ugly lies from a corrupt media. So glad that kind of thing doesn't happen any more.

Six men were captured for the lynching, but all the witnesses suddenly came down with a bad case of dead.

Enter an aptly named hero, Nate Champion. If ever there was a man named for a moment, it was Nate Champion. Don't go by Walken's portrayal in Cimino's movie. He was a good guy. No idea what the film-makers were trying to do with that. Maybe Cimino had big cattle baron backing.

Anyway, to challenge the WSGA, Champion championed the NWFSGA, which stood for Northern Wyoming Farmers and Stock Growers' Association, a group of smaller ranchers and homesteaders organized to protect themselves against big money interests. Oh, what a concept.

Upon hearing about the NWFSGA, The WSGA, doubtlessly suffering from abbreviation envy, immediately sent assassins to kill Nate Champion. That quick. Like the same day, before the new organization had even decided on a letterhead font.

A group of hired killers busted into a cabin where Champion was sleeping. Champion, champ that he was, pulled a pistol out from under his pillow and killed one, wounded two, and sent the others running. They retaliated by ambushing two other ranchers in the coming weeks. The war was looking like a war.

What would a war be without an invasion? A poor war, amirite? The WSGA felt the same way and, à la *Blazing Saddles*, hired the worst killers and nasties they could find. Most came from Texas. They boarded a secret train and then took off on horseback, cutting telegraph wires as they went to keep the invasion secret. They had with them a list of seventy names of people all over the state who were to be killed or hanged—not sure what the difference was, but those were the instructions. Interestingly, a few notables followed the main group of murderers—state senators, a couple of the barons, people who'd help Wyoming become a state and pass the laws to screw over the homesteaders. Big-named fuckers.

Their first act was to go at Nate Champion again. With seventy people this time, they did the job, though it took a lot longer than they expected. Again holed up in a cabin, Nate held them at bay for hours, spending his sieged-down time writing a journal. The invaders—yes, they actually called themselves the invaders—set the place on fire, so Champion ran out with guns a-blazing. He was shot down good and dead. They tacked a note to him saying 'Cattle Thieves Beware,' so you can see they had justification. They accused him of being a cattle thief because 'union organizer' didn't have the same flavor.

The organized locals took offense to the invasion and the murder of their Champion and quickly put together a two-hundred-man posse. That tells you something about the prevailing attitudes in the area. This led to another standoff, this time the odds a little more even when the invaders were surrounded. This happened at a place called the TA Ranch, which was on the now-named Crazy Woman Creek, which is kind of interesting, thematically speaking.

The siege went on for three days. One of the locals went to a nearby fort asking to borrow a cannon, but he was refused and sent away wondering, no doubt, what happened to Western hospitality. He'd gone to the US military, which showed that though the locals were learning and acting locally, they hadn't been wholly woke yet to see the global—or at least national—systems of oppression.

Yes. I'm saying this was a class war.

One of the invaders managed to escape and went to the governor of Wyoming for help. Unlike the hapless cannon-seeking peasant, he was not refused and, being a fucker himself, Governor Barber telegraphed President Benjamin Fucker Harrison telling him that some fuckers were in trouble from some lower-class peons and help was needed.

The posse put together an ingenious wagon siege machine, a wall of thick logs on wheels that could take the fire from the invaders and get close enough to lob sticks of dynamite through their windows. It would have worked, too, if not for those pesky cavalry coming over the hill in just the nick of time. They were there to save the invaders, of course, which most people considered the bad guys. They called themselves invaders, remember. They did that themselves.

The invaders were taken to Fort Just-for-Show and allowed to wander the grounds as long as they promised to come back every night. None of the notables were ever charged, and the rest were bailed out but forgot to return for their trials. Oops. No one was ever held accountable for the invasion, murder, or mayhem. Not a single gunman, and assuredly not the WSGA, thus setting solid precedent for the Ku Klux Klan, Enron, and Lehman Brothers yet to come.

They called that the end of the war, but there were a couple more killings in retaliation. Things mere mellowing until the Spring Creek Raid of 1909, when justice finally decided to visit northern Wyoming and group of ambushing fuckers were lawfully and righteously hanged. Thus, at last, not a goddamn minute too soon, the Wyoming Wild West passed away and law and order took root. More or less.

The WSGA eventually let others join, and their strong-arm monopoly was broken. Cattle is still a big deal in Wyoming. Brands are everything, and stealing cattle may not be a hanging offense officially, but if Roddy Dean's pistol was any indication, it's not for lack of desire.

Taking the side road up the mountain behind Varg's place, following the trail I saw Mandel using the day before, I wondered about new settlers trying to bring change to old settlers who'd brought change to the first peoples, who had done the same in waves to peoples before them. These folks around here now were just following the tradition of fighting to keep things the way they were just changed to.

I get it, though. A little. It takes courage—gumption—to pioneer, to be that famous first adopter to set out and do it, be it a motor car, a smartphone, a toilet or a bleak barren grassland. If things don't go well, you'll be another Crazy Woman, a cautionary tale used to scare the next ones away. Nevertheless, someone will try again and eventually create a new norm everyone comes around to, but while that happens there'll be war—attack and defense and, very often, revenge.

33

THE TRAIL WAS BARELY large enough for my vehicle. One of those bigger things like the Crombys tooled around in would be hard to use.

I was bumped and jostled and bucked, my modern motored machine doing all it could to imitate the horse it replaced, an uppity twisting horse in this case. I felt my kidney smash into my spleen, felt my bowels wrap around both and tighten.

I pulled up a ways to catch my breath on a hairpin curve with a view maybe a quarter of the way up. I activated my scream button taking off the stifling helmet and looked out over the plains.

Referring to my stolen, moist, and crumpled maps, I quickly identified the cabins in the trees below and the road to Bangkok heading north where the fence was still cut.

A reflection pulled my attention. I squinted and made out a man standing at the crossroads. The flash had either been the sun catching on the lenses of the huge binoculars he had, or his bald and shiny head. I recognized Varg Jayger and waved. I couldn't tell if he waved back or used some other gesture. It was pretty far.

My plan was to top the mesa this way by the little medicine wheel and then catch the highway to Miracle Canyon. Checking the map, I saw a miserable climb to the wheel and a relatively easy route around to the bottom of Miracle Canyon. The elevation lines at the top of the canyon suggested that if I approached it from the top, I'd need rappelling equipment to come down. The easier straight path beckoned.

Unlike the trip from the Double Dean, this ride didn't allow me time to muse. It was rocky and bumpy and turny, and I was in a sweaty lather by the time I got to the canyon. I wondered if riding a real horse was as much exercise as an ATV. I thought those things were supposed to make the trip easier. My arms ached.

The trail leading up the canyon wouldn't take the ATV and I gratefully left it at the bottom and started hiking. The Pop-Tarts I'd had for breakfast were fleeing my bloodstream in ever-weakening carbs, and a bottle of water would have been good to have, but why be prepared?

It wasn't long, or maybe it was, until I found a quaint gurgling brook of crystal clear water. I stared at it a long time, sweating under the thinning trees, comparing the pain of water-borne disease versus death by thirst.

Keeping my options open, I followed the stream up another ways or two, and after a while, I was a ways past the tree line looking up a slope of fallen scree. Scree is a real word. Look it up. It's what they call broken rocks at the bottom of crags. Crags is a real word too. That's the kind of place I was in; among scree and crags.

Sweating and thirsty, sore in new places my urban body wasn't familiar with, I sat down to think, catch my breath. Maybe die. People go hiking for fun, I remembered. The world is full of crazy people trying to get creeks named after them.

I saw a TED Talk once about working smarter instead of harder. It was my workout for the day. Remembering the advice from the clip, I studied the cliffs, the crags, and also the scarps. Scarps is a real thing too. I was getting in deep.

Squinting for shadows, I thought I discerned a trail through the loose rock. From a distance with the right light and imagination I thought I could see it. When I got up to it, after getting a good long breather and maybe a little nap, it was invisible. On Indiana Jones-like faith, I stepped forward and my idea was confirmed by consistently finding firm rocks among the scree. When I moved off the path, loose rock slipped away and tried to avalanche me down the slope into the cool, wet, refreshing, and as yet untasted, brook.

I went up a ways, for a while. No way to tell distance or time in the outdoors. It's physically impossible. Around a curve in a crag, up the scarp, I saw a ledge. The trail was petering out, the rocks less certain than before.

I stared at the ledge for a long while trying to suss out a way to reach it. It was fifteen feet up the cliff face, nearly vertical. There were places that could be handholds, which I took to be a good sign that I'd found the lair but a bad sign because one would need actual athletic ability to scale up to it.

There was nothing for it. I had to try.

I followed the firm rocks to the wall and figured that was the start. I felt up and around as if looking for a secret panel and found an impression just above my left shoulder. A smoothed-out indentation at my right knee also looked hopeful.

I know that rock climbing is a thing, like hiking. I've been to REI. I saw an outdoors magazine once. But I'd never done it. Once Nancy, my ex-wife, took me to one of those climbing places up the canyon. The game was to have a husband/wife team compete against other coupled teams of realtors. Nancy was a realtor, and this was supposed to be some kind of team-building exercise. We each had to climb a wooden wall studded with plastic handholds to a tower and then take a zip line down across a pond before scurrying under concertina wire while someone shot live rounds over our heads. Or something like that. I never saw the zip line. I got five feet off the ground, two handholds and one foot, when my hands spurted natural lubricant sweat and I was dangling from the safety wire. In five more attempts, as Connor Anderson zipped and ran and was shot at, I never made it that high again. Nancy was not pleased. Her team lost.

I fondly remembered dangling off the safety cable as I found one hidden handhold after another and paused halfway up, maybe five feet above where I'd started, but what felt like miles over the stream. I hung there for a time, feeling my hands grow sweatier and sweatier, my muscles twitching like electrified frog legs. I tried to find the step below me, to retreat and come back with a crane, but I couldn't find it. Going down, I realized, was harder than going up. I pulled up a foot to another bump that promised perch, trying not to think that with every step of easy up, I would pay back with a harder down.

Reaching blindly to where I thought a handhold should be, I invariably found one. Reach, grab, pull. Another again.

Then I felt nothing. No more handholds. Only a ledge.

I should have been happy I was there, but the ledge was a ledge and not a handhold. I gasped as I realized I'd have to pull myself up. A pull-up, a real, lifesaving pull-up. I'd hated doing those in gym class. They hurt, and who needs to buff up their arms anyway? I got to where I could do three in seventh grade, but after that I couldn't remember doing another. I'd put on a few civilized pounds since then and traded strength for sarcasm. I dared to look down.

The trail, ten feet below, was lost among the other scree. If I dropped, I'm sure I'd find it but only for an instant before gravity and karma took hold and dropped me to the bottom of the abyssal canyon.

I held on as well as I could to the lip of the ledge and tried to poke my knee into a hold only to find it was too slim to get in. Not handicapped accessible. I should report it.

I slid my left knee up the side, my leg stretching out, toeing around for miracles. And I found one. A good solid outcropping I could put my foot on. I could then use one leg to help my arms make the ledge.

I took a deep cleansing breath, cursed the day I came to Wyoming, assessed a long series of poor decisions that led me here, and heaved.

I more or less leaped into the hole, landing my torso into the gap just at the belt line, my legs hanging in open air. It's not very often I thank my lucky stars for being stout, but I did then. The balance was in favor of the belly. Grabbing at rocks and dirt and rodent droppings as I could find, I wriggled like a worried worm until I was in.

I took a moment to catch my breath again. I really need to keep better track of that. Get a leash maybe. My self-congratulations were tempered by an absolute self-disgust for a plethora of reasons ranging from being out of shape to not bringing water to not telling the gang where to find me to not having a will.

Once my eyes adjusted I found myself in a little space about four feet wide, three high and six deep. It sloped upward at the back.

There were footprints in the dust. Not shoe prints. Footprints. They led to the back. Hunched over, I followed them until I found myself in what felt like a closet. The ceiling opened up and I could stand. Just at chest level, another ledge opened into what I sensed was a large room.

I climbed up. Wasn't easy, but I did it.

A teeny-tiny bit of daylight sneaked in, reflecting off hell-knows-what. I found a fire ring by smell. Feeling around the rock circle, I found a box of big kitchen matches. I lit one.

I'd found the lair.

The little fire pit was indeed little, but I found several kerosene lanterns and lit one of those. They were new. He had cans of white gas to go in them. There was a cooler where meat was kept. Not big cuts of anything, more like roadkill leftovers. There were buckets of beans that on closer examination I thought might be animal droppings. They looked like the pile that had appeared in my room the first night. Another bucket looked to have Whoppers in it, those chocolate-malted milk balls. I always loved those, the only candy I'll pay for at the movies. I put some in my pocket for later and eyed the fire pit.

It had blackened coals in the center and a low stack of blackened coals beside it. Upon closer examination, I realized that the blackened coals were in fact black coal. It was rough and rocky, but it was coal, carbon-emitting, planet-destroying, job-making, dirty American coal loved by China and the sixteen circles of cancer devils Dante never got around to mentioning.

There was a cot fashioned out of pine boughs and a ripped sleeping bag stuck to it with sap. There were a couple of knives, some plastic jugs with some unknown liquid in them, a pan with melted chocolate at the bottom as if he had had a fondue. There was a metal bucket that smelled like a chamber pot, a pile of crackers, a heap of drying plants. There was a telltale pile of empty white plastic jars that once held vitamin supplements and twice that many empty orange pill bottles of amoxicillin written out to Craig Carter by a doctor in Sheridan, Wyoming. There were books too, *Of Kings, Queens and Colonies*, the first book of the *Coronam Trilogy*—the man had taste —and a collection of outdoor books from the Floyd library including three scouting books, *Bear*, *Webelos*, and *Boy* along with Jean George's classic, *My*

Side of the Mountain. There was also a pile of magazines next to a stack of kindling: *Woman's Day, Entrepreneur, Field & Stream, Hustler.*

It was lived in, but I had a hard time measuring the duration. It was tidy and yet disheveled. I tried to think of a man living years in that space. The way the cave was formed, with the outer room and the lip going up, would keep it cool in the summer and hold heat in the winter. It was a perfect lair. How lucky the hermit had found it. I wondered how he knew where to look.

There it was again. Who the hell was Dasher the Flasher? Dash, as some people had called him. Deputy Sheriff Craig Carter, Sheridan drug buyer, knew much more than he was saying.

Beside the hole I'd crawled up, I saw a familiar shape that Rawly had called his .50-caliber ammo box. I opened it and looked inside. I made a comparative inventory of what Rawly said he left in them: food (none), foil blanket (none), ammo and gold (present). A leather holster with a gun in it (9mm), and a picture of Kimmy and Rawly on a beach. In the light of the little gas lamp, the thirty Krugerrands brilliantly shone glistening gold. I picked one up and felt its weight before dropping it back in and hearing it plunk.

Something didn't sit right.

I picked up the coin and dropped it again. The plunk was again flat. I tried some others. Plunk plunk plunk.

I fished the coin Rawly had given me and dropped it. Plink.

I was scratching my head with new ideas as I fished my coin out from the bottom of the box among a gallery of pretenders. I turned over the holster and stopped short. Beneath the big black Italian gun was a little silver Italian one, just a teeny .25 semi-automatic. A familiar friend, an exact duplicate of the one I'd given back to Beaumont.

34

I LEFT everything where it was. I was a snoop, not a thief. I looked longingly at the water bottles, wondering what the cure was for dysentery. A rope I'd found wasn't enough to lower me down the cliff, and the sleeping bag was far too small to make a parachute.

I carried the lantern and matches into the anteroom, helpfully placing them handily for the next snoop.

Lying on my belly, I carefully pushed myself backward, feet first, over the ledge. When I was folded over, my toes searched for cracks or bumps as I tried to recall where they were. Coming up, they'd been in natural positions, just a quick reach and feel. My shod feet did not have sensation or dexterity. I found nothing. My arms shook in strain and fear. Gravity pulled.

Still searching, still hoping, I lowered myself down until I was all the way over, my fingers the only thing holding me, dangling like a human plumb-bob.

My next step was to try to find a handhold. That would leave me with one connecting point. I figured I had maybe five seconds to find something before my arm gave out and I was scree. If I hung with both arms like that, I had about a minute. I am not a strong man.

I glanced to my right to look for a likely target when the rock I was going for popped like a party favor. Crack. Gray dust and shards.

"Huh."

I heard the gunshot a moment later.

"Well, that explains it."

There're sitting ducks and then there's hanging by one's fingertips off a cliff face with a sniper trying to kill you. No ducks involved there. No sitting. Just fucked. Hanging fucked.

I lunged with my right hand for the hold, praying there was something to cling there. I never found out. The lunge shifted my weight, and my clenching fingers failed me.

I heard another report midair and crashed at the bottom before the echo was gone.

I'd not died. To be honest, I'd probably fallen all of six feet. It looked much worse from above because the trail, if you could call it that, was so narrow and immediately sloped down toward the valley. When I fell, I hit the trail, had a brief moment of surprise and relief and then tumbled down the slope toward the valley like a pudgy boulder.

Head over heels, somersaults, splays, turns, cartwheels, sliding down with flowing rock, slamming every joint and soft spot on my body into new and interesting edges.

I just kept going. Every time I slowed a little, tried to get my feet under me, surfing the loose rocks like a Waikiki curl, I'd hear another gunshot, twitch the wrong way, slip and tumble on.

What had looked like miles from above felt like hundreds as I fell. It might have been a hundred yards, but it took a hundred years of slashing and crashing before I was splashing in the quaint little brook at the tree line.

Another gunshot, crisp and resounding. Alarming.

On my belly, I splashed down the mud like some crocodile that had had the shit kicked out of it by a gang of methed-out mantis shrimps. I lunged, crawled, swam, and slogged downstream, deeper into cover until I heard no more gunshots. I peed myself, took a deep drink of water, and rolled over. I probably should have done that in a different order, but there it was.

The stream was cool and refreshing after the warm spot had passed and I paused to catch my breath and take inventory of my limbs. I had them all; none seemed broken but every joint and surface was bruised or scraped. Most both. My scream button was bleeding. It'd been ripped open when I bounced my face off rocks.

The shots had come from the canyon lip, not the canyon itself. I think. They'd stopped when I'd put trees between that edge and me.

Muddy, bruised, and bloody, I was thrilled to discover my legs still worked. I tracked down the creek until I found the trail and followed it to my ATV. It took a fraction of the time to get down as it did to get up. I reached for my tile for old time's sake and found that it had been broken in the tumble. It was six large pieces, wet dust and shards.

I slid the helmet on and did not enjoy the experience. I fired up the machine and pointed for home. The jostling tested each wound and bruise as I went. I growled into the visor, searching for more curse words until the machine sputtered and stopped.

Talk about a rookie move. I'd run out of gas. There it was, right on the display, a fuel gauge with a red arrow pointing to E.

"Huh."

AAA was out of the question. My tile was broken. I looked up and down the trail hoping for a passing antelope with a tow rope. Nope. Only mosquitoes.

The map told me I was a ways, a good ways, from civilization. The closest real road was back up Miracle Canyon, but it'd take a miracle to climb to it even without the suppressing fire.

I couldn't remember a time I'd been more sore, injured, and completely bashed up as I was then. I gave some serious thought to finding a hole and burying myself, getting a few hours shut-eye, and, if I was lucky, die, saving someone the trouble of digging the grave.

The drink of water hadn't been enough to sate my thirst, but it was surely enough to infect me with a host of old-timey microbes that would play havoc with my innards for the rest of my life. I was hungry. I remembered the Whoppers and popped a couple in my mouth, before I remembered I didn't have milk to wash them down with.

They weren't Whoppers.

The outside was chocolate, but the interior was not delicious malted milk balls. It was not the sweet, crunchy, special treat I loved, but was a bitter, earthy and squishy nightmare. I spit them out half chewed into my palm. It shifted, moved under its own pressure. There were fibers. There was dirt. There were bugs.

Oh, shit.

Shit.

It was shit.

It was literally chocolate-covered shit.

I scraped my tongue with a sage branch and gargled with sand.

I was not having a good day.

I congratulated myself on not swallowing but then remembered the water and stuck the sage brush down my throat to trigger the gag response to throw up.

The stick was too short. Between pinched fingers, I fed it deep back into my throat. And dropped it. Yep, I dropped the stick down my esophagus. I felt it slide down and into my gut.

"For hell's sake!" I screamed.

I stamped my foot and raised a middle finger to the sky, the trail, the ATV, the trees, the helmet, the wiggling chocolate-covered poo and screamed some more. It was cathartic. I did versions of yelling and stamping for maybe fifteen minutes until my body rebelled in ubiquitous aches and I sat down.

A few minutes later I was calm enough to stick my finger down my throat until I retched up the leafy stick. I was dispirited to see chocolate come up with it but not a lot of water.

"Lovely."

I was in shade behind the mesa, meaning the sun was about to abandon me, like my luck. There was nothing for it. I was walking out or dying. To hell if I was going to die in a place as shitty as this.

I put the helmet on the seat, watching bugs bounce off it even then like it was a beacon. I unbungeed the plastic grocery bag of media, and, after finding a stout walking stick, I set out down the trail.

I had to take it slow. I'd sprained both ankles and both knees, both hips, groin, shoulders, wrists, neck, nasal cavities and intestines. I traded off dragging one foot and then the other in classic mummy shamble. I spit and swore and lamented my state.

Under other circumstances, the trail might have struck me as pretty, idyllic, unpainful, but that was not then. It was a hellscape. The lack of public transportation was a travesty. There were no convenience stores, Subway sandwich shops, gas stations or Starbucks anywhere. What kind of hellscape was this? Aren't we better than this? The butterflies, when not trying to suicide into my mouth, were still annoying, but the wasps and mosquitoes could fuck right off.

The good old days, before technology, was a lot of physical work. Walking was okay from the car to the pancake house, but doing this across Nebraska to California sounded like work. Horses were invented for a reason. Trains and cars and planes and even ATVs were better than this plodding bug-supper bullshit of walking wounded in search of a non-toxic beverage.

This was hard. This was long. This was boring. And it hurt. Everything hurt.

I slipped into odd thoughts, not unrelated to where I was.

Did the Donner Party have any clowns with them that tasted funny? Did Texas Rangers really drink out of dirty hoof prints? How could anyone ride a horse for that long and not give it a name? Outdoor people were strange.

Trudge, ache, drag and bitch. I worked calluses into my hands from the walking stick and plastic bag of books, picked up cactus at my ankles, bug bites around my neck, heatstroke everywhere.

It was late dusk when I got to the crossroads by Varg's place. I paused, waiting for the machine-gun fire to finish off a perfect afternoon. I was, of course, disappointed.

Trudge, ache, drag and bitch, I finally came up behind Perry's cabin. Lights shone in the windows and happy voices carried out into the night just to mock me.

So as not to ruin my mood, I made a quick stop at the splinter shack and tried not to let the presence of real toilet paper—no matter how soft it was—and the wet wipes and hand sanitizer and automatic light brighten me.

I was not happy, and that's how I wanted to be.

I shambled around the front of the house to make a grand entrance and noticed only the Cadillac there. No neighbors this night.

I ripped a blister open throwing my walking stick onto the porch. The sound of it silenced the house and gave me the entrance I wanted.

I threw open the door and stood in the entrance, the wreck I was, hunched, bruised, bloodied, torn. The only thing missing was lightning flashing behind me.

"Hi, Tony," came Garrett's friendly welcome. "Did you eat? We have some trout."

"I caught them," said Standard. He was sitting in the semi-circle in the front room around the fire. "Living off the land."

I stepped farther in, thinking the light hadn't shown the shambles I was.

"What's in the bag?" asked Perry. "Presents?"

"I think he's mad," said Garrett.

"What for?" said Dara. "We didn't do anything. If he wanted to go to the lake with us he shouldn't have slipped away."

"I fell down a mountain."

"It looks like it," said Perry. "The trout really is good. Make sure you eat a small one. Less heavy metals in the smaller ones. Anything larger than a plate is—"

"Look at me. I'm a mess."

"You're working a case," said Perry. "You always look like this at some time during your cases. You're standing up, so this isn't even in the top five."

"Yeah, congratulations on making progress," said Garrett.

"Where's Critter?"

"Garrett let him have a s'more, and now his mouth's glued shut."

"It's going to take some work to clean him up," said Standard. "No digestive tract."

"It was a good gag, though," said Perry. "Hilarious. Like the Cookie Monster but with more seduction and anger."

"He was channeling our time with Kimmy," said Garrett.

"Just do crackers next time," said Dara. "It'll bring down—"

"I was shot at too," I said. "Shot at while I fell down a mountain."

"So it's almost cracked, then?" said Perry. "Well done. Have a fish."

Garrett took the bag from me and peeked inside. "Who's Uri Isaaks?" he said. "Oh, look, a book about s'mores. Dibs."

"Books?" said Dara. "Gimme."

"Any Thoreau?"

"I'll take the one about resumes," said Perry when Garrett lifted it to show everyone.

"Why?"

"Job curious."

"What's left?" said Standard.

"*Gun and Dagger* and *Activities that Don't Suck*."

"That," he said.

The book passed to him.

"Do we have any Bactine?" I said.

"No, but we have vodka."

"I could be really hurt," I whimpered.

"Are you?"

"Could be."

"You look really tired," said Perry.

"I walked miles and miles."

"What happened to your thing?"

"Ran out of gas."

"So you got your exercise," said Dara. "Well done. You'll sleep great tonight. We just sat around a lake taking swims and fishing and eating snacks. Drinking beers, working on s'more-related bits. A real chill day."

"Sorry I missed it," I said.

"You made progress on your case, though."

"Miles and miles and miles."

"Eat a fish and get some sleep."

I shambled into the kitchen and found three small fried fish on a skillet. I slapped one on a paper plate, took three bottles of water and a plastic fork before shambling back into the living room.

"This is everything you need to know about Wyoming right here," said Dara, holding open a book. "The most endangered species in the state of Wyoming is the *Canadian* lynx."

"What does that mean?" I said.

"The state is so out there they don't even get their own lynx."

"That's a stretch." I forked fish. It wasn't bad. The water was better, however. I drank all three. "I have had a hell of a day."

"Poor thing," said Perry.

"Now? Now I get sympathy?"

"Didn't want it going to your head."

"We kind of figured you'd come in looking like that," said Garrett.

"My friends."

"You want me to drive you somewhere?"

"Home?"

"I was thinking a hospital."

"We'll talk in the morning," I said. "I'm heading to bed. You wouldn't believe what I ate today that wasn't fish."

"Chocolate-covered antelope poop?" said Garrett.

"What the hell?" I said.

"That sounds familiar," said Perry.

"Kimmy said the hermit was into that."

"Thanks for the heads-up, a day late. Did she say he was into anything else that might be useful? Like he lived at the far end of a gun range?"

"Sorry," said Garrett. "I couldn't imagine it coming up."

"Do I want to ask how that came up with you and Kimmy?"

"Critter—"

"I don't want to know," I said.

"Second that," said Dara.

"Third."

"Fourth."

"Still, it would have been good to know this morning," said I.

"I just remembered it when you asked what—I mean, who would actually eat such a thing?"

I stared daggers at him while swishing a shot of vodka around my teeth. I split it through the grate of the fireplace and was rewarded with an aesthetically ambivalent sizzling fireball. "Anything else?" I said.

"No. No," he said. "Not that I can remember."

"I'm going—"

"Oh, the hermit slept with guys too," he said. "He was a bi-predator, that's what she called him. Broke hearts of all genders."

"So I missed an opportunity?"

"She said Critter did."

"Good night."

35

THE NEXT DAY Perry was as happy to get up and drive me to Floyd as I was to wake up and ask him to. My sleep was nothing if not painful, finally compelling me out from my sleeping bag at some unknown dark hour to blow air into my mattress for some unknown dark amount of time. When the sun came up and found my eyes like a laser-guided katana I was up for the day, if only for the fact that I couldn't find a surface on my body that didn't hurt so little that I could get back to sleep.

Then I remembered that Deputy Sheriff Craig Carter had told me that kinsfolk were coming for Dasher's body that day. I had a nagging feeling that he wasn't going to fetch me for that event. I think he might have regretted telling me it was happening at all.

"Maybe I'm being paranoid," I said.

"'Bruise-induced paranoia' is a thing," Perry explained, navigating the Caddy through its best bronco imitation down the 'road' leading to a real road. "I read about it."

"No, you didn't."

"I did. I saw a TED Talk by a torture survivor. He said after being tortured, it hurt so badly that he was now forever paranoid of anyone with a water bottle or a car battery, especially if they were asking him questions. He had to quit his job at Jiffy Lube. Couldn't even do the front counter."

"This was a TED Talk? A real TED Talk?"

"Looked like one."

"What was the point of the talk?"

"Never turn your back on a BDSM dominatrix."

"Sounds like good advice. Thanks for sharing."

I couldn't help thinking that Carter had lost his enthusiasm for my help. I suppose punting the mayor's little boys into his spleen was at the root of it, but there was still so much this little town was hiding from me that I was beginning to take it personally, or at least I would if I found out that Carter was planning to ax me out of meeting Dasher's kinsfolk.

"Where are we going?"

"You've been around the town?"

"Driven it. Had breakfast. Been to the Shady motel."

"You said something about a clinic? Is there a hospital? A place where they'd store dead bodies?"

"I saw a meat market."

"How about a funeral home?"

"There's one on Stubbins Street."

"Everything is on Stubbins Street," I said. "Good call."

We drove to Stubbins Street as the sun still cast long shadows from the east and the air still had the annoyingly fresh smell of dew.

"I'm taking it personally," I said.

"What?"

I pointed to Carter's police mobile parked in front of the home.

"Oh," said Perry.

Beside a long black Lincoln with drapes in the windows, there were two other cars. Neither was from out of the state, but since they weren't white pickups, I figured they weren't from around here.

We went in.

The smell of flowers hit us like a wall of fog when nearing the perfume counter at Macy's. Perry and I both took a deep sniff and coughed. Roses and carnations, lilies and baby's breath, thick as grease on a fryer. It was a lot. It was too much.

There was a lectern set up to accept a memory book. Nothing was on it now, but there were no fewer than three cans of aerosol room fresheners behind a little door in the back of the room. Who doesn't open suspicious little doors in funeral homes when they can?

"Explains it," said Perry, his eyes beginning to water.

I heard voices from a side hallway and followed them. Perry, his shirt pulled up to his eyes, was only a step behind me.

We passed a nicely accoutered pew-filled room with casket space and floral wreaths. No body and nobody was there.

The voices came from behind an unmarked but ajar door in the back.

"Slow day?" I said as I entered. "You should have a guy out front in a gorilla costume spinning a sign. Open bay—no waiting. Does wonders in the—"

The looks told me I'd just made a shit joke in a funeral parlor. Even the corpse was unhappy I'd made light of things. There on a metal table with a white sheet covering him from neck to toe was Dasher the Flasher's body, a grim expression telling me that my humor was not appreciated.

The faces turned to me were all in accord deviating only in degree of surprise, disgust and hatred. The mayor was there. That was the hatred.

"I'm Geoffrey Rigor," said a man in a white smock. "I'm the head undertaker." He peeled off a blue rubber glove and offered to shake my hand.

"Rigor?"

"Yes?"

"Can't make this shit up," I said.

"What's that about shit?" said the only other person I didn't recognize, a woman with red-rimmed eyes but no tears. She looked shocked but also familiar.

Sheriff Carter, the other person in the room yet to be named, introduced the woman. "This is Mrs. Tessin," he said.

"Hello." She was a young woman, pretty, short brown hair, ruddy complexion, brown eyes, dressed in tan business casual, blouse and jacket. Her purse was small, matched and alligator.

"I didn't know alligators could be brown," said Mr. No Censor.

"What? Oh, I'm sure it's dyed."

"This is Tony Flaner," said the deputy sheriff finishing the intros. "Looks like a mountain fell on you."

"Something like that."

"It's Mr. Tony Flaner," said Perry. "If she gets an honorific, so does Tony. Don't be sexist."

"And who are you?" asked the mayor.

"I'm Tony's friend. I bought the old Keyshaw place."

"Oh, I heard about you."

"And you are?"

"Mayor Gill Charbone. The man your best friend, Mr. Tony Flaner, attacked on the street the other day."

"What? Tony, is this true?"

"No."

"I knew you couldn't—"

"But I did kick him in his balls."

"What? Really?"

I said, "It's kind of hard to believe, I admit, they being so small."

"Sheriff Carter," said the mayor, "I'd like a word with you in private."

"But, Gill—"

"Now."

The two left us four alone and went into the hall, pulling the door closed behind them.

"Tony, I've got to live here," said Perry. "How could you?"

I showed him the move: weight on left leg, lean back a smidge, and up with the toe of the right shoe. "Like that. It was very liberating."

"But..."

"He started it. He punched me, and I was in a—"

"Excuse me," said Mr. Rigor. "What are you doing here?"

I could see Ms. Tessin had the same question.

"I'm a private investigator looking into the murder of...um, the...the guy who died. Was shot. Without clothes on. Him. You can call me Tony."

"I don't think I will," said Rigor.

"You can call me Heather," said the woman.

"You're the kinsfolk?"

"What do you mean?"

"Are you the one, um...are you here to identify the, uh...body?"

"Yes."

"And?"

"It's my father."

"Oh. Okay," I said. "I am so sorry."

"Who hired you?"

"A government agency kind of thing."

She shook her head.

"Government?" said Perry. "Now you're working for the government. Jesus, Tony. You sell-out deep-state mole, son of a mule-headed—"

"Can we go somewhere and talk?" I asked Heather.

"I trusted you and then you go and work for the man? No wonder you wouldn't tell us."

"I have no background information on the um...um."

"Victim?" said Heather.

"I was reaching for 'hermit,' but I didn't know how much you knew. His nickname isn't so positive."

"Dasher the Flasher," said Heather. "I've heard it."

"What good is a secret hideout if government spies are invited in? You should have come clean. Now what levels of trouble am I in? What have you done?"

Perry's hands flew to his ears and he fell to his knees, distraught.

"Is this something we should be concerned with?" asked Heather.

"I have something that can calm him," said Rigor. "Would he swallow a pill or should I get a hypo?"

There was a knock on the door behind us. We looked at each other and then Rigor pushed past us and opened the door. Sheriff Carter came back in alone. He didn't look happy.

"The door locks when it's closed," he said. "Pity I didn't pull it shut when we came in." He glared at me.

"Ouch," said I.

"I knew it would come to this," said Perry. "Turned in by my best friend. Brainwashed Judas."

"What is he doing?"

"Having a paranoid attack," I said.

He became sensible to the fact that an actual law enforcement official was in the room. He straightened up, sniffed, put on a big smile. "Howdy," he said.

"That was disturbing," said Heather.

"I've seen worse," said Rigor.

"He's a comedian," I said. "What you just witnessed was a joke that took over."

"A joke that took over?"

"He fell into one of his characters, a paranoid guy, and improvised that bit just now. Pretty good, huh?"

"Yeah, I believed it," said Heather. "Not sure it's funny, though."

"Contextually it would be."

"Contextually? Yes," said Perry, nodding slowly. "Yes. Improv. Character. Yes. All that."

"Mr. Flaner, I would like to talk to you outside in the hall, if I may," said Carter.

"No."

"Why not?"

"Because you'll lock me out. I'm on to you. The agency I work for will give you a three-stroke penalty for not informing me that Mrs. Heather Tessin made an identification."

"That just happened."

"But I wasn't invited."

"You don't have a phone."

"And you knew I didn't have a phone."

"How was I to know that?"

"You knew, I know you knew."

"Tony," said Perry, sweat running down his face, "Can we leave the policeman now?"

"Are we done here?" said Carter, his face was red and upset, but it softened when he remembered Heather was there. "I'm sorry," he said. "Take as long as you want."

"I'm done here," she said. "Mr. Rigor, you'll see to the arrangements?"

"I will."

"Where are you shipping him off to?" I asked. "I mean, where are you—was he...the hermit, from? Originally."

I don't want you thinking I was tongue-tied because of a pretty girl. I was tongue-tied because I'd opened with such a shit joke that I felt absolutely exposed. Even I have limits and can recognize poor taste when I step in it. I felt pretty low. There's a time and a place. My bit would have killed on the stage, maybe, but in real life I had been an asshole. Perry's little breakdown, fake or not, took some of the heat from my inane gallows humor, but let's face it, it was a shitty way to begin any conversation. I was kicking myself, and the shock waves were swelling my tongue.

"My dad will be buried here," said Heather. "It's what he would have wanted."

"I'll get right on it, Mrs. Tessin. Sunday, a week from tomorrow?"

"That would be fine," she said. "Thank you."

She sniffled. I felt low.

"I am sorry," I said. "Let me buy you breakfast. I'd like to talk to you."

"For the investigation?"

"Exactly."

Carter cleared his throat.

Heather looked at him. Perry got a little distance by sliding between me and Rigor.

"Oh, are you two not working together?" she asked.

"I was just trying to tell Mr. Flaner that if he isn't out of town by tonight, he'll be in jail tomorrow for attacking the mayor. And this time, the charges will be real."

"Real?" I said. "You mean the last ones were made up? You admit that? In front of four witnesses, three of whom can testify." I cringed inwardly as I realized I'd just made another corpse joke. No one seemed to notice.

"Hallway," he said and opened the door.

I went out. So did Perry and Heather. Rigor remained behind. I heard the sound of an aerosol spray can spurting as the door was pulled shut and locked.

"Better?" I asked.

"Yes," said Carter. "Small towns are gossipy."

"Rigor seemed like a closed-mouth kind of guy."

"He's not."

"But you trust the rest of us?"

"Mrs. Tessin doesn't live here, and she's leaving. You'll be gone by tonight."

"You meant that?"

"Me?" said Perry. "But I live here. Kinda."

"What happened?" I asked.

"An anonymous informant left a message for the mayor saying I hired you to work on the murder."

"What's wrong with that?" said Heather.

"I'm in a pickle. Your father wasn't popular around here," said Carter. "He didn't have many friends. And Mayor Charbone hates Tony."

"About that," I said. "You know what I found in the ah...the lair, hideout of the eh...of Dasher?"

"Coal?" he said in a half whisper.

"You've been there. You little shit."

"Hey—"

"You know a lot more about..." I glanced at Heather again, still feeling low. Her eyes still red, her expression sad. "About...hey, what was his real name, anyway?"

"My father's real name was Dashiell," she said.

"Dashiell," I said, trying it out. "And his last name—" A memory sparked and caught fire. "Severe!" I said.

"No, his name was the same as my maiden one. Stubbins. His name was Dashiell Stubbins. He was born and raised here."

I turned to face Carter, who sheepishly couldn't look me in the face.

"You've got to be out of the county by sundown or I have to arrest you," he said.

"Because you've got to live here?"

"Because I *do* live here."

36

"LET'S take this to Ginger's Café," I said. "I'm hungry."

"Mind if I just go back to the cabin, Tony?" asked Perry, looking none too well.

"Yes, I do mind. You're my ride."

"What happened to your little ATV?" asked Carter.

"Ran out gas on the lone prairie. I'll get Gail to drive me out and get it."

"We can't go to Ginger's," said Carter. "No way."

"More gossips?" asked Heather.

"Oh yes. I'll meet you at the Old Times Saloon. I'll pick up something."

"I want protein," I said. "Bacon, sausage, eggs, steak, ham, chicken. And something with a cheese component."

"Anything else?"

"Coffee."

"Yes, coffee would be nice," said Heather.

"There'll be some in the bar."

With that, Carter got into his cop SUV and headed down Stubbins Street. Perry drove us to the saloon. Heather followed in her own vehicle.

The bar was locked and closed. Mondays it didn't open up until noon. I had no idea what the actual time was, but before noon seemed like a good guess.

We walked around the back and found a delivery man schlepping in kegs.

"Follow my lead," I told the others.

I walked right at him toward the bar as if I owned the place. That's a magic trick. Confidence. If I'd have worried about being caught sneaking in, we would have been, but I looked like we belonged and so we all did.

I held the door open for the others and got grabbed by the delivery guy.

"Who are you?" He was six foot and a bunch, three hundred pounds plus, mostly in his upper torso, arms, and breath. He had eight o'clock shadow from a week before and hair that had been combed by the ceiling of his truck.

"Man, you're ruining my vibe," I said.

"You're not Eddie. You shouldn't be here."

"I'm not Eddie? Well, that's a load off my mind. I'm always being mistaken for him."

He held on to my shoulder. I twisted out.

"I'm Eddie's friend, Tony, and this is Heather and Perry, and the sheriff is coming along soon. Just send him in."

"What's this all about?"

"Eddie gave you a key to make deliveries? Is that it?"

"The owner did. Been doing it for years."

"You probably don't want to be here when the sheriff comes."

"Why?"

"There's been a killing."

"Who?"

"My father," said Heather from the door.

"And the bar's involved?"

"What do you think?"

"Don't you need a warrant?"

"You want to get technical?" I said. "Looks like you are one of the few people who actually have a key to this place. That puts you high on the suspect list. What's your name, anyway?"

"Me? I'm Bruce Merriweather, two Rs and like the rain."

"I'll remember you," I said. "Don't leave town."

"But I don't live here."

"I meant the county."

"I live in Sheridan."

"The state. Don't leave the state."

"I gotta deliver three kegs to Wyola by two. That's across the border in Montana."

"The country. Can you manage that? Don't leave the country? The USA? For a couple days? Don't fly off anywhere?"

"A couple days? Yeah, I can do that. But I got this trip coming up—"

"Okay, good." And with that I confidently went into the bar.

"I don't like this," said Perry. "What if that cop is just setting us for a B&E? He's already threatened to arrest you."

"Perry, he already did."

"Oh, that's right. And now you have the local government after you. This is not what I envisioned when coming out here. You're ruining everything."

"Hey…"

"Do you two need some time together?" asked Heather.

"Nah, we're good. Behave, Perry or I'll mash you."

Perry put his hands in his pockets, a move I recognized from earlier times, meaning he was afraid to leave fingerprints.

We crossed through the back behind the bar. I set a coffee pot to brew while Heather and Perry found a conspicuous table.

"How isn't this B&E?" asked Perry.

"Hush."

He sulked.

"Heather," I said. "Mrs. Tessin, tell me about your father."

"He was born and raised here," she said. "He used to talk about it all the time. He left for college and before his return as Dasher never set foot here."

"Was he a good father?"

"That's blunt."

"You're leaving soon, and I'm on the clock."

"My father was blunt. He was a bad father by modern standards. He was on the spectrum somewhere. Manic depressive. Workaholic. Financially, he did all right for me and my mom until Kiksuye."

"Kiksuye?" said Perry. "That's where I remember it."

"What's Kiksuye?"

"It was his last business. He was an entrepreneur, circling around venture capitalists, making a bit of money here or there until he got an idea of his own and went all in. That idea was Kiksuye Supplement Corporation, KSE on the stock exchange. The logo was a ripped-off sucker-sucking owl—how many licks and all that. Should have seen it coming. Made for suckers."

"He was Kiksuye?" said Perry.

Heather nodded. "What a shit show." And then she laughed.

Perry laughed too.

"Okay, I am officially becoming a third wheel. I've never heard of Kiksway."

"Kiksuye. It means 'to remember' in some language," said Heather. "I honestly don't remember which."

"I can see how you don't know it, Tony," explained Perry. "It was a big thing, cutting edge, and then it tanked and the people involved did everything in their power to make it disappear. They scrubbed the net. Real professional-level hacking. I noticed it because I'm always interested in alternative medicines, and then I was interested in how they scrubbed the web so well. Then I was interested in something else and forgot all about it. The name Stubbins. Of course, I should have remembered."

"Which is a perfect symbol for this whole case. I think everyone knows what happened but me."

"I don't know," said Heather.

"Tell me about the Kiksuye."

"Some of this is private and sensitive and there're legal issues," she said. "I don't know if I should tell you."

"We're safe," I said. "The room has great acoustics, but it's just us. It's not like the table's bugged."

With that, Perry's eyes shifted and searched. He leaned around the chairs, examined the napkin holder and cigarette burns on the tabletop. Then, hands still in his pockets, he slid to his side and looked under the table.

"Tony," he said.

"Let me guess. You have an overwhelming desire for some chewing gum?"

"There is a bug down here."

"Bullshit. You wouldn't know a bug…oh, wait. You would know a bug." I leaned over and he pointed. It was about the size of a dime, stuck to the bottom of the table with a small battery pack.

"Is it on?"

"I think so."

"What could it…" Then I remembered the tape deck under the bar by the gun. I went over and looked again. The gun was gone, but the cassette tape was slowly moving as before.

"Huh."

"Tony, let's go back to the cabin."

"No. That's the first place they'll look."

"Shit? You think so?"

"Yes."

"Fuck."

I reached under the table and opened the battery box and fished out a flat nickel-sized battery. I dropped it on the floor as if it might have fallen on its own.

"This table is right in the usuals' area," I said. "Varg was there, Roddy here. The microphone would have heard everyone."

"Who—"

"Never mind," I said. "It's safe to talk now, Heather. Please, I need to know."

"Kitsuye was sued out of existence. When it collapsed there were criminal charges, allegations of intentional poisoning and obscenity. The FDA went after us like Marines. My father cracked. He jumped bail in Seattle and disappeared."

"When was all this?"

"It exploded, forgive the pun, nine years ago. It took two years for the arrest warrant. That's when Dad disappeared. It bankrupted us. My mom died from shame, I think, the year after that. I was married and hid behind my name."

"What pun?" I said.

"The cases were already forming. The supplement had been on the market a couple of months. The IPO was going well. We had a cadre of marketers out to sell it, promoting it on all social media. Memory enhancement. My father was the poster child. His mind was a steel trap, and he wowed audiences with remembering whole audiences' names, pi to two hundred digits, all kinds of stuff. He claimed it was his supplement."

"But it didn't work?"

"Well, no one had taken the supplement for as long as my father had. His argument was that you have to build it up."

"All right," I said. "What are you not telling me? What's the pun?"

"The TED Talk?" said Perry.

Heather nodded. "People were already getting sick, and lawsuits were brewing. As a PR stunt, one of the partners did a TED Talk explaining the power of memory and the place for traditional natural enhancers in the modern world."

"I never saw it," said Perry. "The video was scrubbed."

"I never saw it, either," said Heather. "But as it was described to me, in the middle of the speech, the speaker shat themselves. Huge diarrhea explosion that could be heard through the whole auditorium, seen on every HD camera pointed at the stage and smelled for days on five floors."

"Oh. My. God."

"That was the end of the company. It filed for bankruptcy, and the agencies began looking into how such a thing could have happened. They dug and accused, and my father finally broke all the way down. My mother said he just went outside one day and she never saw him again. I've been mad at him ever since."

"I take it a lot of people lost money on this?"

"Oh, yes. Millions. They called it the shit show. And some people got sick. Some got very sick. There might have been some deaths. The warrant for my dad was serious. He was in trouble. I was glad of it, wanted him to suffer like he'd made my mom suffer, but lately I've been softer and just wanted to see him again. I can't believe someone killed him."

"We think we know who did it," I said. "With this background, I think I have a motive now too."

"Who?"

"A camper who disappeared right after the killing. I doubt he had any personal reason for the murder, but he might have been a contract killer. The gun used had killed before."

She shook her head and sobbed a little.

I got up and fetched the coffee. I brought over the pot with four cups and all the sweetener and cream I could find. And some Bailey's.

"It won't be long before we catch him," I said. "If that's any comfort."

"Not really."

"There's the sheriff coming," said Perry, peering between the blinds, his coffee untouched because his hands were still in his pockets.

"How did you know to come for the body?"

"An acquaintance sent me a newscast, an old report about the hermit. I watched it and recognized my dad. I sent a man here to see if he could find him."

"You have his eyes," I said.

"You met him?"

"Briefly."

Carter knocked on the door.

"Perry, go get the door," I said.

"How?"

"By taking your hands out of your pockets and turning the knob."

He gave me a crusty look but got up.

"When he was found dead," said Heather, "I got the call and made arrangements."

Perry opened the door with a napkin and Carter strolled in with three plastic bags of Styrofoam to-go boxes.

"The environment hates you," I said.

"Cheyenne said they have a line on Boone," said Carter.

"Boone?" said Heather. "Barney Burger?"

My mouth eased open.

Carter was slow on the uptick. He said, "He's the guy who probably killed your father."

"Can't be him," she said. "He was the man I hired to find him."

"He'll be here later today," said Carter.

"Sheriff," I said. "Mrs. Tessin just dropped an important piece of information."

"We can talk about it after we eat," said the lawman as he passed out boxes of café food and poured himself a coffee. "Dig in."

"I don't want anything," said Heather. "Actually, I think I'll be leaving."

"Wait," I said. "I still don't know why the trouble got so bad, why people got sick. Was it heavy metals?"

"No," she said.

Perry flinched.

"Kitsuye was shit. It was literally shit," she said. "Chocolate-covered—"

"Antelope shit."

37

I WALKED Heather to the front door after she insisted that she was done and had to leave.

"I just need some time," she said.

"But there's food."

"Who can eat?"

Everyone else, apparently, because when I got back, there were only two pieces of bacon left and no sausage.

"Wait," said Carter. "Did she say that Boone worked for her?"

"Yes," I said. "You must have been distracted with breakfast meats. It happens."

"Tony, I want to go home," said Perry. I noticed he'd shifted his chair around the table to be farther from Carter.

As a rule, I'm not a fan of the police. They have a reputation, and not just the one I spread about them. Perry feels the same way. He calls them the blunt edge of the totalitarian state. I like the term blunt edge, but I don't go so far into the conspiracy world as he does. I probably should, but that stuff messes with your mind. Look at Perry trying to eat pancakes holding a fork with a napkin. Cops, however, are the biggest, meanest gang keeping other gangs in check. They take orders from powerful people to keep less powerful people in check. In the Johnson County War, there was a local sheriff of some merit among the defenders, but the invaders had marshals and the "law" was somehow on their side. Not a lot has changed.

I eyed Carter and shook my head. When push came to shove, he'd fallen in line and would do the bidding of the establishment.

"Does knowing who Dasher really was change your ability to actually get off your boot-licking ass and do an investigation yourself?"

"No," said Carter, not even blanching at the epithet. "Makes it worse."

"So out with it," I said.

He shook his head.

"I think Mayor Gill is acting pretty suspicious," I said. "My money's on him."

"We have a suspect."

"No, we don't. Boone is alibied."

"The hell he is. He's a bounty hunter. You had your head turned by a pretty girl. Most murders are done within the family."

"And what was Mrs. Tessin's motive?"

"Shame, hatred, daddy issues."

Perry took a bite of his napkin. It had syrup on it.

"While you're on to the idea of a paid killer, how about you for the mayor?"

"You know I wasn't there."

"Was the mayor?"

"No."

"And how do you know that?"

"Because he was boinking Rawly's wife."

"What? I thought that was you. Are you...ewwww."

"No. Don't even. I'm married. I couldn't—I was the cover. I stood guard and took her home. If anything came of it, we were to say it was me. The mayor's married too."

"Still ick. More ick."

Perry stopped eating and found something interesting across the room. He hummed to show he'd heard nothing.

"This better not leave this room," he said.

I remembered the microphone under the table. Thought about Eddie and Dasher behind the building.

"Tell me about Dashiell Stubbins," I said. "And I'll cut your arm off if you reach for another piece of bacon."

He sipped coffee and leaned back. He took it black, which is a sure sign of mental illness.

"His people go back here a long way. Since it began."

"Floyd Stubbins."

"Yeah, most died out, were ran out, or left. Dashiell's bunch was the last. We went to school together."

"Miss Severe?"

"What about her?"

"She knew Dasher was Stubbins. She called him Dashiell. I missed it at the time."

"Yes. She didn't like him. She kept quiet about it, though. Good egg."

"She called him a shit-eater. I guess she kept up on current affairs better than I."

"He began that habit early. He never was straight in the head. At first he said that by…by doing that, he developed resistance to disease."

"Did he?"

"If coming down with all of them and having to fight them off develops resistance, then he did."

Perry nodded but didn't make eye contact. His hands were back in his pockets.

"We found the cave together," said Carter. "When we were twelve. It was our secret place. There's a coal seam way in the back. It doesn't show on the face of the mountain, but it suggests an edge and a rich vein. The stuff burns well."

"I saw it."

Carter nodded. "I haven't been back there since I was twelve, but I kind of figured that's where he'd go."

"You never talked to him at all?"

"He'd gone off the deep end. I couldn't. He was full-on mad. I thought it was rabies or some other terrible thing, but I think it was losing his wife that did it to him."

"She died after he disappeared."

"But before he showed up back here," he said. "He was not well."

"Why not bring him in, get him some help?"

"He was the devil to catch," said Carter. "And the warrants out for him were serious. They still are. Boone would have made bank if he'd have caught him. He jumped a five-million-dollar bond and is named as an accessory to every kind of white-collar crime I ever heard of and some ugly criminal ones, not the least of which was manslaughter—three counts."

"But he was insane."

"He was always smart and quick. He could talk an Eskimo into an icebox."

"So?"

"So, I didn't want him to go through with that. He was already paying the stiffest penalty I could imagine. I thought he'd die in the hills, a poetic end, but he kept going."

"Because you gave him medicine and bedding."

"Other stuff too. It was good for the community, whether they recognized it or not. Just look at the Crazy Woman Campground. It was bankrupted when Ms. Larsen bought it and now it's one of the area's biggest attractions."

"A campsite?"

"She does a good job. Fishing trips and sightseeing. She once arranged for a parachuting thing over the camp. Didn't work out great, but it made the papers. She talks about making it into a resort with cabins and restaurants. Cattle isn't everything anymore. At least it wasn't. Now though…"

"Coal?"

"Don't hold your breath on that," he said. "Too much disruption. If we were on food stamps, it'd go, but the county knows how much mess it would be."

Perry said, almost in a whisper, "Don't underestimate the greed of entitled men."

"I still like Mayor Gill for the killing," I said. "He's just the kind of shithead who'd do it."

"Why?"

"Well, Dasher said he had secrets, and he told me he was just waiting for the right time to tell them all. Gill's coal thing had to be among them. He was in town enough to see the 'coal country' posters everywhere."

"Weak."

"And he was a local tourist attraction, something to be held up as an alternative revenue source to strip mining."

"I don't think that flies either."

"And I don't like him."

"You don't have to. You can leave."

"So can everyone. So did Dashiell. This place is screwed up."

He shrugged.

"We were best friends for a while," Carter said wistfully. "The best years of my life were spent with him exploring that mesa. He saved my life a few times."

"Really?"

"He was also instrumental in getting me in trouble, but he got me out. Cliffs, a river, that time I got sick after eating…something."

"This is too much."

"The ancient Indians ate antelope droppings. It's medicinal."

"No, they didn't, and no, it isn't."

"How do you know? Have you ever tried it?"

"I know because I'm not an idiot, and I'm an idiot because I did try it. On accident."

"He meant for the best. He really believed it was a miracle drug."

"Wait. Was that antelope poop in your room, Tony?" said Perry, coming out of his invisibility cloak.

"I think so now. The little naked elf was trying to leave me presents."

"You can still buy Kitsuye on eBay," said Perry.

"I know a survivalist who has a stockpile of it."

"Shit."

"Exactly."

"I want to go home, Tony."

"Relax, Perry," I said. "This is a good cop."

He didn't look convinced.

"He's an okay cop."

"A cop who's willing to throw his own marriage under a bus if his boss gets accused of an affair?"

"A cop," I said. "He's a cop, and we're going to be nice because it doesn't take much for him to act like a dick cop, particularly now that he's kissing up to a dick mayor."

"Are you guys going to be a problem?"

"Someone's poking around your police car," said Perry, glancing out the window.

"You should go beat them up," I suggested. "Or at least arrest them on trumped-up charges. Isn't that the usual procedure?"

Carter sneered. "Those are the Isaaks. I'll tell them you're leaving."

"I got this," I said.

Mrs. Isaaks was at the door peeking in when I opened it.

"Hi," I said, coming outside. "I'm Tony Flaner."

"Oh, how just perfect," she said, bringing her hands together. "Sherman, this is Mr. Flaner. You're just who we were looking for."

I felt more than saw Carter behind me in the doorway.

"Did you get the book about our poor Uri?"

"I did."

"Can you help us?"

"Mr. Flaner has to leave the county," said Deputy Sheriff Craig Carter. "Tonight."

"What?"

"Shut up, Craig," I said.

I could hear Carter grind his teeth.

"Your name's Ada, right? I remember you from the other day here at the bar."

"It's a nasty place," she said. "The whole county is nasty—no offense, officer."

"It's okay," I said. "He's nasty too."

Sherman wiped his face with a handkerchief retrieved from his back pocket and stepped up to Carter, really close. "Do you people not know that we went to war with Nazis? They are the bad guys? Unequivocal monsters?"

"We—"

"Then why do you allow fascists to openly run around here?"

"He's a cop," I said as Carter's hand slid to his cuffs. "His job description includes fascist. The mayor is nasty too. Really. They're all nasty."

"I'm beginning to think the worst," said Ada. She took my hands in hers and looked in my eyes. "Do you see what I mean? Because of who we are."

A cold shudder went down my back as I considered what she was saying.

"You think your son might have run afoul of the local color?" I said.

"What else can we think?"

Carter said, "I wouldn't think—"

"No, of course not. So don't start now," I said.

"Mr. Flaner, you're digging—"

"He was a good boy," said Sherman, turning his back squarely on Carter in a clear slight. "He had a mind for business but liked to take shortcuts. I know he saw some business opportunity here—that's what he told his friends—but what it was, we never found out. He disappeared, and we haven't heard from him in years."

"Cattle rustling?" I wondered out loud.

The Isaaks' eyes went big.

"No, too much competition," I said.

"We weren't the best parents," said Ada, "but we love our son."

"How do those two sentences work together?"

Sherman cleared his throat. "We had words," he said. "I told him not to come back until he'd made something of himself and became a success."

"And how would you measure that?"

"Same as his sister's, I guess. Money, power, friends, trophies."

"Yes, Sherman is big on trophies."

"It was stupid," he said. "I'd had the same speech from my father at his age, and it didn't do me any harm."

Ada shook her head.

I said, "Kinda looks like it did."

"It was a family tradition. Goes back to the good..." Sherman let go. I let him.

"I tried to tell them," said Carter. "No one by that name or description around here."

"How do you know that?"

"I'd know. Small town."

"He might have passed through."

"That might have happened, but he's not here now."

"I think he is," said Ada. "Or at least was..."

"I said—"

"She's talking about a grave, you oaf."

"Oh."

"What are you going to do with all the skinheads and Nazis around here?" I said. "Oh, I meant to tell you, one of them unloaded a machine gun at me."

"No, they didn't."

"Yes, they did."

"It's a free country. They have different political views; that doesn't make them criminals."

"Machine gun..."

Sherman turned back around to look at Carter. He didn't say anything, just looked at him. I felt a power coming from him, a righteous anger from a mourning father.

"You should go talk to him," I said to Carter. "I bet Varg knows something. God knows he was quick to get me moving off his property."

Carter's wrinkled blushing face snapped to me. "What? You were trespassing? No wonder he was upset at you."

"He shot at me and not just then, also yesterday at Miracle Canyon."

"You don't trespass on a man's property. He had every right to—" His phone went off in his pocket, or I'm sure he would have rationalized a machine gun murder. He went back inside to take it.

"The country is full of gun nuts," I said.

"Country as in 'not the city,' or country like the USA?" asked Sherman.

"Yes."

"Can we go now, Tony?" It was Perry, his hands in his pockets, sliding sideways toward the Cadillac.

"I'm sorry, Mr. and Mrs. Isaaks. I don't think I can help you," I said. "I'm just not plugged in here. I think the FBI may be needed. The local constabulary isn't interested."

"He has to live here," explained Perry.

Ada's lip quivered. Sherman put his arm around her.

"Please..." Mrs. Isaaks said to me. "Please. He's a pacifist. He wouldn't defend himself if he had to."

"I—"

Carter busted through the door, saving me from whatever I was going to say. "Shooting at the Crazy Woman Campground," he said, sliding into his car.

He spat gravel as he sped away, leaving the four of us to watch.

"I...I should see what's happening. Come on, Perry."

We got in the car and followed Carter out of town. No gravel. In the mirror, I watched the Isaaks disappear into the retreating distance, still holding each other in front of Floyd's Old Time Saloon.

"Too many guns," I said, hoping Mrs. Isaaks, Ada, was wrong about her son.

38

"WE'RE RAVENS NOW?" said Perry.

"What do you mean?"

"Ravens fly toward the sound of gunfire. An act that goes against all instinct."

"They've learned to recognize a dinner bell."

"Why are we going?"

"Mostly to get away from those people," I said.

To Perry's credit, he drove toward the gunfire, albeit not at a great rate of speed. Five below the speed limit, which any American will tell you is teeth-grindingly slow.

"Do you think their son's dead?"

"I don't know. For such a tight-knit community, there is an extraordinary amount of tension."

"They don't like strangers."

"There is that."

"For a place this tightly knit, no way a boy like the Isaaks' kid could go unnoticed. And they have actual Nazis here."

"Yeah," I said, wondering if I already had an idea where his body was hidden.

"What do you want to bet the Nazis are involved in the shooting?" Perry said.

"They're not. It's just the stupid Cromby brats putting holes in their million-dollar camper."

"Then why did Carter book it out of there so fast?"

"Same reason we did, I bet," I said. "To get away from an uncomfortable situation."

I needed to go to the campground, anyway, hoping Gail would help me retrieve the stranded ATV. It was probably time to return the rental anyway. Carter had made it pretty clear that I was no longer welcome. I wondered if he'd pay me. I never did get the contract or the money upfront. He might just dick out of his obligation. Probably would.

We saw the police lights flashing from the highway. Carter had parked his SUV sideways across the road as if barricading it.

"He's going whole hog," said Perry.

"Thanks for the rural color commentary," I said. "Do you even know what that means?"

"Gluttony?"

"Why not."

Perry pulled next to the dumpsters at the front end of the park and we got out.

We heard a gunshot. It was not a pop from the little gun Bunny had had. It was a loud thing. Perry ducked behind the car. Channeling Poe, I wandered weak and weary toward the shooting.

Carter was hunkered behind his police mobile. I joined him.

"'Sup?" I said.

"Flaner?"

"Yes?"

"What are you—" Another shot. Some sobs.

"Beaumont, let him go!" Carter said.

"Beaumont?" I said.

"He's shot his father."

"What?"

"They were arguing about something. Roddy got winged in the arm, managed to get to the office. Gail called it in, and now Beaumont is in there too."

"Where's Gail?"

"Haven't seen her."

Another big-gun shot.

"I figure that's Roddy firing back," he said. "Beaumont has that little .25."

"And Roddy has a big .357."

"Yeah...wait. Dasher?"

"You just putting this together?" I said. "He was on your list."

"But I took him off."

"What changed your mind?"

"Boone."

"Because he's black?"

"Because he's a bounty hunter, and it was his gun."

"We don't know it was his gun," I said.

Another shot.

"Boys, you've got to come out of there!" shouted Carter over the hood.

The sound of a small gun going off.

"What in the world could they be arguing about?" said Carter.

"You're telling me you have no idea? Couldn't wager a wild guess?"

"What? Dasher?"

I heard Gail shriek, and I stood up.

"Flaner!" Carter reached to pull me back but missed.

"Hey, you fuckwads!" I yelled at the office. "I'm coming in. If anyone shoots me, I'm going to be royally pissed."

"Flaner!" Deputy Sheriff Carter followed me, careful to stay behind me. Behind me, as in using me as a human shield. Cops.

I walked to the porch. Two white pickups were parked to the side. One had girl silhouette mudflats and a rifle in the back window, the other was the one I'd seen on the trail with an ATV strapped down in the bed. Down the road, I saw the Crombys, each with a gun of their own: Bunny with a little derringer, Terrance with a 9mm, Maxine with a rifle and finally Penn with what looked like a .50 anti-tank gun on a biped. I didn't see Lynson.

"Don't you guys shoot me, either," I called to them.

Each registered a different level of disappointment on their scary faces.

No one shot at me, and I got to the door of the office. I pulled it open and found Carter standing next to me.

"Shamed you into some balls, eh?" I said.

"Stick it."

From inside, I heard sobbing.

"Gail?" I went in. "Gail?"

"Here," she called.

I followed her voice into the front room, Carter behind me. Yes, behind me, brave be-badged soul that he was.

Gail was kneeling over Roddy Dean, tending a bloody arm. Beaumont sat on the couch his face in his hands, bawling. There were two guns on the table. One was the little silver thing I'd given back to Beaumont; the other was a big silver thing that looked exactly like the one I saw with Boone's clothes.

"Huh."

"Call an ambulance," said Carter.

"No," said Roddy. "It's just a scratch."

"You're not hip enough to quote Monty Python," I said. "You're an idiot."

"I don't like you," said the rancher.

Carter took up the two guns and put his back in the holster.

"Is that a .357?" I asked.

"Yes."

"Huh."

"He did it," moaned Beaumont. "He killed Dash."

"No, I didn't," said Roddy, holding his arm and trying to stand up.

"You did, you bigoted murderer!"

"Mrs. Larsen, call an ambulance," said Carter.

"Ms.," she corrected him and disappeared into the kitchen.

"What happened here?" asked the sheriff, helping Roddy to a chair.

"Just a little family squabble, Craig," he said. "Nothing to see here. No charges."

"You murdering bastard!" Beaumont reached for a gun from the table but they were no longer there.

Gail called from the kitchen, "They're an hour out on another call. Maybe you should drive him."

"Okay. Tell them to expect me. Come on, you two."

"Hold up," I said. "Beaumont, why do you think your father killed Dashiell?"

The young man's eyes went large and soft. "You know him, then?"

"Not like you did," said Roddy, spitting on me. "Queer."

"Me?" I said.

He glowered. "Queer!"

Beaumont's face went red.

"He set up a blind at the little medicine wheel," Beaumont said. "I told him that Dash liked to dance there in the rain. Only he knew it. The night of the killing, he left me, and I didn't see him again until the next day. He was covered in mud and guilt. You rotten murdering bastard! No wonder Mom left you!"

"Is this true?" I asked Roddy.

"The boy's crazy. He needs help. He's—"

Beaumont threw himself past me and onto his father. He landed several blows to his nose before Carter pulled him off and remembered he carried handcuffs.

"You bastard!" screamed Beaumont, tears running down his face. "You're in the past, old man. My past! I'll never speak to you again, but I'll speak at you at your trial. You can count on it."

"Remember which side your bread's buttered on, boy."

"Rot in hell!"

Carter led Beaumont out to his car.

"It was that A-rab!" Roddy yelled after him. "I didn't do it!"

"A-rab?" I said. "Are you trying to get me to punch you, too?"

"The bartender. He was there. He did it. I saw him up at the little medicine wheel that night, standing over the body."

"Bullshit."

"He shot at me."

"Pull the other one."

"True. I didn't kill that faggot."

I punched him in his arm, not hard, more of a friendly little smack that wouldn't have hurt anyone who didn't already have an oozing gunshot wound there.

"Ahhhh! Sonovabitch!" he yelled.

Another tap. "Mind your manners," I said.

"What's going on in there?" called Carter.

"Diversity training," I called back.

Roddy said, "He fell in with a bad crowd. Got pulled into the agenda. Ouch!"

It was Gail that time. She handed me a wet wipe for the blood on my knuckles.

"Is it true?" I asked him. "Did Beaumont tell you about the dance?"

"Yes."

"You built the blind at the wheel to ambush him?"

"I ain't talking without—Ouch!"

"What's all that screaming?" Perry poked his head in the door.

"Angst," I hollered back. "Growing pains."

"Looks like a gunshot."

"They're everywhere," said Gail, pointing. There were indeed several new additions to the wall and seat covers.

"Roddy, did you go up to the medicine wheel that night to kill the hermit?"

"I didn't kill him," he said. "I was there and saw the bartender standing over the body. He shot at me when I called out."

"I don't believe you."

"He had a laser gun!"

"Calm down, Roddy. This ain't *Star Wars*."

"Eddie?" said Perry. "He's the killer?"

"Or this piece of trash," I said. "Maybe."

"Maybe?" said Gail. "There was a gunfight in my house. These people suck."

"What were they doing here?" I said. "What happened?"

"They came looking for a fight," said Gail.

"Those stuck-up campers poached on my land," said Roddy.

"He means the Crombys."

"Killed two doe out on my back third. Left the carcasses to rot. I came to have a word with them about it."

"Why not call the cops?" I asked.

"That's not how we do things around here."

"Guns," said Perry.

"Guns," I agreed.

Carter came back inside. "Come on, Roddy, you're next."

"Ain't no reason to go arresting me," he said.

"Gail?"

She looked from the shot man to the sheriff and hesitated.

"You've got to live here?" I said.

"They shot up my house. Book 'em."

"But first, let's get you to the doctor."

We followed Carter out the door. Beaumont was in the back, restrained and weeping. Roddy, he put him in the front seat beside him, uncuffed. I helped slide him in, doing the customary head push so he didn't bump it. I might have slipped and hit his hurt arm.

"Did you know about Dashiell dancing in the rain at the little medicine wheel?" I asked Carter.

"No. Never heard of that before."

"It was his new thing," moaned Beaumont. "To wash away the sins. He'd just begun it. It was his secret thing."

"He was dead when I got there," said Roddy.

"Why did you mention the dance in the bar?"

"I only mentioned it once."

"Why?"

"To throw opportunity onto others."

"I don't follow," said the deputy sheriff.

"That is why you'll never be sheriff," I said.

"Hey, no reason to be uncivil."

"Fucking murdering inbred asshole!" screamed Beaumont from the backseat.

"Beaumont, you might want to find a different approach than heredity," I offered and sniffed. "Maybe his hygiene. Yeah, that'll stick." I closed Roddy's door.

Carter swung his vehicle around and sped off, leaving his customary asshole gravel plume behind him. Man, it's hard to like cops.

The Crombys watched the vehicle go and then disappointedly shuffled back to their land yacht. Lynson poked his head out of the far bathroom where he'd hidden and followed them.

"Those people," I said to Gail as I jogged up the steps to the porch.

"They lucked out. The Deans were here for them."

"Start from the top," I said and took one of the seats at the bistro table. Perry took one beside me. Gail remained standing, probably because there were no more chairs.

"They arrived together. Roddy was in a state," Gail said. "Beaumont looked bored and moody."

"So his usual self?"

She laughed. "Yeah, I guess. Poor kid having such a jerk for a father. I'm shocked he's stayed here as long as he has. He should have recognized that these people would never accept him. Being gay just isn't something that's done out here. This town is in the past, left behind by the rest of the world."

"You knew he was gay?"

"Everyone knew he was gay," said Gail. "But no one talked about it, see? If you don't talk about it, it's not real."

"What if you act on it?" I asked.

"Then your father might get upset."

"Roddy went to that camp to make accusations about poaching?" said Perry, pointing to the Cromby's glampsite.

"He did."

"What happened?" I said.

"He accused them of killing deer on his property. Penn Cromby replied he wouldn't kill anything so common. Lots of name-calling. It went on for a while. Roddy thought it might have been his kid because the animals were so shot up, no man would do that. Penn told him to prove it. There was some shoving and shouting and then Roddy turned around to go to the truck, I think to get a gun."

"What did the Crombys do?"

"They got theirs."

"And Beaumont?"

"He went inside to get a drink from my sink while it was all happening. When he came out, his father was still yelling and I asked him about the gun under the seat."

"What gun? What seat?"

"That big silver gun you saw before. I saw it under the driver's side seat of Roddy's car. I asked Beaumont if it was a .357. He said his father had one of those, but it wasn't silver. I showed him what I was talking about. He fished it out and opened it. Several spent shells."

"That set him off?"

"No," said Gail. "He looked worried and asked me why I wanted to know about the caliber."

"What did you say?"

"I told him that was the kind of gun that killed Dashiell."

39

PERRY WANTED TO LEAVE. He let me know by saying, "Tony, I want to leave."

"It's been a busy day," said Gail. "And it's barely noon."

"Hey, I gotta ask you a favor," I said. "You know the ATV I borrowed?"

"Rented," she said. "Yes, I know you left it on the trail."

"How do you know that?"

"Varg Jayger called me and said he saw it by his property."

"How'd he know it was yours?"

"It has my name on it—well, the campground's."

"Oh, you Crazy Woman!" I said.

"Don't be cute."

"Hey, Ms. Larsen, let him be cute," said Perry. "He rushed in to save you, you know."

"You did?"

"I did," said I.

"I thought that was Carter."

"He followed me in. Didn't you notice?"

"I was otherwise distracted. Once the shooting stopped and the crying went into overdrive, I had blood to deal with."

"Well, he did," said Perry.

"Thank you."

"Don't tell Allie," I said to Perry.

"I won't."

Gail's eyebrow went up. "So that's her name."

"What about the ATV?"

"Go get it."

"Can I borrow a gas can? And some gas?"

"In the shed."

We left her to spackle bullet holes and think insurance claims, and followed the path of ATVs to a little shed wherein were gas cans, and, just to prove a rule, one actually had gas in it.

"Can you drive me there?" I asked Perry.

"Can I?"

"Um, actually, no. Not in the Caddy. But you can get me close. It's just behind Varg Jayger's place."

"How about we go the long way around?"

"Your car still wouldn't make it. Come on. Strength in numbers."

"I want to go home."

"To do what?"

"Well, we haven't even opened the bomb shelter yet."

"There's plenty of time for that."

"No, there isn't," said Perry. "Sounds like we have to leave tonight."

"Don't believe everything you hear."

"What is it with you and cops?"

"Me?" I said. "You're the one who wet himself being at the same table with one."

"Did not."

"Did too."

"I have bladder problems."

We laughed and I put the can in the trunk of Perry's car.

"It's just up the road," I said. "Opposite way of the law."

"Thank God."

We pulled out of the park without digging a trench in the gravel proving it can be done, and headed past Perry's turnoff looking for the Nazis.

"Do you think Eddie could have done it?" asked Perry. "He seemed okay."

"What about the microphone?"

"Oh, shit," he said. "Yeah, that's totally not okay. Man, what a jerk. He did it."

"Why?"

"Because he's sneaky."

I didn't think that was a good enough motivation for killing anyone, but Eddie was again on my radar. He had to be. Roddy put him there.

"There," I said, pointing to a barbed wire-strewn gate. "That's got to be it."

We got out in front of a chain-link gate with a motorized opener.

"Place looks like some kind of camp."

"Prepping Nazis," I said. "Your neighbors."

"Don't remind me. What now?"

"We knock?"

"Is this the guy who shot at you with a machine gun earlier?"

"Yes, but then I hadn't knocked."

"How many bullets?"

"I didn't count. Two guns full. Maybe three. How many in a gun?"

Perry shook his head. "Forget it. Buy Ms. Larsen a new—"

Before he could finish, the air exploded with the roar of motorcycles. Subtle as an H-Bomb, and nearly as pleasant, the sound shook the gravel and sent plumes of dust up the road like smoke signals warning of a coming cavalry.

Perry and I stepped back as the sound came at us, covering our ears and screaming at each other unable to hear a thing.

"...hermetic fallopian tubes!" I think Perry said. "Assuming Epcot gerrymandering terrier noodle snouts!"

"I couldn't agree more!" I said.

"Who's got acne?"

The gates shook and parted. We peered in, expecting to see Beelzebub and Beatrice on beagles, but it was only three skinhead Nazi types sterilizing their testes with acoustically weaponized Harley-Davidsons. I pictured little bald spermies getting rattled to death by the vibrations of unmuffled motorcycles and felt a little happier.

The three roared up and looked us up and down. They squinted at Perry's Cadillac, adjusted their guns—of course they wore guns—and then rode away without even a sunset. We watched them vanish down the lonely road for a long while until, like their deodorant, they were only a memory.

When we turned around, there was Varg Jayger himself standing right behind us. He'd surprised us enough to make us jump, so we did. He'd snuck right up on us, which wouldn't have been hard with those god-awful loud bikes nearby. He could have approached with the Trojans' marching band and still made us wet ourselves like that.

"Someone needs to put a bell on you," I said.

"What?"

"I said...eh, forgot it."

He stood there in big heavy boots laced above his ankles, steel-tipped. Baggy camouflage cargo pants bumpy with pockets in the Arctic Alpine motif, helpful for July blizzards. He wore a green army surplus tank top that did a good job of showing his heavily tattooed torso. His face had been inked more than a sixteenth-century peace pact, but he'd really given his shoulders over to the effect. He had Celtic knots on one, a swooping Valkyrie on the other, spears aiming down his bicep. He had dials on his chest, little stars I'd seen in a movie once. They were some kind of Russian mafia thing. I couldn't imagine that little shit having such connections. I stepped up and saw they were compasses, not stars at all. The one on his right breast pointed east, the other, I guess to blow the viewer's mind, pointed west.

"What?" he said.

I tried to imagine what his family thought of his aesthetics. Even if they were racist skinhead alt-right stormtrooper wannabes like him, family photos had to be rough. And what was the meaning of the 1488 under his eye? Was that his PIN number he kept forgetting? Did he have to use a mirror to buy groceries?

These are the kinds of questions that always came up when I saw unfamiliar facial tattoos representing poor life choices, and normally I wouldn't hesitate to ask about them, but since the man underneath them was a steel-toed-booted skinhead with a gun on his hip and had previously tried to kill me with a machine gun, I thought I would save my questions for another time.

"Hey, Varg," I said. "Remember me? From the bar and also from behind your house when you tried to murder me?"

"What?"

I said it again louder. Seriously, motorcycle noise is a menace.

"What do you want?" he responded.

"I've come for the ATV that was left behind your house by someone. Who it might have been is anyone's guess."

He squinted and shifted his weight. Though I was closer to him than I'd ever been before, looking right at the tattoo lines around his eyes—he's a Gemini apparently—I couldn't read through his mask.

"I have gas," I said.

"What?"

"Perry."

Perry opened the trunk and showed the gas can.

"Gail Larsen from the campground sent us."

"Crazy Woman," he said.

"You're one to judge."

He squinted again. Maybe he sneered. Who knew?

I tried to be afraid of him. It made sense. He'd shot at me. I'd been afraid of his deaf friends, but I couldn't see Varg as anything but a poser punk. Maybe it was his height, maybe it was not having a vibrating motor between his legs, but even watching him feel up his gun handle, I couldn't help myself.

"Listen, gerbils," I said. "Gail said you called her about the machine. Do you have it?"

"Gerbils are small rodents, not a famous National Socialist," he said.

"Your point?"

"Tony…" Perry wasn't as confident as I felt and moved to the other side of the car.

"She said she'd lent it to you," said Varg.

"Shows what you know."

"She didn't lend it to you?"

"Me? No."

"Oh."

"She rented it."

"I don't like you."

"I am sorry to hear that, I was about to invite you to my bris."

He sneered at that. I think. Maybe snarled. A smile of some kind? There were teeth involved.

"Maybe we should take the long way around," said Perry. "This car can take it."

"Are you going to make my friend, my white male heterosexual friend, drive his classic white American car, across treacherous axle-breaking back roads like some bi-curious foreigner?"

"What?"

"Mind if we get the ATV?" I pointed past him up the path toward his cabin to help clear up the point. "I figure it's about a hundred steps that way."

"You'd save us a load of time," said Perry.

"Be a chap. Let us walk your lonely driveway. We promise not to bring up feminism, gun control, or the Nuremberg trials. Promise."

"You're a funny guy."

"Ha! Told you, Perry. I'm funny."

"Perry?" said Varg. "As in Perry Whitehouse?"

"Yes," said my friend.

"I saw you at some Indian casino. You were awesome."

"Eh...I don't remember seeing you, but then again, the lights were pretty bright."

"I didn't look like this then," he said.

"What did you look like?"

"Picture me without the tattoos."

I tried. I couldn't.

"Why don't you have a Netflix special yet?" he asked

"Cell phones," said I.

"What?"

"He's joking," said Perry. "He's a comedian too."

"I heard he was a cop."

"A private investigator," said Perry. "Not a cop. Can't make arrests. Isn't even licensed in this state."

"Oh?"

"Oh," I said.

"I heard you were working on the hermit thing."

"You heard right."

"Am I a suspect?"

"No way," said Perry. "Not even—"

"Yes."

"Why?"

"The murder happened up at the little medicine wheel, which is right up behind your place."

"A ways up, but so?"

"So you're a gun-toting, trigger-fingered Nazi with delusions of adequacy."

"What?"

"And you said he'd stolen from you."

"He broke into my place once. That wasn't enough to kill someone over."

"Just bending your grass got me shot at."

He laughed. "You tell the sheriff about that?"

"I did."

"What did he say?"

"He wanted to know if I'd press charges, so he could lock you up for the betterment of society. I told him I'd wait and see."

"He said you had it coming for stepping on my property, didn't he?"

I squinted.

He smiled.

"I don't like you either," I said.

"Can we just get the machine?" asked Perry. "I really want to go home, and Tony won't let me until this thing is handled."

"You can go," said Varg. "I'll walk your friend to the machine and see he gets it moving."

"Good with me." Perry dropped the gas can where he stood and was in the car and peeling out before I could say "abandoned to fascists."

40

IT WASN'T A HUNDRED STEPS. It was much more. I'd call it a ways.

After Perry sped away, leaving me to my fate even after hearing me taunt the little man and knowing he'd shot at me earlier, I followed Varg down a long, winding dirt road. Shaded by aspens and cottonwoods, it was actually a pretty walk with the sun peeking in between breezy leaves. I smelled grass and fresh water, mud, bark. Soil.

"What the hell happened to you? Get beat up?"

"Whatever do you mean?" I said.

"You just had the big bump before. Now you look like you were a paint-ball target."

"It's all this country air."

"You're the king of the non sequitur."

"You're assuming I wear underwear."

He shook his head and walked. I shifted the gas can to my other hand and followed. It was heavy and suddenly the little nature walk with the master race felt like exercise.

"I didn't kill the hermit," said Varg after a minute or two.

"Why do you say that?"

He paused, no doubt trying to fix my response to his statement. "Because I didn't," he said.

"You're hardly an unimpeachable witness." I really should learn to shut up. I braced myself for a slug when Varg held up a moment.

"I live alone here."

"On all this land? Way out here? How very serial killer." Really, I was asking for it.

"I was home when it happened."

"How do you know when it happened?"

"I heard it was during the fireworks."

"This place is better than Instagram."

"I was at the fair during the afternoon," he explained in a calm, almost friendly way. "But when the clouds started coming in, I rushed home."

"Why did you rush home?"

"Reasons."

"Reasons?"

"Reasons."

"Glad we cleared that up." I flinched again but again no violence.

We walked on. I reached for my now-tattered map and tried to orient myself.

"What the hell are you doing?" asked Varg.

"Getting directions. I think we're lost. I'm supposed to follow the drinking gourd."

"Give me that!" He ripped it out of my hands.

"What gives?"

"What?"

"Give it back."

"I'm taking you across my land as a courtesy. You are not allowed to take notes, record locations, count steps or do any other such espionage stuff."

"I'm just trying to get my bearings. Seems like we've been walking a long time."

"That's because you're fat."

"Yeah, well at least I don't look like a truck stop shit-house door."

"What does that mean?"

"It means you're covered in repulsive graffiti."

"Aren't you judgmental."

"Says the Nazi."

He paused. I braced.

"Do I have to blindfold you?" he asked.

"Not unless you take me to dinner first and I get to pick the feather duster."

"What?"

"Give me back my map. I'll be good."

He put it in his gun holster. I guess it was more convenient than any of the eighty-three other pockets his pants offered.

We walked on. I made mental notes of locations and counted my steps.

"I met with some people at the fair," Varg said.

"Eighty-six, eighty-sev—"

"What are you counting?"

"Shrubs. You have a lot of shrubs."

"No, I don't."

"Well, you could have a nice shrubbery over there, two levels. Set it off with a herring tree."

He stopped and scowled.

"I'll shut up," I promised.

"I didn't kill him. I know you think I did."

"Actually, I should tell you that Roddy Dean was just arrested for suspicion of the crime."

"Really? He was arrested? For that?"

"Wait, now that you mention it, maybe not. He went away in a police vehicle, but that might have been to go to the hospital. But he is high on the list."

"Why?"

"His son said he did it."

"Beaumont?"

"Has he other sons?"

"No, but he wishes he had."

"Go on."

"He could have done it. Hell yes, he could have. Real redneck."

"Says the Nazi."

"I know you're saying that to bug me," said Varg,

"And...?"

"You can stop now."

"Said the Nazi."

"Please."

"Sure. Fine. Is that the best alibi you have? Alone fondling your guns?"

We turned a bend and I finally saw the house I'd seen before. I guess it was set far back on the property. I don't have a sense for the area, but the lots out here were pretty large. Baby ranches. Lots of woodland, creek, and critters, ideal for wildlife and wildfires.

"She ran calling Wildfire!" I sang.

"Who did?"

"The song."

"Why are you singing that?"

"Got distracted."

Before the house on the road was a camper, one of those big pull-behind things. White sides. An awning. I think you need something called a fifth-wheel to move it, a fifth wheel being a visiting cousin during a swinger's orgy.

"Nice camper."

"I was here," he said. "That's all I can tell you."

"In the house or the camper?"

He held up then and looked at me suspiciously.

"Okay, now I'm suspicious."

"What?"

"Why do you need two living spaces?" I asked.

"None of your business."

I studied the two choices. If I had to choose one to live in, it wouldn't be the house with its boarded-up windows. The camper looked far more inviting. There were nice curtains waving in open windows, a little tea set on a bistro table. A welcome mat at the door.

"What did Dasher do to you, exactly—you know the thing he did that wasn't worthy of killing?"

"He broke into my...house."

"House or camper?"

"Why?"

"Just trying to pinpoint the coordinates for the airstrike."

"You're getting on my nerves."

"Said the Nazi."

Okay, that time I think he really thought about punching me.

"I'm not a violent man," he said.

"Said the—"

"Don't."

"Guy who shot at me with a machine gun."

"You're a grudge holder, aren't you?"

"My bad."

Hidden behind some pines was a garage-sized aluminum shed with closed doors. Tire tracks leading to the door suggested it housed vehicles. Another shed was actually built into the front of the house, maybe like an airlock, or extra storage. A fifty-gallon drum lay on its side, a common enough yard ornament for recluses and rednecks, but this one was pretty new. Another was blue. I'd seen a similar blue one at Rawly's for rainwater.

"Let me guess," I said. "All your survival stores are in the house, and you live out of the camper when there's a low chance of Armageddon."

"That's it," he said. Which told me it wasn't.

"Dasher?" I said.

"He broke into my house and went through my things. I caught him."

"Trespassing? And you didn't shoot him?"

"No, I didn't shoot him."

"Shoot at him?"

"Not that either."

"Was he naked? Was that why you didn't shoot him? You admired his cock? Couldn't bring yourself to deprive the world of that?"

"I told you I'm not a violent man."

"Said the—"

"I could see he wasn't armed. Okay?"

"Okay..."

"All he did was yell at me, accuse me of wasting my potential, polluting my mind and memory with shit."

"Shit? Did he really say shit?"

"No, I'm paraphrasing."

"Too bad."

"Why?"

"No reason," I said. "Go on."

"What aren't you telling me?"

"Oh there's bunches, but first you. How'd it end?"

"I told him to leave, get off my property. He ran off."

"Holy hell, what is that smell?"

It was the same stink I'd encountered before. A window cleaner smell. We were coming into the backyard, following the trail that would lead out to the back road, the one I'd come in before.

"I got sewer issues," he said. "Stink. It's why I came home that night."

"To smell your own stink?"

"I'm trying to help you," he said.

"Sounds like you're trying to get out of a murder rap."

"I keep the smell mostly contained," he said. "When there's a storm, particularly when it rains, it's a good time to let the smell out without offending the neighbors."

"You worry about offending your neighbors?"

"Yes."

"You're a skinhead survivalist gun nut, why would you care?"

"Who said I was a gun nut?"

I bent down and picked up some cartridges from the ground. "Remember these?" I said.

He shrugged. "I didn't do it."

"I saw you standing right there with an automatic weapon. Who was it, then?"

"No, the hermit. I didn't do that."

I dropped the casings back to the ground like sand through an hourglass.

"Can you find your own way out of here now?"

"I don't know. It'll be hard to remember without a hailstorm of bullets flying past me."

"Want me to do it again?"

"Nah, I need to improve my navigation skills." I held out my hand.

"What?"

"My map."

He dug into his holster and gave it to me.

"Do you have a pencil?" I asked.

"No, why?"

"I guess I'll just have to remember three hundred twenty-two paces from the gate."

"Are you joking?" It wasn't sarcastic, he really wanted to know.

"Yes, I'm joking. It's how I handle stress. That and pissing myself. Oh, and running away. Sarcasm mostly, but peeing myself in a pinch."

"And you're not a cop?"

"I don't look like a cop."

"Then why count steps?"

"Dasher was right, you have been messing with your memory."

"Just joking?"

"Yes. To get a rise out of you."

"That's not very nice."

"Said the Nazi."

"I'm not a Nazi!"

The statement took me aback.

"I'm taken aback."

"I'm not a Nazi."

"Says the man with swastikas on his face."

He stared at me with some kind of emotion. Fear, frustrations, toothache. Hard to tell under all that ink.

"Just an Aryan Brother then? An alt-righty?"

He stared daggers at me.

"Don't tell me you've fallen so low...that...say it ain't so—you're not a..." I gulped. "A *Libertarian?*"

"You're trying to piss me off."

"Actually, at this point I'm still testing boundaries."

"Why?"

"Reasons."

"Reasons?"

"Reasons."

Varg smiled, a warm grin. Actually human beneath all that hateful iconography.

"Well, bye," I said.

"Bye."

I'd maybe taken five steps when he called me back.

"Hey, you."

"The name's Flaner," I said. "Tony Flaner."

"Right. I forgot."

"Say it."

"What?"

"My name."

"Tony Flaner."

"No, say it like I said it."

He shook his head, the humanity rising up again. I blinked.

"You're Flaner, Tony Flaner."

"That's it."

"License to annoy."

"Bingo," I said. "What was it you wanted to say?"

"You didn't ask me if I heard anything that night."

"The night of the killing?"

"What other night?"

"Did you hear something?"

"Yes."

"What? Fireworks and thunder?"

"That," he said. "I also thought I heard shooting from on top of the mountain, but I can't be sure."

"Would you swear to that in a court of law?"

"No, I just said I can't be sure."

"Right."

"Tell me, Flaner, are you on drugs? Because I've seen people on drugs and you're acting weird."

"Me? No. It's just my personal..." I trailed off as I realized I was a little dizzy. "That stink isn't doing me any good."

"Yeah, the containment broke."

"I'll leave. You can fish your urinal mints out of your cesspool without me. Do you have a cesspool?"

"No."

"Smells like you do."

"I heard vehicles on the road," he said.

"When?"

"The night of the killing."

"Who was it?"

"I don't know. I only heard it."

"Go on." I pulled my shirt up over my face.

"Before the rain started, I heard an ATV moving on the road from the south. I think it was Rawly's. He has a really expensive one. Sounds different than the run-of-the-mill machines like most people have. After that, about half an hour later, I heard a truck down the road by the Bar Shield pasture."

"Where the cows were stolen?"

"Steers."

I ground my teeth.

"Shortly after the truck, I heard another ATV coming from the south toward the park turnoff. Couldn't have been twenty minutes later that I heard another ATV, this time from the north coming the same way. I figured kids were going up there to do drugs."

"What kind of drugs?"

He ignored me. I didn't blame him.

"Then, still before the fireworks started, maybe ten minutes before, Rawly came back down. And..."

"What?"

"Maybe he had a trailer," he said. "On a long lead or something. I heard gravel crunching."

"A trailer?"

He shrugged. "Can't explain it."

"Try."

"A rolling."

"A drum? Like those suspicious ones in front of your house?"

He went white, which was a trick behind his blackface.

"Well?" I said.

"Maybe. A mountain bike maybe. A wagon."

"And?"

"And that's it. The fireworks started, a storm blew through. I was dealing with my stuff."

"Did you hear any more?"

"No. I was inside by then."

"So the gist of what you're sayin' is that there was a lot of traffic."

"Yes. Truck down by the fence. Smaller things up the back trail."

"Back trail?"

"There's a good road that leads to the little medicine wheel. Much easier."

"But more visible."

"Yes."

"Would all that traffic have seen each other?"

"I didn't see lights. If they were running dark, they might not. Probably wouldn't, actually. Plus there are lots of turnouts. The trail leads to the wheel but also to a bunch of other places."

"Like Miracle Canyon?"

"That's one of the places."

"Is it usually so crowded on the trail at night?"

"Hell no. It was one for the books."

"Weren't you curious? Why didn't you come out and see what was going on?"

"We like to be left alone out here. We mind our own business."

"Says the Nazi who just snitched."

41

THE ATV WAS FARTHER AWAY than I thought. It took me a spell to go the ways, and when I arrived, I was tuckered out, I can tell you.

The sun was high and bright, making the landscape cruelly beautiful to my sweat-stung eyes. The smell of sage wafted on the too-little-to-cool breeze, and the cicadas were just loud enough to coax an exertion headache. My tongue tasted like a shoe, my arms were stretched to twice their length by alternating the gas can between them and had turned a nice shade to peeling red between the yellow-blue bruises and scabs. A rock in my instep was competing with the blister on my heel to be the most annoying. Nine out of ten podiatrists agree I was not having a good time.

I slumped to the ground by the vehicle, caught my breath, and wiped sweat off my brow with my peeling arms. I'm not a big hat guy or a small hat guy. I mean, I'm not a hat guy, but I began to understand why the fashion had taken hold out in the West.

I hadn't given myself the luxury to ruminate on Varg or the developments at the Crazy Woman Campground during the walk because it would have interfered with my misery. Taking a rest, however, finally crawling under the chassis to find a little goddamn shade, I allowed myself to consider the situation and try to fit any of it together.

The big deal was what Varg had heard that night. The traffic out behind his house was important and would have been damn useful to have known about before I'd been kicked out of town. It was the kind of information that a regular cop would have discovered right out of the gate by talking to the neighbors. Granted, the little medicine wheel was miles away and much more easily approached by the main road, but as the crow flies, Varg's place had to be the closest permanent human habitation to it.

What did it all mean? Who was it? I had some ideas. Rawly was in the mix. He'd told me he'd gone up there. The other two—or were there three? —I wasn't so sure. I had suspicions and conjectures, theories and stratagems, blisters and sunburns, but not enough. Beaumont accused his father, who accused Eddie. Meanwhile, bounty hunter Boone was coming to town to talk to Carter.

Boone.

Was coming to town.

To talk to Carter.

Carter was not a good client, witness, cop, husband, or tour guide, but now that I was officially off the case, I could be sure that he would not invite me to the interview with Boone.

Which should have been okay.

The case was over for me. It'd been a rousing success. I'd taken it for something to do in this boredom gulag they called the country, and now I didn't need it because I was being chased out of town. That's a win, isn't it? A certain symmetry. What began with a Hobson's choice ended with another. Push and pull. Life in balance, Tony's law of momentum.

But I'd been shot at on multiple occasions. I'd fallen down a mountain, brushed my teeth with brush, and eaten antelope poop. I'd been hit and hit on. I'd heat-stroked across dirt roads two days running, and I had to steal my showers.

Strange that these things did not serve to make me happy to leave. They should have. Really. Look at that list. It's sick. I should have done a happy dance to think I'd sleep in my own bed tomorrow night, but instead, I felt a familiar screwing in my brain, that 'quitting parasite' that had so ruled my life once, that very worm of personal responsibility that had originally sent me down this path of detective work.

There were a lot of similarities between that first case with the finger trap and this one. Lonely misunderstood people whom the world was quick to write off and forget but who had people who cared enough to look into it. Me before, Craig Carter, deputy sheriff, now. Dasher's daughter, after a fashion, another. And Beaumont. The tears in his eyes were beyond anger. They were betrayal. They were loss. They were real and heartfelt.

Maybe the case was wrapped up. Maybe Eddie would confess, or Roddy, or Boone, but I wanted to be there when that happened. Besides, the killing wasn't the only thing going on around this happy little small American town. It was a nest of vice. Least I could do for the rest of the country was fuck with it a little.

Plus I didn't want to go back to Perry's "cabin" again. I'd find a flushing toilet in town.

I quickly filled the gas tank from the heavy red plastic container and only spilled about half. For safety's sake, I pushed the machine down the road ten feet or so before I started it. After five feet I realized the brake was on, so you can guess how that went.

I mounted my steed feeling like some cowboy of old—not the ones who hanged innocent women but the ones from drive-in movies who had clear moral compasses.

Off I went, buzzing down the trail, looking for the turn-off to Mandel's "vacant" house, it being the only one on the road besides Perry's that wasn't fenced, gated, and guarded with machine gun nests. On that rough dirt road, I couldn't achieve a speed fast enough to keep the spooked grasshoppers from leaping into me. They'd bred and multiplied since the day before. Maybe it was the heat. Maybe they were planning some kind of Egyptian plague to demand more straw from Pharaoh. Grasshoppers love straw. That might have been it, but I didn't stay to find out. Instead I drove to the turnoff and zipped by the house and then down the road to the highway. I kept to the shoulder, maxing out at my stupid twenty-four miles per hour on the straightaways, hoping not to be flattened by a texting truck driver trying to connect to a new hentai site his good buddy had turned him on to from channel thirty-five, ten-four, watch for smokeys.

I could have dropped the gas can off at the campground, but Gail had been pretty clear about bringing the machine back to her filled up. I assumed that went for gas cans as well. I waved at the turnoff, thinking of the warm shower I hadn't had that day, and went into Floyd.

The gas station and Floyd's Old Times Saloon were on the left. On the right was the strip mall with realtor, Prospector Paradise, salon, and the police station. Parked in front of those was Carter's cop-mobile but also a black Lexus.

I stopped at the gas station, refilled the can and the machine while considering how best to approach the sheriff's office. Landing on no real plan, I parked next to the luxury car, peeled off my helmet, hurting in a thousand different ways, and strolled into the office. Deputy Veronica was behind the desk. When she looked up to see me, her face twisted into a malicious glare.

"Little early for Halloween isn't it?" I said. Surprisingly, that didn't calm her down.

"You're a sniveling thief," she said.

"Sniveling? What does that even mean?"

"It means you snivel."

"Is that like a sniffle? Maybe with a fever?"

"No."

"So how does one snivel? Do I snivel now? Is it a nasal thing or a gait? Can snakes snivel? How about goats? Steers—don't call them cows. Stealth motorcycles? Worms and condors?"

"You stole my maps."

"Yours? Oh man, I'm sorry. I didn't know they were yours. I thought they belonged to the sheriff's department and were therefore part of the commons, being a taxpayer as I am."

"You're not a taxpayer in Wyoming."

"The hell I'm not. Four percent sales tax paid at Ginger's Café, and don't get me started on gas prices."

She took a deep breath and sighed.

"Was that a snivel?"

She shook her head.

"A shnork?"

She glared.

"A snupdog?" I offered.

"What's a snoop dogg?"

"Nothing much, what a-snup with you?" I said.

It took her a moment, but a smile crossed her lips, painting her in mirth and malice.

"Where are the maps?"

"Here." I handed them over.

She took them, opened them, saw dust fall from the folds onto her desk, held them up to peer through the tears and fixated on a stain. "What is that?"

"Blood."

"Yours?"

"Yes."

"Cool."

I expected her to give them back, but she kept them and put them into her desk drawer.

"Carter asked me to come by to talk to Boone."

"Who?"

"Barney Burger."

She shook her head.

"He's the only Black guy in the county, and he's behind that door, right there, at this moment."

"Not ringing a bell."

Her phone rang.

"How about now?"

"Sheriff's office," she said.

I leaned really close over the counter as if I had something very important to whisper, but then I shrieked and pointed suddenly to the left. She turned her head to look, and I was around the counter and down the hall before she could put the phone down.

"Excuse me, excuse me!" she called after me.

Deputy Sheriff Craig Carter's office door was closed, but I'd used doorknobs before, so it was no big thing to burst in.

"What the hell?" said Carter, standing up from behind his desk.

"Lassie fell down a well! Where's Timmy?"

"What?" That question was posed by the guy I'd kicked in the crotch after he'd punched me in the torso. The mayor. Mayor Gill Charbone. He sat in front of the desk, and beside him was Boone. Everyone was looking at me, so my ploy had worked.

"What ploy?" asked Boone.

"Why do you want us to look at you?" said Gill.

"For hell's sake," was my unbridled response.

"Flaner, you shouldn't be here," said Carter.

Gill turned to Carter. "I thought he was leaving town."

"Carter gave me the day to wrap things up," I said. "He needed time to heat the tar. I assume he already had feathers. Did you ever find a rail, Craig?"

"Get out of here."

"Hey, Boone," I said, offering the man my hand. He stood up and took it. "How goes the third degree?"

"Not much to say, really. I've been roasted by better, petted by worse."

"What is that supposed to mean?" said the mayor.

"Why are you here, Gill? Planning another rendezvous with the constable?"

He looked at Carter.

"Um, Tony," said the sheriff. "You should go."

"Sorry, Craig." Veronica was in the doorway. "He just ran past me."

"We get that."

"Should I arrest him?" She had a twinkle in her eye.

There was a long pause that didn't bode well.

"So tell me about the gun," I said to Boone.

He settled back in his chair. I moved inside, sat on the edge of Carter's desk, crossing my legs and knocking over the paper clips again.

"Tell me that's just mud on your pants," said Carter.

"Haven't checked," I said. "Though in truth, I had the shit scared out of me earlier. Oh, and I was playing in some coal recently. Could that be it?"

The mayor pretended not to hear me.

"I said, I was playing in some coal yesterday."

Boone said, "I was just telling these folks that I lost a gun."

"I saw you had a big one in the shower," I said.

"A big what?" said the mayor.

"Under my towel," said Boone, which didn't calm the mayor one little bit. "You remember the towel, Mr. Flaner? It was dry and clean when I came in. Moist and muddy when I came out. Seriously. Learn to use soap."

The mayor's mouth fell open. Hicks.

"That's true, sheriff and crooked bureaucrat," I said. "I did see the gun before." I winked at Boone to show I had his back and maybe suggest it was a good thing I'd borrowed his towel. "A big silver thing, like the one pulled out of Roddy Dean's car."

"Sounds like mine, all right. It's a .357. The kind of weapon Rick uses in *The Walking Dead*."

"This it?" Carter opened a drawer and took out a big silver gun. He passed it to Boone.

Calmer than I would ever be in the same situation, he took the gun, opened the cylinder, shut it, spun it, sited down the barrel out the window, and said, "It's mine. Serial number checks out."

"It has been used in previous killings," I said. Carter gave me a look that could have caused internal bleeding in a weaker man. I guess that was supposed to be a secret.

"Really? I bought it used." Boone passed the empty gun back to Carter.

"Tell me about the night of the killing," I said.

"The Fourth of July? You saw me. I went to the carnival. Saw some of the rodeo. Saw Charbone there talk coal, saw Flaner speak truth to power."

"Thanks."

"I saw you there too," said Charbone.

"I did too," said Carter.

"That's because he's the only Black guy in the county," I said. They didn't respond.

"I left early and went back to my camp."

"Why'd you leave early?" asked Carter.

"Didn't feel welcome. Plus a storm was coming."

"Which was your campsite?"

"The one by the pool."

I was right.

"Right about the campsite?"

"Yes." I really had to control my censor. I kept speaking my thoughts out loud.

"Your friends are probably used to it," said Boone.

I ground my teeth. "When did you notice your gun missing?"

"Earlier in the day. The only places I could have lost it were the shower or the latrine. It wasn't in the shower, and if it was in the latrine, it could stay there."

"Don't they have flush toilets?"

"I'd used one up the mountain that day."

"What were you doing up the mountain?"

"Looking for Dashiell Stubbins. It's what his daughter, my employer, hired me to do."

"Where were you looking?"

"South side of the park. I heard the sheriff had told some newspaper guy that he stayed around there."

"He lied."

"Craig, we're going to have to have a long talk about this," said the mayor.

"I thought it might have been stolen. It's not my style to drop things. I figured whoever took it had more need of it than I did," he said.

"That's an interesting way of seeing it," said the mayor.

"It's how I grew up."

"You were a thief."

"I grew up," he said. "Anyway, I let it go and spent the evening in front of my tent. When the fireworks came on, I watched them poolside in the reflection of the cool water."

"Were you alone?"

"No," he said. "That butler fellow came by and shared some drinks with me."

"How do you know him?"

"I'd asked him earlier if those little brat children could have stolen my gun. He said he'd look for me. If they had it, I wanted it back."

I smiled. I liked Boone's style. The mayor was about to have a coronary, however, if his face was any indication.

"Lynson said he hadn't found it but would keep looking. I told him to keep it on the down low. No need to alarm anyone and guns are as common as cigarettes out here."

"Plus, you had another gun," I said.

He smiled. "You know?"

"I'm in the business."

"That's right. You're a gumshoe."

"You're probably strapped right now," I said.

"You know I am."

"Jesus," said the mayor, jumping out of his chair.

"Now there's a racist reaction," said I.

"What? No. I um…" The mayor sat back down and patted Boone on the knee. "I'm just spooked by guns," he said.

"Did you see anyone else?" I said to Boone.

"People came from the fair back to the camp. Sparklers and fireworks. Too cold to swim. Not a body there. Oh, I saw your friends," he said. "At least I think they were your friends. You'd come in with them."

"You noticed that?"

"I'm in the business." He winked at me.

I winked back, though I think he did it better.

"Pretty quick to forgive losing such a nice gun," said the mayor.

"Easy come, easy go."

"But when the shooting happened the next day…" I said.

"There was no more work to do," said Boone. "Job was over, so I left."

"And you were a stranger in town, tanner than most, different, urban, suspicious, and missing a gun that actually might turn out to be the murder weapon."

"There was that too," he said.

42

I'D CHANGED the subject from me being there when I wasn't supposed to be to Boone, and it had thrown them off. After Boone explained why he'd left the day after the shooting, Deputy Carter and Mayor Charbone remembered, and I was politely escorted out of the room by Veronica, who was stronger than she looked.

"I'm going to have a drink across the street," I said. The lady cop bent my arm behind my back in a very unladylike fashion and led me out. "Come on over when you're done," I said to no one in particular. "We'll do some karaoke."

Veronica took me right out the door, shut it and waited while I admired the sidewalk. Mandel had duct-taped a piece of cardboard over his broken window, which did nothing to improve the strip mall ambiance. Gail came out of The Sophisticated Cowgirl beauty parlor, and I had to do a double-take to recognize her.

"You've changed your...everything," I said. Smooth.

"Just hair and nails. A girl has to splurge once in a while."

"Celebrating?"

"I think I'm ready to rejoin the workforce. This country stuff is too dull. I miss the corporate ladder, the power lunches. A couple years of this is enough."

"I was just getting used to it."

"You were?"

"No. Not really. I don't know if I have more rock bites or bug bites. I'm sunburned and dirty. But I haven't thought about computers or phones in a while, so that's something."

"Why is that something?"

"It just is."

"How?"

"I don't know."

She laughed. "Hey, I have an idea. Since you're leaving, why don't we have a campsite party tonight? I'll light a bonfire, invite some neighbors, and we'll have some drinks. We can fire off some leftover fireworks. Maybe swim. Bring your friends."

"Can I have a shower while I'm there?"

She laughed. "Of course."

"Actually, that sounds nice," I said. "It's either that or cabin fever."

"Excellent."

"What time?"

"Do you have a watch?"

"No."

"Evening."

"That works," I said.

She took her new hairdo, manicured nails, and freshly facialized pores, got in a white truck and left. I glanced back into the sheriff's office and saw Veronica still standing sentinel at the door.

I waved.

She scowled.

I moved.

And nearly walked into Jack Mandel coming out of the gold shop.

"Hey."

"Hey," I said.

"How's business?"

"Good."

I noticed that his gold shop hours were by appointment only.

"Isn't it hard to get customers like that?" I said, pointing to the sign.

"Don't need many to keep the doors open."

"Cheap rundown strip mall. Look at that window. You should talk to a realtor and move."

"That's funny." He wasn't laughing. "Hey, is it true you're leaving town?"

"Who knows?"

"What? I heard the Carter told you to leave."

"He did, but what does that mean, really?"

He offered a forced guffaw. Just one.

"Hey..." he said.

"Hey back."

"Hey, if you are staying around for a while, I'd appreciate it if you didn't tell everyone about the other day."

"What about the other day?"

"The other day."

"With your motorcycle?"

"That's it."

"Why?"

"Hey, it's...you know."

"Nope."

"Um."

I watched him making up a story. He had that look-up-into-the-distance stare, signifying that the trolls in his brain were fabricating whole cloth. "It's not very cowboy, you know."

"The motorcycle?"

"Exactly. I have an image."

I examined his five-thousand-dollar suit. "And a silenced motorcycle doesn't help sell houses to country folk?"

"Hey, exactly." Guffaw. Then awkward silence, then he pushed past me, saying, "Hey thanks," before getting into his truck.

He'd given me his tell as if I needed to know he was lying. Once he got nervous, out came the bales of hay.

Mandel was one of the pieces that I had a handle on, maybe, but hadn't handled, if you know what I mean.

I walked across the highway between a Peterbilt going ninety and a Florida sports car going twenty.

There were three or four people in the bar I didn't know. One couple sitting together looked like tourists—sunburned, shades instead of hats, drinking tall cold drinks. Two men were at the bugged table, talking quietly and glancing at me as I came in. They looked to be horse-trading. Really. Actual horse-traders. Quaint.

The battery I'd dropped beneath that table was no longer there.

Amir "Eddie" Rahat was behind the bar and nodded a hello when I came in. I moseyed up because that's how you approach a bar in northern Wyoming.

"Set me up," I said.

"Gin and Fresca."

"Two umbrellas," I said and scratched myself for effect.

He rolled his eyes and made me a beverage.

Presenting it to me with a napkin and a flourish, he said, "So how goes the sleuthing?"

"The deputy is chasing me off."

"I heard that. Why?"

"You know why. You know everything."

"That's a stretch."

"Okay, then you know a lot of things. Some of which you probably should have told me."

He looked surprised. Maybe he was.

"You haven't heard, then?" I asked.

"About what?"

I sipped my drink. I considered it for a moment. It was a new take on an old recipe. I remember reading that the late great Hunter S. Thompson drank gin and grapefruit juice. He also drank Crown Royal and just about everything else. No, not just about. He did *all* the drugs, but one of the things I saw he drank was the old favorite gin and grapefruit juice. It's a fine concoction if you don't mind the calories. Fruit juice is liquid sugar. Then came the soda pop revolution or the soft drink wars, depending on your state of origin. Bubbly beverages became ubiquitous and synonymous with Americana. This naturally led to the obesity epidemic and then to diet sodas, which may or may not help your insulin spike, but at least have a zero somewhere on the can. And no one has to squeeze nothing. And it's consistent. A Fresca and gin in Wyoming tastes pretty much like the same drink in Salt Lake City or aboard an Alaskan cruise ship, the only room for difference being the ice and the proportion of alcohol. What I'm saying and what I thought when I drank that cool refreshing drink on that hot dusty day was that this was a traditional beverage of old, improved for today, quick and good, different—better in most ways, worse only in some, an overall achievement.

"I agree, soft drinks revolutionized hard drinks."

I blinked and inwardly cursed my brain and mouth.

"Remember the day after Dasher was killed?" I asked.

"What about it?"

"You suggested that the rancher Pilana was a good suspect."

"He'd come in that morning complaining about stolen cattle and actually said that he'd kill the man who did it if he found out."

"He looks like a rancher, doesn't he?"

"Yes."

"All the ranchers look like ranchers?"

"Well, if you put it that way, yeah." He polished a clean glass with a dirty towel. Hilarity ensued.

"I can see how you'd make the mistake, it being dark and all."

"What mistake?"

"Can I have some nachos?"

"What?" he said. "Tell me."

"Nachos?"

He glared at me.

"You were at the little medicine wheel the night Dasher was killed."

"Whoa, hold up there."

"You were seen."

"By Pilana? He's the killer."

"It wasn't Pilana."

"Who?"

"Roddy Dean says he saw you there standing over the body and then shooting at him."

He stared. I waited for the lie. When it didn't come fast enough, I pressed.

"He said it was you. Even called out your gun, laser sight and all."

"He had the advantage of the lightning," Eddie said.

"How so?"

"It flashed behind him. I only saw a silhouette, the hat, the rifle. A rancher."

"So you shot at him?"

"He'd just killed Dasher, and I'd come upon the body. He was going to shoot me as a witness. It was self-defense."

"You saw him kill Dasher?"

"No. But I think I heard the shots from the parking lot."

"Why were you there, Eddie?"

"I wanted to talk to Dasher. I'd heard Roddy mention that he could be found up there during a storm, and I wanted to talk to him."

"About what?"

"I told you. I didn't want him telling the town what I was doing."

"So you brought a gun?"

"It was dark. I'm a minority."

"Uh-huh," I said. "Not sure I buy that."

"I got there and found him dead. A heaping steaming pile of crap on top of him. The lightning showed a figure, and I panicked. I shot and ran."

"You didn't hit him."

"The laser sight is shit."

"Shit. Ha!"

"What?"

"Did you see anyone else?"

"I didn't stay long enough to look."

I sipped and thought, then said, "You're lucky you missed, or you'd be in jail like the Deans."

"The Deans? Both? They killed him?"

"What did you really need to talk to him about, Eddie? With a gun."

He swallowed and hesitated. He looked around, maybe to see if Dara was there. The door opened behind me, and I turned to see Deputy Sheriff Carter stroll in.

"I'll get those nachos for you," Eddie said. "Sorry you have to leave town so soon."

Carter signaled me to join him. The horse traders were leaving, and he headed that way. I diverted him to the opposite side of the room by pretending to tie my shoe and made sure that table wasn't bugged. I didn't know if anything would be juicy enough to merit the precaution, but that's what precautions are for. There was no bug.

"Come to apologize?" I asked.

"No."

Eddie brought over a bottle of beer and another gin and Fresca. I still had half to go on my first one.

"Do you believe Boone?"

He shrugged. "Not too far. He admitted to owning the murder weapon."

"Have we checked the gun already?"

"No, but it makes sense."

"So you think it was him?"

"It's hard. He's got to be suspect number one. I told him not to leave town. He was agreeable to it, which says something." Carter then noticed Eddie standing at the table. "Yes?"

He twitched his head as if coming out of a dream and looked at me. "Still want those nachos, Tony?"

"Sure."

He left us, his cheeks the color of Carter's neck.

"Mr. Burger got a room at the Shady Tree Motel."

"Not the gray cell?"

"He's an officer of the court," said the deputy. "That's more than you are, even back where your license is good."

"Well, a little piece of paper never stopped me from being brilliant. I've done some of my best work without it."

"You mean being a pain in the ass?"

"Oh, okay. We're sliding into that cop-hates-PI thing again. What happened to you needing my help?"

"It blew up in my face. The mayor knows, and that's the worst it can get. My job is on the line for you hitting him and for me overstepping in the death of an indigent."

"Dashiell Stubbins, great-great-grandson of the town's father, is an indigent?"

"Yes."

So much for tradition.

"Let sleeping dogs lie," he grumbled. "Should have never gotten involved."

"You asked me to."

"I was talking about myself." He tipped his bottle. I sipped my second fruity drink, my first still unfinished. Hardcore tough. That's me.

I saw hurt in Carter's eyes.

"This town has no secrets, you know," I said. "People come here to get away from that kind of thing, and yet Floyd is a hive of gossip."

"Most people know things, but not everything's talked about. We have manners."

"Are you talking about Beaumont?"

He grunted.

"What happened to the Deans by the way?"

"Roddy's at the hospital in Sheridan. Beaumont is in jail."

"Are you going to arrest Roddy?"

"I'm thinking about it," he said. "First I have to talk to Eddie."

"About what?" said the barman with a plate of nachos.

"Where were you the night the hermit was killed."

"I was at the fair, then I went home and went to sleep."

"Did you stay for the fireworks?"

"No. Wait. Yes. Yes, I did. Big storm."

I glanced at Carter. He was believing the barkeep. I glared at Eddie.

"Why do you ask?" he said and shot me a glare back.

"Checking on things," Carter said.

"I'm leaving town after the summer, by the way," said Eddie. "Going back to school."

"Good to have goals."

He placed the plate in front of me and shot me another look before returning to the bar, cheeks still a-blush.

"So?" I said.

"So Roddy's got some explaining to do."

I was shocked. "Out of curiosity, why don't you believe Roddy? He's a local. Eddie's an itinerant bartender."

"That's no way to look at things," said Carter.

"Their stories are diametrically opposite. Someone is lying."

"And?"

"And the question still stands. Why Eddie over Roddy?"

"Roddy has a temper. He had the most motive of anyone I know. It's his word against Eddie's, and he's shown himself to be untrustworthy."

I thought to tell Carter that Eddie had already confessed to me that he'd been up at the Little Medicine Wheel that night and was thus, ipso facto, ad nauseum, lying. I'd told Eddie I'd not snitch, but I couldn't let it go. I was about to challenge Carter's discernment and slide in the word "untrustworthyer" which I'd just lit upon when Eddie appeared with another gin and Fresca.

"What's all this I hear about the hermit being related to that diet supplement Kiksuye?"

"You know about that?"

"I heard things," he said.

I rubbed my temples.

"Nothing to get killed over," Carter said.

Eddie nodded, then remembered he had a glass. He put it on the table next to my other two. Then he left.

"What is worth getting killed over?" I asked.

"Money, reputation, revenge. A woman."

"Rustling?"

"Maybe. But there's reputation there too. Can't live here with that on you."

"You'd run them out on a rail?"

"Wouldn't have to," he said. "Speaking of which, shouldn't you be gone already?"

"Free country."

"You have to leave town right away. I can't defend you."

"When did you ever?"

He didn't like that question. I didn't care.

"What about Dasher's murder?"

"You stirred the pot enough that I can finish it," he said.

I sipped from my third gin and Fresca. "No, you can't."

"It doesn't matter. Can't bring him back. He was a ghost before; he's a ghost now."

"Cowboy poetry," I said.

"There've been other complaints about you."

"Like what?"

"I can't say."

"More anonymous callers?"

"Some," he said. "Mandel."

"What did he accuse me of?"

"Breaking and entering."

"And you believed him?"

"Is he lying?"

"No, but why does Eddie get a pass and I don't?"

"You're sneaky."

"You're an idiot."

"That was uncalled for."

"It's what we got."

"Go home, Mr. Flaner." He rose to go.

"Hold up," I said.

"Why?"

"I'm leaving first."

"Why?"

I got up without another word, sticking him with the check, wondering if he'd notice that Eddie had brought me three drinks without me finishing one and maybe, just maybe, in some alternate timeline, find that suspicious.

43

IT WAS dusk when I got back to Perry's place and found the gang all in a foul mood. Dara was reading *Resumes that Don't Suck* and turning the pages like each one was a 4chan post. Garrett was on a lounge chair, his legs pulled up and wrapped in his arms, looking small and scared. Perry and Standard were in the kitchen.

"Hey, Standard," I said. "Are you done with your Thoreau phase yet?"

"I pulled a two-inch splinter out of my ass this afternoon," he said. "What do you think?"

Perry nodded.

"Then we're leaving?"

"Thank God," said Dara.

"I don't feel well," said Garrett.

"Two inches?" I said.

"At least," said Perry. "Nasty. Got it in the outhouse."

"Ouch. You should get a shot for that."

"Can we get shots?" came Garrett's urgent voice from the other room. "Is there a place in town to get shots? Did you see one?"

"In Floyd? I doubt it. Probably have to go to a bigger town. You got a splinter too?"

"No," he said miserably.

"Oh? Oh. Ah…you're kidding," I said.

He moaned.

"There's a party out at the Crazy Woman Campground starting like right now. Some of your neighbors should be there. You can say hi, goodbye, Perry."

"We're leaving then?" he said.

"Looks like."

"Thank fuck," said Dara.

"Eloquent as ever, my dear."

"I'm not your dear," she said, tossing the book aside. "Let's go."

"Garrett?" I said.

"I'll stay here. I want to try and pee again."

"Sounds like you have a full night," said I.

We took the Caddy. Perry had learned where most of the bumps were, so we arrived without broken necks or bruised asses. We parked just as the sun set.

The place was hopping around a large fire in the center of the grounds. A genuine bonfire without the bones showed us the way. We parked next to a row of white pickups and sauntered forward.

I recognized many of the thirty or so people there. There was Jack Mandel standing nervously by James Rawly, who watched his wife, Kimmy, talking to the Crombys, Penn, and Maxine while her eyes slaked up and down Lynson's torso, bringing a blush to the butler that was visible in the firelight. To my surprise, Varg Jayger was there sitting alone nursing a beer. Flickering flames made the hieroglyphics on his skin actually look menacing and not just stupid. Gail was there, of course, in her new hair and nails. She was talking to some strangers I didn't know whose swimsuits suggested either that they had plans to swim or had missed wash day.

Gail signaled us over and kicked open a cooler full of beers for us.

"Microbrews," came Perry's exclamation.

"Help yourself," Gail said. "It's time to unwind."

"Hey, Tony!" Rawly approached me with his arms out like we were old war buddies. He hugged me. "How's it been?"

"Since yesterday? Oh, it's been amazing."

"Hasn't it, though?"

He stole a glance toward the Crombys and his wife but turned it back to me. "Drink with me." It was a plea more than an invitation.

"I'd love to."

"Great."

"You too, Perry," he said. "And your friends."

"What about my little dog?"

"If you have one."

I couldn't see anything, but the sound of motorcycles came from the road up by the dumpster. Varg got up and strolled quickly to the parking lot, his hands firm in his jacket pockets.

We all sat down around the fire.

"Hey, Kimmy!" said Rawly. "Look who's here."

She looked over, confused.

"Tony and Perry."

"That's nice," she said and went back to talking to Maxine and looking at Lynson.

Rawly looked at me and I thought I heard something break.

"Can you pee?" I asked him.

"What?"

"Never mind," I said. "You're a lucky man."

"Am I?"

"Hey, Penn," I said. "Bring Maxine over and visit."

Penn raised a tall glass of what I assumed had once been mint julep but now was ice water, put his arm around his much younger wife and came over, leaving Kimmy to goggle at the butler without distraction.

A gunshot came from inside the Crombys' super-silo RV. The couple didn't even flinch. Lynson however did, and quickly went to see what the children were up to.

I introduced Dara and Standard to the Crombys, and Mandel came and sat down across the fire from us, as far from Rawly as possible while still being in the group.

The strangers talked about the wildlife they saw, comparing it to what they had in Biloxi. Penn talked about hunting in Louisiana once, and Maxine mentioned there was a nice restaurant in New Orleans.

After a while of nonsense, the worm in the back of my head bit to remind me I was a detective and I still hadn't figured it out.

"Figured out what?" said Maxine.

"The hermit," I grumbled. Damn censor.

"What kind of sensors?"

"What's to know?" said Gail. "About the hermit?"

"I heard he was actually a local," said Mandel. "Dashiell Stubbins."

"Dashiell Stubbins?" said Rawly. "I know that name."

"Me too," said Cromby. "Something about a TED Talk."

"Perry?" I said.

"Why me?"

"Why not?"

"No."

"Me?"

"If you must."

"Okay, I will."

"Good. Go ahead."

"I will," I said.

"Fine." Now Perry was moping.

"Here it—"

"What?" said Cromby.

"You know him from your occupations," I said to Rawly and Penn.

"Hunter?"

"Prepper?"

"Venture capitalist."

"Oh, right."

"Kitsuye," I said. "A memory enhancement medicine that is in fact antelope droppings."

"Real antelope droppings?" said Dara.

"Accept no substitute. Stubbins owned the company, and it tanked hard. I guess he went insane—well, more insane—as it fell apart. Not a stretch really, since I'd bet he'd been on the road there for a while. Selling chocolate-covered antelope crap isn't exactly taught in business school."

"What about business school?" asked Varg, coming back into the firelight.

"They don't teach you to sell shit there," said Maxine.

"You can sell anything to anyone," Varg said. "There's always a market."

"Even shit?"

"Even shit."

"Even if they know it's shit?" I asked.

"Why not?"

"But it's shit."

"Ever hear of cigarettes? Reality TV?"

"Touché," said I.

Varg took a seat next to Mandel on the log. The realtor scooted over a little.

"Who needs a fresh one?" called Gail.

A bunch of hands went up.

"What's that about a TED Talk?" said Standard.

"Perry."

"No."

"I remember that," said Maxine. "Oh my god. It was so terrible."

"You saw it?"

Her face grew animated, maybe a little cruel. "She shit her pants right on stage. Didn't even know it happened until the smell. Ran off stage, leaving a trail of...well, you get it."

"The real scary thing about that was how the internet erased it," said Perry.

"You can't erase the internet," said Varg, taking a beer from Gail. "Everyone knows that."

"But you can scrub it," said Perry.

"Bullshit."

"True story."

"How?"

"Disney," he said.

"Here we go," said Dara.

"You know where he's going with this?" I asked her.

"Do I need to?"

"It'll be interesting."

"Walt Disney," said Perry. "He froze his head after he died, thinking that future technology would be able to revive him."

"And?"

"And...don't you see?"

"No."

"PR problem."

"And?"

"What happens if you Google 'Disney Frozen'?"

"You learn about a kooky media man?" I offered.

"No. You see a happy little snowman with Elsa and a reindeer."

"You're saying they made a billion-dollar animated blockbuster movie just to skew search engine results away from an embarrassment?"

"Of course. Why else?"

We all shared a look around the fire.

"Ingenious," I said.

Standard shook his head. "What can be more embarrassing than shitting yourself in public?"

"On a TED Talk?"

Lynson finally came back from the camper. "I tried to put the kids to bed, but Terrance says he's going hunting with you later tonight."

"Oh," said Penn, looking around at us to see if anyone had heard that, and seeing we all had said, "He means snipe hunting. We're going to hunt some snipes later."

"I'll tell him he's wrong," said the butler.

"I'll tell him myself." Penn retreated to his expensive bullet-ridden camper.

Lynson took a seat next to Kimmy. Her leg brushed his and then stayed there. I heard Rawly's jaw grind.

"So," I said. "All ready for the apocalypse?" It was an open question, a great conversation starter in some places. Like that one.

"I have munitions and food and water and just about everything I need for the end of the world," said Rawly. "Which is any day now."

"And you, Varg?"

"We'll see."

"Perry?"

"I'm just getting started."

"You should have stuff in your secret bomb shelter," said Rawly. "That's where it was kept."

Everyone nodded, indicating either that everyone knew that's where you keep your apocalypse supplies and or that everyone knew about Perry's "secret" bomb shelter. Maybe both.

"We haven't gotten in there yet," he admitted. "It's locked. We might need Geraldo Rivera."

"Who?" said Maxine.

I felt old.

"We'll do that before we go," I promised.

"That's right," said Mandel. "You're leaving."

"You'll be missed," said Gail. "Lots of excitement with you around."

"Really?" said Dara.

"A shooting right here," said Gail.

"And another up Miracle Canyon and a third at Varg's place," I offered.

"You're the Nazi fuck who shot at Tony?" said Dara.

Varg belched.

"Maybe I'll stay," I said.

Mandel went white. His eyes shifted from me to Rawly.

"Carter said you had to go," said Gail. "I've never known him to say something like that and not mean it."

"I think he means it," I said. "That doesn't mean I have to do what he says. I have a reputation to uphold."

"You're famous for being a pain in the ass," said Gail. "I saw it on the internet."

"Well, if it's on the internet, it's got to be true."

"I don't know how you guys do it," said Standard. "This simplified old-style living is hard."

"Who said anything about old-style living?" said Maxine. "Our RV has its own satellite. That chair is electric. All the comforts of a four-star hotel."

"Even a pool boy," cooed Kimmy.

Teeth ground.

"It's cool for a while," said Standard, "but outhouses and no running water?"

They all stared at him.

"Really," he said.

"That sucks," said Gail. "Who sold it to you?"

All eyes went to Mandel, who hid himself behind a beer bottle, spilling some down his cheek.

"It was a good deal," he said. "The Kayshaws were in a hurry to sell. That's the trick. Have time to get the price you want. That's why I think we should find your price, Ms. Larsen, and stick to it."

"You're selling?" asked Rawly.

"I've had enough," she said. "This place has been a good investment but too much work."

"You'll clear six figures easy."

"I thought you said nothing sells out here," I said.

"Things will be better now," Mandel explained. "As long as you're not in a hurry to sell."

"How does a hurry to sell mean it's okay to bilk a buyer?" asked Maxine.

He swallowed more beer. "It was a good deal," he said.

"Would have been better with water."

"A fixer-upper. You've got a start. A nice secret bomb shelter. It's a blank slate."

"Realtors are not far from con men," I said.

Penn Cromby came back wearing a light camouflage jacket. Or did he?

"What'd I miss?"

"Con-men talk," said Maxine.

"Business," he said. "Caveat emptor. People with money make money. The rich have an innate—"

"Excuse me." I got up eager to be elsewhere. Perry followed me to the bathroom.

"How are you liking your neighbors?" I asked him.

"They suck."

"Even Gail?"

"She's leaving."

"So's Cromby."

"Maxine said he was looking for a cabin up here."

"When?"

"The other night."

"Sell him yours."

"Maybe I will."

We enjoyed a splinterless urinal experience and then returned to the campfire, where a conversation was still in progress.

"It's patience," explained Penn.

"It's an ambush," said Dara.

"What are we talking about?"

"Penn is explaining about blinds," said Lynson.

Kimmy turned and stretched out her leg, her foot accidentally brushing Lynson's crotch and staying there.

"A hunter builds a blind and then uses patience to wait for game," said Penn. "It's much harder than you think."

"To shoot an unarmed animal?"

"Patience is a virtue and hard to come by," said Penn. "Real hunters have it. They can wait as long as they have to for the right moment."

"What kind of honor is there in shooting an animal?" asked Dara. "If you were a real man, you'd go after a deer with a pair of antlers. A rabbit with your front teeth."

"That's not how it works," he said. "And honor is a personal matter."

"It is anything but that," said Dara. "That's self-esteem. Honor is a subset of reputation, which is how other people perceive you. It's in the damn definition."

"Oh really?" he said.

"Really," said Varg.

"Yep," said Standard. "She's right."

Penn coughed and stammered. "Well, it's a—"

"Tony?" said Perry. "You okay?"

Everyone turned to regard me, faces full of worry, confusion. Relief?

"I'm just, um...thinking," I said. "Let's go back to the house."

44

MAYBE THE MOOD was strained to begin with, but I definitely felt that my exit from the fireside had put an end to the party. That's the kind of guy I am.

Perry took control and told the gang that they could stay but that the Caddy was leaving. That got them moving after a last raid on the micro-brews for the drive.

"What is it?" said Perry.

"I got a feeling."

"Ooooo. You figured it out, haven't you?" His headlights turned off the highway and onto the obstacle course he called a road.

"There's something, but I...I...I...I...I...I..."

"It's not like you to lose language skills, Flaner," said Dara.

"I...can't put my finger on it."

"So why'd we have to go?"

"You could have stayed. I just needed to get away."

"You could have wandered around, taken your shower, and we could all still be partying," said Standard.

"Didn't you feel it?" said Perry. "The tension?"

"No."

"No."

"Yes," I said.

"Where from?" said Standard.

"Everywhere," said Perry. "Rawly was on edge."

"His problem."

"And," said Perry, "in case you didn't notice, we were drinking with a Nazi."

"I thought we were open-minded," said Standard.

Dara said, "What do you call three guys sharing a drink with a Nazi?"

"What?"

"Nazis."

"He said he wasn't a Nazi," I said, rolling that over my mind.

"Has he looked in a mirror?"

"And the realtor," I said.

"What about him?" said Perry. "Is he the guy?"

I sighed and braced myself as best I could as Perry caromed the Caddy through rut and bump.

"I feel like everything's been bounced up, is floating in the air. I just need to chill and wait for it all to land and then I can sort it out."

"We still have booze," said Dara.

"That'll do," said Standard.

The house was dark, the night warm, but breezes pushed moist air from the creek that gave us a chill as we went to the door.

"I'm going to walk around for a minute," I said. "You guys go in and drink."

"Gee, thanks, Dad," said Dara.

The gang went in and the lights came on. I walked behind the house, gravity taking me more than intention. A low moaning stopped me short, and I paused to listen.

It was coming from the outhouse.

I crept closer and heard crying.

"Garrett?" I said.

"Who's there?"

"It's me, Tony. Are you all right in there?"

Sniffle. Pause. "No."

"It hurts to pee?"

"Oh, yeah."

"Dude, you should have used a condom."

More crying.

"We're leaving in the morning," I said, wondering if it were true. I still hadn't decided. "We'll get you a shot, and you'll be right as rain in no time."

"What is it?"

"If I had to guess, I'd say the clap. Very curable. Very common. No shame."

"Really?"

"Sure."

"How do you know? Have you had it?"

"Hell no. What do you think I am?"

He let out a loud howl.

'Sorry," I said. "I've never had an STD, but you're in good company."

"Yeah? Like who?"

"Half of Big Horn County—from the same source, I'd wager."

He bawled.

"But I read about it once."

"I feel so stupid," he said. "And burny."

"Sorry, dude."

"It smells like shit in here."

"It's a shithouse. Why don't you come out?"

"I'm not done."

"Well, okay then. When you are, come inside and get drunk. That'll help."

"Really?"

"Sure."

"I should fumigate Critter," he said.

"Yeah, probably."

I left him to moan and shriek and wandered to the creek by moonlight. Kimmy and Rawly were on my list of floating questions, but not as high as they could be. Them, at least, I thought I had figured out. An old story with new morals, but it was all a web.

My head swirled with details, faces, and June bug scabs. I didn't try to catch any one thread, just let them sway and sputter, land and gel. I didn't notice the creek until I'd stepped in it. A cow stirred from the wallow I'd seen before. There was a strong smell of bovine. Cow patties, to be precise.

I looked at my wrist to see the time and saw, in the darkness, my wrist. My hand slid into my pocket, and I felt tile shards and a Krugerrand. Old habits coming back. I missed the internet.

By the time I got back to the cabin, my brain had rebelled against random thoughts and all I could think of was booze and dry socks. The gang was in the front room, drinking like the booze had to be finished that night.

"We can't take it back to Utah," Perry said. "That's considered smuggling since we bought it in Wyoming."

"You could pay the Utah tax on it," said Standard, a little slurringly.

"We don't have time to wait in some state customs line," said Garrett, who was back and drinking whiskey neat, not his usual flavor.

"It'll put us on a watch list."

Garrett offered me a sip. I recoiled like he was a leper, and his lip quivered. Feeling sheepish, I took a sip and felt it burn down my gullet. The twitch in my groin was psychosomatic. I hoped.

"We should pack tonight," said Garrett, "so we can get an early start in the morning."

"We haven't even seen the secret bomb shelter yet," said Perry.

"No time like the present," I said.

We grabbed flashlights, and Perry led us to the master bedroom where he'd been sleeping. His big Wyoming king inflatable bed lay in the middle with his sleeping bag across it, looking like a piece of nylon bacon on a Mississippi raft.

In the closet, Perry lifted the trap door to reveal the stairs I'd seen before. They disappeared into darkness as before. Perry flicked on his flashlight and down we went.

"No light?"

"No light."

He gave me a pencil flashlight. I hesitated. "This doesn't count," I said.

"Count as what?"

"Using technology."

"No. Of course not. I won't allow an open flame down here, so unless you can bioluminesce, use this."

"Any time, Flaner," came Dara from behind us. "Sooner we can get this shit done, the sooner I can pack, we can leave, and I can get into therapy."

I was a little apprehensive and very surprised to realize I hadn't explored down here at all. Where was my curiosity for the unknown? My love of dark places and bomb shelters? Oh, right. I don't have those things. Though I moved like I was entering Dracula's tomb, the others apparently were familiar with the area and were more interested in not spilling their drinks than showing me around.

"Where's your drink, Garrett?" I asked.

"I'm feeling the one I had. Any more and I might have to pee again."

"Gotcha."

The stairs led steeply down for at least two stories and then leveled into a short hall. Perry shone his light on a large plain door at the end with a keypad.

"There it is," he said.

"Shit," said I. "I was hoping for something easier to pick."

"You have a lock pick set with you?"

"No, but some locks don't need them. Rocks work really well, usually, and I saw a rock just out by the—"

The explosion was deafening, and I swear reached us before the flash of light did.

All the carefully managed drinks found airtime as we jumped out of our shorts.

Before the ringing in our ears really had time to register or the smell of gunsmoke fully reached us in a billowing black cloud plummeting down the stairs, we saw the lights above flicker off, followed by another explosion of light and sound.

Someone may have been screaming. Probably me. It was hard to hear.

I looked around for an exit, but this was a dead end hall. I said something in sub-frequency that not even I heard and headed back up into the house.

Before I was halfway up the stairs, I smelled gasoline and saw bright orange flames through the doorway. I could see the flames were already reaching the ceiling of the closet above and spreading down like inverted apricot syrup.

I stumbled back down, catching my friends as I went.

In a moment, the smoke had reached us. The only light was from flashlights and reflected flashing bursts from upstairs.

Another explosion. Then another. Loud and bright. Sparks in the gloom and more smoke to thicken that. The lights diminished taking with them the breathable air. Muffled noise and diffused light, flame and crackling inferno—terrible input carried to our shocked senses on suffocating black smoke.

I ran to the door and pulled at the handle. It didn't open.

I stared at the key lock as I felt my friends around me, coughing and shrinking from the encroaching fire.

The night had gone from rushed to interesting and now to terrifying while my thoughts had gone from rushed to pensive to surprisingly crisp. Some mechanism kicked in above the flight-or-flight subroutine, and time slowed to near *Matrix* bullet-dodge level. I waited for my life to pass before me, hoping to catch a glimpse of Allie, my gal, and Randy, my son, but my eyes filled with the keypad by the door. I trained my light on a sticker peeling up from the heat above the panel: Pearson and Son Survivalist Security and Time Shares.

I pressed 1-2-3-4, and the door opened. A gust of cool air filled the corridor for a moment, which felt great until it was sucked up by the fire like water down an unstoppered drain.

I pushed Perry through and grabbed at the others, counting heads: Garrett, Standard, Dara—Critter on the floor. I gasped for air, and my chest hurt. That couldn't be good.

The clarity was gone, and I was shitting little green lizards as I grabbed at the puppet, losing my orientation in the blinding smoke.

I bumped into a wall, then the stairs. Smelling my hair singe, I crawled as fast as I could into another wall, caromed off it like a five to the side pocket, and finally found the doorway.

"All here?" I gasped, but still my hearing hadn't returned.

Flashlights flickered in the gloom, and I saw my friends.

I pulled the door shut, pressed an inviting green button beside it and heard something latch. A refreshing hiss told me that there were either snakes in the wall or we were hermetically sealed.

I slumped over, coughing like I'd swallowed coals. The world was ringing in my forehead and my eyes were blurry—flash-burned retinas and smoke-coated corneas.

I sat, eyes closed, until my breath came back and the distant sounds of yelling made me look up.

I found my flashlight and saw each of them bent over and coughing like me. We were all in one piece. Some of us had less hair than an hour ago. All of us had bloodshot eyes.

The walls rumbled. The door behind us grew hot. I moved into the room and looked around.

It was a big, bare square space thirty feet to a side with a low concrete ceiling, maybe seven feet. It smelled like moist cement and wood smoke. There was a door opposite the one we came in in the back. Again, no lights. Not even fixtures. It was as bare as the rest of the house had been—not a shelf or a box, no military-grade full-on MASH-level triage center as promised. There was one thing, however: a single exercise bike in the middle of the room.

"I've seen more welcoming oubliettes," I said, the ringing in my ears fading to only a three-alarm fire.

"You've never seen an oubliette," said Perry.

"I saw *Labyrinth*."

"Fair cop."

"What the hell is going on!" screamed Dara.

"Grenades," said Perry. Maybe yelled.

Garrett took Critter from me and nodded a thanks. Standard stood shaking all over, a wet spot on his crotch.

"Understandable," I said.

"What?"

I pointed.

"Ah shit!" he said.

"That too?" said Dara. Like a top, he spun around to try to get a look at his derrière. "Say it ain't so."

He looked at me for help. I gave him the okay sign.

That problem settled. We all kind of just looked at each other for a while.

"No food down here," said Garrett finally.

"And where does that door lead?" I said.

While eerie sounds of creaking and crumbling filtered down to us from above, we moved farther in and checked out the bike.

It was hooked up to an inverter and a car battery. A dusty copy of an excellent short story collection called *Little Visible Delight* was on the seat. A matchbook marked the page where a story called *The Point* began. It looked good, haunting, and strangely appropriate.

"Do you feel that?" I said. "A breeze."

"Coming from down the hall."

I shone my light back the way we came and saw smoke beginning to seep under the not-so-hermetically-sealed door. A crash accompanied it.

"I saw grenades at Rawly's house," I said.

"I bet that Nazi has a collection," said Dara. "Why did we drink with him?"

"Not sure that connects, but it is a good question."

The door at the end of the hall was locked, but I used the same code to open it, 1-2-3-4.

"How are these locks powered?"

"Batteries, I'd guess," said Perry. "Lucky for us they're not dead."

"Or we would be."

"You had to say it, didn't you, Garrett?"

"It was Critter."

The puppet nodded. His mouth was unstuck from the s'mores.

I let the others go first to be polite and since it could be dangerous. I had a thought to examine the lock again to find the mechanical override it must have, but the breeze was a full-on gust as the house fire fed after the air into the room.

It was a long straight corridor, six feet wide and seven tall.

"Anyone claustrophobic?" asked Critter.

"I'm going to mash you," said Standard.

"There's a puddle here," said Perry, "and water trickling down the wall."

"Your secret bomb shelter leaks," said Dara. "Poor craftsmanship."

"Could be an asset," said Garrett. "Water is life."

"A ladder."

We shone our lights to where the corridor ended in a metal ladder leading up a three-foot round vertical shaft.

The wind was coming from there.

"See anything?"

"No," said Perry.

"I'll go," I said.

"Why you?"

"There might be a lock."

"I can count to four too," said Standard.

"It might be five."

"Okay, you go."

I put my little flashlight in my teeth and scaled the ladder. It was maybe twenty feet, maybe thirty. My palms were sweaty when I got to the end, where what looked like a submarine hatch awaited me.

"There's a hatch!" I called down.

No answer.

I tried to turn the valve. It didn't move. I tried it the other way, and it did.

"Yeah, guys, I—look out!"

I'd dropped the light.

I heard the crash and shatter on the concrete below

"Watch it, dickhead!"

The wheel was turned all the way, but the hatch wouldn't open. I pushed. It moved but sprang back. I ascended another couple rungs to get more leverage and put my shoulder to it. It moved again, then I felt deliberate resistance back into me. I knocked on it with my knuckles.

"Hullo? Howdy? 'Sup?"

I heard nothing back.

I tried it again, shoulder and push. It opened.

A wet slurry of mud and manure rained down the hole. It was a cold, slimy splashing rain of grit and sludge. It put my mind immediately to my earlier thought of all the clues floating in the air, waiting to come down. I laughed and paused and felt it doing just that. There was clarity in the mud, a crystallizing of potential and possibility.

"What the hell, Flaner?" came Standard's voice from below.

"It's just a little muck!" I called back.

"It got all over Dara," Garrett warned.

"I'll get you for this, Flaner!" she yelled. "Don't you think I won't."

I poked my head out and recognized the creek and the path and the cow from before giving me the stink eye as I emerged from its wallow.

I rolled out and crawled to the stream and lowered myself into it. I could hear distant sirens and see a bright orange light toward the house. I was only there a moment. The water was too cold, my thoughts too fast. Not wanting to force it, I concentrated on getting my friends out of the hole.

Even in the moonlight, I could see malice on Dara's brown-streaked face. "If anyone hears about this..." she threatened.

I pointed her to the creek as the others arrived.

"What?" said Garrett. "Tony, why are you grinning?"

"Perry," said Standard. "Tony's losing it. I think it's shock. Don't worry, Tony. You done good. Let it all out."

"Is it shock?" said Garrett.

"No," said Perry. "I don't think so."

45

THE HOUSE WAS A TOTAL LOSS. We saw that instantly when we came off the trail as the second fire engine rolled up. They wrapped us in blankets and gave us delicious oxygen and bottles of water from Walmart.

Everyone gave a quick report to Carter about explosions and the fire and of luck we had being so close to an actual bomb shelter. He arranged rooms for us at the Shady Tree Motel and told us not to leave town.

"Oh, now we're welcome?"

That made him pause. "Oh, right."

"Come here, Carter," I said. "I gotta talk to you."

I led him away from the firefighters and my friends who were already getting into the Caddy to relocate. I told the cop what I needed him to do, whom I needed rounded up, and where to bring them. "The saloon, at high noon, tomorrow." I squinted when I said it to give it the proper Western punctuation.

He wasn't happy about it, but he didn't need to be. I was done with this town, and I could finish my business in an hour. High noon sounded good, plus it would mean I'd get to sleep in on a real bed.

———

It was everything I'd hoped it would be.

When I rolled over around eleven the next morning, I felt like a new man. I sprang out of bed before remembering my many bumps and bruises. I stopped springing when my ankle reminded me. I went to the bathroom, flushed the toilet three times, used it, flushed four more just to hear the blessed sound. I got in the shower, opened a vial of shampoo, unwrapped a mini-soap and scrubbed smoke and grime and blood and dust and guts and poo and whatever else Wyoming had stuck to me.

I'd washed my clothes the night before in the sink, and they were mostly dry. They smelled like shampoo and body wash, but they were better than before.

I put myself together, admired my bruises in the mirror—June bug wound was still angry, black eyes peeping out, scratch down my cheek, scratches all over.

"Perfect," I said. And left the hotel at 11:50.

I wanted to arrive just as the clock struck the hour, when I'd mosey in bow-legged. I had a gob of spit ready to make the illusion complete. I stood outside the door, counting the many vehicles there and listening to low conversation inside, waiting for the clock to chime.

Finally, Garrett poked his head out. "Are you coming in? It's ten past."

"Ah shit," I said. "I was hoping for a clock chime or a noon bell or something."

"Why?"

"Never mind."

I followed him in, forgetting to bowleg, not squinting and spitless. I looked around the room to make sure they were all there. My friends were in a booth sipping drinks and eating nachos. Deputy Sheriff Craig Carter sat at the bar beside Mayor Gill Charbone. Roddy Dean was there, his arm in a cast. He sat by Jack Mandel, his ass in a suit, at the usual table. Gail Larsen was in her usual booth in the back. Beaumont was with her, his back to his father but his eyes followed me. Kim and James Rawly were there at another table. They looked stressed. The Crombys were there, Penn and Maxine and Lynson. No idea where the children were. Probably locked in their cages. Boone sat at the other end of the bar, sipping something cool and refreshing out of a highball glass, while Eddie opened a Fresca for me in anticipation. Varg Jayger sat at his usual table by the window, sipping a beer, looking out from his ink-stain of a face.

"Where're the others?" I said to Carter.

"Veronica's hunting them down now. Be here in a minute."

"And that other cop from Lovell?"

"Jake? You really wanted him?"

"Yeah, I did."

"I'm here," said the deputy coming out of the bathroom, shaking water from his hands.

I took in the faces, nibbled a nacho, strutted for effect, bowleggedly, and squinted of course.

"What the hell is he doing?" said Boone.

"I'm getting in the mood."

"For what?" said Maxine.

"For the reveal."

"The what?" said Rawly.

"I'm a detective. This is what we do. When we solve a crime, we bring everyone together to explain it."

"No, we don't," said Boone.

"Never heard of that at all," said Carter.

Deputy Jake from Lovell shook his head in disbelief. "That is not how it's done. Ever."

"Shhhhh!" I said. "My case, my way."

"He always does this," said Dara.

"Yeah, it's usually pretty good," said Perry. "Though people have been known to be killed during them."

"Get on with it," said Varg. "I have business this afternoon."

He was joined by a chorus of "get on with it's".

"Shhhhh!"

They quieted down.

I put my squint back on, paced another step or two, washed down the nacho with a gin and Fresca Eddie brought to me. After a loud, commercial-worthy refreshing "Aahhhh," I began.

"Before spending these days in Big Horn County, I often asked myself why anyone would want to live in a place like this. Now that I have had a chance to experience it, I have to ask it again."

"Hey," said the mayor. "This is 'Merica."

"Cool it, coal king," I said. "Why would anyone live here? To hide is one reason. If I were looking for a place to disappear, to get away from creditors, start my life again, I might consider this place. If I had all that happening, had grown up here, had friends here, and was clinically insane, this place would be perfect."

"You're talking about the hermit?" said Rawly.

"I am. Dasher the Flasher, formerly Dashiell Stubbins."

"Like the road?"

"Yes. He's a son of the pioneers of Floyd. Great-grandson or something. He grew up here."

Carter rearranged his hat, sipped his beer.

"And to make matters even more perfect, this town is positively stupid in its isolationist fantasies."

"We do tend to mind our own business out here," said Roddy.

"The hell you do. This place is worse than a sewing circle on K Street."

"What's there to gossip about?"

"Plenty. This place is swimming in old-fashioned lies, cheats, and crimes. Some of the secrets are open, others are pretty well hidden, but this place is a nest of villainy."

"I'm just visiting," said Penn.

"Shhhh."

"Okay, what do you have?" said Carter. "Out with it."

"Ah, okay, now here's the rub. I have stories to tell, things I have deduced and figured out. Since I have done all this without the benefit of the internet or screen time beyond watching a single three-minute video, which I did not activate"—I gave my friends a good emphatic glare—"what I'm going to tell you all now is 'conjecture.'" I made air quotes. "It's right, you'll see it's right, you'll know it's right. You'll be amazed, but unless someone"— here I looked pointedly at the two law officers in the room, particularly Jake, who didn't live in Floyd—"unless someone with *authority* follows up on all this, these crimes will go unpunished because after my accusations, I'm leaving."

"So this is all hearsay?"

"The proofs won't be hard to find. I have some, and I can swear to it. Fuck it. There, see?"

"I heard you were with the USTA," said Maxine. "Who told you to do all this?"

Mayor Charbonne said, "You're not even licensed here."

"I asked him to look into it," said Carter.

Mayor Gill grumbled.

"It's okay, Mr. Flaner," said Carter. "Pull it all out. You're free to speak."

"Oh, he's gonna," said Dara. "I never knew anyone to stop Tony from speaking when he wanted to. Ever."

"Thank you, peanut gallery," I said.

Perry nibbled a nacho.

"Carter knew Dashiell had returned. He's been helping him survive for years, mostly by giving him antibiotics to help him survive his, shall we say, eccentric diet."

"When he was a kid he said that God shaped some poop like candy to teach us its goodness," said Carter. "I'm not sure why he thought clothes were bad."

"He was never playing with a full deck," I said. "That's why he went into venture capitalism."

"Hey, don't besmirch what you don't understand," said Cromby.

"Penn," said Rawly. "You know what he's talking about."

That shut him up.

"The librarian, Ms. Severe, knew Dasher the Flasher was Dashiell Stubbins. I should have caught the slip of the tongue when I was with her."

"Library? What were you doing there?" It was Standard trying to catch me out on my technology fast.

"Book stuff." I wondered if anyone had ever been told to avoid pages for a fortnight to show they weren't addicted to reading. Oh, the good ol' days.

"Get on with it," said Beaumont. "We already know who killed him. Just say it and tell us where we can find the clues to lock the bastard up."

"I'm getting there," I said. "Dasher, for all his eccentricities, was friendly. Loving even. Endowed like a god, smelling like a goat, he pleasured the people of Big Horn County. I don't know everyone he played with, but some of you are in this room."

Nobody stirred or gasped, so I knew I was on solid footing.

"The Rawlys," I said.

James Rawly looked up with a bright red face and forced a friendly wink. Kimmy smirked bemusedly.

I said, "Kimmy loves you, James. I think. But she can't stay on the porch. It's why you moved out here in the first place, thinking a small town—or better yet, isolation in a bunker—could curtail her...hobby. Alas and alack, it was not the case."

Rawly's face held a lifeless smile that looked cemented on.

"Dasher and Kimmy hooked up at some time," I said. "And you knew about it, James."

Same smile, dying eyes.

"That's motive. Means and opportunity show up by your own admission that you have little recollection of the night of the murder and found one of your many guns had been fired empty the next day."

"I remember some of it," he said. "I remember caching and coming back. Having a drink, then another, then waking up."

"So diminished capacity as a defense?" said Carter.

"He didn't do it," I said.

"I didn't?"

"No. I think if you were to kill anyone it would be yourself and Kimmy. Probably in that order. No. James Rawly, you're a broken man. Get a hold of yourself. Find a divorce attorney and thank God you haven't slept with your wife lately because she's got a raging case of clap."

The mayor let out a gasp. Out of the corner of my eye I saw Garrett shift uncomfortably in the booth.

"Which brings us to Mayor Gill Charbone. A late-comer in the parade of suspects, this weaselly little artifact from the Industrial Age had reason to kill Dasher. The hermit knew about the coal deposits in the park and would stand in the way of any development there, bare-assed naked and howling all he knew about the shady deal the mayor was pushing through. I'm sure he saw surveyors."

"She has the clap?" Gill said.

"Dasher knew all the secrets. He saw everyone and everything. Using his super antelope-enhanced memory, he processed and stored it all. He understood enough to be dangerous. Anyone with a big enough secret was threatened by the hermit. If he ever came forward or said the wrong thing to the right person, reputations and fortunes could be lost."

"Kimmy?" said the mayor.

"Mayor Charbone," I said, snapping my fingers in his face. "Gill. Am I close?"

"With motive? Maybe. Sure. But I'd never...plus, I didn't...I wasn't there."

"That's where Kimmy comes in," I said. "Mayor Gill Charbone was boinking Rawly's wife the night of the murder, as told to me by a reliable witness and lookout."

"Who shall be nameless?" asked Varg.

"It was Deputy Sheriff Craig Carter," I said. "which means it's a conspiracy, but not for murder. What I mean is that here we have alibis for the mayor, Carter and Kimmy."

"Why would Kimmy want to kill Dasher?" said Garrett.

"Maybe she was spurned by the best lay she ever had."

Kimmy's face for the first time showed something other than wicked amusement. She tightened and looked away.

"Damn," I said. "Got it in one. But anyway, they're out."

"Why would Carter want to kill his friend?" asked Beaumont.

"Mercy killing? Orders from Gill? Pressure from the townsfolk who feared him or didn't like him? But he didn't do it."

"I resent that," said Carter.

"Okay. You did it. Happy now?"

"No I resent the—"

"Shhhh."

He rearranged his hat again.

"Of the people in town who had complained about Dasher in one form or another, several are here. First, there's Roddy Dean, representing the stolen cattle lobby. Varg Jayger, innocent little homeowner who'd had his cabin broken into. And then there's Jack Mandel, realtor and gold digger."

"I thought that was Kimmy," said Standard.

"She had all the gold she needed. She digs other things," said Dara.

"Dasher kept real estate prices down," said Mandel. "I was only voicing public concern."

"I wasn't the only one complaining about losing cattle," said Roddy.

"I have a right to complain," said Varg.

"Secrets secrets secrets," I said. "Old-fashioned crimes, new-fashioned crimes, old loves and new."

I paused for dramatic effect, giving myself a moment to ready the next wave of accusations and giving Veronica time to escort the last participants into the bar. I'd seen them pull up.

The quiet lingered, irritating everyone. Roddy was about to say something, taking one of those I-know-better-than-you deep breaths old people take before lecturing you for an hour, but then the door jangled and an angel got its wings.

Deputy Veronica escorted two people inside.

"Everyone, I'd like to introduce Mr. And Mrs. Isaaks, Sherman and Ada. They're here looking for their son."

Everyone stared.

"Isn't anyone going to say hello?" I asked.

"Hello," said Mr. Isaaks.

"Don't you have a hello for your parents? Stand up, Varg, and give them a hug. They've missed you."

46

THE TATTOOED SKINHEAD had sunk low into his seat the moment the couple came in. He remained half under the table as Mr. and Mrs. Isaaks scanned the room, trying to find who it was I was talking about. By following the stares of the others, they landed on Varg under the window.

"Uri?" said Sherman. "Is that you?"

"It's not what it looks like," he said.

"Uri?" said Ada. "You're a Nazi?"

"Mom, it—"

"You were bar mitzvahed."

"He's Jewish?" said Eddie. "Wow, I didn't see that one coming."

His father stared at him. His mother slowly moved forward and hugged him.

I said, "Varg Jayger is really Uri Issaks, entrepreneur businessman who's found a niche market for his wares and is making a killing."

"Killing? He's the killer?"

"No," I said. "He had reason to fear Dasher. The hermit broke into his laboratory house behind his camper and discovered he was making drugs. Amphetamines, to be precise."

"A drug lab?" said Carter. "In Big Horn County?"

"If you'd ever bothered to shake down the skinheads that keep wandering through Floyd, you'd have figured this out a long time ago."

"I sold drugs to skinheaded freaks," said Uri, looking like a skinheaded freak. "Not to nice people."

"A good disguise," I said. "Even after studying the pictures your parents gave me, it took me a long time to find you under all that racist ink."

"I've made two million three hundred and sixteen thousand dollars, Dad," he said. "Can Rachel say she did as well?"

"It's not about the money. Look at you."

"It'll cost me twelve thousand at most to have all this removed. I already have a guy lined up to do it in Tulsa. I was going to leave at the end of the summer. Believe it or not, Mom and Dad, this kept me safe."

"That kind of money makes for a nice motive," said Roddy. "And his place is situated by the back trail that leads to the little medicine wheel."

"He's a pacifist," I said. "He uses blanks to scare people off."

"I wondered how he missed you," said Standard.

"Don't sound so disappointed. On the night of the killing, he heard movement on that trail, but he didn't know what it meant. Those noises are his alibi."

"What did he hear?" said Maxine.

"He heard ATVs and a truck down by the Pilana pasture."

"He can't swear to that," said Roddy.

"Shhhh," I said. "This is where you come in."

He was going to say something, but my stare shut him up.

"Roddy and Beaumont Dean are cattle rustlers," I said. "This is one of the secrets that's been more or less kept, though I'd wager that besides the Deans and myself, there is at least one other person in this room who knew that."

"Who?" said Perry.

"Getting to that."

"Oh, yeah," he said and took another chip.

"If this goes on much longer I'm going to be drunk," said Gail. "Eddie, bring me another."

The barkeep made her another drink but not before dropping a glass onto the floor and breaking it.

"Using the cover of the fair, fireworks, and foul weather, the Deans rustled Ollie and Hardy, Pilana's prized steers. But Roddy left Beaumont to do the work himself and took an ATV up to the little medicine wheel to kill Dasher."

"I knew it!" screamed Beaumont, springing to his feet. "That's what he did. He pulled down his rifle, took the Honda and disappeared for a while."

"I didn't kill him!" screamed Roddy. "Eddie did!"

"You went up there to kill him," I said.

"Because Dasher knew about the cattle thefts?" said Gail.

"There are few crimes in Wyoming more stigmatized than cattle rustling. They hanged people for that, fought class wars—murder, mayhem, injustice. It's a tradition. Had Dasher told his friend Carter about Dean's midnight forays into others' pastures, he'd be done here. Roddy sold the animals to Magnus Meats down in Cheyenne, by the way. Their truck was in town the day it happened, and I found a card on Roddy's desk. Anyway, if the town found out, even this backward place—especially this backward place—he could never live it down. That's one of the problems with small towns. People know one another. They remember. It would be social death to him if not an actual rope."

"Makes sense," said Gail.

"But that's not why he wanted to kill Dasher."

"Why did he then?" asked Maxine.

"Because he hated that Dasher and his son were lovers."

"Dasher and Beaumont?" said Rawly.

"Whereas rustling was a stigma he was willing to face, and Dasher had been an easy scapegoat to hang the crimes on, Roddy hated that his son was gay. He couldn't kill his own offspring, but he could destroy the emblem of it."

"He told me he'd do it," said Beaumont. "I gave him my gun to protect himself."

"Wait, so Roddy had a double motive and admits he was up there?" said Carter. "That'll do it." He reached for his handcuffs.

"It wasn't me. Yes I went up there to…to talk to Dasher, but he was dead. It was that Arab, Eddie. I saw him there."

"Why would I want to kill the hermit?" said the barkeep, a tug in his voice.

"Secrets, secrets, secrets," I said.

"Don't," said Eddie.

"You had reason to kill the hermit as well."

"A year's work…"

"Eddie is here to do research for a graduate project."

"He's studying rednecks," said Dara.

"We're just like ordinary folks," said Mayor Charbone.

The room laughed at him. He blushed.

"This bar is a laboratory. Eddie eavesdrops and observes and records what he hears. It'll be a great paper."

Eddie polished a swizzle stick with a dirty towel and gave me a quick, hateful look.

"Jig's up, Eddie," I told him. "Fess up for what you've done or risk a murder charge. We friends?"

He pretended not to hear me, but I knew that the acoustics in this room delivered every nuanced syllable to his ears, and he'd have a recording of it later for posterity.

"He's learned so much, in fact, that he's mirrored the hermit in knowing all the secrets. Dasher knew what Eddie was up to, knew that he knew about the rustling, about the drugs and about a lot of other things."

"How?"

"He's bugged that table." I pointed. "And records everything. Dasher found him listening to the recordings and knew what that meant."

"Isn't it illegal to record conversations?" said Gail.

"If one party wants to record, that's okay," said Carter, "but by the sound of this, he recorded conversations that he wasn't a part of. That is illegal. Arrest-worthy."

Mandel poked up from under the table and held a bug for everyone to see.

"Shit," I said. "Real evidence. That kind of ruins the mood."

"I drove up there to talk to him," said Eddie. "To reason with him. He threatened to tell everyone I was a spy and said I was weak for having to record it. I should be able to just remember it all like him."

"You took your gun," I said. "The gun I found the next day still smelling of gunpowder, having been fired recently."

"I fired at Roddy," he said. "I thought he was the killer and was afraid."

Eddie came up with the gun, and the room froze. Carter's hand was on his holster. Jake's gun was out and pointing.

"Here's the gun," said Eddie. "I just wanted to show you. It has a laser sight, see?"

"That's what I saw," said Roddy.

Eddie handed the gun butt-first to Carter, who took it quick.

"Am I making an arrest now?" he said to me.

"For Dasher's murder? No."

"Jesus," said Varg.

His parents scowled at that.

"Sorry."

"Up at the little medicine wheel," I went on, "Carter and I found a blind. For a while I thought it was Penn Cromby's, but it was yours, wasn't it, Roddy?"

"Yeah, I built it that morning."

"My blind?" said Penn, finally showing some interest. "Are you suggesting that I had some reason to kill the hermit?"

"Yes. Yes, I am. Yes, you did."

"What possible reason?"

"The most dangerous game," I said. "You're a poacher of endangered species."

"What?" said Carter.

"Knew it," said Gail.

"How dare you!" said Penn, standing up. Maxine rolled her eyes.

"You printed off a picture of the hermit and used it for target practice. He'd be a great kill for a big hunter like you."

"You can't slander me like this."

"Sure I can. I found the dead end of a Canadian lynx in your trashcan. I know there's no such thing as lynx season. The first day I met you, you asked if I'd seen any one of five endangered species—species that were in a library book you'd checked out naming them all as endangered."

"You had no right to go through my garbage."

"I was looking for tissue. Sue me."

He stared.

"But that lynx is your alibi. You were out shooting a kitty that night and not Dasher."

He didn't say anything.

"Plus, you didn't know where to find him, and there my friends, is the crux of the problem."

"How?" said Mandel.

"First, let's clear up Boone here," I said, gesturing to the Black man sitting at the bar. "Can you ever not look cool?"

"Not to my knowledge," he said.

"Boone is a bounty hunter. He was hired by Heather Stubbins Tessin, Dashiell's daughter. I apologize for not having her here. Her father was a crap dad and screwed over her family. There's motive. But since I forgot to invite her, she'll have to be represented by her means and opportunity."

"Me?" said Boone.

"You."

He nodded and rolled the ice around his glass. So cool.

"The weapon that killed Dasher, that put three bullets into him, was from Boone's gun."

"Then why isn't the n—I mean, guy, locked up?" said Roddy.

"You fucking racist," said Varg, squinting at the rancher beneath his swastikas.

Eddie said, "I'll admit to the bug, but I'm no murderer. Tony, say something."

"Eddie's gun is the wrong caliber," I said. "It's a .32."

Carter nodded.

"Rawly only uses 9mm in all his small arms. Makes it a point of pride."

"Only reasonable thing to do," he said.

"Roddy there has a .357 of his own. I know this because he pointed it at me. Boone's gun, the murder weapon, was also found in Roddy's truck. But he was being framed."

"Ignorant gay-boy son of mine!" spat Roddy.

"Someone smack him," I said.

Dara pushed Garrett out of the booth, walked over, and smacked Roddy upside the head.

"He had a rifle when he went to kill Dasher. The blind was rifle range, not pistol. He had a rifle. Eddie saw him with it. I assume it was the same rifle you have in the rear window of your truck, the same rifle you used to shoot at me in Miracle Canyon when you thought your son and I were lovers."

"You can't—" He was cut off by another smack from Dara.

"Plus, it would make either murder look like a hunting accident. Maybe implicate Cromby."

Roddy opened his mouth but held up as Dara's hand drew back.

"I lost the gun," said Boone.

"Likely story," said Mandel.

"Boone said he watched the fireworks poolside with you, Lynson. Is that right?"

Lynson looked nervous. He threw a look at Maxine and Penn, who ignored him.

"That's right. We watched the whole show and then hung out a while before turning in."

"Where are the kids, by the way?"

"Bunny accidentally shot Terrance in the calf," said Maxine, "after Terrance accidentally stabbed her in the thigh. They're at the clinic."

"There's a clinic?" said Garrett. "Where?"

"Lovely," said Gail.

"I still like Roddy for the killing," said Carter.

"I don't like him for much at all," said I. "To call his views old-fashioned is an insult to rumble seats."

"What about Mandel?" said Rawly. "Does he figure into this anymore?"

"Sorry, Rawly. He does."

"How?"

"The night of the killing, he knew you'd be making a cache," I said. "He followed you. He has a silenced motorbike for the deed. He stores it next door to you, Rawly. I think he's been raiding your caches for years."

"Why?"

I tossed the Krugerrand on his table.

"I found a cache of yours in Dasher's cave. It had fake Krugerrands in it. I bet if you dig up a couple of your caches, especially the last one, and inspect the gold coins, you'll find they're not worth the time to throw down a well."

"How did he know where and when…"

"Kimmy at first, maybe."

"I didn't," she objected.

"Maybe not on purpose. Maybe not at all, but you did sleep with him."

"So?"

"So there's gold in them there hills."

"I always cache them at night," Rawly said. "When there are storms especially. To conceal the place."

"So Mandel knew what you'd be up to that night and followed you."

"I didn't see him."

"He didn't hit the cache that night. My guess is he just saw where it was. He hit it the day after. I saw him coming down the trail. He was spooked as all hell. Deathly afraid of running into you."

"He shot at me," said Mandel.

"So that's what happened to your ammo, Rawly."

"I don't remember."

"Don't need to. The gesture was made and interpreted by Mandel, who afterward tried hard to pin the murder on you."

"Why?"

"He thought you suspected him."

"I did," he said.

"How many times have you sold Rawly the same coins?" said Perry.

He didn't answer.

Boone said, "So what happened? How'd my gun get used?"

"Shit," I said.

"Because there was shit on the body?" said Carter. "I wondered about that."

"That and shit. Country life has a lot of shit in it. Manure, droppings, poop—it's all about shit."

They waited. I guess I wasn't being clear.

"Carter hired me on the QT, and yet some citizen called Mayor Dip-Shit Charbone and narced us out."

"The name's Gill," said the mayor.

"Mayor Dip-Shit Gill," I corrected myself. "Who could have told on us, I wonder?"

"And who knew to follow you up to Miracle Canyon?" said Gail.

"Oh, that was covered. It was Roddy," I said. "I foolishly mentioned I was going there when I talked to him. So on him is an attempted murder, for those of you keeping track."

Carter nodded. Jake looked concerned. Concern was good.

"Here's another reason it wasn't Cromby or Boone or Rawly."

"What's that?"

"None of them knew where to find Dasher that night."

"He was hell to find," said Mandel. "How did anyone know?"

"Well, Beaumont knew," said Roddy.

"Fuck off, Dad."

"Roddy heard it from his son. Half drunk and already planning to kill him, he mentioned that in this bar, at that bugged table right there, that Dasher dances in the rain at the medicine wheel. He called it the medicine wheel, not identifying it as the little one. Only a local would know there were two and realize it had to be the less frequented one. The big medicine wheel is the closest thing you have to a tourist attraction, not the kind of place a hermit would like under any circumstances."

"I told him about the rain dance," said Beaumont. "I don't know why."

"Because it was a beautiful thing," I said. "And you wanted to show your father the beauty you saw in your friend."

Beaumont sniffled. He'd been the only one in all of Big Horn County who'd actually cried over the death of the man, the hermit, the friend, Dashiell Stubbins.

"The storm was coming. The fireworks would be a great distraction: cover for a shooting should the noise echo below."

"Who knew about it?"

"My friends and I were in the bar when he said it."

"That rancher," said Perry. "The barkeep, the skinhead. Wait. And Ms. Larsen."

All eyes turned to Gail.

"Me?"

"You. I saw the owl logo on your coffee mug."

"What? You're suggesting that I killed the flasher? Why? How? I was fishing a dead animal out of the pool at the time."

"Nope, Lynson and Boone were both at the pool that night. They'd have seen you. And just to be sure, I looked in your dumpster. No dead badger."

"You can't honestly—"

"You knew the back trails better than the locals. Carter and I had shown you that we were working together. We'd even mentioned the caliber and the gun. The gun, by the way, that you had stolen from Boone that day and later planted in Roddy's truck when they came by to fight with Cromby."

"I didn't even know he had a gun."

"I knew he had it. Dasher knew he had it. Frankly, Boone, you really need to be more careful. You left it in the damn shower."

"Lesson learned."

"Why would I want to kill anyone?"

"Revenge," I said. "An old-fashioned motive if ever I heard one."

"I'm not even from here."

"No. But you moved here after you saw the news story about the hermit. You recognized Dashiell Stubbins and moved in for the long game. The campground was a blind. You sat back and played patience, waiting for your moment. It's why you knew all the trails. You'd explored them all looking for him."

"This is stupid."

"When you found out that I was on the case afterward, you hit on me to distract me or maybe get information. Confuse me. It worked after a fashion —*after a fashion*," I repeated for my friends. "I was confused."

"Normal," said Perry.

"Still stupid."

"Humiliating," I said.

She stared daggers at me.

"Maxine said it last night. She mentioned she'd seen the infamous TED Talk where one of Dashiell's partners had shit themselves publicly. She said it was a woman. That woman was you."

Silence.

"It's hard enough to be a woman in a man's world. Venture capitalists are probably the worst brand of shysters and hucksters out there right now, but that's where the action is. You were quick to jump on the Kiksuye, be an early adopter, join at the ground level. Be a pioneer, take a chance with the promise of riches. But it all went to shit. Disaster—professional, personal, spiritual. Medical."

She sipped her drink and looked at all the faces in the room, then back at me. "No one thought to test the damn thing. Talk about shortcuts."

"The danger of early adoption," I said.

"Last night, I heard you say that, Maxine," said Gail. "I saw your wheels turning, Tony. I knew enough about you from your media to fear you. I sensed you'd figured it out, or were about to. Sorry about your cabin, Perry. Had I known about Tony before, I'd have waited for you to leave and caught Dashiell in the next storm."

"He wouldn't have been there," said Roddy.

Dara slapped him. With a closed fist. On the throat.

"Jesus!" said Varg.

Gail giggled. "I thought I was smart getting you and your friends out of your place so I could use that trail."

"What's your real name?" I said.

"Gwyneth Lorten. I was going places. I was interviewed for *Forbes* and *Business Day*."

Maxine looked Gail up and down. "I don't see it," she said.

"I was thirty pounds lighter, dyed hair, in designer glasses, and a thousand-dollar suit. Confident. Determined."

There was a moment of mournful quiet.

"Those weren't grenades last night, were they?" I said.

"No. They were those godawful fireworks that hurt you to watch."

"That's right," said Varg/Uri. "She said she had fireworks but never fired any off last night."

"Yes, she did," said Perry.

"Another, Eddie," said Gail, holding up her glass.

Eddie looked at me. I nodded. He poured.

"I'm sorry, Gail—Gwyneth," I said.

"You can call me Gail."

"I get it. When Dara got drenched climbing out of the bomb shelter last night, she was mad as a snake, threatening vengeance. That was the final piece. Long time in coming. Should have happened sooner, but with so damn much crime and shit, pun intended, how could I think straight?"

I finished my gin and Fresca. I could still taste the alcohol but just barely.

"He ruined me," said Gail. "And not just me."

"A little mental health care would have gone a long way," I said. "At least in the beginning."

Carter didn't look at me.

The room shifted and waited. Beaumont wept. Mandel stared into space. The mayor cringed when he crossed his legs as if it hurt. Rawly stared at Kimmy, the blank smile gone. Kimmy smiled and then her smile faded. The Isaaks huddled and gaped. The Crombys reached for their phones but put them back when the stillness didn't break. Roddy scowled.

Finally Gail broke the silence. "I had to crap on him," she said. "You know I had to."

47

WE DROVE north across the state line into Montana that afternoon, going the opposite way of home to see the famous landmark.

The Little Bighorn Battlefield, as it was now called, wasn't far and even though Garrett was uncomfortable, his clinic shot not doing anything yet, and we were tired, anxious to be on our way, we couldn't pass on the chance to see where history had happened.

It was a beautiful day. The sky a deep western blueberry, the ground green in waving grass, gray in spindly brush. Tawny rocks. The air carried smells of hot dust and dry sage. A distant hope of rain in the hint of ozone, or maybe someone's air condenser had malfunctioned. It was lonely out there, easy to get lost in the low rolling hills.

There was little conversation, everyone in their own thoughts. I was replaying the morning, Perry still strangely upbeat after losing his cabin.

"Why aren't you pitching a fit about your house being blown up?" I asked.

"Because it would have happened even if it had been a real house."

"And?"

"It doesn't matter that I was suckered."

"Is that all?"

"And I'm done with that place."

We were all done with that place. Whatever sheen the simple life had presented, whatever noble savagery we thought we might find—isolation, innocence, quiet—it was not in Big Horn County. Or it had been but was hell and gone now. I was ready to get back to drive-thrus and computer screens, showers, ice, pizza delivery, soft beds and sheets. So were the others. Since we had nothing to pack and no reason to stay after I finished my show, we left after Garrett's shot.

I'd given Jake, the deputy from Lovell, one of my business cards. Then I poured myself a tall glass of ice water from behind the bar, noting the recorder still turning and toasted the town's suspects and villains.

Veronica asked, "Who do we arrest?"

Carter, as if unable to find words, pointed to Gail.

Veronica shook her head. "I mean, who else?"

I knew that would be a problem. Everyone in the room had done something culpable if not outright illegal. Even the sheriff and mayor. Probably especially them. Even Veronica could be tagged as an accomplice of some kind with the coal and the hermit coverup, the police harassment of visitors and so on. Lynson too could be investigated for knowing of a crime and not reporting it. I don't know if temporary butlers have servant/master privilege, but someone might test that.

That was the thing. I didn't know what they'd do with any of it. I'd unloaded my theories and conclusions, but except for the confessions I'd wrung out of the guilty consciences and the one piece of hard evidence Eddie had left under the table, I was peddling speculation, recounting a history in an area afflicted with deep selective historical amnesia. I couldn't be sure that the truth, any of it, in any form, would leave that barroom.

Would Boone feel obliged to report back to Heather what I'd said if Carter put conditions on him? Could the politics of the small town separate a murder from the rest of it, punish Gail while keeping the coal quiet, the longstanding tolerance of skinheads and drug dealing, rustling and poaching? Black eyes a-plenty coming their way if they didn't.

The key of course would be Deputy Sheriff Craig Carter. He'd be the one to drive the bus now, off a cliff, into the open, or down a hole. Jake from Lovell had my card, but I knew he'd do "a favor" for his friends in Floyd if asked to. That was part of the reason I wanted to get out of town as fast as possible. Me and the gang were loose threads if they changed it up too much. Not that we were in danger, but we might have been in danger. Floyd was a strange, isolationist place, a stanch counterposition to the myth of the welcoming West. Even now, the murder of the hermit was surely pulling unwanted attention to the area. That little television clip would be replayed with an update, and someone might have something new to say.

I shook my head, realizing I'd fallen into a daydream of paranoia, a prepper mentality of conspiracy and injustice, hoping for the worst. I was already planning a press release if things got hairy. It's easy to get in your head out there. Something about the wide open spaces that makes one feel small and vulnerable. It feels lonely. People aren't meant to be so lonely. Even Dasher, a hermit, came down from his cave for affection and company once in a while. I thought of Rawly's bunker and how Kimmy would scratch the walls to get out, even if it meant chancing the zombie horde.

Perry paid the fee for the car to park, and still quiet, we got out and wandered up the path past the gift shop toward the famous hill. To our right were crosses of dead servicemen, not from the 1876 affair but from after. The ground was a national cemetery now, like Arlington but more lonely.

This place used to be called Custer's Last Stand but was changed to The Little Bighorn Battleground to suggest there might have been two sides to the issue. A lot of people dislike political correctness like that, but I don't. It's correctness. Here at least, in the renaming of the place, was an attempt to remember some of the buried truths, an attempt to treat national moral amnesia.

I doubt there's a more famous event of American Western expansion than the Battle of Little Bighorn. It is a good example of the power of propaganda to become myth. Ironically it was used to rally more people to move West, touching on patriotism and honor to show our manifest destiny. I'm sure there were some folks who argued against it, seeing the massacre as, oh, I don't know, a cautionary tale? Suggesting danger and hardship? Brutal death? But history ignored them, and the hearty pioneering colonizers, the early adopters of the moment, are held up as heroes, their sins forgiven by time and reality of conquest.

It's an eerie place, the Little Bighorn Battlefield, at least it was when we were there. I doubt it's ever a picnic. The grass shuffled and hummed from the wind, giving speech to the invisible. Crosses littered the landscape marking where soldiers had fallen. It was still pretty one-sided, but there were a couple of Indian monuments to show where one of the other side had died. Maybe there just weren't that many of them, but I suspect it had more to do with who was writing the history. The Little Bighorn Battlefield National Monument—the nation in question symbolized the stars and stripes, not a medicine wheel.

Custer and his gang of killers were on assignment to massacre Indians and sow terror everywhere they went. Really. They were there to murder the natives. Drive them off. Make way for the whites who were even then flooding in. It had been a full-time job for the cavalry for a while, employment for Civil War washouts with sociopathic bloodlust. Custer anyone?

I won't go into too much detail about the battle because there's been more ink dedicated to this American embarrassment than the rest of our wars combined.

The campaign of 1876 had the army punishing the natives for being alive, and worse, trying to survive, and even worse still, using white shirts in the hope it would help them survive. An advance party found a band of Amerindians chilling out on the Little Bighorn River on June 25th. These were Dakota, Lakota, Northern Cheyenne, and Arapaho, to be precise. They'd gotten together because they shared the same problem: murderous white people.

Luckily for the tribes, they had scouts so the village was alerted and on guard when snipers started shooting into it willy-nilly, because why not? The Amerindians didn't take enormous casualties from it, but it did, unsurprisingly, piss them off.

Then the US attacked outright. Yes, the US attacked the village. To make a long story short, the tribes resisted the attack, saving their families, pushing the cavalry back and eradicating some of them in the process.

There was always to be a massacre at the Little Bighorn. It just didn't pan out as planned. The massacre of the Little Bighorn was self-defense. The rest is history.

It's easy to get wrapped up in "they were there first," but no one had been there first. The "modern" tribes were newcomers themselves and the whites just newer-comers. Maybe a better arrangement could have been discovered that didn't include genocide, but that's not the code of the West. Greed and violence—now there's a code America can get behind.

I see it as old versus new, both terms relative as hell. Good ol' days versus move aside. A simple struggle, but when the stakes became life and death, compromise and patience, empathy and simple human decency get tossed out the wagon. Even then, there were soldiers who knew they were murdering people and not just "savages."

But I digress.

I looked at the marker where Custer himself fell, just on the hill. His was surrounded by lots of other markers, places where other soldiers had fallen. Murderers murdered.

The guns, I think, speak to the situation. The cavalry had state-of-the-art weapons: model 1873 .45 carbines, while the natives had older Winchester .44 repeaters, a sports gun by most accounts. The carbines would have turned the Civil War on its head, a great weapon with a lot of punch and great range. The only thing the Winchesters had in their favor was they could shoot more than once without reloading. The battle was at close quarters, which was the Indian way. No sniping across a river at women and children as a rule. Here at least, in that battle, the older guns were superior.

Though treeless, the hilly ground gave real cover, and the Indians, for the most part, didn't stay still to be shot. They kept to their horses while the cavalry dismounted to fight in a line, another tactic held over from the Civil War. Their horses were run off in short order, and the fate of Custer's Killers was pretty much sealed. They were killed by a man. Heavily outnumbered, suffering a dozen tactical miscalculations, not the least of which was facing an overwhelming force of righteously angry people fighting for their very lives. A traveling skirmish is what the natives wanted and that is what they got, and what they ultimately won, to the shock of a nation who didn't think of the natives as people at all. I mean, why were they so mad? It was only their families being killed.

But of course the narrative was, and in many ways continues to be, different since it tarnishes the myth of the Wild West, a time of enthusiasm for white America. These were the good ol' days, weren't they?

I thought of Dashiell Stubbins, his already frayed and troubled mind breaking. Not from what he was doing—I'm sure he truly believed that antelope poop was an effective supplement. I'm convinced of it. But he broke because of the destruction of his world, his career and wealth and reputation and family. A world turned upside down. Of course he fled home, led on by a memory of innocence and adventure, a place that even then seemed rock solid and unperturbed. But it was a fiction. The place was always dirty.

The West continues to inspire hope. It brings people thinking they can be the ones to restart the world when this one finally and gloriously gets erased by zombies. It brings people who think that roughing it was somehow morally superior to convenience. It still has its cattle barons, still wallows in outdated technology, even when it is literally killing the planet. The myth lives on. It strikes me as a surrender to nostalgia, worship of a fiction that never was. Selective memory and rose-colored glasses.

But underneath it all, there are still people. People who value friendship and company, people who still suffer the perennial sins of greed, lust, sloth, and wrath. Oh, the wrath.

Today had been a turning point for Floyd and Big Horn County, Wyoming, at least for a few of its inhabitants. I'd brought to them a crisis long in the making, showing old crimes and new. They'd have to go on from that now. Rawly and Kimmy, Penn and Maxine, their monster children and hopefully angry game wardens. Mandel, the con man, unmasked. Varg, an American snake-oil success story—sell out your morals, pride, history, and people—all to make a buck. Carter and his debts of childhood affection and modern politics. Mayor Gill exposed in his corruption. Cattle rustlers, divided by a new sensibility shown in Beaumont's pain and stoicism and the outdated bigotry in his father. Gail had no remorse; she'd suffered insult too great to go unanswered and so had answered it with a gun, another Western trope come true.

I was feeling pretty good about myself. I'd been hit on and stayed true to my gal. I'd solved a murder, uncovered deviltry, avoided the clap, gained a pretty gold coin. I felt satisfied and reinvigorated, even though I couldn't help but feel I'd peeled back a Band-Aid. I'm not sure I'd be thanked for what I'd done. Or paid. All I was sure about was that I did it all without computers. I hadn't thought about my phone in hours or reached for my tile in days. Day. I'd proved to myself and my weak friends that I could break the addiction to technology. I could survive and even sleuth without it, like the Good Ol' Days®. That was something, I guess, a point of bragging, maybe, but it was bullshit.

I remembered a picture I'd seen on the internet showing a crowd of people on a train all staring into their phones like zombies, absolutely no interpersonal conversation to be seen. Next to that picture was one of a train from fifty years earlier showing people staring into their newspapers in the same exact way, no conversation, everyone in their own worlds. Same shit, different day.

A LOOK AT BOOK SIX:
THE REAL DEAL

Tony must face sticky mud, stickier orgies and the Rapture itself to uncover the Real Deal.

In this captivating tale, Eugene, Oregon, known for its vibrant counterculture and unconventional charm, becomes the backdrop for a convergence of competing cults. As the Merry Pranksters revel in their mischievous antics and the spirit of the world hangs in the balance, Tony finds himself in the midst of a psychic soiree hosted by a mysterious mushroom millionaire. Little does Tony know that this enigmatic figure shares a troubling connection with his girlfriend, raising questions and stirring suspicions.

With a blend of humor and uncertainty, Tony faces the muddy obstacles of Eugene, where even the Roman cement would blush at the thickness of the mud. Amidst the swirling incense and fervent devotion, Tony must navigate sticky situations, outrageous orgies, and a series of unsettling events that involve brainwashing, kidnapping, and multiple murders. Can he rise above his mid-life crisis, embrace his inner hero, and uncover the truth behind the facade?

Prepare for a mind-bending journey where reality intertwines with the mystical, secrets lurk behind closed eyes, and the fate of the world hangs in the balance. Will Tony be able to separate fact from fiction, or will he succumb to the allure of a world-building mastermind? It's a whirlwind of suspense, laughter, and unexpected twists as Tony faces his greatest challenge yet—the quest for the Real Deal.

Immerse yourself in the wild and whimsical world of Eugene, Oregon, as you join Tony and his eclectic gang in a New Age gathering like no other.

AVAILABLE NOVEMBER 2023

ACKNOWLEDGMENTS

Thanks for reading. You're an awesome human being for reading. No really, reading is cool. Reading literally makes you a better person. It's science— brainwaves and stuff. And reading my writing, well, that makes you a certain special kind of wonderful. I am humbled by, and grateful to, and playful, with all of you.

Special gratitude I offer to my editor, Audrey Hammer and her editor, my best alpha reader, Craig Kingsman. Thanks also to Michelle, who shall be nameless. Thanks to my students who inspire me and remind me why words are cool, reading makes you a better person, and how giving back is salvation.

Remember to join my 'Seldom-Used Mailing List®' at *www.johnny-worthen.com* for the occasional update.

Stay safe. Stay sane and never take any shit too seriously.

ACKNOWLEDGMENTS

ABOUT THE AUTHOR

Johnny Worthen is an award-winning and best-selling author of books and stories. Trained in stand-up comedy, modern literary criticism and cultural studies, he writes upmarket multi-genre fiction, symbolized by his love of tie-dye and good words.

"I wear tie-dye for my friends, but I write what I like to read," he says. "This guarantees me at least one fan and easy dressing in the morning."

Johnny teaches writing at the University of Utah and lives in a house with his wife, sons and assorted cats. There's also a lawn.